Shadow
Play

Also by Ger Gallagher

Broken Passions

A Life Left Untold

Shadow Play

Ger Gallagher

POOLBEG

Published 2007
by Poolbeg Press Ltd
123 Grange Hill, Baldoyle
Dublin 13, Ireland
E-mail: poolbeg@poolbeg.com
www.poolbeg.com

Typeset by Patricia Hope in Bembo 11.4/15

Printed by
Litografia Rosés, S.A., Spain

Note on the Author

Ger Gallagher lives in Dublin with her husband and two daughters. *Shadow Play* is her third novel.

Acknowledgements

While I sit at home scribbling all year, there is a group of people working very hard to ensure that my story will be packaged, bound and sitting in a bookshop waiting to be read.

I would like to extend a huge thanks to those people – Paula, Kieran and the team at Poolbeg – for all the work they do on my behalf.

To my editor, Gaye Shortland, this is the third book you have edited for me, and each one has been a thoroughly enlightening and enjoyable experience.

To the booksellers throughout the country, your support is greatly appreciated.

Thank you again to everyone at the Tyrone Guthrie Centre, Annaghmakerrig for your unique kindness and hospitality.

To my family and friends, I couldn't wish for any better.

But my biggest thanks goes to you, the reader. My dream was to write – and you have made that dream come true.

For my girls, Jessie & Eve,
with all my love.

Then

I was eleven when my mother passed away, and Lizzie was
only seven. When Daddy came home from the hospital I
thought he looked different but it was only because he
hadn't shaved. His hair stuck out at the sides and his chin

I can still recall the nights my mother came into my room as if it were yesterday. The scent of Pears soap and starchy vanilla hung in the air as she slipped into my bed and pulled me close to her. I never once asked why she came, I only cared that she was there. I nestled into her warmth and revelled in our stolen moments of intimacy while baby Claire slept soundly in the other room. Sometimes I fell back to sleep immediately; other times I lay awake and looked at the shadows on the wall that were cast by the chestnut tree outside the window. I never liked to close my curtains at night, preferring the hypnotic effect of the swaying branches as they waved me back into my dreams. If the night was windy and I couldn't get back to sleep, Mum would whisper a story about the fairies that lived in the shadows of the fluttering leaves. Good fairies that would always protect me from any harm, is what she used to say.

Then

I was eleven when my mother passed away and Claire was only seven. When Daddy came home from the hospital I thought he looked different but it was only because he hadn't shaved. His hair stuck out at the sides and his chin was covered with silvery bristles. He had gone with Mum during the night in the ambulance. His face crumpled up as he delivered the terrible news. "Your mother has gone to heaven."

Auntie Rita bustled around us and I remember how much I wished she'd stop fussing – her movements were only making the pain inside my head worse. I sat at the kitchen table and stared at the wrinkly skim of milk that had formed on top of the mug of drinking chocolate, which sat untouched in front of me. Claire sat on Daddy's knee clutching her Peter Rabbit and sucking her thumb as if nothing of any great importance had happened.

Auntie Rita came to live with us when her husband Norman ran off on her. I was only eight at the time but, even then, I remember feeling resentful about how she barged her way into our family. Rita liked to make an entrance. She didn't walk into a room – she bustled in, causing a palpable stir in the air around her, letting everyone know she was there. She made a very theatrical entrance the day she arrived at our house, clutching a suitcase and blowing her nose into a handkerchief. Daddy wasn't there so Mum ushered her into his study and they stayed in there for ages. Claire was having her afternoon nap and I sat alone on the stairs and strained to hear what they were saying but only the murmur of hushed voices reached my ears. Later that evening Daddy hit the roof. Not only had the women violated the strictest rule of the house by entering his hallowed study, but Auntie Rita had had the temerity to smoke her cigarettes there as well.

"What happened to Mum?" I finally found the voice to ask on that dreadful morning.

Daddy reached over and put his hand on my arm. "Her heart stopped beating," he said gravely.

"Drink your chocolate," Auntie Rita said. "You'll feel better after you've had something hot to drink."

It was then that I realised that she was about to step into my mother's shoes and I was seized with an overwhelming desire to throw the mug of murky liquid over her head. A few minutes later she removed the mug from the kitchen table without saying another word, as if she'd guessed what I was thinking.

Later that day Mrs Whyte came over and took me up to her house to play with her daughter, Lainey. Her real name was Elaine, but her mum always called her Lainey. Mr Whyte had died when she was only a baby, leaving poor Mrs Whyte all alone with her little girl. I liked their house – it smelt of baking and freshly cut grass – and although Lainey was two years younger than me, she was always nice to be with. I spent a lot of time in their house after Mum died and it was during that time that Lainey and I formed the beginnings of a very special friendship, one which has lasted until now.

Now

Yesterday was Daddy's birthday; he turned sixty-eight. Not an age one does anything special to celebrate, but Rita marked the occasion by inviting us around for tea. They have dinner at lunch-time and tea at six o'clock sharp every day. Since Daddy retired, they've lived their lives like clockwork toys – at any given moment I can tell where they are and what they are doing. For instance, it is now half past four on Thursday afternoon, so I know that they're playing bridge in the church hall with the active retirement group, along with all the other retired married couples. Except Daddy and Rita aren't married – they are only related by marriage.

I drove through town yesterday afternoon looking for a parking space whilst racking my brains for an idea of what to buy Daddy for his birthday. I had decided earlier in the day on a golf sweater but as I approached the corner of the street where the golf shop was, I suddenly went off the idea. He had lots of golf clothing and another golf sweater seemed like such a thoughtless gift – how many of them had I bought for him over the years? I hadn't checked with Claire to see what she was getting him but doubtless it was another fascinating law book that they could both discuss in depth. A car pulled out of a parking space right outside Golf Links and I put my indicator on and dispelled any doubts from my mind about the suitability of a golf sweater.

I had grabbed my bag and made to get out of the car when I spotted Richard on the other side of the street with a person I could only presume was from the Shields case. They were both clutching their take-away coffees and Richard was speaking with a serious expression etched across his forehead while the other man listened intently. At three thousand euro a day, he looked like he was taking in every word. Richard is a barrister and is working on a tribunal representing Shields, one of the largest multi-national technology companies in the world. They have been accused of breaking anti-competitive laws by abusing their monopoly position to squeeze out their competitors. The case has taken up every hour of his life for the past year and there doesn't seem to be any end in sight. I stared across at them and studied my husband closely. He had improved with age, not that he had ever needed much improving in the looks department, but at the age of fifty-two he still had a full head of wavy brown hair with only a sprinkling of grey. He certainly looked a lot younger than most of his peers. His suit jacket, I noticed, was slightly crumpled at the back but it was an expensive well-cut suit and, despite the creases, he wore it well. He is exactly twelve years older than me and as we move through our marriage that age gap is closing. When we first met I was twenty-five and my friends all seemed slightly taken aback that I would go for a man who was approaching forty – back when forty was old. Now I am that age and I smile to myself when I think of how we fool ourselves by believing that we are still young, no matter what age we are. My father had probably woken up that morning and convinced himself that sixty-eight wasn't old – after all, he probably still felt the same inside as he did thirty years ago.

I prepared to leave the car and run across to him, but changed my mind. I checked myself in the rear-view mirror and saw that I looked a bit of a mess. My hair needed to be washed, and I was still wearing the raggy old tracksuit that I'd been working in all afternoon while I weeded the garden. Instead, I watched and admired my husband's show of chivalry as he opened the door of the Shields building and allowed a lady to leave before he entered and disappeared from view.

We have no children. I find this difficult to say without stumbling over the words as if they were pieces of concrete in my mouth. Our married life has been divided into two parts, the first where I delayed starting a family because I simply didn't feel the desire to be bogged down with kids. I suffered a time delay in the release of that maternal hormone, the one that sends women in their thirties into a spin about getting pregnant. Whatever the process is called, it simply didn't happen to me until I was thirty-six. I was too busy, heading up the creative department at Task Advertising Agency. It simply never occurred to me that I might not be able to have children. When we started trying four years ago, it soon became apparent that something was definitely wrong. After a year of nothing happening, we succumbed to the dreaded fertility tests. I remember rushing to the hospital with Richard's freshly produced and, as it turned out, healthy sperm, to have it analysed while it was still warm as it were. There was nothing wrong there: he had an abundance of live ones bursting to fertilise my ailing eggs which is where they discovered the problem was lurking. My reproductive system was a medical train crash. It was all traced back to a burst appendix when I was twelve years old. Apparently the poison that had leaked from the offending organ had spent years rotting one of my ovaries and rendering the other one as good as useless.

Turning forty was particularly difficult. It is an age for most women that marks the beginning of the end of their reproductive cycle. I found myself gazing longingly into buggies as they were pushed past me in the street. In supermarket queues I smiled at babies as I bit down on my quivering lower lip to stop myself from blubbering out loud. I began to understand how those women felt, the ones you hear about on the news who steal babies from hospitals.

Richard didn't take the news as badly as I did. Although I suspect he hid a lot of his disappointment when he saw how devastated I was. Still, we have each other and we are discussing the possibility of adopting a Chinese baby. At first I wasn't enthusiastic about the idea. It was Lainey who suggested it, and got all the information from the adoption board. We put our names down two years ago as we both agreed that there was no harm in applying – it was something we could always change our minds about along the way. But with each new stage of the process I become more and more excited. Richard is not keen on the idea of adoption. Even in the early days of our trying for a baby, he never got overly excited at the prospect of us having a baby. Unlike me, he has remained steadfastly temperate on the subject of children. He has promised to go along with whatever I want but says he can't pretend to have feelings for a child that he has never seen before. We have had two meetings with the adoption board and they have deemed us suitable candidates to continue with the process. It is a lengthy process, whereby we will be put through the wringer as a couple to test our suitability as parents. Richard hates the idea of having to suffer any interviews or meetings where he'll be expected to share aspects of his personal life with strangers. I try to tip the scales over to the positive side by reminding him that we'll have a baby at the end of it all, but sometimes Richard's negatives win out which makes me wonder if we're doing the right thing.

Rita had a ham salad prepared for the four of us at exactly six on the button. Claire, as always, was late. We waited until she rushed in the door at twenty-five past six to begin the feast of mixed leaves and honey-baked ham. Claire is a solicitor and works for a large firm that deals mostly with personal injuries – or ambulance chasers as my father prefers to call them. Law is something that runs in the blood in our family; my grandfather was a solicitor and Daddy was a high court judge until his recent retirement. I preferred the frivolity of the world of advertising but made up for my lack of achievement by marrying a barrister.

"I like your hair," I said as we all sat down to tea.

Claire and I are complete opposites when it comes to our colouring and features. She has brown wavy hair down to her shoulders which is highlighted with delicate tones of copper. Her eyes are large and brown like Daddy's and her skin is sallow, almost Italian-looking. I look like my mother. My hair is fair. I get highlights now but as a child it was white. My eyes are an unremarkable shade of blue. My skin is also fair and sensitive to sunlight or anything perfumed.

Claire ran her fingers through her freshly blow-dried hair. "Thanks," she said, "I just had it done."

"That will explain your tardiness," Daddy remarked as he sawed through his slice of ham.

Claire looked over at him and smiled sweetly. "I'm so sorry, Daddy. I didn't realise I was late."

Daddy didn't look up from his food. "We eat at six every evening. You know that."

Rita shuffled about on her chair and chirped, "Your father sleeps better if he eats early in the evening."

Rita always addresses Daddy as "your father". I don't believe I have ever heard her call him anything else. I sometimes wonder what she must call him when they are in bed together. Does she say things like: "Would Father like sex tonight?" or "Could Father possibly stop snoring in my ear?"

Claire looked at me and rolled her eyes up to heaven. We both knew that when Daddy got into one of his moods it was hard to coax him out of it.

"How is Richard?" Rita asked cheerfully.

"He's fine. He's sorry he's couldn't make it over this evening but things have been really busy with the tribunal. I hardly see him myself these days." It was true. We were like ships that passed in the night. The Shields people had taken him over completely; when he wasn't down at the law library, he was back at their offices burning the midnight oil, or having dinner with them. Most nights I was asleep by the time he got home.

Claire reached down and pulled Daddy's birthday present out of a bag.

"Here you are," she said, handing it to him. "Happy birthday!"

Daddy put his knife and fork down and gave a little snorting sound that resembled a laugh. He took the parcel and carefully began to unwrap it. Inside the tissue paper lay a dress shirt and a pair of gold monogrammed cufflinks. Daddy looked over at Claire and cracked a smile.

"It's for the law society dinner next month," she said, returning his smile. "I figured you could do with a new one."

"I certainly could," he said, shaking out the shirt to hold it up to him. "What do you think, Rita? Will it fit me?"

Rita reached over and examined the size label. "Yes, it's a seventeen collar, exactly your size."

"Thank you, dear," he said, making an unsuccessful attempt to fold the shirt.

Rita took it from him and returned it to the nest of tissue paper. "Your father badly needed a new dress shirt. Well done, Claire!"

I grabbed the bag with the golf sweater, feeling guilty that I hadn't bothered to wrap it nicely. "Happy birthday, Daddy."

He looked at me in surprise, as if he wasn't expecting anything else.

"It's nothing much," I said, apologising before he even saw it. "You're so hard to buy for."

He took the bag and stuck his head inside. "I know what this is," he said with a chuckle as he pulled the sweater out.

Rita clapped her hands together with delight when she saw the navy thermal-lined jumper, and Daddy positively beamed as he held it up for all of us to see. I looked over at Rita, feeling slightly baffled at their gleeful reaction. It wasn't like I'd bought him a Rolex.

"Your father lost the one you got him last year, and he's been so cross about it. He's called the golf club several times but no one's found it. It's a perfect present, Liz."

Alarm bells started ringing in my head. I'd bought him one last year? I had absolutely no memory of what I had given him for his birthday last year but now that Rita mentioned it, I did have a vague recollection of a taupe sweater with a similar lining, but only very vague. How could I have given him the same present two years in a row?

Claire looked over at me and started to laugh.

Daddy reached over and patted my hand, "Thank you, Lizzy dear," he said reassuringly. "I loved that sweater, and this one looks every bit as nice."

I looked back at Claire and shrugged my shoulders. "I'm definitely losing it," I muttered to myself as I reached for my glass of wine.

Claire's eyes had a shine to them that suggested she might be in love. I have noticed that with women when they're in the first stages of a new relationship. Their eyes glisten with a special kind of contentment carried on the first flush of love.

Rita brought the birthday cake into the room and we sang a rather flat "Happy Birthday" to Daddy before he blew out the candles.

Later on, Claire loaded the plates into the dishwasher, while I made coffee and Rita buzzed about organising cups and saucers, probably wishing that we'd get out of her pristine kitchen. Rita hated anyone helping in the kitchen. I caught a glimpse of Claire's boots and lifted the leg of her trousers to get a better look.

"I don't believe it," I said indignantly. "When did you get them?"

Claire looked down at her feet. "The other day. Why?"

"I have the same pair ordered," I whined.

Claire gave me a smug grin. "Well, as you have them ordered I'll allow you to make the purchase, but you're not to wear them at the same time as me."

It was always the same. If you put the two of us in a clothes shop anywhere on earth we would buy the same things; it must be some genetic pairing we have in our sense of dress. Anytime I see something unusual or am spending over the odds on an item of clothing, I generally ring Claire from the dressing-room and check that she hasn't been in before me and bought that particular thing.

"Fine," I sighed. "I'll check with you before I wear them."

Claire scraped some coleslaw off a plate half-heartedly, afraid that a speck of mayonnaise might fly off and ruin her silk shirt. Housework is not my sister's strong point. Perhaps it's because when Claire was growing up, Rita was always two paces behind her to pick up that dirty pair of jeans and race down to the sink to wash them. I don't believe Claire ever so much as made a bed in her life. She lives alone in an apartment that she only ever sleeps in, yet has a cleaning lady twice a week.

Rita rushed over from the other side of the kitchen and wrestled the messy plate from Claire's beautifully manicured hands.

"Don't bother with those, love," she said. "I'll look after them later." She grabbed a tray laden with cups and saucers and turned towards the door. "Come on back inside, you two! Leave the rest of that to me."

I washed my hands and looked over at Claire as I dried them on a towel.

"What?" she asked.

I smiled at her. "Who is he?" I asked.

Claire immediately seemed to lose her lustrous glow. "What are you talking about?"

"Come on," I pressed. "I can always tell when you've met someone new."

Claire glared at me indignantly. "Well, this time you're wrong. I haven't met anyone."

I could see that I had upset her and instantly realised that my assumption had been taken as an insult. "I just thought that you looked so well – you have that newly-in-love glow about you."

Claire averted her eyes. "It doesn't always take a man to make me look good, Liz."

"I didn't mean it to sound like that. It's just that you look really well and I thought that maybe you'd met someone."

Claire stared at the floor. "I don't have anyone in my life right now and I'm beginning to think that I never will," she whispered.

"Oh, Claire," I said moving towards her, "of course you will! You just haven't met the right one yet." I wanted to throw myself on top of the kitchen knife for being so insensitive.

Claire seemed to have such a great life, always flying here there and everywhere. There were always male admirers in abundance, but never the right one. She had wasted five years on James, a married man with two children who never had any intention of leaving his wife for her, even though Claire was convinced that some day he would. Ever since she had seen the light and given him his marching orders, Claire hadn't managed to find the right partner.

I reached out and gave her arm a squeeze. "Sorry, I really didn't mean to upset you."

She forced a smile and looked up at me. "I know," she said.

"The right guy will come along soon," I reassured her.

I took her arm and we walked back into the dining room to join Daddy and Rita.

Then

I wake to see the shape of my mother lying beside me. Her long fair hair is loose around her shoulders and I feel her

13

breath on my cheek. She sniffs quickly. It is a wet sniff and I can tell, even though it is dark, that she is crying again.

"What's wrong, Mum?" I ask.

Another sniffle. "Nothing, sweetheart. Did I wake you?"

I don't know why I am awake. I can't tell what woke me.

"Why are you crying?" I ask.

There is a silence as my mother breathes in deeply and I can tell that she's trying to think of something to say.

"I'm feeling sad tonight," she whispers.

"Why?"

I hear her swallow loudly.

"I don't know why. Don't you ever feel sad and not know why?"

I think about this for a few seconds. "Not really."

She moves closer to me and slips her arm across my tummy. "Well, sometimes grown-ups feel sad for no reason and it helps to have a cry."

I put my hand on her arm that is rising and falling with the rhythm of my breathing.

She kisses the side of my head. "You take all my sadness away," she whispers into my ear.

I turn my head towards her. "Doesn't Daddy take it away?"

"No," she answers, a little too quickly.

We stare over at the wall and look at the shadow of the chestnut tree, the branches swaying slightly against the floral wallpaper.

"Mum, do fairies really live in the tree?"

"Yes, they do."

"Will they make my wishes come true?"

"Only if you wish very hard."

I look at the fluttering reflections of the leaves and close my eyes so tight that they feel like a mass of crinkled skin.

"What are you wishing for?" she asks.

"I'm wishing that they'll take your sadness away."

Her grip tightens around my waist and she rests her head in the crook of my shoulder.

"I love you so much, Lizzy," she whispers.

"I love you too, Mum."

Now

We live in the suburbs, in a house that is far too big for us. They were the first newly built houses in the city to sell for a million euro and were known thereafter as the "million-euro houses". We have five bedrooms, but only use one. On occasion I will move into the spare room if Richard has had too much to drink and his snoring disturbs me. Or if we've had a fight, one of us, usually Richard, will stamp into the spare bedroom and spend the night sleeping alone. Downstairs, there are rooms that we hardly ever go into. For instance, the dining-room, which I only ever use twice or three times a year. I prefer to use the kitchen when we are entertaining – it's brighter and more welcoming. When we have dinner parties in the dining-room I usually end up becoming grumpy and frazzled. It's too far away from the kitchen and I end up spending the evening sprinting up and down the hall in an attempt to get things from the oven to the table while they are hot.

Richard is the most undomesticated person on God's earth. During these dinner parties, he is usually to be found chomping on a cigar, oblivious to any panic that might be unfolding in the kitchen. His mother brought him up to believe that on no account was he ever to undertake any kind of domestic chore – that territory was hers and all hers – and Richard gladly obeyed.

There are thirty houses in the estate and surrounding these houses are high granite walls with security cameras peeping out from the corners. I am reminded by my neighbours that it is not an estate, it is a development, but I think that sounds pretentious, so I continue to refer to it as an estate, much to their annoyance.

I don't know many of my neighbours because until a year ago I worked full-time, and was never around for the power walks or coffee mornings. My next-door neighbours Brenda and Tom are a great couple, and before Richard took on this Shields case we saw each other quite a lot. Tom is in the motor business and Brenda stays at home with her three kids.

Brenda got pregnant unexpectedly last year and I found it really difficult to be around her. They hadn't planned on having another child, and the news came as a complete shock to her. Of course she had every right to moan about it, but I found it impossible to sympathise and started avoiding her.

When she was a few months into the pregnancy she came to the door one day looking really worried. I invited her in and she burst into tears.

"Oh God, Liz, I'm so sorry!" she blurted.

I stood looking at her and instantly all my anger disappeared.

"I never thought of how this would make you feel. Here I am giving out stink about being pregnant and all the time you . . ." She looked down and ran her hand across her stomach.

It was true. I'd wanted to choke her every time she had started on about how this pregnancy had ruined her life, but when I saw her standing there in such a state, I knew that she hadn't meant to cause me any hurt.

"Brenda, I really appreciate you saying that." I took her into the kitchen and sat her down.

She wiped her eyes with a tissue and looked over at me. "I've been so wrapped up in myself that I just never stopped to think about how you could be feeling. Please say you forgive me!"

I smiled at her tone of desperation. "Of course I forgive you. This is something I have to get over too, and your calling in today has really helped."

"Oh good," she said, blowing her nose in a piece of kitchen roll. "I don't know how I could have been so insensitive. It was only when Lainey pointed it out that I realised what a stupid cow I've been."

I should have known that Lainey had something to do with it. Her finely tuned sense of righteousness allowed her to see things that most people were oblivious to. She must have taken Brenda aside and asked her to ease off on the moaning. This would have all have been handled with sensitivity and carefully chosen words so as not to offend Brenda. Lainey put herself out on a limb for people she cared about and it made me feel lucky to have her as a friend.

Brenda had her third boy six months ago and most mornings we walk the park, taking turns to push the buggy uphill. Brenda usually gives me a run-down of every mouthful of food she had to eat the day before. We then calculate how many pounds she has to lose on her latest diet before she reaches her target weight, which started off at size zero – but has crept up to a more realistic size twelve.

On the second of May we will have been married fourteen years. Richard got home quite early last night – nine o'clock has become early. I was surprised when I heard his key in the door. He came into the living room, dropped his briefcase on the floor and collapsed onto the couch beside me.

"Half day?" I joked.

He sighed heavily and put his feet up on the coffee table.

"Glass of wine?"

He looked at me and nodded wearily.

We sipped our wine and looked at a repeat episode of *The Sopranos* and it occurred to me that I couldn't remember the last time we'd watched television together. Wasn't that what most married couples did every evening? Chilled out and watched TV? It also occurred to me that it had been at least three weeks since we'd had sex.

"Richard, you have to cut back your hours at work."

He looked at me as if I had just asked for a divorce.

"Well, it's crazy," I continued. "We never spend any time together any more. What's the point in working twenty-four hours a day? Who's benefiting from all of this? Certainly not us."

He leaned forward and put his glass down on the table.

"It won't be for much longer," he said guiltily. "I know I've been gone all the time, but I promise I'll make it up to you."

"Oh Richard, stop treating me like a child! You know as

well as I do that this is going to go on indefinitely. You have to pare back your hours and start living like a normal human being again. What's going to happen when we get this baby? You'll never see it." I stopped talking and sipped my wine. I didn't want this to turn into an argument but his patronising attitude was beginning to grate on my nerves. "Speaking of which, we have an appointment to see someone in the adoption board next Thursday afternoon."

Did I imagine it or did his face drop?

"I'm not sure if I can make it on Thursday. I think we may be in court. I'll check the diary tomorrow and let you know. Is it necessary for me to be there?"

My mouth fell open. "Richard, this is something we're meant to be doing together. It's not like we're buying a new car or a sofa – it's a child. It's our child." He pushed his hair back off his forehead, looking slightly startled at my reaction. "Are you suggesting that I go to the meeting alone? Because I don't think that would look too good. Are you telling me that you're not interested in adopting? Because if you are, I need to know now. Before I get my hopes up."

The wine had gone to my head. I was getting stupid and emotional and making unreasonable presumptions. Richard took the glass from my hand and set it down on the table beside his. He put his arms around me and held me tightly. I put my head on his shoulder and relaxed into his body.

"Sorry," he whispered. "I didn't mean it to sound like that. You're right. I need to pare back my hours and start living a life again."

Later in bed we lay together with limbs entwined. Our lovemaking had lost the frantic urgency of those early years of marriage but had been replaced instead with an easy intimacy that had become so familiar to both of us. The anger I felt at his earlier comments had vanished and was replaced with a peaceful afterglow.

The Task Advertising Agency have asked me to go back to work for them. I was not surprised when I got the call as I'd heard that David Fenlon had been headhunted by another agency. David had been my successor and hailed as the new Messiah by Brian Davies, the Managing Director. But only months after my departure, word had filtered back to me that things were not working out very well between them.

Brian called me last week and asked me to go back, there and then.

"I won't beat around the bush, Liz," he said in his usual matter-of-fact way. "We really need you back again."

I had left to start a family. For some inexplicable reason I thought that if I gave up my job I might have a better chance of getting pregnant. That was before I knew about my infertility. It had never occurred to me to go back again, which means that I was probably ready to leave the job anyway. It's funny, after working there for twelve years I never once missed it after I left.

I felt slightly panicked at Brian's offer, and wondered if perhaps returning to the company would compound my feelings of failure. Everyone there knew why I'd left.

"Please think about it. If you agree to come back you'll be made a partner with immediate effect."

I smiled to myself, thinking he must be really desperate. I'd spent years fighting my corner to make partner but

Brian never gave in. The fact that I was a woman had ruled me out automatically.

"Wow, Brian, what's come over you?" I laughed.

"I'm serious, Liz. Don't make me grovel. I really need you back – the department's in a mess."

I should have been excited, but I wasn't. I didn't have my baby. It would be like returning to work after maternity leave without having had the child. I knew what it would do to me.

"I can't do it, Brian," I said flatly.

I heard him exhale loudly.

"Say you'll at least think about it."

"I'll think about it but I know that I'm not going to change my mind."

"I won't go away," he barked before hanging up.

Dinner in Lainey's is always such a feast. When Lainey decided to learn how to cook she did it as she does everything else in her life – perfectly. She has attended every cookery school in the country and could probably show most of them a thing or two by now. Lainey leads a charmed life but, unlike most people who do, she thoroughly deserves hers because she is such a genuinely good person. She falls in age exactly halfway between Claire and me, and as a result we argued over her all the time when we were growing up.

"She's more my age," Claire would point out.

"She's too old to be your friend. You're just a baby to her!" was my reasoning.

"Find someone else your own age to play with. You're too old for her!" she would respond.

And so on and so forth, but the funny thing is that Lainey seemed to be just as much Claire's friend as mine and even now, if we were both to be perfectly honest, we still get jealous over who spends more time with her.

Lainey met Peter Chambers when they were in college and it was a real live case of love at first sight. They say they both knew they were going to marry each other on their first date. Peter went into his father's engineering business and has done really well. They live in a beautiful house overlooking the sea and have two beautiful daughters. Yes, indeed, they live that charmed life that everyone strives to achieve.

Peter was away on a golf trip last weekend so Lainey cooked dinner for me, Claire and Brenda. Brenda was delighted to get away from the three boys for an evening, Claire had no plans and I presumed, quite rightly, that Richard would be working late again.

We were greeted by Lainey's two girls Alannah and Jenny, who opened the front door for us. They smiled angelically as I handed them a bag of sweets and some colouring pencils. They turned and sprinted upstairs before their mother saw the bag of goodies and told them not to eat sweets before bedtime. Lainey came out of the kitchen looking every bit the domestic goddess. Her trim size ten figure was clad in the most gorgeous wrap dress and her silky dark hair fell about her shoulders in loose curls.

"Hi, come on in. Your sister's beaten you to the first glass of wine."

In the kitchen Claire was perched on a stool at the island. Her legs were crossed and I immediately spotted the new boots and was glad I'd made the last-minute decision not to wear mine.

Brenda looked around at the New-England-style hand-painted kitchen with envy. "Every time I come here I fall in love all over again with this kitchen."

We all looked around and agreed with her; it was such a warm and welcoming place to be.

"Tom would kill me if he heard me complaining, but I'm so sorry I went for all that streamlined stainless-steel stuff – this is so much nicer," Brenda said, running her hand along the walnut butcher's block.

"You're right," I agreed. "He *would* kill you, after all the expense you went to with that kitchen. It just goes to show, you only ever want what you can't have."

"I suppose that's true," Brenda said, raising her glass. "I'm just spoilt."

We sat down to a starter of goat's cheese and sun-dried-tomato tartlets.

"Please tell me you bought these!" said Claire as she cut into hers.

Lainey laughed at the suggestion.

Claire put her face closer to her plate. "You didn't seriously make them yourself?" she exclaimed, lifting the cheese with her fork to get a closer look at the pastry.

"Oh this is so delicious!" said Brenda, not caring where the food came from.

"Yes, I made them myself," Lainey announced proudly.

"Jesus, Lainey, if I am reincarnated I want to come back to earth as your husband," Claire said as she reached across for some freshly baked bread. "Imagine getting handed food like this every day!"

Brenda pulled a pen and some paper from her handbag and had begun to demand the recipe when we were interrupted by Alannah and Jenny who came running into the kitchen to show their mother the pictures they had drawn. Evidence of the chocolate buttons I had given them was smeared all over their little faces.

"Girls," said Lainey sternly, "did you take chocolate without asking?"

They grinned impishly and pointed to me.

"Sorry," I said. "I'd forgotten how messy kiddies can be."

"Go upstairs and wash your faces," Lainey said, shooing them away from the table. Then she looked over at me and narrowed her eyes. "Wait till you adopt your baby – I'll bring the cheapest sticky toffees every time I visit."

Brenda shot me a worried glance and Claire lowered her head, but Lainey locked her eyes on mine.

"How are the interviews going?" she asked.

I shrugged my shoulders. "We've been given the go-ahead to proceed. We had an interview last Thursday which went really well. Now we have medicals to do, if I can get Richard to commit himself to a day."

"Just make the appointment and tell him he has to be there," said Lainey.

"I just can't wait for it to happen," Brenda said, giving my hand a quick squeeze.

"How long do they think it will take?" Claire asked without taking her eyes off her plate.

"It could be anything up to eighteen months," I answered. "Maybe even longer – there are tons of hurdles to overcome."

Claire nodded but I could tell she wasn't comfortable with the conversation. Although she'd always made it clear that she wasn't interested in having children, I thought I saw

24

a look of sadness in her eyes. Even if she was to change her mind about having a child, she still had no man in her life and it made me feel a little smug, as if I was gloating.

"Claire! I hate you for looking so good in that dress," Brenda exclaimed.

All eyes turned to Claire and the little black dress she was wearing.

"Thank you," she said with a grin. "I'll take that as a compliment."

Brenda grabbed a handful of flab around her middle and groaned. "Will I ever see the day that I can fit into something as gorgeous as that?"

"Don't be ridiculous!" quipped Lainey. "You'll be there in no time. Look how much weight you've lost already."

"Lainey's right," I agreed, trying to steer Brenda off the subject of her never-ending diet.

The main course was another culinary triumph. Medallions of beef in a brandy sauce with baby potatoes – she even managed to make a bowl of peas look sexy by tossing in pieces of feta cheese and prosciutto ham. After too much food and wine we sat back and talked about the summer holidays that were almost upon us.

Brenda and Tom were taking the kids to Disney in June.

Lainey and Peter had bought a villa in the south of France and they were spending July and August there.

Claire hadn't made any holiday plans and I was glad we hadn't either. Otherwise I'd feel compelled to invite her along. She had joined us in Portugal for a week last summer. We rented a huge villa, and there was more than enough room for the three of us. When I invited her, I'd hoped she would bring a partner, as once again I'd suspected that there might be a man on the scene. But she came alone and, although I enjoyed her company, I felt that three was definitely a crowd. While he has never actually said it, I know that Richard isn't overly fond of Claire. I can see it sometimes when they are in conversation. Claire likes to argue a point to the nth degree, she enjoys a heated exchange and gets great pleasure in finding someone who will rise to the challenge of the debate. But Richard finds this tiresome and confrontational and after living with both of them for two weeks in that villa, my brain was fried.

"Take some time off and come over and stay with us," said Lainey. "There's plenty of room."

"I don't know how I'm fixed for holidays at the moment, but thanks for the offer. I might take you up on it for a few days," Claire said.

"What about you, Liz?" asked Lainey, and all heads turned to me.

"I really can't plan anything with this damn tribunal. It's our wedding anniversary in two weeks and I'm thinking of booking a few days in Italy, in the hotel where we honeymooned."

"Oh, that sounds so romantic!" Brenda said wistfully.

"I have to pin Richard down and make sure he's free before I book anything."

"How long will you go for?" asked Claire.

"I was thinking from Thursday to Monday. That way it will take in a weekend and Richard might find it easier to get away."

"You'd better get your skates on," Brenda said. "The flights are getting busy this time of year."

"Yes, I'm going to talk to him tomorrow and get moving on it."

"That will be nice," said Lainey. "Like a second honeymoon."

"Yes, it will. We've been spending so little time together. I think we really need to get away. Besides, if I take up the offer Brian Davies made to me, it may be the last holiday I'll have in a while."

All three looked over at me.

"What offer?" asked Claire, her eyebrows arched with curiosity.

"He rang me yesterday and wants me to go back to Task."

The three of them moved closer.

"I don't believe you," exclaimed Brenda. "What about the hot shot that took over?"

"Didn't work out," I said with a self-satisfied grin.

"What are you going to do?" asked Lainey.

"I don't know," I said, thinking out loud. I had thought about nothing else since the call, but couldn't come to any decision. "He's so desperate to have me back that he's offered to make me a partner."

Lainey clapped her hands together. "Well done! You should have got it a long time ago – but better late than never. It took someone else to fill your shoes to show them what a good job you were doing."

I smiled at her enthusiasm.

"When will you start?" asked Claire.

"Oh, I'm nowhere near making a decision yet. In fact I more or less told him that I wasn't interested – although he didn't sound like he was taking no for an answer."

"Why not go back?" said Brenda.

"Well, the reason I left was . . ."

Lainey reached across and rested her hand on mine. "You left to have a baby."

I nodded my head and was conscious of the silence that had descended across the table.

"You're still going to have that baby. It's just going to take a little longer," Lainey said, giving my hand a reassuring squeeze.

"How would you feel about working full-time again?" asked Brenda.

"I really don't know. At first I was so sure that I didn't want it, but now I'm beginning to think that it might be good for me."

"If you like," Brenda continued, "you could come next door and mind my three kids and I'll take the job at Task. I used to be so envious, looking out the window at you every morning, while I was still in my dressing-gown making bottles. You used to step into your car looking like a vision from *Vogue*. I'd watch you pull out of your driveway and go back to picking pieces of Liga out of my hair, and promise myself that some day I'd look glamorous again."

I laughed at this. There were days when the kids were younger when it was not unusual to find Brenda still in her dressing-gown at three o'clock in the afternoon.

"Done!" I said, clinking my glass against Brenda's. "You've got the job."

"Seriously," said Claire, "you should go back. It would give you something else to focus on."

I bristled at her remark. "You make me sound like a 'desperate housewife'."

"I didn't mean to," said Claire, making no apologies as usual. "What I meant was, if the adoption process is going to take a while, then it might be good for you to have something else going on in your life. You can always give it up when the child arrives. What does Richard think?"

It suddenly occurred to me that I hadn't told Richard.

"I haven't spoken to him about it."

"He doesn't know yet!" Brenda said, looking shocked.

She found it hard to understand our relationship. I could go for days without talking to Richard and had become used to it, whereas Brenda rang Tom at least four times every day even though he was always home by six thirty. If one of the boys had a fall or an unexpected bill arrived in the post, Brenda was straight on the blower to Tom.

I threw my hands in the air. "He had his mobile switched off and I didn't bother leaving a message and I was asleep when he got in last night. Anyway, I don't want to tell him until I've made up my mind. Richard would probably love me to go back to work – anything to take my mind off the baby."

"He still isn't sure, is he?" commented the all-knowing Lainey.

I didn't want to agree with her, it sounded too definite. "I don't know," I said quietly. "He just doesn't share my enthusiasm. All these interviews, followed by a trip to China, is putting him off big time. You know Richard! He doesn't understand why we can't pop out to the local supermarket and buy one."

"I don't think there's anything unusual about that," said Brenda. "It's not the same for guys. They don't experience the same longing as women do when it comes to having kids. Tom was exactly the same, but as soon as the boys came along, that all changed. Believe me, as soon as you get this baby, Richard will change overnight."

"Do you think so?" I said, desperately wanting this to be true.

"Definitely! As soon as he sets eyes on that little child he'll be a different man."

"Well, don't any of you say a word to him about Task ringing me until I have my mind made up. I don't want him bullying me back to work."

"Agreed," said Lainey, as she pulled the cork from another bottle of wine.

I lay alone in bed when I got home, my heart racing from too much red wine. Richard was entertaining a client who was over from the Shields office in London, and was still not back from dinner. I thought of the look on Claire's face when I spoke of the adoption and wondered if I'd ever reach a point in my life when I didn't feel compelled to protect her. She was a grown woman now, and had made her own choices in life. The fact that she was without a partner was nobody's fault but her own. All those years with James were a waste of time, but she knew this when she was dating him. Now she was alone and seemed to turn her nose up at every man that showed the slightest bit of interest in her. I had tried so hard to set her up with men that I thought she might like, but every one of them had been met with utter disdain.

I am about to adopt a baby, yet my sister is making me feel guilty about it. Or is it really my sister that makes me feel this way? Perhaps it is a misplaced sense of responsibility that I have felt towards her for as long as I can remember.

Then

Auntie Rita is crying in the kitchen because Uncle Norman has run off with all of their money. Mum went with her to the bank today and the manager told her what Uncle Norman had done. He's gone to America and he's never coming back. I don't really know why Auntie Rita is crying so much because I don't think she ever liked Uncle Norman. They were always fighting and shouting at each other and Auntie Rita was always arriving at our house asking to stay the night because they'd had another row. I think she's more upset about losing the money than she is about losing Uncle Norman. Mum says that we have plenty of money to help her out and that Rita can stay with us as long as she likes because we have a spare room. I wish we didn't have a spare room. I don't like it when Auntie Rita stays with us. She's bossy and I hate the smell of her cigarettes. At first Daddy forbade her to smoke in the house, but now she just ignores him and puffs her smoke all over the place. Mum tells me to be nice to Rita because she's going through a hard time, but how can you be nice to someone you hate?

Auntie Rita doesn't like me very much either – she gets really annoyed when I sit at the table and listen to what she is saying to Mum.

"Can't she go out to the garden to play?" she says, nodding her head in my direction.

Mum looks at me and smiles but I don't move from the table. It's our table and Auntie Rita is only a guest – she should be the one to go and play in the garden with her stinky cigarettes. So, Rita stops talking and glares at me and I glare right back.

I hate her cooking.

Now that she is living with us Auntie Rita insists on sharing the cooking with Mum, so twice a week she makes us our dinner. Last week she made spaghetti bolognese with big lumps of tomatoes that made me want to choke.

I looked over at Mum and pleaded with my eyes, but she shook her head and whispered, "Lizzy, it's rude not to eat it after Rita going to so much bother."

I pushed it around my plate until it looked like cow dung and then just looking at it made me feel sick. Mum never makes me eat her dinners and they taste much nicer, so why should I have to eat Auntie Rita's slop?

"Look at that!" Rita exclaimed at the top of her voice. "Lizzy hasn't touched her dinner. Look at Claire's plate, she's eaten everything."

Claire's legs swung backwards and forwards as she smiled at us.

Daddy looked over and examined my plate. "Eat up, Lizzy."

Again I looked over at Mum but she just turned away.

"I don't like it," I whispered.

"Nonsense, all kids like my spaghetti bolognese. Now eat up before it gets cold!"

I took another spoonful but it wouldn't go down my throat. I chewed it for ages but it sat in my mouth and wouldn't go down. When no one was looking I let it fall out of my mouth back on to my plate, but Rita saw me.

"Oh for heavens sake, Lizzy! It can't be that bad," she said crossly.

I began to cry. "I just don't want to eat it."

Mum jumped up as if she couldn't stand it any more and took my plate away.

"She'll never get used to new food if you keep shovelling fish-fingers and chips into her day after day," Rita said while Mum scraped the cow dung into the bin.

"She's right, you know," said Daddy, wagging his fork at me. "You should educate your palate and start trying new things."

Mum swung around from the sink, looking really fed up with the two of them. "Well, today she tried spaghetti bolognese and guess what? She doesn't like it."

Daddy and Rita looked at each other in surprise as Mum stormed out of the kitchen. I jumped down from my chair and ran out after her in case Rita tried to make me eat anything else.

Auntie Rita is renting her house to some students, which means she won't be leaving us any time soon. She wants to rent out her house so she can have some money to live on instead of taking it from Mum and Daddy. The good news is that she has started a new job as a secretary so she is out all day. I think Mum is happy about that because she seems more relaxed during the daytimes – she doesn't have to listen to Rita bleating on about what she should and shouldn't be doing. I am on my summer holidays from school, and yesterday Mum made a picnic and we sat at the end of the back garden and ate it. It was just the three of us – me, Mum and Claire. When Claire had fallen asleep on the rug I told Mum that I hated Auntie Rita but she said that I was never to say that again, that I was just being unkind. I didn't say anything else because it seemed to upset Mum and I hate it when she gets upset.

Claire is starting school when the summer holidays are

over – last night, she tried on her new uniform when Daddy came home from work and he took a photograph of her. Rita kept cooing and kissing her and making her twirl around. She told Claire that she looked as pretty as a picture. She never says that about me.

Last night there was a storm and the branches of the chestnut tree blew so hard that they almost came through my bedroom window. I woke with a start and thought that someone was trying to break into my room. Mum pulled me back down beside her and told me it was only the wind. She'd been crying again. She'd been crying so hard that her breathing was all jerky and uneven like Claire's when she's had a tantrum.

"Will the fairies be blown out of the tree?" I asked.

"No, they hide inside the trunk when the wind blows."

"Are you feeling sad again?"

"Just a little."

"Will you feel better in the morning?"

"Yes, now go back to sleep."

I lay there but I could feel her sadness seeping in through my skin and I couldn't get back to sleep. Sometimes I wish Mum would take her sadness into Claire's bed, but I suppose Claire's too little to do anything about it.

Now

"Richard," I began. "Do you realise that we have been married almost fourteen years?"

He looked over at me as if I'd just accused him of murder.

"Well, I'm only stating a fact. Don't look so surprised," I said, laughing at his reaction.

"Christ," he muttered, "I thought you were going to tell

me that I'd missed our anniversary. But, of course, no, it's not yet."

"That's exactly what I want to talk to you about," I said, putting my hairbrush down.

We were going for the medical that had been arranged for the adoption board and for the first time in ages we were getting up together.

Richard concentrated on putting a knot in his tie as he spoke. "What? Our anniversary?"

"Let's go back to Portofino," I said with a rush of excitement. It was only then that I realised how much I really wanted us to go.

He swung around to me, holding the knot of his tie in place. "When?"

"Richard! For our anniversary! I've checked availability, and there are some seats on the flight left. The hotel is holding a room for me."

He didn't say anything for a few moments, then he swung back to the mirror. "I'd love nothing better, sweetheart, but you know how things are at the moment. It's impossible to get away."

I could feel a lump form in my throat and felt immediately stupid for feeling so disappointed. I knew how busy he was. He turned back to face me and I tried to blink back the tears that were threatening to fall.

"Oh God, Liz, I'm sorry. How long have you been thinking about this?"

I shrugged my shoulders and tried to brush it off as a passing thought. "Not very long – it just seemed like a nice idea." My voice sounded choked and there was no hiding the fact that I was about to crack up.

Richard rushed over and put his arms around me. "Don't get upset, Liz! Look, I'll check a few dates and see if I can manage to get away. How long were you thinking of?"

"Just a few days, maybe a long weekend. Richard, we never see each other any more. It's beginning to feel like we have no life together."

He tightened his grip on me and his voice sounded shaky. "I'm sorry, love. You're right. You go ahead and book it and I'll just have to make the time."

We proceeded to get ready in silence. I felt like a spoilt child that had got what she'd wanted by sulking and blubbering. I hadn't meant to put a gun to his head to make him spend time with me, but that's exactly what it felt like.

We were taking the early morning flight, so the taxi arrived to take us to the airport at 5 a.m. We walked about the house bleary-eyed, making sure windows were closed and doors were locked. We both sat in the back of the taxi and stared out at the deserted early-morning streets that would soon be heaving with rush-hour traffic. Richard's eyes were puffy and he looked tired. I had gone to bed early and only had a vague memory of him getting into bed very late. I was glad I'd pushed for this weekend – it would do him good to get away from it all.

"Tired?" I asked.

He nodded grumpily as he switched on his mobile phone and checked for messages. "I was with Damian Jones last night. We've a lot more ground to cover before this case gets heard next week."

Damian was from the Shields office in London and was

over in Dublin working on something for the tribunal. It had been on my mind to invite him over for dinner some night, but I still hadn't got around to it. I made a mental note to do so as soon as we returned from Italy. The poor guy was holed up in an apartment and seemed to do nothing but work – it would be a nice gesture to invite him over. Another reason I wanted to invite him over was because Richard had mentioned that he was recently divorced, and was reasonably good-looking. I hadn't met him myself so would have to rely on Richard's judgement in the looks department. I would have to ask a few more people, so that Claire couldn't accuse me of trying to fix her up – although that was exactly what I'd be trying to do.

Although it was an unearthly hour of the morning, Dublin airport looked like a supermarket on Christmas Eve, with queues snaking back as far as the eye could see.

Richard scowled at the scene and proceeded to scour the board for the number of our check-in desk. He located it and, gripping my arm firmly, negotiated our way through the throng.

The queue moved with surprising speed and fifteen minutes later we were browsing through the duty-free shops. As we walked towards our boarding gate, Richard put his hand up to his chest and began to beat it frantically. I dropped my magazine and grabbed ahold of his arm.

"What's wrong?" I cried.

His whole face had contorted and the first thing I thought of was a heart attack.

"Richard, are you all right?"

Some passers-by had slowed down to see what was happening.

He dropped his briefcase on the floor and put his hand inside his jacket. "My phone," he moaned.

I stared at him in disbelief, feeling the rush of adrenaline subside as my brain registered the false alarm. "Your phone?"

"Christ Almighty! I think I left it in the taxi."

"Jesus, Richard. I thought you were having a heart attack," I said, bending down to pick up my magazine.

"I will have a heart attack if I've left it there." He picked up the briefcase and balanced it on his knee before opening it. "Shit, shit, shit," he muttered as he threw the contents of his briefcase around. "It's not here," he said as he snapped the case closed.

"Richard, take it easy. If we ring the taxi company now, they can probably locate it," I said, taking control of the situation.

He looked at me blankly and glanced at his watch. "I can't go without it. I haven't told anyone in Shields that I'm going away today. You've no idea the amount of work we have to get through before next week. Damian would do his nut if he knew I was planning on spending the next two days on a weekend break in Italy. I need that phone beside me day and night. Ring the cab company on your phone and see if they have it."

After waiting twenty minutes while Richard paced the floor of the departure lounge like a lunatic, the cab company rang back to say that they had located our driver but no phone had been found.

"That's it," said Richard on hearing this. "I can't leave the country without that phone. All my numbers are keyed into it – I'm screwed without it."

The final call for our flight was announced and I looked him squarely in the eye.

"Are you saying that we have to cancel our trip because you have no phone?"

He jumped from one foot to the other, looking utterly agitated, and ran a finger under his shirt collar. "Liz," he pleaded, "what can I do? We're in court next Thursday and the outcome will decide whether we press ahead with this case. It's only a phone, but I need to be at the other end of it twenty-four hours a day."

"You can use my phone. You can contact the office when we land and get all of your numbers faxed over. You can stop behaving as if your life depends on it, and get on that plane now."

He looked at me in surprise as another final call was made for our flight. The boarding gate, that had been heaving with passengers minutes earlier, was now empty except for two airline staff who were giving us murderous glares.

"Don't do this to me, Richard," I said sternly.

He looked over at the airline staff and back to me, as if he was going to make a run for it.

"Just get on the plane," I said, surprised by the even tone of my voice.

Without saying anything, Richard turned around and walked towards the two irate flight attendants, and handed them our boarding cards.

Nothing had changed in the fourteen years since we'd last been there. I had requested the same room at the Grand

Hotel Mare and it was just as beautiful as I had remembered. The sun glistened across the sparkling azure sea as we ate breakfast on our terrace. Richard had still not adjusted to living without his phone and things had been tense between us since our arrival. I began to question whether I had done the right thing, dragging him off on the weekend before an important court hearing. He had called the cab company at least ten times but there was still no sign of the damn thing.

"How about a swim?" I suggested lazily, as I drained the remains of coffee.

"Maybe later," Richard replied. "I need to make a few calls first."

"My phone is on charge beside the television."

"I'll make them from the room phone."

Down at the pool most of the sun beds were vacant. The summer season had not yet begun and the hotel was at its most peaceful. I dived into the crystal-clear water and felt a rush of blood to my head as the coolness penetrated my body. After five lengths, I felt slightly less guilty about the amount of food I had eaten the night before and convinced myself that I had worked off all the excess calories. Not being a strong swimmer, I was also completely out of breath. I dried off and fell back into the comforting warmth of the sun bed. I flicked though my magazine and read a four-page spread about a celebrity I'd never heard of, before turning over onto my stomach to let the warm rays of sun fall across my back. Although I had only just risen after nine hours' sleep, I felt my eyes growing heavy and gave in to the wave of laziness that washed over me.

The crash of water woke me with a start. I jumped up

and looked around the place in silent panic. The noise of someone jumping into the pool had woken me. I quickly wiped the stream of dribble from the side of my face and hoped that I hadn't been snoring. I looked at my watch – it was almost one o'clock – I had been asleep for over an hour. The beds on either side of me were both empty. No sign of Richard. I grabbed my kaftan and pulled it on before gathering my things together and heading back to the room.

Richard was sitting on the balcony thumbing through some papers. He turned to me and smiled as I stepped from the bedroom on to the baking terrace.

"Well, it's the Sleeping Beauty!"

I put my hand to my face, conscious of the fact that there were probably Alice-Cooper-style gashes etched into my cheeks as a result of my mid-morning coma.

"Could you see me from here?" I asked, peering over the balcony, trying to locate where'd I'd been sitting.

"No," Richard said casually, "but I could hear you."

"Oh, stop it!" I exclaimed. "Richard, please tell me you couldn't!"

He began to chuckle and looked back down to his work.

I bent down and put my hand over the papers to get his full attention.

"Was I snoring?" I had a very unpleasant vision of me lying unconscious on the sun bed, snoring like a pig. It was something I did quite regularly, especially when I fell into a deep sleep. When we were kids, Lainey used to throw things at me on the nights I stayed over in her house and my snoring woke her. In fact, I still have a tiny scar near my ear, from the time she threw a stiletto at me.

Richard looked up at me and burst out laughing.

"Stop teasing," I demanded. "Was I snoring down at the pool? You didn't really hear me from up here, did you?"

He packed his papers tightly into a bundle and put them on top of his briefcase, prolonging my misery. "Not exactly from here," he said, beginning to laugh again. "I went down and had a swim and sat beside you for a few minutes. You were dead to the world, so I just reached over and closed your mouth gently. The people beside the pool were delighted – apparently there'd been complaints to the management all morning about the noise of the road works."

I buried my face in my hands and groaned. "Oh God! I'm not leaving the room for the rest of the weekend. Why didn't you wake me?"

Richard couldn't keep it in any longer and erupted into an uncontrollable schoolboy's giggle. I looked over at him and saw that he'd been winding me up.

I picked up his bundle of papers and hit him over the head with them.

"You little shit!" I said, trying not to laugh, but it was impossible to keep a straight face. "Oh my God! That would have been so embarrassing! You big liar! Were you even down at the pool at all?"

Richard leaned over and kissed my forehead. "Yes, my love, I was, and you looked too peaceful to wake, so I left you be."

"And I wasn't snoring?" I asked, just to be sure.

"Not even a little grunt," he assured me.

"Happy Anniversary," I said as the waiter poured the champagne.

I had booked the restaurant where we had eaten on the first night of our honeymoon, and apart from a few new waiters, it hadn't changed at all.

Richard raised his glass and smiled over at me. "You look more beautiful than you did on our wedding night."

My face flushed with the compliment, aided by too much sun that day. "You don't look too bad yourself."

Richard had managed to tear himself away from his briefcase for the afternoon and we'd lounged around the pool for a couple of hours after lunch. All my feelings of guilt at dragging him away from work had disappeared as I watched him relax and just do nothing but lie in the sun and unwind. Already, I could see the difference those few hours had made. His grey pallor had been replaced with a healthy tan – Richard only had to look at the sun for his skin to turn a nutty brown. He reached across the table and put his hand on top of mine.

"I love you, honey," he whispered.

Dinner was superb. The three waiters that were assigned to our table hovered around us like demented mosquitoes.

As the last of the champagne was poured into our glasses, I realised that Richard had drunk most of the bottle by himself. I was still trying to get through my second glass. Champagne and too much sun were a bad combination and I could feel myself getting woozy.

Richard's eyes had that misty look that he sometimes gets when he's had too much to drink.

"Honey, why don't you have some water?" I said. "You'll get dehydrated."

He smiled a clownish smile and drained the last of his

champagne before reaching for his glass of red wine. "To hell with it," he slurred. "It's our honeymoon."

"No, dear, it's our anniversary. We had our honeymoon fourteen years ago."

He slid his hand across the table, knocking over his empty champagne glass. One of our waiters scurried over and plucked the glass from the table with one swift movement. Richard took my hand and laced his fingers through mine.

"I love you, Liz. You know that, don't you?"

I smiled at his foolish expression. "I do know that," I said.

"I'm a shitty husband and I don't deserve you," he said, his grin now fading to a frown.

I tightened my grip on his hand. "You are not a shitty husband," I reassured him. "Richard, why would you say that?"

His face drooped despondently. "I don't spend enough time with you. I haven't given you any support about the adoption. I am a shithead." (The 'shithead' was pronounced with a little too much emphasis on the sh, making it sound like 'shed'.)

He said this a little too loudly and I looked around at the handful of diners in the restaurant and smiled at them apologetically.

"Richard, stop it. I love you and that's all that matters. I know that when we get the baby things will change. You'll feel differently, and you'll have more time to spend at home. Things are just hectic right now and I understand."

He looked at me with his big brown doleful eyes, and I suddenly wanted to put my arms around him and hold him close to me.

"You do?" he said.

"Yes. I do."

We got a taxi back to the hotel and I steered my very unsteady husband of fourteen years into the elevator and up to our room. By the time I had taken off my make-up and slipped into the silk nightie I had bought especially for the occasion, Richard was lying on the bed in a drunken coma still wearing his clothes.

The following morning was our last day and Richard stayed in the room for most of it. He sat on the terrace for the morning sipping Alka-Seltzer, looking a little the worse for wear. He did manage to join me down at the pool for an hour, but Shields were having a problem and he spent most of the afternoon back in the bedroom on a conference call.

Am I a demanding woman? I asked myself this question as I sat alone and gazed at the ripples that the gentle breeze created on the surface of the swimming pool.

Had I been pressurising him too much about the baby? Did I set him off on a guilt trip for spending too much time away from me? Was I responsible for the look of misery on his face the night before as he confessed to being such a bad husband? It had filled me with guilt. Perhaps Claire was right when she'd said I was too focused on this baby. The last thing I wanted to do was neglect Richard, or make him feel inadequate. After all, he was only trying to make a living. He had always provided me with everything I wanted and I'd never had to worry about money matters since the day we were married.

The sun disappeared behind a cloud and I shivered slightly as I felt the chill of the breeze against my bare arms.

Was I being unreasonable? I wondered, as I threw my hat and sun lotion into my bag and prepared to go back up to the room to pack. Perhaps I was.

Then

I hear a shrill ring in the distance. In my dream there is a telephone ringing that no one can find. I look for it in the garden but it's not there. Claire searches through the toy box in the den but she can't find it either. Daddy is looking for it in his office, but still the telephone continues to ring.

I open my eyes and Mum is sitting up in the bed beside me.

"Go back to sleep. I'll get it." She leaves the room to answer the telephone that is on the locker beside her bed.

We have two telephones. One is on the hall table and the other is in their bedroom in case Daddy gets a call in the middle of the night for an emergency sitting in court. He got a call once, before they got the phone put in their bedroom and he fell down the stairs trying to get to it in time and sprained his ankle.

I get out of bed and follow her out to the landing but she turns at her bedroom door and stares back at me crossly.

"Get back to bed!" she hisses.

The telephone is still ringing.

Claire appears from her bedroom and begins to cry.

I stand there in a daze and watch the landing fill up with people. First it was just Mum and me. Now Daddy and Claire and Rita are all standing there like ghosts in the darkness and the phone has stopped ringing because Mum has answered it.

Rita picks up Claire and takes her back to bed.

Mum appears at her bedroom door. "It's for you," she mumbles and brushes past Daddy without looking at him. She grips my hand and pulls me quickly back into my bedroom.

We lie together and listen while Daddy gets dressed in the room next to us.

I can feel Mum's chest tighten as I rest my head on her shoulder, and wait for her tears to come.

Now I know I can never take away her sadness.

"Why was Daddy in Auntie Rita's room?"

I hear her muffled sobs as she buries her head into the pillow and I put my arms around her neck.

I don't say anything else. I lie back and stare at the wall and concentrate on the shadows of the fluttering leaves as they wave me back to sleep.

Now

Linda Simms sits behind her desk and smiles at us. We are spruced up for the occasion. I have on my grey Dolce & Gabanna trouser suit and I have carefully picked out the clothes that Richard is wearing. Linda will be our adoption liaison counsellor. She will lead us through the maze of bureaucracy, paperwork and emotions until the day we finally get our baby. I desperately want her to like us. I want her to think that we would make the best parents possible. I lace my fingers together in order to stop my hands from shaking and try to exude an air of composure.

"How old will she be?" I hear myself ask. We already know that our child will be a girl.

"Anywhere between six months and one year," she answers.

"How long will it be before we can take her home?"

"From the time she is handed to you in China, it usually takes about four weeks until the paperwork is finalised."

I nod my head and smile back at her. I don't want to bombard her with too many inquiries.

"You both must be very excited."

"Yes," I gush, "we are."

I look over at Richard but he does not meet my gaze. He seems to be examining his watchstrap. I silently implore him to ask her something. Anything. Just to prove he has his heart set on this baby. He has not opened his mouth since entering the office.

Linda picks up her pen and begins to write something down.

"Now," she says, looking at the form in front of her. "Your referees are Tom and Brenda Power and Peter and Lainey Chambers. Is that correct?"

I say nothing and wait for Richard to answer. A second passes before he realises what I am doing. He clears his throat.

"Yes, yes, that's correct," he says, straightening up in his chair.

"And they have known both of you for some time?"

He looks over at me and searches my face for the right answer.

"We've known the Chambers since we started dating," I said. "Lainey was a neighbour of mine, we grew up together. The Powers are our next-door neighbours. We've known them for eight years."

Linda is writing as I speak. "Okay, that seems to be fine," she says as she moves on to another form. "How soon do you think you can get the references to me?"

Again Richard gives me a hapless glance.

"I'll have them within a week or two," I answer. "It'll take them that long to write down all the wonderful things about us." I give a nervous giggle and feel immediately foolish for trying to make light of the situation.

Linda smiles over at me and glances down at the new set of forms in her hand.

"There will be medicals to take, but both your medical records are excellent, so there shouldn't be any problem there."

She puts down her pen and looks over at us. "Do either of you have anything else you want to ask?'"

Please, Richard. Surprise me. Anything.

"No?" she says, clicking the top of her pen.

"No," I say. "I think you've answered everything for us."

She stands up and stretches out her arm to me.

"Thank you for calling in," she says as she shakes my hand. She turns to Richard. "You'll have a social worker appointed to you in the near future. I'll be in touch with you about it."

Richard shakes her hand and we say goodbye.

Out on the street I feel my anger rise with every step we take.

Richard checks his precious watch again and turns to me. "I thought we could stop off for lunch but that took a lot longer than I expected. I'd better fly."

I stop walking and glare at him.

"What?" he says, looking at me with an uncertain smile.

"Could you not afford an hour out of your schedule to give to our baby?"

His head jerks back in surprise. "What are you talking about?"

Tears sting the back of my eyes and I want so badly to slap his face.

"One hour is all that meeting took, and you sat there and stared at your bloody watch as if we were boring you."

"That's not fair, Liz. I told you I had a meeting this afternoon."

"I don't care about your meeting!" I shouted. "This is about us getting a baby and you sat there as if you couldn't give a damn whether it happens or not." I stop and check myself when a woman passing by stares straight at us, making me aware that I am raising my voice in the middle of a street.

Richard throws his hands in the air and gives a long exasperated sigh. "For God's sake, Liz! Stop being so dramatic. So I checked my watch a few times, what's wrong with that?"

I chew my lower lip and swallow hard and wonder once again if I'm being unreasonable. I don't know any more.

"Just go back to work," I say almost inaudibly, waving him away.

He steps closer to me and cranes his neck to meet my eye. I look away immediately, too hurt to hear his explanation or apology. His phone begins to ring and I can see that he wants to answer it, but he is torn between it and me. He stands in front of me and we both listen as it rings.

"You're overreacting," he says and rubs my arm awkwardly as if he is afraid that I might slap it away.

I don't. I stand like a block of ice and stare at his breast pocket where his mobile phone is still ringing. Then I turn and walk away.

We always meet in Daphne's for coffee. It isn't a very fashionable place and it could certainly do with a face-lift, but they make the best scones in the world. When I arrived, Lainey was sitting in the corner at our favourite table waving over at me.

"Hi," she said, leaning over to kiss my cheek.

"Brenda just rang – she's running a bit late."

"Let's go ahead and order without her, I'm dying for a cup of coffee," I said as I settled into the chair.

"You look great," beamed Lainey. "Any news?"

"Thanks," I answered, patting down my freshly cut hair. I had risen early which was unusual for me on a Saturday, and had already had my hair cut and highlighted.

"No news really," I said.

Lainey looked disappointed. "Did you decide about Task? Are you going back?"

We gave our order to the waitress and I turned back to answer her question.

"The truth is I haven't decided yet. I've given myself another week to make up my mind."

"Which way are you swaying?"

I paused for a moment and tried to think of which way I was swaying. Every way really. One minute I wanted to go back and the next minute I was certain that I didn't. I felt completely stumped.

"I'm not being evasive, but I just can't make up my mind," I said.

"I know how you feel. Sometimes it's difficult to go back to things that you thought were over," Lainey said as she took her handbag off the table to make room for the coffees.

"Yes, that's it. I really thought that part of my life was over and I was moving on to other things. Now it almost seems like a step backwards."

"Being made partner of one of the biggest ad agencies in town is hardly a step backwards."

"I know. It's not about the job. I suppose it's just where I am in my life right now. I thought things were going to work out so differently."

Brenda breezed in with a huge smile on her face and threw her shopping bags in the corner.

"Someone's been busy," I said, eyeing the bags.

Brenda flopped down onto the chair, looking chuffed with herself.

"I just bought two pairs of fab shoes and a new outfit," she announced with unashamed glee.

"Good for you," said Lainey as she rummaged through the bags. "Oh these are gorgeous!" she exclaimed, pulling out a pair of red wedge-heeled suede shoes.

"I've lost five pounds and decided to treat myself," Brenda said, patting her stomach. "At last that baby weight is beginning to shift."

Brenda had put on a lot of weight with her last pregnancy and she was determined to lose it, even if it meant starving herself. She had picked at nuts and salads for the past three months and finally the results were beginning to show.

"Just a coffee for me," she said to the waitress. "Now,

what do you have to tell us? Or should we wait till Claire arrives?"

I laughed at their curiosity. They were waiting for some big announcement and what I had to say wasn't exactly earth-shattering.

"No, we don't have to wait for Claire," I said. "I want to ask the two of you something."

They leaned in to the table and waited for me to continue.

"Would both of you supply Richard and me with character references for the adoption board?"

They sat back, looking slightly disappointed with my request.

"Of course," Lainey said.

"Sure," echoed Brenda. "Is that it?"

I laughed again. "Yes, that's it. I'm sorry it isn't something more exciting."

"It is exciting," said Lainey. "You just sounded a bit secretive on the phone. We thought you might have had a bit of gossip."

"What sort of things do we have to say about you?" Brenda asked.

"Oh, just the truth. That we're the most perfect couple you've ever met and what a fantastic mother I'm going to be. That sort of thing," I said with a grin.

"No problem," said Brenda. "I was always a great liar."

"Actually I wanted to ask you something else before Claire gets here. Richard has a client over from the London office. He's staying here in the company apartment and I want to invite him over to dinner. I've been trying to get around to it for weeks but something always gets in the way.

I feel a bit sorry for the guy – he seems to spend his free evenings, not that there's many of them, wandering around town on his own. Would Saturday week suit both of you?"

"I think so. I'll just check with Peter and see if he's free," said Lainey, scribbling it into her diary.

"Yes," Brenda said quickly. "We'd love to come. Why before Claire arrives? Aren't you inviting her?"

"Of course I am. This guy had a short-lived marriage with no kids and is now single. According to Richard, he's also very nice and reasonably good-looking. I thought it would be good for Claire to meet him. But I don't want to make it sound like a set-up – she's a bit touchy about being single at the moment so . . ."

"Here's Claire," said Lainey, nudging me in the ribs. "Grab that chair beside you."

Claire walked over and waved a hand in the air. "Hi, all, sorry I'm late!"

She pulled out the chair and sank down into it. Dark rings circled her eyes making her look as if she hadn't slept for days. It had been three weeks since we had seen each other and I knew just by looking at her that she wasn't well.

"How have you been?" I asked.

"Crap," she answered. "I've had a cold for weeks that I can't get seem to get rid of."

"Have you been off work?" asked Lainey.

Claire rolled her eyes up to heaven. "No such luck. I've hardly been out of the place – things are hectic at the moment."

"Why don't you take a few days off next month and come down to France with us?" asked Lainey.

"That's just what I need," said Claire, her eyes glazing over at the very thought of it.

"Well, why don't you? Just book a ticket and come," insisted Lainey.

Claire hesitated for a moment.

"Really, Claire, you need a break. You've been working far too hard lately." Lainey tilted her head to one side and waited for an answer.

"Are you sure I wouldn't be intruding?" Claire asked.

Lainey gave a broad smile. "Not at all! We'd be thrilled to have you."

"I'll probably only make it down for a long weekend, but thanks, I could certainly do with a break."

"Peter will be delighted. He'll be able to clear off and play golf and we'll have some quality retail time together." Lainey clasped her hands together like a child.

"I'll check out some flights and get back to you about it," said Claire, brightening up a little at the prospect of a holiday. "Did you decide about Task yet?" she asked, turning to me.

I looked over at Lainey and gave a weak smile. "We were just talking about it. I haven't made a decision yet. I'm giving myself another week."

"What did Richard say?" said Claire.

"I haven't told him yet."

The three of them looked at me incredulously and waited for an explanation. I hesitated for a moment, wondering whether to smile and gloss over the situation or to tell the truth. The truth seemed like a better idea.

"Richard has no interest in adopting this baby. The further along the process goes, the less he seems to care about it. I'm doing it all on my own. Going back to work is going back to the way things used to be and I know that's what he wants. If he knows that I'm thinking about it, he'll push me to accept the offer in the hope that I'll forget about the adoption. You might think I'm jumping to conclusions but I know Richard, and I know he would love me to go back to work and stop nagging him about this baby."

There was a heavy silence.

"You'll have to talk to him Liz," said Lainey.

"It certainly sounds like you have a lot to clear up," Brenda added.

Claire pulled at the corner of the tablecloth and I waited to hear what she had to throw in. She was hopeless in these situations. It was always me telling her what to do about her life, never the other way round.

"Maybe you should postpone the adoption and go back to work for a while," she said at last. "It might give you a better perspective on the situation and give Richard some time to think about it. He has to want this child too."

"That might not be a bad idea," said Brenda.

I fiddled with my napkin and felt a sinking feeling of regret in my stomach. I was sorry I had said anything. If that was all that Claire had to offer then she really had no idea of how strongly I felt about getting this child.

"It might not be a bad idea if I was ten years younger, but sadly I can't afford the luxury of that option. I'm forty years of age. I can't waste any more time."

The three of them hopped about on their seats at this.

"Lots of women are having babies well into their forties these days," Brenda said.

"There's a woman in the UK that's nearly sixty and she's pregnant," chirped Lainey.

I put my hands up to stop any more unhelpful comments.

"Yes, thank you, I know all that, but foreign adoptions take time and I could be waiting another two or three years by the time I get a child." I listened to myself and realised that I was saying I, not we. "By the time *we* get our child."

"I'm sorry," said Claire. "That wasn't a very helpful suggestion, was it?"

I looked over and smiled at her. "No, not really."

Did I imagine it, or did her eyes get watery for a split second?

Richard undressed quietly while I lay in bed pretending to sleep. I knew I had to talk to him yet I had no idea how to begin. I had to word this carefully. I had to be firm and employ a strategy that would prevent him from changing my mind in any way. He has always had a way of sounding so much more pragmatic than me, and there have been times that I have allowed myself to be led blindly into situations that I didn't want to be in.

He pulled back his side of the duvet and climbed in beside me.

"Richard," I whispered.

"Did I wake you?"

I turned to face him in the darkness. "No, I was already awake. We need to talk."

I felt his body stiffen even though we were not touching.

"I didn't tell you this because I needed time to think about it. Brian Davies rang me a few weeks ago. He wants

57

me to come back to work. He's offered to make me partner if I agree."

He breathed out deeply and I waited for a second while he processed this information.

"Why are you only telling me now?"

Not the reaction I'd expected.

"I needed to think about it first and make my own decision. I didn't want to be influenced by you."

Another loud exhalation.

"You mean 'bullied'."

"No, I just wanted some time to mull it over before I talked to you about it."

"Well, congratulations on being made partner, if you decide to go back."

I could tell by the tone of his voice that he was annoyed.

"Richard, I'm so confused. I know it's a great offer and I should be pleased but I feel that by accepting it I'm somehow going back to a place that I thought I'd left for good."

He moved closer to me and slipped his arm around my stomach.

"Only you can make the decision, Liz. I'll support you whatever you decide."

"I still want this baby, Richard. I want it with all my heart. Sometimes I dream about her waiting for us in her little cot in an orphanage and I wake with this terrible longing inside. It's so strong that I can almost feel her, Richard."

I felt the muscles in his forearm tighten against my skin.

"You don't feel anything like that, do you?"

There. I'd said it. The problem was now articulated and therefore real.

"No, I don't," he said hoarsely.

I could feel my heart sinking down into the depths of the mattress.

"We can't adopt a baby if you feel that way, Richard."

His silence filled the air. He took his arm from around me and rolled on to his back.

"Liz, I don't know what to say. I can't lie about it, I just don't feel any emotion towards this baby and I can't say if I ever will. Even in the beginning, when we were trying for a child, I never felt as strongly as you did about it. I just thought it would happen and I'd deal with it as we went along. I can't explain it, but I could never see myself as a father. And now, with all this adoption business, well, it's made it seem all the more complicated. It seems wrong, going to such lengths to get a child that I've no real longing for. Maybe it's because I'm so busy at the moment that I just can't think straight. If we could even wait until next year until after the tribunal is over and I have some time to invest in it." He made it sound like a property deal. "Liz?"

"Yes."

"How about it? Put it off until next year."

"You really think you might feel differently about it then?"

"Yes."

"You're positive you don't want to forget about it altogether?" I tried to disguise my disappointment but there was an undeniable shake in my voice.

Richard turned back to me and stroked my hair. "I know how much this means to you, Liz, but I need a little more time."

"Okay, we'll put it off until next year," I said, quietly calculating that next year was only six months away.

Then

I must spend the entire day in my room today.

Yesterday it was my birthday. Mum made a special hedgehog cake from her recipe book and used chocolate fingers for the spikes. I allowed Claire to stick some of the candles in the cake. Ten candles, one for every year.

It was a hot afternoon and Mum put the picnic rug at the end of the garden and we made daisy chains. I made mine on my own and Mum helped Claire because Claire's fingernails are not long enough to open the stems of the daisies.

"Where's my birthday girl?" Daddy shouted from the kitchen window.

He was never home from work before tea. I felt so happy to see him that I sprinted up the garden and into the kitchen to meet him. I threw my arms around his waist and buried my face in his stomach.

"Well now, Miss," he said, picking me up.

My feet dangled down to his knees. I am getting too tall for Daddy to pick me up but it felt good, swinging with my arms around his neck like a big monkey.

"Have you been a good girl?"

Claire ran into the kitchen and put her arms around one of Daddy's legs, almost toppling us over. "I'm a good girl, Daddy!" she shouted at him.

Mum stood at the back door, her arms folded across her chest, smiling in at us.

"Lizzie's been a very good girl," she said, pulling Claire away from us.

"In that case, come with me," he said, planting me on the floor and taking me by the hand out into the hall. My heart jumped up into my mouth when I saw what was standing there. I dug my nails into the palm of Daddy's hand with excitement. It was pink and shiny and had sparkly streamers that hung from the handlebars. My very own grown-up new bicycle.

I stood and stared at it in disbelief. I'd been begging them to get me a new bike for ages, but Daddy said that there was nothing wrong with the one I had.

"Do you like it, Lizzy?" Mum asked from behind me.

"Yes," I whispered.

Claire came running out of the kitchen and headed straight for the bicycle.

"I want it!" she screamed.

She began to climb up on it, but it was too big for her and it wobbled precariously against the wall. Daddy went over and pulled her away gently.

"This is for your big sister," he said. "When you are a big girl we'll get one for you."

Claire struggled out of his grip. "I want it, I want it!" she screamed.

Mum went over and picked her up but Claire cried even harder.

"You can have my old one, Claire," I said, but she was crying too loud to hear me.

"She's tired," said Mum as she walked away with Claire struggling in her arms. "I'll take her upstairs for a while."

I went over and ran my hand along the cool metal of the handlebars.

"Let's take it outside to the garden and see if that saddle is the right height for you," Daddy said, taking the bicycle from against the wall and steering it through the kitchen.

Outside in the garden he took a spanner from the tool shed and lowered the saddle until my feet could touch the ground. The streamers on the handlebars fluttered in the warm breeze as I cycled around the garden feeling giddy with excitement. After three laps at high speed, I stopped and grinned over at Daddy as he filmed me with his cine camera. I waved to the camera and shouted thank-you over and over again.

Daddy put the camera down on the picnic rug and came over to me.

"I love it, Daddy. Thank you."

He bent down and kissed me on the forehead. "You've been a very good girl, Lizzy. You deserve a new bicycle. Happy birthday."

Mum came out of the kitchen with Claire who was carrying a jug of lemonade and spilling lots of it out on the grass as she walked towards us.

"I have lemonade!" she cried out. Her face was still red and blotchy from crying but the lemonade had made her forget about the bicycle.

The four of us sat on the rug and drank our lemonade in the sunshine. Mum sat next to Daddy wearing her new yellow sundress that made her look so pretty. I looked over at both of them and wished that it could be like this forever. Lemonade, sunshine, my birthday – and no Auntie Rita.

"Yoohoo!" she cried from the top of the garden. "I hope you haven't started the party without me." She teetered towards us in her high heels, clutching my birthday present.

I looked over at her and wished that I could run her over with my new bicycle.

"Happy birthday, darling," she said, planting a wet lipsticky kiss on my cheek.

I wiped it away as soon as she turned to plonk herself down on the rug, in between Mum and Dad. I stared at the wrapped gift on my lap and wanted to throw it over the back wall, but they were all looking down at it, waiting for me to open it.

"Well, go on, open it," ordered Rita as she fished about in her bag for cigarettes.

Mum looked over at me and forced a weak smile.

I slowly tore the paper open and unfolded a disgusting Aran cardigan with pukey brown leather buttons. I held it up and stared at it.

Rita gripped an unlit cigarette between her teeth and snatched the cardigan from me.

"It should fit," she said, holding it up to me. "I got it a size bigger because the lady in the shop said that they shrink after the first wash."

"Rita, you shouldn't have gone to that expense. It's lovely, isn't it, Lizzy?"

I looked over at Mum as she tried to compensate for my silence and I felt my face go red.

"Yes, very nice indeed," Daddy said, glaring over at me.

"Thank you," I said, stuffing the cardigan back into the pink wrapping paper.

"Try it on," barked Rita. "I can take it back tomorrow if it's not the right size."

I looked across at Mum and made my eyes bigger to show her that I didn't want to.

"Just slip it on over your T-shirt," Mum said.

I fingered the scratchy wool and thought that I would

63

rather die than put it against my bare arms. "Can I wait until later?"

Mum looked over at Rita awkwardly. "It's a bit hot now. She'll try it on later, before she goes to bed."

Rita flicked her lighter open and lit her cigarette – she took a giant suck from it and stuck her nose in the air.

"It wouldn't kill her to slip it on for a second," she mumbled as she blew the smoke out.

"Here," said Daddy, grabbing the cardigan and undoing the pukey buttons. "Try it on now and see if it fits."

My throat felt tight and I bit down hard on my lip.

"I don't want to try it on now," I whispered over to Mum.

Mum jumped up from the rug and pulled the cardigan from Daddy's hands.

"She's too hot to try it on now," she said with her back teeth clenched tightly. "We'll do it later." She glared down at Daddy for a few seconds before turning to walk away. "I'll go and get a start on the dinner," I heard her say as she rushed back up the garden towards the kitchen clutching the cardigan to her chest.

The scratchy wool made my teeth feel strange even though the cardigan was nowhere near my mouth. Once the first stitch had come undone the whole thing began to unravel of its own accord. The tiny nail scissors had taken on a life of its own and it ripped through the wool with surprising ease. I was barely moving my fingers yet the hole was getting bigger and bigger before my eyes.

The floor outside my bedroom door creaked and I took a firm grip of the scissors and threw it onto the floor and stared down in horror at what it had done to my birthday present. I stuffed the cardigan under my bottom and sat with my legs swinging against the side of the bed.

Rita pushed open the door and walked in.

"Well, has the Birthday Girl cooled down enough to try on her cardigan?"

My heart clattered inside my chest as if it was going to burst open. I sat on the bed and didn't move. Her beady eyes scanned the room and stopped as she spotted the sleeve dangling down beside my leg. With one fluid movement she crossed the room and yanked it from under me.

"Come on, Lizzy," she said, pulling me off the bed. "Try it on now, so I can bring it back and change it for another size if it doesn't fit."

One arm was forced into the sleeve, then the other. I stood like a statue and waited for her reaction. First her face went a funny shade of pink, then her hand shot up to her mouth as she spotted the scissors on the floor and realised what I'd done. The first sharp tug brought the cardigan down to my elbows, making me feel as if I was trapped in a straitjacket. It came clean away on the second tug. As she freed me from the scratchy wool she took the opportunity to give me a rough thump between the shoulder blades that sent me flying across the room.

"You spiteful little bitch!" she spat, as she bent down to pick up the scissors.

We stood staring at each other for a couple of seconds. It must have been all the hatred that came pouring out of my eyes that made her give a little shiver before she went charging out of the room.

"Denis! Maria!" she bawled. Her footsteps sounded like

an elephant's as she pounded down the stairs, waving the cardigan in one hand and the scissors in the other.

I stayed in my room and listened to the muffled voices in the front room below me. At first it was only Auntie Rita, shouting things like, "Look at this!" and "She's gone too far this time!" Then came the soothing voice of my father, as he tried to calm her down. Rita's voice was hysterical, she sounded exactly the same way as she did when Uncle Norman ran away, and I began to really get scared that maybe I *had* gone too far. The odd thing was that I hadn't really wanted to do it. It was as if the scissors had wanted to cut a hole in the cardigan even more than I did. I heard Mum raise her voice. This was followed by the sound of Daddy's heavy footsteps as he walked out into the hall.

"I'll deal with this!" he shouted back to them.

Thump, thump, thump! His angry feet stamped upstairs and into my room.

Once inside, he closed the door and looked over at me. He had an odd expression on his face, as if he wasn't quite sure how to approach me.

He walked across and sat down on the bed beside me.

"What's got into you, Lizzy?"

I looked down at my hands and didn't answer.

"That was a most destructive thing to do. Rita is very upset about it. Indeed we all are."

I looked up at him but couldn't think of anything to say, so I looked back down at my hands again.

"I want you to go downstairs and apologise to her right away. I can't understand why you did such a thing but at least if you say sorry it will go some way towards making Rita feel a little better."

I wanted so badly to say I would apologise if he stopped going into her room at night and making Mum so sad, but the words were stuck at the back of my throat and refused to come out.

"Off you go now," he said, patting my back gently.

I stayed on the bed and didn't move.

"Lizzy," he said sternly, "go downstairs and say you're sorry."

I shook my head and felt my heart start to pump again.

Daddy took a deep breath and cracked his knuckles loudly.

"Don't make this any more difficult for yourself, young lady. Just tell her that you are sorry."

I shook my head again and fixed my gaze on the piece of frayed carpet at my feet.

Daddy stood up and stared down at the top of my head. I could tell by the way his hands were bunched into two fists that he was furious with me.

"You will not leave this room until you are ready to apologise to Rita. What you did this evening is unforgivable, and I will not tolerate that kind of behaviour in my house." He walked out and I gave a jump as he slammed the bedroom door behind him.

Now

The dust is still settling after our marvellous dinner party. Claire and Damian didn't get it together and, going by her reaction, my matchmaking skills are obviously not what they used to be. The evening started out very well. Brenda and Tom arrived in their usual high spirits. Brenda was wearing yet another new outfit to celebrate the fact that she had lost another three pounds. It was a wrap cardigan in deep pink, which she wore with a pair of loose white linen trousers. We had enjoyed a week of sunshine and Brenda had made the most of it, decamping to the garden with the children. The colours of her new outfit complemented her healthy glow.

"You look stunning," I said, as I poured them each a glass of champagne.

Tom beamed over at his wife, looking every bit the proud husband.

"Well, she deserves to," he said, raising his glass in her direction. "The poor girl has tortured herself to get her figure back."

Brenda swatted his remark away with a flick of her hand. "It's only a diet," she said with a laugh, uncomfortable with the attention she was receiving.

"Well, whatever you're doing – it's working. You look brilliant," I agreed.

We decided at the last minute to eat out on the patio. The weather had been so good it seemed a shame to eat indoors. I had set the table in the dining room the night before and had been toying with the idea of moving outdoors all day. It was only when Richard came home (an hour late) that I decided to switch to al fresco. Not that he had been in any way instrumental in the decision. He had come home, hot and bothered, wearing a suit that looked as if he'd slept in it, and not looking in any way up to entertaining. I, on the other hand, was wearing a very summery halter-neck silk dress and had had my hair cut and blow-dried for the occasion.

"You look nice," Richard mumbled as he flung his briefcase on the hall table.

"Thank you," I said, picking his tie off the floor. Not wanting to start an argument before our evening began, I kept my voice light and even. "Sweetheart, the others will be here in twenty minutes. Why don't you have a shower and change and then help me to set up the table outside. It's too nice an evening to eat in the dining room."

Richard looked over my shoulder and out through the kitchen patio doors, where I had started to set the table.

"I don't know if there's any gas for the patio heater," he said, undoing the top button of his shirt.

"I checked it. There's enough for this evening. Did you give Damian directions?"

He started to climb the stairs. "Mmh?"

"Directions. For Damian to find the house?"

"Yes, he knows where it is," he answered, and continued to walk up to the bedroom.

I'd kept the menu simple, keeping within my very limited culinary boundaries. Caesar salad to start with, then barbecued steaks and salad with baked potatoes. That way, nothing could go wrong. Or so I thought.

Next to arrive was Damian. The taxi had dropped him off at the wrong house but he had recognised Richard's car and found us easily. I opened the door and was pleasantly surprised at my first glance. He was good-looking in a middling type of way. Not tall, but not too small either. Brown hair parted to the side, a little too neatly, but that could be easily fixed. He was dressed smartly, in a white shirt and beige chinos and wore sandy-coloured suede shoes. Actually the shoes were what I looked at first, as I knew that Claire always looked at the shoes a guy was wearing, before she even considered his looks or personality. Not the size. She just had a thing about men and what kind of shoes they wore. If, for example, a guy arrived to take her out when we were younger and she didn't like his shoes, she would fly upstairs to my bedroom in a blind panic, moaning something like, *"He's wearing Gola runners!"*

As if this piece of information was pertinent to the night ahead.

I shook hands with Damian and accepted his generous offering of wine and flowers and felt a flush of excitement at the prospect of introducing him to my sister. When I led him out to the patio, I saw that Richard had arrived down from the bedroom. He looked better after showering. His hair was still wet and combed back off his forehead and his face was relaxed into a smile as he chatted to Tom and Brenda about the tribunal.

"We keep seeing you on the *Six O'Clock News* walking into the tribunal with all the legal eagles," Brenda said with a laugh. "The boys wave furiously at the TV and they're so disappointed when you don't wave back."

Richard tore the cellophane wrapping off a cigar and smiled over at Brenda.

"Perhaps I'll try to send them a secret greeting some day next week – maybe a quick wink to the camera!"

Richard stood up and introduced Damian to the others and I turned back to the kitchen as the doorbell went again. I opened the door to find Peter and Lainey looking like a pair of film stars. Peter was in his designer casuals and Lainey was wearing a strappy Missoni dress in the most amazing shades of burnt orange.

"God," I gasped, "you look just like Catherine Zeta Jones!"

Lainey gave an unladylike snort and belted the side of my arm. "Give over," she said, stepping into the hall.

Peter followed, looking proud as punch. "See? I told you it was nice," he said. "She was going to take it back to the shop but I persuaded her to keep it."

"Well, you did the right thing, Peter. It looks gorgeous. I covet it!"

Out on the patio, the others were all laughing at a work incident that Tom was recounting. I introduced Peter and Lainey to Damian and noticed that Richard hadn't poured him a drink yet.

"Oh, Damian, you haven't got a drink," I said, giving Richard the eye.

Richard balanced his cigar on the ashtray and went to heave himself out of his chair, but I told him to stay where he was and poured more champagne for everyone.

Tom continued his story and had us all laughing loudly as he told of how a customer had parked his new Jag in the forecourt, only to see it minutes later being driven out on to the main road on the back of a multi-vehicle truck on the way to Cork.

At eight o'clock the sun began to set but the patio was still baking from the heat of the day. Damian fitted in really well with the company and didn't take offence at Tom's slightly offbeat sense of humour. Tom swore incessantly and could tell jokes all evening, if Brenda allowed him – one more outrageous than the next. I glanced at my watch again at twenty to nine. As usual, Claire was late and I tried to suppress my annoyance at her lack of consideration. I had told her more than once that I intended to serve dinner at eight thirty. In fact, I wasn't planning to eat till ten, but if I had told Claire that, she wouldn't have arrived until eleven.

Richard pressed at the buttons of the gas barbecue, trying without any success to ignite the flame.

"Jesus, Liz," said Tom, "have you not got this bucko housetrained yet?"

Richard held in the knob to release the gas and pressed the button repeatedly, until it sounded like it was going to snap off. He tried to smile at the remark and get the damn thing lit before Tom came over to highlight his incompetence. Tom swaggered over and gave Richard a gentle nudge out of the way, making a big deal of rolling up his sleeves and pretending to spit into the palms of his hands. He clicked the ignite button and held it in for a few seconds and to his delight, and my relief, we heard the whoosh of the flames as the barbecue lit up. He took a bow and was given a round of applause by everyone. This was followed by the sound of the doorbell. I went to get up, but Richard motioned for me to stay put.

"I'll get it, Liz," he said, trying to shake off his embarrassment.

Any other time he would have made the effort to laugh along with the rest of us, but being made to look anything but a genius in front of a work colleague was no laughing matter for Richard.

"Will I give you a hand, Richard?" Tom said, grinning at us as we tried to stifle our laughs.

"Thank you, Tom," Richard said evenly, "I think I can manage to open the door by myself, but I'll call you if I have any difficulty."

He walked in through the kitchen and Lainey and Brenda released a wave of suppressed giggles. Richard, as we all knew, could get very touchy if anyone dared to make a clown of him. Self-deprecation was not a quality he possessed, and Tom always managed to re-discover this fact, especially when he'd had a few drinks. I looked over at him and realised that he was quite pissed. I had opened a second bottle of champagne and Tom had been lowering it like beer. Brenda quickly picked up on my thoughts and plucked the glass of champagne from his hand.

"Don't drink any more until you've had something to eat," she said firmly. "You'll be under the table before dinner is served."

Richard appeared again followed by Claire. I stood up and tried to hide my disappointment at how crap she looked. I hadn't told her about Damian, of course, but it never occurred to me that she wouldn't make the effort to look nice when she knew that the others were coming. It was so unlike Claire – she wouldn't put out the bin without freshening up her lipstick. She wore a pair of denims and battered deck shoes that were very unflattering. The green sloppy T-shirt looked as if she had picked it up in a charity shop and actually made her look dumpy. I felt so deflated as I introduced her to Damian. To top it all off, she'd gone and had her hair chopped up to her shoulders in a blunt bob that looked very badly cut.

There was a chorus of greetings from the gathered company, as Richard offered her his chair and went in search of another one.

"Damian, this is my sister Claire," I announced flatly.

Damian stood up and shook Claire's hand.

"Pleased to meet you," he said politely.

"Hi," Claire said casually as she flopped into the cushioned garden chair.

"How are you?" Lainey asked. "Have you managed to shake off that flu?"

Claire rolled her eyes up to heaven. "Not quite. Though the echinacea you gave me has definitely helped."

"It's an odd time of the year to have a dose like that," remarked Brenda.

"A few days of rest and relaxation in France will knock it on the head once and for all," said Lainey.

"When are you off?" Tom asked, as Richard handed him a beer.

"Myself, Peter and the kids are going on Tuesday and Claire is joining us the following Saturday."

Brenda smiled over at them. "A few days of Lainey's hospitality should have you right as rain."

I could see by the temperature gauge on the barbecue that it was ready for the steaks and I went inside to the kitchen to get a start on the food. Richard strolled in behind me to get a beer for himself.

"Make sure everyone has a drink," I said.

He reached for the corkscrew and took a bottle of white wine from the fridge.

"Although, maybe kill the champagne," I added. "It's gone straight to everyone's head. I think it's the heat."

He pulled the cork from the bottle and poured a glass for me.

"Need any help?" he asked.

"No thanks, I think I have everything under control." I smiled over at him, then whispered, "Pity about Claire."

Richard looked at me blankly.

"About how she turned up," I continued, keeping an eye on the patio door. "She looks like something the cat dragged in."

"Ah, Liz, give her a break. She just said she has a rotten dose," said Richard, making me feel like a right bitch.

"Well, the one night I had someone interesting to introduce her to and she shows up looking so dowdy!"

Richard gave me a disparaging look and his eyes narrowed into a frown.

"Is that what tonight is about?" he asked, the penny finally dropping.

"Not really," I shrugged my shoulders nonchalantly. "But it would be nice if they hit it off." I looked at Richard and raised my eyebrows mischievously.

"Liz," he lowered his voice and glanced over at the door, "I will not have you trying to pair off my work colleagues with your sister."

"Relax," I said, taking the plate of steaks from the fridge. "I don't think she'll be sweeping him off his feet tonight."

"Liz! Please don't try to push them together all evening. It's embarrassing for Damian."

"Here," I pushed the plate of meat into his hands. "Put these on the barbecue, and let me organise our guests. And don't worry! I'll be the soul of discretion. Damian won't have any idea of what I'm up to."

Richard looked down at the meat and back to me with a puzzled expression.

"Just throw them on the barbecue and close the lid," I instructed.

He turned and walked out of the kitchen, gripping the sides of the plate as if it might run away from him.

Brenda came in and took two bowls of salad from the counter.

"I'll kill Tom," she muttered.

"Oh leave him alone. He's just unwinding after a busy week," I said, trying to soften her up. Being in the motor trade, Saturday was often a very busy day for Tom.

She dressed the salads, both arms flapping vigorously as she tossed the vinaigrette through the shaved parmesan and mixed leaves of rocket and rapidly wilting baby spinach. "He's as high as a kite out there! He just admitted to having two pints on the way home. Honestly, sometimes I feel more like his mother than his wife, the way I have to constantly nag him to keep him on the straight and narrow!"

I went over and took the wooden salad spoons from her and placed them at the side of the bowl. "Well, if it's any consolation, your husband is the best dinner guest in the world. He can talk to anyone about anything at any time – and that's why we all love him. Listen."

We both stayed quiet and cocked our heads towards the patio doors. The only voice that could be heard was Tom's as he told a story about a bungled raid on his showrooms last year.

"You see? Tom is the life and soul of the party. If he wasn't here, there'd be no fun."

Brenda looked at me and fought hard to disguise the girlish smile that spread across her face. She could never stay mad with him for very long. "If he wasn't here," she said, lifting a bowl of salad from the counter and thrusting it into my hands, "other people might be able to get a word in edgeways." With this, she took another bowl and marched back out to the others.

Darkness fell, but the evening stayed warm and sultry. I kept waiting for the temperature to fall before I lit the patio heater, but there was no need. What an unexpected treat, to sit outdoors after midnight enjoying the African heat that had mistakenly been carried to our shores by a rogue south-westerly breeze.

The food had tasted remarkably good, enhanced by the candlelit al-fresco atmosphere. Everyone looked content. Everyone, that is, except Claire. I had decided to abort my plan of pairing her off with Damian. I could see there was no chemistry between them. Dressed the way she was, it was obvious that she wasn't in flirting mode. I only hoped that she was kicking herself for not making more of an effort when she saw how nice he was. They had ended up sitting beside each other without any meddling on my part. I looked around the table, feeling relaxed now that the serving was over. Richard was deep in conversation with Peter about the Shields case. I checked Peter's face for any sign of boredom, but he seemed to be genuinely interested in what Richard was saying.

Lainey and Brenda were debating over whether a girl in their gym had succumbed to Botox.

"She looks frozen all the time. She must have had it," said Lainey.

"No, she doesn't. She looks great," Brenda argued. "I'd love to get it done."

Lainey gave her a scowl. "If I hear you've gone and ruined your lovely face with that poison, I'll never speak to you again."

Brenda lifted her glass and giggled. She had calmed down about her husband's earlier alcohol intake and looked as if she had decided to join him in his inebriation.

"I'm having everything done," she announced. "Lipo-suction, collagen injections, Botox, the whole shooting match!"

"Oh, what the hell!" Lainey said with a laugh. "If it works, I'll join you. You'll look like Sylvester Stallone's mum and I'll look like Joan Rivers."

At the end of the table Tom was trying to explain the rules of GAA to Damian so he could watch the big match the following day. Poor Damian tried to follow Tom's ramblings but I could see that, although he was finding it amusing, he was also completely lost. Claire was just lost. She sat between Tom and Damian with a vacant look on her face as she feigned interest in the discussion. I could tell she didn't want to be there. As I watched her sitting there, I was reminded of someone else for a fleeting second – but I couldn't think who. I stood up and gathered the dessert dishes together and went to make some coffee.

Tom stood too. "Will I get the guitar?" he asked, with a beaming smile.

Everyone gave excited claps and whoops of approval, drowning out Brenda's protestations. Tom knew every song that had ever been written and could play the guitar all night long. Unfortunately, Brenda knew that was exactly what would happen – he would play until the sun came up if he had an audience.

Tom didn't wait for any further encouragement and ran next door to get his guitar before Brenda had a chance to stop him.

Lainey followed me into the kitchen with more dishes.

"Make that nice and strong," she said, nodding towards the canister of coffee in my hand. "We all need it!" Then moving towards me she said in a whisper, "Hey, Damian's really nice, isn't he?"

"Yes, he seems to fit in really well. It's a pity Claire isn't giving him the time of day," I said despondently. "She looks as if the evening won't end soon enough."

Lainey sighed as she arranged some cups on a tray for me. "Why do you bother, Liz? You know how she feels about being set up on dates."

"I'm only thinking about what's best for her — and it's not very often a suitable guy comes along."

Lainey glanced out towards the party. "I think you picked a bad night to work your magic. Claire looks worn out — she's working far too hard. I haven't seen her look so wrecked in a long time. "

"You think?" I asked, feeling selfish at my earlier comments about her appearance.

"I don't know what to think," said Lainey. "I'm hoping that a few days in France might do her some good."

I pushed down the stick of the cafetière and smiled. "You mean a few days of you pampering her."

"Something like that," Lainey replied. "Some nice meals and late-night chats are probably all she needs, just to remind her that there's more to life than work."

I immediately felt a rush of guilt. I hadn't noticed that Claire had been working any harder than usual, or that she needed a holiday. Not for the first time in recent weeks, I wondered if I was too wrapped up in myself and neglecting the people who meant so much to me.

Tom appeared at the kitchen door holding his guitar. Clenched between his teeth was a red rose which he had swiped from a vase in the hall. Strumming a Spanish tune loudly, he walked past us with his head held high, out to the patio where the others were beating their fists on the table with raucous shouts of "*Olé!*"

"Come on," said Lainey, lifting the tray of coffee cups. "I'll talk to you about it another time. I don't want to miss this."

I placed the coffee pot on the table as Tom began to strum the opening cords of the Eddie Cochrane song "C'mon, everybody". I looked over to see if Damian had had enough, but he was clapping in time to the tune and looked as if he was really enjoying himself. The only person who looked miserable was Claire, and I found myself wishing that I hadn't invited her. At least no one else seemed to be affected by her mood, as everyone joined in the chorus and shouted, "*C'mon, everybody!*" Just as I went to sit down, I remembered the box of mint chocolates that Lainey had brought and I slipped back into the kitchen to get them. As I reached up into the press, I heard footsteps and turned to see Claire standing behind me. Her arms were folded tightly against her chest and she looked furious.

I looked at her and shrugged my shoulders. "Don't you like his music?"

Claire looked outside and back to me again. "What do you think you're playing at?" she hissed.

I opened my mouth to answer but closed it again and allowed her to continue with her tirade.

"Why is *he* here?" she said, pointing towards the patio with an outstretched arm.

"Damian?" I asked.

"Yes, Damian," she said scornfully.

"He works with Richard. He's staying over here while he's working on the Shields case and I thought it would be nice to include him." I kept my voice light and breezy and acted like I hadn't a clue what she was on about.

"Yes, I know who he *is,* Liz. I asked you what he was *doing* here."

Thankfully, Tom had launched straight into a Van Morrison number and his singing was loud enough to drown out Claire's rising voice.

I tried to think of an excuse, or a suitable explanation that would make my matchmaking seem like an accident, but I was so annoyed with her sulking all night, and now this uncalled-for confrontation in the middle of my dinner party, that I couldn't be bothered conjuring up a story. "I thought you might like to meet him. He's recently divorced and seems like a really nice guy, that's all."

For a moment I thought she was going to slap me. Her face turned pink with fury, like it used to when she was a kid, just before she threw a tantrum.

"When are you going to get it into your thick head that I'm not interested in any of your corporate divorcees?"

I took a step back, shocked at her anger. "For God's sake, Claire, I didn't think anything of it – it was just a dinner party. You don't have to lose the head over it."

"I'm sick of you and your manipulative ways," she continued. "Who do you think you are? Cilla fucking Black? Trying to fix people's lives with your pathetic blind dates!" She was now shouting at me and it was only a matter of seconds before Tom would take a break from the guitar and everyone outside would get an earful.

"Claire, calm down," I said, reaching out to grab her arm in an attempt to steer her towards the hall. But she shook me away with a flick of her wrist. "What's really wrong, Claire?" I asked rather bravely, considering the state she had worked herself up to.

"Oh, it's me, is it?" she said, with an ugly sneer. "Nothing whatsoever to do with you and your interfering, controlling ways?"

"Claire, I know you. I know you've been down about something for a while now. If there is anything wrong I wish you'd tell me."

"You're unbelievable, Liz," she said, her voice straining to keep the tears at bay. "I'm annoyed because you have once again forced me into a situation that I don't want to be in. You know, it may come as a surprise to you, but if I'd felt like having a date with me tonight, there are plenty of guys I could have brought. But I chose not to. Have you ever thought of what it looks like to our friends? Here comes Saint Liz again, trying to fix her sad old sister up with another charming dinner guest."

I gave a sharp laugh. "Clare, it's happened only once or twice in the past that I've invited you to dinner with a single guy who I thought you might like."

"And I didn't like it, did I? So when are you going to get the message and give up trying? It's not such a tragedy being single, Liz. I'm quite happy on my own. In fact, the only time that I'm not happy is when you do something like this to make me feel like there's something wrong with me."

The guitar stopped, followed by loud applause from everyone. I looked out nervously.

"Don't worry," Claire said, running her hand through her hair. "I'm not going to make a scene and ruin your party. I'm going home."

I didn't argue. Eager for her to leave I followed her out to the hall and waited while she rummaged about in her bag for her car keys.

"I didn't mean to upset you," I said, hoping that that would be enough of an apology.

She took her keys from her bag and stared at me reproachfully. "Just stay out of my life, Liz."

There was no point in saying anything else. She opened the front door and marched out, slamming it behind her. I stood still for a moment in the empty hall, her shrill words still ringing in my ears. I walked back into the kitchen feeling slightly stunned. Outside, the sing-song was now in full swing and Brenda had joined Tom in a rendition of the Frank and Nancy Sinatra song "Something Stupid".

I went out and sat down quietly and poured myself a cup of coffee.

Richard looked over at me and mouthed, *Where's Claire?*

Gone home, I mouthed back.

He gave a drunken nod of his head and lifted his shoulders slightly as if to say, who cares?

Then

I go to ballet classes with Lainey on Saturday mornings. Sometimes Lainey's mum drives us, but if it isn't raining, we walk. Mum doesn't know how to drive. Daddy keeps at her to learn. He says that he'll teach her, but Mum says she wouldn't have the confidence to drive a car on her own.

Auntie Rita knows how to drive and when Uncle Norman ran off, he left his car behind, so she drives that now. It's an orange Ford Capri and she parks it in our driveway beside Daddy's Mercedes. I wish she wouldn't park it there, because now all the neighbours must know that she's living with us.

I walked home from ballet with Lainey and we stopped at the shops and spent our pocket money on Black Jacks and Cola Cubes. Lainey could afford to buy *Jackie* magazine because she gets more pocket money than me. Anyway, I'm not allowed to buy *Jackie*. Mum saw an ad for sanitary towels in a copy that Lainey left lying around in our house, and she told me that I'm not old enough to read magazines like that yet. She never said anything about the sanitary towels, but I know that's why she doesn't want me buying it. Lainey told me about periods when Mrs Whyte told her the facts of life, but I never said anything about it to Mum. I expect she'll tell me about it some day soon and I wouldn't like to spoil it by telling her that I already know. I don't really care that I'm not allowed to buy *Jackie*, because Lainey lets me read hers on the way home from ballet.

I took the key from under the hall doormat and let myself into the house. Rita's car was in the driveway but Daddy's was gone. The house was quiet and I found Mum in the front room, sitting up very straight on the couch with the curtains closed.

"Mum?"

She looked at me but through me at the same time, as if she was asleep with her eyes open.

"Hello, pet," she said, stretching out her arms for a hug.

I am far too old for hugs, but I can't bring myself to say this to Mum. Maybe when I start buying *Jackie* I'll tell her.

"How was ballet?"

"Fine," I said, pulling back. "Where's Claire?"

"Daddy popped her up to Maura's a little while ago." Maura is Lainey's mum. We call her Mrs Whyte but Mum and Daddy call her Maura.

Mum's hands were clasped together tightly in her lap, as if she was pressing something between her palms.

"Is Rita here?"

"No. Daddy's teaching her how to play golf today. They'll be gone for a few hours."

I didn't care where they were, just so long as they were gone.

Mum's face looked strained, like she was trying to smile but couldn't.

"Why have you got the curtains closed?" I asked, moving over to the window to open them.

"Don't!" Mum said quickly.

I looked back at her.

"Leave them closed," she said.

"But it's daytime. They should be open," I tried to explain.

"I know," she said, looking down at her white knuckles. "Just leave them closed."

I sat down beside her and leaned in towards her and we stayed like that until my neck began to feel stiff.

"Are you okay?" I asked.

She nodded her head slowly. "Yes, pet. I'm fine."

"Can I call for Lainey?"

"Of course you can," she said with a sleepy smile.

85

I stayed in Lainey's for most of the day. Her mum made us spaghetti hoops on toast for lunch and we ate it in the garden. We had cola made from their new Soda Stream, and Lainey showed me and Claire how to make the fizz come down our nose. We had just started playing hopscotch in the driveway when I saw Daddy's car come down the road. I left Lainey's house and ran down to meet him. Then I felt a pang of guilt as it was almost teatime, and I'd forgotten that Mum had been alone all day. I let myself into the house before Daddy and Rita got out of the car and went into the front room to find Mum still sitting in the same position with the curtains drawn.

She looked at me and gave me the saddest smile I've ever seen. Daddy came in behind me and dumped his golf clubs in the hall. He walked into the darkened sitting room and glared over at Mum.

"Where's Claire?" he asked sharply.

"In Whytes'," I told him.

He kept his eyes firmly fixed on Mum and stamped across the room, then flung the curtains open roughly. The evening sun came pouring into the room, throwing the couch where Mum was sitting, into a pool of light. It was what she had been trying to avoid all day. She put her hand up to shield her eyes and I wished that he'd close the curtains again because I could see how awful she looked. Her skin was a dull greyish colour and strands of greasy hair were stuck to the side of her face.

"I told you not to leave her there all day, Maria. Remember?"

Mum shook her head and seemed to snap out of the dream she was in. "What time is it?" she asked.

I glanced at my digital wristwatch. "Six fourteen."

Mum rubbed her forehead, looking slightly bewildered.

Rita had now entered the room and clasped a hand over her mouth dramatically.

"Maria, have you been sitting here all day?" she asked.

Mum looked over at me as if she expected me to answer for her.

"I suppose I have," she said.

"What about Claire?" Rita said, looking around the room.

"She's in Maura's," Mum said.

"I asked Maura to watch her for an hour," said Daddy. "You promised you'd go and pick her up after Lizzy got home from ballet."

Mum stared into the empty fire grate as he spoke. "I forgot," she whispered to herself.

Daddy turned his back on us and stared out the window, his hands held tightly by his sides like a soldier.

Auntie Rita grabbed my hand. "Come on," she said, tugging at me. "We'll go and get Claire."

Mum appeared oblivious to the air of tension that pervaded the room. She was still lost in her foggy thoughts and didn't seem to notice that Daddy was about to explode. I was frightened for her and pulled my hand out of Rita's. "I'll stay here," I said.

Rita went to say something, but Daddy swung around from his position at the window and shouted at the top of his voice, "Don't you bloody well start! Go with Rita and get your sister!"

Rita squeezed my hand so tightly that all my knuckles bunched together, making me wince. She pulled me out of the house and we walked quickly up to Whytes', neither of us saying a word. Lainey's mum opened the door – she didn't invite us in but Rita barged past her anyway. Claire came running down the hall and into Rita's arms. I hate when she does that. She never does it to Mum, but whenever Rita comes into a room or gets home from work, Claire always runs into her arms. Sometimes I think that Claire likes Rita more than she likes Mum and it makes me feel like thumping her. After Rita smothered Claire with kisses, she turned to Mrs Whyte and began to explain how Mum was meant to have collected Claire when I got home from ballet but had forgotten. She threw her hands in the air and rolled her eyes around when she said this, to show Mrs Whyte how stupid Mum was. But Mrs Whyte didn't smile or agree with Rita – she just nodded her head and said that it was no problem and that Claire could come and play any time she liked. That put Rita in her box. She huffed and puffed a few more times, about how embarrassed she was and how she was sure that Mrs Whyte must be sick of the sight of us, but Lainey's mum just patted my head and said that she could never be sick of girls that were as good as us.

When we got back to the house Mum had left the front room. Instead, Daddy was sitting on the couch where she had been, wiping his eyes with a handkerchief. I expect Mum had said something to make him cry and I was glad. It was good to see him upset for a change. The three of us stood there staring at him.

Daddy blew his nose loudly and stuffed his handkerchief back into his trouser pocket, ignoring us.

"Who'd like some cocoa?" asked Rita cheerily.

"Me!" Claire yelled.

Rita shooed us out of the room and walked down the hall towards the kitchen. I didn't feel like cocoa, so I turned the other way and went upstairs to my room. Mum was lying on top of my bed – she turned and gave me a dreamy smile. I climbed up and hugged her.

"Is Claire all right?" she asked.

"She's fine. I don't know what all the fuss is about," I said, trying to show her that I was on her side.

Mum kissed my forehead and turned over on to her back.

"Rita's just making a fuss over nothing, as usual," I said warily. Mum never liked me saying anything bad about Rita.

"It's my fault," Mum said with a sigh. "I shouldn't have left her there all day."

"But she was fine!" I protested. "Lainey's mum looked after her, and I took care of her too."

Mum took my hand and squeezed it gently between hers. "You're such a good girl, Lizzy. You take such good care of your sister. Promise me you'll always take care of her."

I didn't like the way Mum was speaking. She sounded as if she might be going away somewhere.

"Promise?"

"I promise," I said softly.

The day was drawing to a close and my bedroom was bathed in a soft yellow light. I rested my head in the crook of Mum's neck and we lay in silence as the light faded and watched the shadows of the leaves and branches on the wall, as they bowed and swayed in the gentle breeze.

Now

I picked the telephone up but put it down again and went back into the kitchen. I boiled the kettle to make more coffee, but decided that I didn't want any. I went back out to the hall and reached for the phone again, but decided to hang out a wash first. Delay tactics. I looked at the clock. It was almost eleven. I knew I'd have to leave soon or I would be late for yet another medical that had been arranged by the adoption board. I forced myself to dial Brian's direct number and let it ring, one, two, three times before he answered.

"Brian Davies," he barked.

"It's Liz."

"Liz! How are you? When are you coming back?" he said in his usual cocky manner.

"I want the rest of the summer off. I'll come back mid-September."

"Thank God!" I could almost see him punching the air with a closed fist, the way he always did when he secured a deal. "I knew you wouldn't be able to stay away from us for too long!"

"Well, there you go. You were right," I said with a smile. I like Brian, I can list at least one hundred ways that he annoys me, but at the end of the day he's a good guy to work for.

"Liz, you don't know what this means to me. I didn't mention this when we spoke last, but you'll probably hear about it anyway."

"What?"

All the delight of my return to the company had vanished from his voice.

"We've lost the Browne account," he said morbidly.

"Jesus!" They were our most important client. Browne's was the biggest sportswear manufacturer in the country, and Task had always taken great pride in the fact that they had managed to hold on to their account for almost ten years despite vicious competition from other ad agencies.

"I hear they're giving a few agencies a shot at it."

A silence followed that left me in no doubt about how Brian was taking this.

"How did it happen?" I asked, dumbfounded.

He exhaled a long noisy breath down the line. "That incompetent asshole, David Fenlon. The account was in trouble for a while and he didn't come to me. Stupid prick thought he was clever enough to fix it himself."

I had been baffled the day that Brian announced who my successor would be. Fenlon had been heading up the creative dept of Draper Good, a large ad agency and Task's main competitor. After me, the obvious choice would have been Susie Wilkes. She had worked in Task for eight years and had proved herself to be a brilliant creative force. But Brian, in his infinite wisdom, had given the position to an outsider and in my opinion, a lesser candidate.

I should have felt a certain amount of satisfaction at Fenlon's failure, but the Browne account was too important to the company.

"Brian, I'm shocked. What are you going to do?"

"Don't know," he said sharply. "At least I've got you back on board. Any chance you could get back before September?"

Here we go, I thought. I knew it would happen.

"I'll think about it, Brian. I might be able to start sometime in August, but no sooner than that."

"I should never have let you leave in the first place," he said in a rare show of emotion.

"You couldn't have stopped me."

"Any sign of the baby?" he asked quickly, thinking ahead.

"Not in the near future. But it's definitely going to happen."

"Welcome back, partner. You're the best news I've had all year. I'll give you a call in a week or two and we'll have lunch and discuss the finer details."

It's been three weeks since my botched attempt at setting my sister up with Damian Jones. He obviously didn't notice what was going on, because he sent us a thank-you card, saying that it was the best night he'd had in a long time. Claire, needless to say, did not send a thank-you card. I have called her three times since the night in question, but each time her machine has picked up and each time I have left a grovelling apology, but to no avail. I even had a sneaking suspicion while I was leaving my last message that she was listening to me as her machine recorded. Yesterday, I finally got through to her.

"Hello."

I knew by the tone of her voice that she knew it was me calling, and I could tell that she was still annoyed.

"Hi," I said breezily, choosing to ignore the frosty vibe that was trickling down the telephone line. "I've been trying to get you for weeks. Every time I call you at the office you're either out or in a meeting."

"I know. It's been very busy lately."

"How are you?" I asked, trying to break the ice.

"Fine," she said with a sigh. "Looking forward to the break."

Lainey had been on from France and told me that Claire was joining her for the weekend.

"That's right," I said. "You're off tomorrow, you lucky thing."

"Yes. I had a text from Lainey to say the weather is lovely – I can't wait."

A few seconds of silence followed and I couldn't think of anything else to say. I certainly wasn't going to bring up the dinner party again. If Claire wanted to make an issue of it I wasn't going to go there. I had made my apologies.

"Well. Have a good weekend and give me a call when you get back. I want to have Daddy and Rita over some evening so we'll try to arrange a date."

Claire had never cooked a meal for Daddy and Rita. I doubt very much that they had even been in her apartment more than once or twice. Any get-togethers were always suggested and arranged by me. That's not a complaint. It's just the way it's always been.

"Okay. See you soon," she said flatly.

"Bye."

I put down the phone, wanting to strangle her. How long did she plan to continue sulking? She didn't even acknowledge the fact that I had left my profuse apologies on her answering machine. There is nothing more I can do but wait until she comes around. It's not that I'm being stubborn but apart from crawling up to her front door and throwing myself at her feet, I can't think of anything else I can do to make her realise that I am truly sorry.

Our medicals were scheduled for different times because Richard couldn't make the appointment that had been scheduled for both of us. They went through me with a fine comb. I sucked and blew into machines that measured my lung capacity. Although what they want to know that for is beyond me — perhaps they want to know how loud I'll be able to shout at my child! I ran on a treadmill like a white mouse until my face looked like a beetroot. This is to ascertain if I am fit enough to keep up with a toddler should it break loose on a busy street. I ran my little legs off to prove to them that I'm more than able to match the athletic prowess of a two-year-old.

When I'd finished at the hospital, I felt lonely. I wanted to talk to someone, but Lainey and Claire were away, and Brenda needs at least two weeks' notice to meet for coffee because she has to arrange baby-sitters.

I went into a café beside the hospital and ordered a cup of coffee. I took out my phone and went to dial Claire's number. I figured she'd be in the airport by now, about to leave for France. I scrolled down to her number but lost my nerve. I remembered the icy tone in her voice and threw the phone back into my bag. I didn't want to risk another stand-off before she left. It would only put me in bad humour.

I left the café and noticed that there was a very stylish-looking salon across the road. I walked over and enquired if there was anyone free to give me a blow-dry and, as it happened, there was.

I arrived back home to find Richard's car in the driveway. It was five thirty on a Friday evening. Richard was never home at that time. The first thing I thought of was that he might be sick, but I found him sitting out on the patio with a glass of wine in his hand.

"How come you're home so early?"

He shrugged his shoulders and smiled over at me.

"Just wanted to get home early on a Friday," he said, pouring me a glass of wine. "Come on," he pulled out a chair for me, "sit down and enjoy a sundowner. It's a lovely evening."

I sat down beside him and he handed me my glass.

"How did the medical go?"

"Fine," I answered.

He leaned over and lifted a stray hair that had fallen across my forehead.

"You look nice," he said.

I smiled bashfully.

"Want to go out to dinner?"

"Oh, that would be nice. I didn't get a chance to do any shopping today, and I didn't know you'd be home this early."

"Good," he said, looking very pleased with himself. "I booked The Bistro for nine o'clock."

The Bistro was a local restaurant that specialised in fish dishes. It was small and simple but required booking weeks in advance. We never ate there for the simple reason that we always left it too late to reserve a table.

"When did you book it?" I asked excitedly.

A smile widened across his face. "I could say that I booked it weeks ago, but I don't think you'd believe me."

I laughed. He was right.

"I rang just half an hour ago and they happened to have a cancellation," he admitted. But I could tell from the way he kept smiling that he was nonetheless delighted with his brainwave.

"You're a genius," I said, leaning over to kiss him.

We sat in the warm evening sunshine that was slowly

receding from the patio and chatted about this and that. Something we rarely ever did any more. I told Richard about my telephone conversation with Claire and how she was still mad with me.

"Just leave her alone for a while. It'll blow over. You know Claire and her moods – she's basically just a spoilt brat. The more you apologise, the more she'll just draw the whole thing out. Leave it be for a while and the whole thing will be forgotten about."

Wise words from my husband.

"You're probably right," I agreed. "She's gone to visit Lainey in France this weekend – perhaps some time away will mellow her."

Richard drained the last of his wine and set the glass back down on the table. He stood up and gave my shoulders a gentle squeeze. "I'd better go up and get ready."

I sat and thought about what he had said. Even though it was true, I didn't like to hear him criticise Claire. It surprised me how defensive I felt towards her – almost like an involuntary emotion. I couldn't help it – she was my little sister and I would always feel duty bound to protect her.

The Bistro is in the village about half a mile away and at the last minute we decided to leave the car and walk. It's the kind of restaurant where people stop eating and crane their necks when somebody walks in the door, to see if it is a person of any importance. We didn't seem to drum up any interest amongst the diners and, after a quick once-over, they got back to their meals. A couple from the house opposite ours waved over, but apart from that we knew nobody there.

"Great." Richard settled into his chair and glanced around the room. "Sometimes this place can be a bit too local. You can spend an entire evening saying hello to people you hardly know."

"I know what you mean," I replied, as I spotted another neighbour.

We skipped the starters as we were eating quite late. Richard ordered a particularly nice bottle of white wine and both of us relaxed and enjoyed each other's company.

After our main course, I told Richard about my telephone conversation with Brian Davies. His eyes widened when I told him about the Browne account.

"Christ, it sounds like you'll be walking into a war zone. Do you think you'll be up to it?"

"Oh God! I hope so," I said, feeling a knot begin to form in my stomach.

Richard gave a laugh. "Davies must be sick, having to beg you to come back again after he waved you off so dismissively."

It was true. Brian Davies had taken my resignation very personally. His marriage had split up years ago and Task had become his family, with me as his eldest daughter. He barely spoke to me in the weeks before I left and refused to come to my farewell dinner. Instead, he switched his attentions to my replacement, David Fenlon – the new wonder kid, letting me know just how dispensable I was. But I knew Brian, and felt sorry for him because I knew he really was hurting at my decision to leave.

"Poor Brian! I can't imagine it was easy for him, having to swallow his pride and ask me back. But I feel I've been very straight with him – I didn't make him beg."

Richard smiled at me. "You were always too easy on the

guy. This time round just remember you're a partner and he'll need to treat you right."

I felt a rush of excitement. It was the first time I had let myself believe it was really happening. "Wow. Partner! Can you believe it?"

His hand rested on mine and he patted it lightly. "Of course I can believe it. Well done, my love."

The night was clear and starry as we walked home. We held hands and fell into step with each other in an easy silence, the way we used to when we were first married. At home, we made love, something else we hadn't done in a while, and afterwards fell into a deep sleep.

Then

Claire has asthma and when she wakes up at night she cries alot. Rita has to give her an inhaler and make her suck air from it. Claire doesn't like the inhaler and screams even louder when Rita tries to get her to take it. Mum is tired all the time because the doctor put her on new medicine that makes her dopey. Daddy took me into his study to try to explain why she has to take the medicine.

"Your mother is very sick, Lizzy," he said, pacing the floor with his hands held behind his back.

"Will she have to go to hospital?" I asked, praying that he would say no.

He stopped and twisted his mouth tightly. He always did this when anyone asked him a difficult question.

"Not for the moment," he answered. "This medicine makes her very tired and she'll be sleeping a lot while she's on it."

I nodded my head.

"Mrs Whyte will bring Claire home from school from now on."

I didn't have to ask why. Claire gets off an hour earlier than me because she's in junior infants, and last week Mum fell asleep and didn't wake up in time to collect her. The school rang the house but Mum didn't answer the phone. They had to contact Daddy at court and he had to ring Rita in work and Rita came to the school and brought both of us home. That night there was a big row and Daddy stormed out of the house and didn't come back until after I had fallen asleep.

Mrs Whyte has offered to mind us after school to give Mum a chance to get some rest.

I'm glad about this, even though I'm annoyed with Lainey for telling her mum what happened. Last Wednesday, when I got home from school Claire was locked in her room. I could hear her screaming before I even got into the hall. They were the kind of screams that she does when she is scared of something. I ran upstairs and tried to open her door but it was locked. Claire was banging on the door and screeching her head off. The key was in the lock and I turned it, and Claire opened the door and ran into my arms clutching Peter Rabbit tightly to her chest. Her whole body shook as she began to sob uncontrollably. I took her downstairs and got her a glass of milk and some biscuits and tried to get her to speak. After a while, she told me that she had gone into her room to get Peter Rabbit, like she does every day when she gets in from school, and someone had locked the door behind her. I lied and told her it wasn't locked – that it had just got stuck. Claire eventually calmed down and ate the plate of biscuits quietly. When she stopped sobbing completely and the red blotches on her face had died down, I crept upstairs to my room. Mum was lying on the bed staring into space – she didn't move her head when I opened the door. I went over and sat on the edge of the bed but she didn't look at me. The faraway look in her eyes scared me and I shook her arm to let her know I was there. Her head turned slowly and a scary smile spread across her face as she focused on me.

"Claire was locked in her room," I said.

She blinked a few times as if she didn't know who I was talking about.

"Mum, are you feeling all right?"

Her eyes looked glassy, like Minny's before she died. Minny was our cat but she got cat flu and died. I could tell that Mum wasn't in the mood for talking because she closed her eyes and looked as if she'd fallen back asleep. I crept out of the room and took Claire up to Mrs Whyte's. Later that afternoon, when we were up in Lainey's bedroom and out of earshot – I told her about Mum locking Claire into the bedroom, but made her swear not to tell anyone else.

"Is there anything you want to talk to me about?" Daddy said later that evening, looking at me like he was reading my mind.

I thought about telling him, but decided not to. There had been too many rows in our house recently and that would only cause another one.

"Is the medicine going to make Mum better?" I said instead.

Daddy's mouth twisted into a mass of wrinkles and he stared down at his shoes trying to think of an answer.

"Will it take away her sadness?"

This made him look up very quickly and to my utter dismay his eyes filled with tears. He walked over to me and pulled me tightly in to him. Daddy never gives hugs or kisses and it felt strange to have my face buried into his chest, smelling his strange musty smell. I kept my head tilted back slightly and my eyes focused on the ink stain that was on the breast pocket of his shirt. He took a big gulp of air and pulled me tighter.

"Yes, Lizzy," he gasped, "we all hope it will take her sadness away."

After a few moments of being caught in his grasp, I pulled away politely and forced a smile. Daddy pulled his handkerchief out and, while he was blowing big hoots into it, I slipped out of the study and raced upstairs to my bedroom.

Lainey's house is the best in the world. And after my Mum, Mrs Whyte is the best mum in the world. When we come in from school the smell of cooking fills the house and Mrs Whyte always has something nice for lunch. Today it was chicken sandwiches and Bird's trifle for dessert. She even waited for us to get home so we could take turns putting the sprinkles on top. While Lainey and I did our homework, Mrs Whyte persuaded Claire to have a bath. Claire hates having baths and screams the house down when she's having her hair washed, but she let Mrs Whyte bath her and wash her hair. When she came down, she looked so nice and clean. All the black dirt from around her ankles had been washed off and her hair looked soft and silky. Mrs Whyte dressed Claire in a pair of Lainey's old pyjamas and had her ready for bed when Rita called to collect us.

We are usually sitting in the front room watching

Jackanory when Rita calls. I hate that time of day, when I know I have to leave the Whytes' warm house and go back home. Our house is always in darkness at that time of the evening and the fire hasn't been lit so it's cold. I usually go and wake Mum while Rita bustles around downstairs getting Daddy's dinner. Most days, Mum is asleep when we get in, but recently she hasn't been as tired. Yesterday, she was sitting up reading when I got home and she had lit the fire in the front room. Rita says that Mum's medicine is finally "kicking in". The doctor gave her too much to begin with and that's why she was acting so dopey.

Now

I had lunch with Brian Davies this week. We met in The Green Room, his favourite restaurant. It's a stuffy gentlemen's club that has been in existence for centuries. Because of the exorbitant prices, Brian usually reserves it for his more important clients. I was touched at his blatant attempt to win me over. Years of experience had taught me that Brian was not a believer in free lunches – there was always an angle. He swaggered into the restaurant and over to where I had already been seated. He hugged me tightly and planted a big kiss on my cheek.

"You're looking far too good, Liz," he said, pulling out a chair for himself. "It's time you came back to work."

He looked over and examined me closely. "Honestly. I've never seen you looking so well."

"Stop," I said, shaking out my napkin. "Your backside has hardly touched the chair and already you're overdoing it on the compliments."

"Okay," he said, raising his hands. "But I mean it. You look," he searched for the word, "radiant."

I grinned like a schoolgirl. "Thank you."

He pulled at the knot of his tie and gave a long sigh. "It's good to see you."

Brian did not look radiant. There were dark fleshy bags under his eyes that indicated how exhausted he was.

"You look a bit stressed," I ventured.

He looked over at me and I noticed that all the energy he had mustered up for our initial greeting had disappeared, leaving him looking like a deflated balloon.

"It's been a rough few weeks," he said, reaching for a glass of water. "I let David Fenlon go last week."

I sat forward on my chair, agog. "You fired him?"

"Yes."

"But I heard he'd been headhunted by . . ." I tried to think of the company but couldn't.

Brian made a clicking noise with his tongue. "Headhunted, my arse. That's the line he's putting out. After I'm finished with him, no other agency in the country will want to touch him."

"How did he take it?"

"I've already received a solicitor's letter. He's suing me for unfair dismissal," Brian said with a snort. "Unfair dismissal! It's me that should be suing him for running my business into the ground."

"What happened?"

Brian shook his head and grabbed the menu as the waitress approached.

"Caesar salad and the medallions of beef to follow," he said without looking at her.

I ordered the same, anxious for him to get on with the story.

"What about some wine?" he asked, reaching for the wine list.

"No thanks. It's too early in the day for me."

He dropped the menu. "You're right. We'll stick to water."

When the waitress had walked away I pulled my chair closer to the table and continued. "Well, go on. What happened?"

Brian brought his shoulders up stiffly and let them drop again. "Nothing happened. That's why I'm in this mess. Nothing bloody well happened – the lazy bastard sat on his arse and bled his expense account dry."

A dark shadow passed over his face and he looked as if he was about to kill someone. "Did you know he had a drug problem?"

"Fenlon!" I said with a gasp. It had never occurred to me, yet hearing it did not surprise me either. He was such a flash git. He had started in the business around the same time as me, and had earned himself quite a reputation in the world of advertising. He always drove the flashiest sports cars he could get his hands on, and dressed in the very best designer wear. He had remained unmarried and always, always had the most beautiful women on his arm. I fancied him for about ten minutes when I first met him, but as soon as he opened his mouth I lost interest. The guy was completely in love with himself.

"Yep," Brian said, twisting his napkin as though it was Fenlon's neck. "He's very fond of the nose candy. Apparently he spends a small fortune every week stuffing cocaine up his nose."

"How did he survive all those years in Draper Good?"

Fenlon had come from the most prestigious ad agency in the country. Draper Good had a reputation for only employing the very best.

Brian let out a loud guffaw. "That had me baffled all right! Until I discovered that Tony Good, chief partner, is Fenlon's uncle. They were only too delighted to see the back of him."

Our salads arrived and Brian grabbed his knife and fork like a farmer about to pitch a bale of hay. That was about halfway down the list of things that annoyed me about him. He ate every meal as if he had never seen a plate of food before.

"So what now?" I asked.

Brian stared at the tablecloth for a few moments before throwing down his cutlery. "Shit!" he exclaimed. "I'm so fucking angry, Liz." He looked close to tears. "How could I have been so stupid?"

"Brian, everyone makes mistakes with employees. It was a bad call, but surely you can move on and put it down to experience?"

"Fucking expensive experience," he muttered.

"I know the Browne account is gone, but we'll get it back," I said, trying to sound positive, "and if we don't, well, there are plenty of others to chase out there."

"Oh, Liz," he sighed. "Browne's is only the half of it."

"What do you mean?"

He took his fork up and began to poke at the lettuce on his plate. "I gave him free rein. I trusted him completely – never once checked up on him. He's in debt to the company to the tune of two hundred and fifty thousand euro."

"What?" I almost shouted.

Brian nodded his head wearily. "And, because I made the idiot partner, I am now obliged to make a settlement in order to get rid of him."

He had always taken financial losses very hard. In all the years I had known Brian I had seen him go through some tough times. Several health scares and a car accident that almost killed him. But nothing had hit him harder than the financial losses he incurred during his very messy divorce. After turning a blind eye to his extra-marital affairs for years, his wife decided to put an end to their marriage. And while she was at it, she also decided to hit her husband where she knew it would hurt him most, his wallet. Poor Brian was devastated. Not about losing his wife – in fact, he got over her very quickly. He could deal with losing people because he never got emotionally attached to them. But his money was a very different matter.

"The whole thing is a mess. There's no team left to fight for the account. Susie's lost interest since Fenlon came on the scene. I know she's been looking around for somewhere else to go since I passed her over."

I knew this to be true but didn't want to compound his misery any further.

"If you can prove that Fenlon abused his access to expenses then you might get away with having to buy him out," I said hopefully.

Brian gave me a half-smile. "I've already thought of that – my solicitor's looking into it."

He went back to pushing his salad around his plate, looking totally dejected.

"Look, Brian, it could have been a lot worse. He was only

there for ten months. You can easily dust yourself off and start over again. God knows, it's not the first time someone's tried to shaft you. I'll be back soon and we'll pull through it."

He looked at me for a moment, trying to decide whether to go with my optimism or remain wallowing in his anger. He shovelled the last of the salad into his mouth and put his knife and fork together on the plate.

"You're right," he said, reaching for a bread roll and tearing off a lump. "I've been letting that little shithead get the better of me."

"That's more like it," I said, trying to coax him into higher spirits. "You can't let it eat you up."

"Anyway," he said, brushing breadcrumbs off his hands, "enough about my problems. Let's talk turkey."

I gave a laugh at his sudden turnabout.

"I'm making you partner and giving you exactly the same as Fenlon. You'll have the same salary, holidays and benefits. I'm having the contract drawn up at the moment and I'll post it out next week. All right?"

Brian had started David Fenlon on almost twice my salary and it had been a bitter parting pill to swallow.

I felt a surge of self-satisfaction wash over me but tried not to show it. "All right," I said in a business-like tone. "But Brian, be sure about one thing. I am getting this baby, and when it happens, I will need time off. If you're not happy with that, then say something now."

"Any idea when it's going to happen?" he asked.

"No. It'll probably take another year or so. It's a slow process."

I could see the relief spread over his face. "Well, a year

is a long time. Let's just take things as they come, but when the time comes you will be entitled to whatever maternity leave is these days."

"Thank you," I said.

The waitress arrived with our meals and I could see that Brian was feeling a lot better.

"Maybe we will have that glass of wine," I suggested.

"Yes," he said quickly. "We need to have something to celebrate your promotion. In fact, let's have a glass of champagne." He turned to the waitress and ordered two glasses of Dom Pérignon.

The owner of the restaurant arrived over moments later and made a big fuss over opening the snipes of champagne. I looked around uncomfortably and saw the curious stares we were attracting.

"Christ, Brian, everyone will think that you've proposed to me!"

"It's better than that," Brian said, lifting his glass with a mischievous grin. "I've got the woman I want and I don't even have to marry you!" He clinked his glass against mine and looked around at the smiling faces of the other diners. "She said yes!" he said in a loud voice.

A chorus of "Oohs" and "Aahs" rippled around the dining-room while I tried to stop myself from choking on the champagne.

I finally got around to making that call to Rita to invite her and Daddy over for lunch. I hate ringing the house because no matter where Rita is, she will run as soon as she hears the phone begin to ring. If she is at the end of the garden, she'll drop whatever she's doing and charge into the house and up the hall as if her life depends on it. I let it ring several times and had visions of her falling and breaking a hip. But thankfully, after the sixth or seventh ring, Rita picked it up, out of breath.

"Sorry, Rita. Did I call at a bad time?"

"No, no. I was upstairs changing the bed-linen," she said trying to steady her breathing.

"Don't you have a phone by the bed?"

"Yes, but the line's gone all crackly, I can't hear anyone properly on it."

"How are you and Daddy?" I asked dutifully.

"Fine, dear," she answered.

"I'm ringing to invite you over to lunch next Saturday."

"What a coincidence!" she exclaimed. "Your father and I were just talking about the same thing last night. He's got all these vouchers to use up at the golf club and he was just saying that he'd like to take you and Claire out to lunch."

"Well, whatever you like. I'm quite happy to have it here."

"No, no. He's out playing golf at the moment but I'll talk to him about it when he gets home. Was it this Saturday you were thinking of?"

"Yes. I've checked with Claire and she's free. Richard is too." I said this, knowing that Richard hadn't really given me a straight answer but I'd never have them over if I waited around for a definite yes or no from him.

Rita rang back that evening and confirmed the golf club for Saturday. Richard's face dropped when I told him and I could tell immediately that he was trying to think up an excuse not to go.

"Claire's going as well?"

"Yes. What difference does that make?"

"Well, I'd only be in the way. It'll give you all a chance to catch up," he said, jumping at the opportunity to get out of it.

Richard and Daddy had never really hit it off in the way I'd hoped they would. In fact, they just tolerated each other. Although he had never said anything derogatory about Richard, I always thought that Daddy was disappointed with my choice of partner. He'd never really made a huge effort to get to know Richard. They play golf together once or twice a year but, apart from that, much to my disappointment, there has never been any great fondness between them. It's a pity, because in a way they are very alike.

"You are part of the family, Richard," I remarked. "It might give you a chance to catch up as well. You hardly ever see Daddy and Rita."

His back was turned to me but I could see his shoulders droop with my request.

"Liz, you know I'll be like a third wheel. Why don't you just go and enjoy yourself? I'm meeting Damian at ten on Saturday morning to go over some things for court on Monday. If I finish up early, I might pop in for a coffee afterwards. How about that?"

"Fine," I said.

What was the point? If he didn't want to come then why should I make him? After all, he had never tried to force his family on me. But both his parents were dead. They died within a year of each other, shortly before we were married. His only sister, Judy, lives in Canada with her husband and four children. We have visited them twice, but they rarely ever come home. Birthday and Christmas cards are really the only contact we have with them. I suppose it was unfair that I expected Richard to tag along to every family get together. Although, a little more willingness on his part occasionally would be nice.

"You're not just saying that?" he asked, putting his arms around my waist.

We kissed and I straightened his tie. "No. It's fine," I said, sounding mildly begrudging. "But do try to make it for coffee. I know Rita and Daddy would like to see you."

Then

I hate the golf club. Rita loves it. She smiles and waves like crazy at everyone whenever we walk in. We have to stop at loads of tables and listen to adults yapping their heads off about rubbish. Rita points to us and everyone tilts their heads and smiles as she tells them about Mum. Rita has had her hair done and is wearing her best stripy dress which makes her look like a big deckchair. When she opens her mouth to laugh, I can see patches of red lipstick on her front teeth. Daddy has brought us here for lunch – it's a treat after our visit to Mum this morning. Rita has made me wear my tartan dress with the collar that digs into my neck. It is too short for me – even Mum asked me what I was doing wearing it.

Mum is in hospital. The medicine she was on made her heart beat too quickly and she couldn't breathe properly. I woke to find her clinging to the side of the bed one night, gasping frantically, as if there was no air in the room. Daddy took her to the hospital and came home the next morning without her. She has to stay there until they fix her heartbeat and make it steady again. She's already been there for two weeks and the doctor still won't tell us when she can come home.

Rita has taken some time off work until Mum is better. At first I felt my heart sink when she told us that she would be home all day to look after us, but it hasn't been too bad because she is being especially nice to me and I don't have to eat any dinners I don't like. Rita never stops cleaning. The house is sparkling and smells of Mr Sheen and bleach all the time. I don't like her being there and I wish Mum was out of hospital, but it is nice to come home from school and have everything perfect, like the fire lit and the lunch made and someone there to help with homework. But that's the only part I like. At night when I'm going to bed I get a funny pain deep inside my stomach, like I want to get sick, but I know I'm not going to. I haven't told anyone about it – I know it's just a lonely pain because I want Mum back.

I think Daddy is relieved that Mum isn't at home. He comes home from work in really good humour and sometimes I feel like reminding him that she's only in hospital and will be coming home soon. I definitely think that he doesn't love Mum any more. If he did, he'd be more upset about her being sick and he doesn't seem one bit upset. I think that Rita cares more about polishing and scrubbing then she does about Mum.

Claire doesn't miss her at all. Sometimes I think Claire thinks that Rita is our mum. Mum was tired when we went to see her last week. She lay back in the bed and smiled at us but didn't say very much. Daddy said it was because the nurse had just given her an injection that made her sleepy. We stood at the side of the bed and looked at her as she drifted in and out of sleep – she looked so pretty in her blue nightie with her golden hair all loose around the pillow. When she had fallen asleep, Daddy told us to kiss her before we left. I leaned over and kissed her cheek. I could smell her soapy skin and feel her warm breath on my face and I wanted so badly to climb in beside her and put my arms around her. I got the funny pain in my stomach and tried to blink back my tears because I didn't want Daddy to see me cry. When I moved away, Daddy picked Claire up and told her to give Mum a kiss, but Claire squirmed in his arms and buried her face in his shoulder. Daddy tried to turn her face around and bent down so she could kiss Mum but Claire turned her face the other way and tightened her grip on his neck. He stood there for a few moments, not knowing what to do. Luckily, Mum was fast asleep and didn't see anything.

I said nothing in the car on the way home, but when we were getting ready for bed that night I went into the bathroom while Claire was brushing her teeth.

"Claire, do you miss Mum?" I asked crossly.

Claire took the toothbrush out of her mouth and looked at me blankly. "No," she answered.

I glared at her as she continued to brush her teeth. When she finished I swung her around and held her tightly by the shoulders.

"Why wouldn't you kiss Mum goodnight?" I shouted in her face.

Claire tried to wriggle away from me but I had a good grip of her.

"Get off me," she whined.

"Why? Tell me why you wouldn't kiss Mum goodnight?"

"I didn't want to," she cried.

I let go of one shoulder and with my free hand I drew back and walloped her across the face. Her screaming echoed around the house as I stormed out of the bathroom. Daddy and Rita came running up the stairs as if the house had caught fire.

I listened in my bedroom as Claire wailed her heart out. "Lizzy hit me. Lizzy hit me!" she repeated over and over again. I could hear the low-pitched tone of Rita's voice as she murmured some comforting words. When Claire finally stopped screaming, Rita put her to bed and read her a story.

Daddy came into my room and I prepared myself for a stinking row, but he just sat beside me on the bed and said nothing for ages. Eventually, he put his arm around me and said, "You mustn't be angry with Claire. She's just a baby."

"She's almost six," I said, kicking my legs against the side of the bed.

"You're older, Lizzy. You understand that Mum is in hospital because she's sick."

"So does Claire."

"She doesn't really understand, Lizzy, not the way you do. Claire is angry with your mother because she's not at home with us and that's why she wouldn't kiss her this evening."

"She doesn't miss her," I whispered.

Daddy hugged me close to him and my throat felt like it would burst from all the tears that had clogged up inside it.

"Claire misses Mum every bit as much as you do — she just doesn't show it the same way because she's so young."

114

He straightened up and looked at me squarely. "Now Lizzy," he said gravely, "I want you to promise me that you'll never hit your sister again."

I hung my head in shame at the thought of what I'd done. It was the first time I had ever raised a hand to her.

"I promise."

"Good," Daddy said, standing up.

I lay back on my bed after he left and stared across at the ghostly shadows of the branches on my wall. The leaves are all gone now because it's November and the shapes look black and eerie. I look for a sign that something might be peeking out at me, but I can't see anything, just spiky branches like sticks of charcoal banging against one another. I know it's just a baby story and that I'm really too big to believe in such things any more – but I can't stop believing that there are fairies out there, watching over me. I got into bed and stared at the shadows until I felt my eyes getting heavy and tired. "Please make Mum get better," I whispered into the shadows, before falling asleep.

Now

The golf club is still filled with the same old dinosaurs that were there thirty years ago. The place does not hold fond memories for me. It reminds me of silent Sunday lunches where I was made to sit in my over-starched dress listening to adult conversations. As I entered the dining-room I spotted Daddy and Rita being led to their usual window table. Claire was sitting there already. The three of them exchanged kisses and I looked on, feeling slightly nervous as I made my way over.

"Hello, dear," said Rita as she saw me approaching, and stretched her arms out to give me a warm hug. The overpowering scent of her perfume invaded my nostrils.

"Hello, Lizzy," Daddy said, reaching over to kiss me. The bony edge of his high cheekbone swept the side of my face like a razor blade.

Claire observed our greetings and sat back down on the far side of the table, waving at me perfunctorily.

We hadn't seen each other since the night she had stormed out of my house and I sensed a chill in her gaze. She looked a lot better than she had that night, her skin lightly tanned from her weekend in the south of France, her complexion healthier.

"How was France?" I asked, trying to ignore her hostile stare as we all settled around the table.

"Good," she snipped.

"Is Lainey's house beautiful?" asked Rita. "Her mother told me it was like a palace."

Mrs Whyte still lived beside Rita and Daddy. They didn't see much of each other but when they did, their conversation was restricted to the children – because outside of us they didn't have very much in common. I had always been under the impression that Mrs Whyte was never overly fond of Rita.

"It's out of this world," said Claire. "I'm looking into buying a place out there myself. Not one as big as Lainey's of course, but something smaller in the same area."

"Oh, how nice," exclaimed Rita as she grabbed ahold of Daddy's arm. "Wouldn't that be nice, dear! A place in the sun."

Daddy reached for a bread roll and tore it apart. "Nice indeed," he snorted, not bothering to hide his disdain. Buying property abroad was something my father considered a foolish extravagance.

"I've already been on to an estate agent in Cannes," Claire continued, ignoring Daddy's disapproval. "He's sending me some brochures next week."

I could hear her little voice crying, *I want it. I want it!*

I pursed my lips, forcing a smile, and tried to look surprised, but I wasn't. I had guessed that when she saw Lainey's place in France, my sister would come home wanting it.

Daddy lifted his menu and squinted at the print through his bifocals. "Are we going to order or is Richard coming?" he asked, looking over at me accusingly.

"Sorry, Richard won't be able to make it. He's stuck in a meeting this morning, but he said he'll try to make it over for coffee." This came out in an apologetic gush and I was instantly annoyed with myself. It wasn't my fault that Richard wasn't joining us, but Daddy's glare made it impossible for me to feel any other way.

"Oh well," he said with a sigh, "let's just order then."

"Yes, let's!" Rita echoed excitedly. "The lamb is very good at the moment." She was looking at the menu that only ever offered salmon or lamb. The golf club served good lamb in the spring and mutton for the rest of the year. Some days, if the wind blew in the right direction, you could smell the lamb fat from the car park.

"I'll have the salmon," I said to the waitress.

"Me too," said Claire, suppressing a smile as she read my thoughts.

"That's two salmon and two lamb," Daddy said to the waitress. "And is everyone having the soup?"

"Not me," said Claire.

Daddy looked at her impatiently. "Well, have something else then?"

"No, thank you. A main course is more than enough for me. I'm not used to eating at this time of day."

"Very well then." He turned back to the waitress. He lifted three fingers. "Three soup," he said in a raised voice, as if the waitress were both deaf and stupid. "Two salmon," he bent one finger, leaving two held up, "and two lamb." She gave him a withering look, scribbled on her notepad and left without a word.

Daddy's mouth opened in disbelief as he waved his menu after her. "I never ordered the wine," he said, turning back to us.

Rita reached across and patted his arm. "Don't worry, dear. She'll be back shortly."

"Bloody staff they have here now," he said crossly. "They're only short of telling you to go and serve yourself."

I sipped my water and wondered why I had bothered to come. It was never any different these days – Daddy moaning while Rita clucked over him.

He eventually ordered the wine. Claire didn't want any of that either, which clearly annoyed him further. "Have a glass with your lunch," he ordered.

"No, thank you," Claire insisted.

That's the difference between the two of us. I'd just have the damn glass of wine to shut him up, whereas Claire would dig her heels in and flatly refuse.

Our starters arrived and as we tucked in, Claire stood up and went to the bathroom.

I had noticed it, but said nothing. I didn't have to – Rita said it for me. "Claire's put on weight," she said matter-of-factly.

She looked over at me for a comment. Claire had always been stick thin, too thin, in my opinion. Although she never admitted to being on a diet at any time, she was always obsessed with things like fat content and calories and spent ages reading the labels on food packaging. It used to drive me mad when we were younger. She used to delight in telling me how many calories were in a Mars bar, just as I was about to ram the last piece down my neck.

"Yes, she has," I said.

Rita nodded contently. My answer seemed to satisfy her. "It's about time she filled out. That child was always too skinny."

I smiled to myself. Rita still talked about us as if we were children. She didn't seem to understand that after the age of seventeen most women don't want to fill out any more. "She looks like a damn boy with her hair cut like that," said Daddy.

We both ignored his comment.

Rita chased a cherry tomato around her plate with her fork. "Having some flesh on you in my day was considered attractive. Women these days are far too thin. I think Claire looks very well with –"

I jumped in quickly when I spotted Claire walking back towards us. "Yes," I said, cutting her off. "Are you taking any holidays this summer?"

Rita speared the tomato and looked over at me quizzically but soon realised what I was doing as Claire settled back into her seat.

"No plans yet, have we, dear?" she said, looking to Daddy.

He grunted something about Kerry and kept eating.

"Claire, we were just saying how the little bit of weight suits you."

Christ, the woman doesn't know when to shut up! She's like a dog with a friggin' bone once she gets started.

Claire blushed and shook out her napkin nervously. "It's all the fast food I've been eating lately. I get in late in the evenings and can't be bothered cooking for myself." Her tone was almost confessional, as she twisted the corner of the napkin into a sharp point. "And then, Lainey's cooking in the South of France didn't help matters either. It's back to the gym next week," she added with a strained smile.

"Ooh," cooed Rita, "don't start dieting and losing any more weight. I was just saying to Lizzy, in my day, a little weight on a woman was considered attractive."

Rita had always been a little on the heavy side whereas Mum had been tall and willowy, but Rita's confidence and self-belief allowed her to think that she had the better figure of the two.

Thankfully Daddy saw fit to change the conversation and began to talk to Claire about an ongoing case in the Supreme Court. Rita started to tell me about a new hairdressing salon that had opened in town which was doing specials for pensioners on Thursdays. I half-listened to what she was saying, which is all I ever did with her. I often wondered had she come to accept my lack of concentration, or had she simply failed to ever notice. I expect lots of people do the same with her, because giving Rita your full attention is like having your head stuck in a paper bag with fifty bluebottles buzzing around inside it. Claire seemed to be doing the same to Daddy. I could tell from the way her eyes wandered away from his gaze that her concentration was not wholly on what he was saying. What had happened to her? My beautiful little sister who people stopped on the street to admire when we were kids. Why wasn't she married to a successful husband and living a charmed life like everyone thought she would? What went wrong that she has ended up approaching the age of forty with no one in her life? I gazed over at her chopped hair and my face began to flush as the thought struck me that she might be gay.

I grabbed my glass of water and turned back to Rita who had moved on to low-energy light bulbs and how they were saving on their electricity bill by using them.

My God! Was Claire gay? It all added up. Men being off limits, getting touchy about anyone trying to set her up with a date, and this new butch look. I gave a sideways glance and let my eyes glide over her, trying to hide the feeling of dismay that was bubbling up inside me. Claire met my gaze and looked as if she knew what I was thinking. For a split second our eyes locked and we were suddenly strangers.

I tuned in and out of Rita's conversation as I picked my way through lunch, trying to digest my new theory about Claire. I tried not to look at her too much in case she might see right through to my thoughts. Claire's good at that sometimes. I'm no good at hiding things – I can't pretend that things are any other way than what they are and there have been times when Claire has been able to tell exactly what I'm thinking. After lunch, while the waitress cleared the plates from the table, Claire gave me a questioning look. I felt my face go red and looked away quickly, hoping she wasn't reading the thoughts that were racing through my head.

All the way home in the car I turned it over and over in my mind. It all seemed to make sense. The way Claire had distanced herself from me and Daddy and Rita in the past year or two – being gay would have forced her to do that. God knows, it would be shocking enough for me, but I doubt that Daddy and Rita even knew what gay was. I thought of how isolated Claire must be feeling and immediately felt a pang of guilt. I was so wrapped up in my own life that I had never once stopped to think of her and whether she was all right or not. I had always assumed that she was the one living the high life, filled with fun and happiness. Of course, I could be wrong.

My mind was jolted back to the present, as the guy behind me blew his horn to let me know that the traffic lights had turned green.

Richard called me that evening to say that he was still in the office and would eat in town. I waited for him to get home but by the time he came in at a quarter past eleven my excitement had waned and I was annoyed with him for being so late.

"Hi," he said, as he walked into the front room. "Still up?"

I looked at him sternly. "It is Saturday night. I stayed up in the hope that you'd be home at a reasonable hour and we could have a few glasses of wine and chat, but obviously, you prefer your colleagues' company than mine."

Richard looked crushed. "Come on, Liz," he said wearily. "Don't start on at me. It's been a long day."

"Richard!" I exclaimed loudly, surprising myself with how angry I had suddenly become. "You should have come to lunch with us today. It's been months since you've seen Daddy and Rita. This Shields case has got out of hand – you act as if they own you."

He came over to the couch and flopped down beside me and reached for the empty wineglass I had placed there for him earlier. He lifted the half-empty bottle of wine and poured himself a glass.

"I'm sick of it," I said, trying not to sound whiney.

He looked at me as if he were about to cry. "So am I," he said quietly, and took a long draught of his wine. "Sick and tired of it," he added.

We both sat there in silence.

"I don't want to pressurise you," I whispered, "but we need to start spending more time together."

He shut his eyes tightly and massaged the bridge of his nose. "I know, love. Believe it or not I made a decision last week to do just that. As soon as this tribunal is over, I'm taking a few months off."

Great, I thought to myself. I'll be back to work by then.

He reached for my hand and even though I felt like slapping it away, I didn't have the heart to do it. I looked at his face and saw the lines that had appeared around his eyes and mouth in recent months. For the first time ever, he looked his age.

We finished the wine and went to bed. Just as I was about to drift into sleep I remembered what I had wanted to tell him. I could tell that he was still awake by the way he was breathing.

"Richard, Claire came to lunch with us today."

He gave a low murmur to let me know he was listening.

"I think she might be gay."

My words seemed to shake him into wakefulness and he turned with a jerk as if I had prodded him.

"What?" he asked in a strangled whisper.

"Claire. I think she might be gay."

"For God's sake, Liz, what the hell are you talking about?"

I seized on his reaction and rolled over towards him, propping myself up on the pillow with one arm.

"I know it sounds crazy, but it's just something that struck me about her today and it seems to explain everything."

"Like what?"

"Oh, just little things that have happened recently. I haven't mentioned them to you because you're never around when I'm thinking about them."

"Thinking about what?" he asked, sounding totally confused.

"Well, I know that over the past year or so, I haven't seen as much of Claire as I used to. We used to meet up to go shopping all the time and all those winter breaks when we went to the Canaries, they just stopped. I thought it was because we were both just too busy – but today I realised that Claire has pushed me out of her life. It happened so gradually that I never really stopped to think about it. Then there's the whole thing about her not dating anyone and getting upset if anyone tries to fix her up with someone. And you have to admit, she's beginning to look like a lesbian."

Richard let out a loud yawn. "Liz, you have always meddled with her love life and she just gets upset when you interfere. I've been telling you that for years."

"It's more than just upset. I know Claire, and not talking for weeks on end is just not her style. Believe me, when she's upset she just lets fly."

Richard pulled the duvet under his chin and settled into his sleeping position. He ran his hand up and down my arm and kissed me on the cheek.

"Liz," he said gently, "why do you feel you have to get so involved in her life? She's an adult, and you have to get used to the fact that you may not be the person she always turns to. Just stand back and give her some space."

"Do you think I'm interfering?" I asked. The thought had never occurred to me. I was just concerned for her. I certainly didn't want to appear to be sticking my nose in her business.

Richard gave my arm a reassuring squeeze. "No, I don't. I think you're just a big sister who cares too much."

"So you don't think she could be gay?"

Richard gave another yawn. "No, I wouldn't say she is."

I felt slightly deflated at his reaction. Could I be that wrong? She was after all my sister and whether we chose to or not, we could read each other like maps. It was something that Richard would never fully understand.

125

Then

There are a lot of things happening that I don't understand. A good thing that happened is that Mum came home from hospital and I'm happy about that. An odd thing that happened is that Rita moved back to her own house. I should be happy about it − but I felt a bit sorry for her the day she packed up and left. Before that, there had been lots of whispering between her and Daddy behind closed doors and I knew by their cross hissy voices that they were arguing. At night, when Mum was in hospital, I could hear them talking in Daddy's bedroom. At first it was always a low murmur but after a while Rita's voice grew louder as she tried to talk over Daddy. Claire woke on one of these nights. Her asthma has got way worse and I was afraid that she would hear Rita in Daddy's room. I could hear Claire moaning and wheezing, so I went in to her and brought her into my bed. I gave her the inhaler and counted with her as she gulped the clean air into her lungs. I had taken Claire into my bed a few times recently when she woke at night, because I didn't want her to hear the arguing.

"One, two, three, breathe," I whispered to her, as I pressed the button on the inhaler.

Claire cried and gulped at the same time.

Daddy's voice got louder and I tried to talk at the same time so Claire wouldn't hear them. Rita sounded like she was crying.

Claire's ragged breathing evened out and she calmed down and lay back on the pillow. I nestled closer to her and kept talking − saying anything to drown out the rise and fall of the voices coming through the wall.

"Lizzy, close the curtains," Claire whispered to me.

"If I close them the fairies won't be able to see in and watch over us – look," I said, raising a finger in the dark to point at the swaying shadows of the branches.

"What fairies?"

"Well," I said, trying my best to sound the way Mum did, although it seemed like a lifetime since she had told me any stories, "inside that tree are fairies. Good fairies that grant wishes and look over you while you sleep, so nothing bad can happen."

Although it was dark, I could sense that I had grabbed Claire's full attention.

"Really?" she asked, her little voice full of wonder.

"Really," I answered, delighted to have someone to share my secret with. "Look at the branches, the way they move to and fro. They do that because the fairies are jumping from leaf to leaf. They come out to play at night but they are so tiny we can't see them."

"What kind of wishes do they grant?"

"All kinds of wishes. Just ask them whatever you want, inside your head, but don't tell anyone what you've asked for."

"Have they granted wishes for you?"

"Yes," I assured her, "plenty of times."

"Like what?"

"I can't tell," I said, remembering Mum's words.

Daddy and Rita's voices came clamouring through the wall again and I could feel my heart pounding with panic. I tried to think of some excuse why they would be in the same bedroom arguing in the middle of the night.

"Rita's crying," said Claire without a hint of surprise.

127

"That's not Rita," I said, trying to make up something quickly.

"Yes, it is," Claire insisted.

"It's only the radio," I said, because Rita often listened to radio plays in her bedroom in the evenings.

"It's Rita. She's in Daddy's room and she's crying," said Claire hugging her Peter Rabbit tight to her chest.

"She's not crying. Sometimes she goes into Daddy's room so she can help him with his work." This is what I used to say to myself in the beginning, before I knew what was really happening.

Claire turned on the pillow and faced me.

"No, Lizzy," she said matter-of-factly. "Rita goes into Daddy's room to sleep in his bed. I hear her at night when she creeps across the landing. His door creaks when she opens it and it always wakes me."

I felt myself burning up inside. I couldn't believe that she knew. Claire didn't understand what she was saying even though she was speaking the truth. All the nights I'd tried to hide it from her, talking my head off, telling her stories, anything to send her back off to sleep before they made any noises. And all the time, she knew.

"Well, maybe she does," I said, "but you must promise never to speak to anyone about it. Not Mum or Lainey or anyone. Promise?"

"Promise," said Claire sleepily.

I stared across at the shadows and shut my eyes as tight as I could and wished that Rita would vanish or die or be kidnapped by gypsies on her way home from work some day.

The following morning, we ate breakfast together in total silence. Daddy frowned into his bowl of Weetabix.

Rita stood in the corner beside the kettle staring into space, clutching a mug of coffee to her bosom. Daddy scowled over at Rita as he stood up to carry his bowl over to the sink. He cleared his throat loudly and Rita starting blinking quickly as if she was trying hard not to cry.

"Girls," he said sternly.

We turned our sleepy faces towards him and waited for him to continue.

He placed his bowl down on the drainer and came back to the table.

"Mummy is coming home from hospital tomorrow."

I felt my heart fill up like a balloon about to burst. Claire looked at me blankly and went back to scraping the last of her Rice Krispies from the side of her bowl.

Daddy pushed his chair back in towards the table and stood clutching the back of it, looking from me to Claire. He threw Rita a worried look, as if he wanted her to say something, but she turned her back on him and began to wash her mug under the tap.

"Yes," he said sharply. "Mummy's coming home and Auntie Rita is going back to live in her own house."

My heart was now a hot air balloon, floating in the sky. Mum home, Rita gone. My wish had been granted. There was a brief silence before Claire jumped off her chair and rushed over to Rita, wrapping her arms around Rita's waist and burying her head into Rita's stomach.

"Don't go! I don't want you to go!" she wailed.

Rita had two big tears rolling down her cheeks. She blubbered something about having to and looked across at Daddy who turned away. Daddy always hated tears. I wanted to laugh out loud and slide down the banisters, but

I didn't dare to even smile. Rita took Claire by the hand and led her towards the kitchen door. "Come on, sweetheart. It's time to put on your uniform or you'll be late for school," she gasped through her tears.

I was left alone with Daddy who was still staring at the wall with one hand now clutching his briefcase. He turned to me and stood there like a giant statue.

"You'll be happy to see your mother again," he said solemnly.

I nodded my head, almost afraid to admit it. "Will you?" I asked.

He drummed his fingers against the battered leather briefcase and his eyebrows knitted together in a tight frown. "Of course. I'll be delighted to see her," he said, but I could tell he was lying and it made me hate him. He cleared his throat with some short noisy coughs. "It will be terrific to have Mummy back again. Claire is upset, understandably, because she'll miss Rita. We all will."

I looked up at him and felt a hot flash of anger rush through me. "I won't," I said, staring at him defiantly. He glowered at me and I saw his fist tighten around the handle of his briefcase, his big knuckles turning white. I stiffened in my chair and cast my eyes downwards and prepared to receive a slap. Instead, when I looked back up, I saw the kitchen door being pulled closed and heard the angry click of Daddy's shoes as he marched down the hall and out of the house.

Now

Daddy and Rita have gone to Kerry for two weeks to stay in their house by the beach. Daddy bought it when Mum was still alive, but over the years it has fallen into a state of disrepair. Last time I saw it, it had begun to resemble a New Age hippy squat. I don't know how they bear to stay in it. I remember happy times in that house, when Mum was well and it was just the four of us. Daddy loves the place and always said he wanted to retire there, but summer holidays are all he ever manages. Claire sometimes goes with them but I find it hard to go back. It holds too many memories.

The car journey takes them six hours from door to door and they are always very tired when they arrive. I spent the morning baking a ham and packed it into a picnic basket with some fresh rolls and a flask of coffee. On the way to their house, I stopped at our local deli and bought an apple tart and popped that in too. It would save them having to go shopping when they arrived at the house. I knew that by the time they got there, neither of them would be fit for anything.

Rita was bundling a pile of bed-linen into the boot of the car when I arrived. Her face was pink with nervous anticipation as she fussed about, trying not to forget anything.

"Hello, dear," she cried, straightening up from the car boot. A single bead of perspiration rolled down her forehead. She shielded her eyes from the sun and looked down at the picnic basket.

"Just thought I'd bring you some food for this evening. It'll save you shopping when you get there."

Her face broke into a huge smile. "What a pet you are. I was just thinking that I should have made something for tonight, but we've been so busy this week, I never got a chance to do anything."

"Well," I said, thrusting the basket into her hands, "now you don't have to. Happy holiday!"

She took the basket and put it on the back seat of the car. She was wearing one of her holiday dresses, which must have been about ten years old. She had about four of them that were pulled from the back of the wardrobe every summer to be worn during the holidays. The one she was wearing was blue with big white polka dots. It was belted at the waist and flared out into a full skirt that reached just below the knee. It made her look like a character from an Enid Blyton story.

"Come in and say hello to your father. He's going potty looking for his fishing rod. He's gone and pulled the garden shed apart but I don't think it's in there."

We walked into the house and down through the dark hall to the kitchen.

Rita looked out the window and clapped her hands together excitedly. "Oh look, he's found it!"

I moved over beside her and we looked out at Daddy who was walking up the garden clutching the fishing rod, muttering something to himself.

"Lizzy's here!" Rita shouted as she rapped on the window-pane.

Daddy looked up and tried to read her lips as she rapped on the window again which completely drowned out her voice.

"Lizzy's here. She brought us a picnic!"

Daddy stopped as he reached the patio outside the window and looked in at the two of us with a puzzled expression.

"Wait till he gets inside. He can't hear you," I said, trying not to let my irritation show.

Why would she scream out at him and bang at the

window when he would be inside the kitchen in less than ten seconds?

Daddy walked in through the back door and smiled as he shook the rod at us.

"I knew the damn thing was out there. Hello, Lizzy, what are you doing here? Didn't you know we were leaving this morning?"

Rita looked at me and rolled her eyes up to heaven. "Of course she knows. She brought us a lovely picnic basket full of food for this evening, so we won't have to go shopping when we get there."

Daddy stopped fiddling with the tangled line of the rod and looked over at me in surprise. "Really?" he said.

"Yes," Rita gushed. "Isn't she a pet?" She turned to me and gave me a pat on the back. "You're so thoughtful, Lizzy."

I began to blush at their show of appreciation. "It's nothing really. Just some ham and bread and stuff."

Daddy stayed perfectly still and kept looking at me. "That's so good of you, darling," he said, his large brown eyes softening as he looked at me in a way I am not used to. It is not often that my father is touched by anything people do for him and I felt slightly uncomfortable standing there under his benign gaze.

I broke the awkward moment by hoisting my handbag over my shoulder. "Well, I hope you both have a lovely time. Don't forget your mobile phones, so we can stay in touch."

The phone began to ring and Daddy and Rita looked at each other in wonderment.

"Are you expecting any calls?" Rita asked.

Daddy shook his head. "No."

The shrill ring echoed around the hall. Rita immediately broke into a gallop and raced out to answer it.

We listened to her voice from the kitchen.

"Hello. Yes, this is she." Then she let out a loud whoop. "Hello, Lainey dear! How are you? Yes, yes, she is. We're off to Kerry this morning. Thank you. Yes, I'll get her, dear. Just a moment."

The phone receiver was dropped onto the hall table with a clunk and Rita broke into a run again, back to the kitchen.

"It's for you, Lizzy. It's Lainey."

I went out to the hall and picked up.

"I'm spying on you," said Lainey with a laugh.

"Where are you?"

"I'm up in Mum's with the girls. I saw your car outside the house. Why don't you come up for a coffee? Mum would love to see you."

"I'll be up in a few minutes," I said before hanging up.

I went back into the kitchen, glad to have an excuse to leave the two of them to their last-minute fussing.

"Lainey's invited me up to her Mum's for a coffee. So I'll go now."

The two of them walked me out to the gate and we hugged and said our goodbyes in the warm sunshine.

Daddy put his arms around me and held me for a split second more than was usual.

"You're a good girl, Lizzy," he whispered into my ear.

For a second I was nine years old again and Daddy had told me I was a good girl. It's funny how it still had the same effect all these years later. I felt a warm glow rush through me as I revelled in his fleeting show of affection. I walked up to Mrs Whyte's house and waved back at the two of them before turning into the driveway. Rita's arm was linked through Daddy's as she waved back frantically with her free arm. When did I stop hating her? All the bitter resentment I had felt towards her had faded with age. I think I inadvertently reached a stage when I knew that I had wreaked sufficient punishment on her. The sheer venom I had stored up inside me for her alone, had whittled down to nothing over the years. This is the woman who usurped her sister from the most hallowed throne of wife and mother. She is the woman who I made a career of tormenting through all of my teenage years. Every underage drink, every cigarette, every sordid encounter with unsuitable young men and later every illicit drug was all done in a desperate attempt to break Rita down and destroy her relationship with my father. To let her know that however hard she tried, she would never take the place of my mother. How I triumphed on those nights as I lay in bed and listened to them argue over something I had done! My heart would lift at the sound of Rita's sobbing through the bedroom wall. Back then, my only aim in life was to inflict as much misery and pain as possible on her.

The front door was opened by a joyous Mrs Whyte.

"Lizzy!" she cried, throwing her arms around me, making me feel awful that I hadn't called to see her in months.

She took my arm and led me through the hall into the familiar bright airy kitchen where Lainey was sitting, a mug of coffee cupped between her hands.

"Sit down, sit down," Mrs Whyte said, pushing me into a chair. "I'll get you some coffee."

Lainey stood up and put on the kettle. "You go on, Mum, or you'll never get out of here." She turned to me and smiled. "Mum is taking the girls into town – they were meant to leave an hour ago."

"Well, if you're happy to get the coffee, I'll go on so." Mrs Whyte looked over and beamed at the two of us. "It's so nice to see you, Lizzy. It's been too long."

I tried to calculate how old she must be. She was a good bit older than Mum, and Mum would have been sixty-five now – making Mrs Whyte over seventy. She looked nowhere near that age. Her hair was a mixture of grey and blonde and cut in a stylish bob. No summer frocks for her! She had always had great taste in clothes and I admired her smart beige trousers and cashmere twin set.

Outside in the garden Alannah and Jenny ran around in circles trying to catch Trixie, Mrs Whyte's beloved West Highland Terrier. They shrieked with delight as the dog ran through their legs and around the garden, delighted with some youngsters to play with.

They came running into the kitchen when their gran called to them.

"Hi, Auntie Liz!" they said, running into my arms. "Are you coming into town with us?"

They looked the picture of health and happiness with gap-toothed smiles and skin that had turned golden from their stay in France.

"No, girls, she's staying here with me. Now run upstairs and wash your hands before you go," said Lainey.

The girls bustled out the door and we listened to their footsteps tramping up the stairs.

"There's some chicken in the fridge if you want to make

a sandwich, and there's a fruit cake in that tin beside the kettle," said Mrs Whyte as she took her handbag off the table.

"Thanks, Mum," said Lainey. "We'll help ourselves."

The girls came running back into the kitchen, rubbing their damp hands on the legs of their trousers. "Ready!" they said in unison.

"We'll be back later. See you then," said Mrs Whyte. "Goodbye, Liz, pet, I'm sorry I'm in such a rush. Call up and see me the next time you're visiting home."

"I will," I promised, standing up to kiss her.

We sat back down at the table and listened to their excited chatter in the hall, about what they were going to do in town. The front door closed behind them and Lainey looked over at me with a wide-eyed smile.

"Oh my God! I thought she'd never go. I've been here for hours, waiting for them to leave. They were meant to go at ten o'clock. Look," she said pointing to her wristwatch. "It's nearly twelve."

I laughed at her exasperation.

"Mum's got so doddery lately. It takes her ages to do the smallest of things."

"I find that with Daddy and Rita as well. I suppose they're getting old and slowing down."

Lainey nodded her head in agreement. "I worry about her in this house all alone. I just presume that she's all right and able to look after herself, like she always did. But, when she came to France, I realised that she's not young any more. She couldn't open milk cartons or take the lids off any jars – and it made me wonder what she does when she's here on her own."

The kettle clicked off and Lainey went over to make my coffee.

"I know what you mean," I said. "We presume that our parents will always stay the same and it's a shock when they begin to get old."

"I'll have to keep an eye on her and maybe start dropping hints about her coming to live with us. I've spoken about it to Peter and he'd be happy to have her.

As Lainey moved about the kitchen I stared at her silk smocked top enviously.

"I love that top."

Lainey looked down at it and smiled. "I found the best shop in Cannes. You'll have to come over for a few days before you go back to work and we'll give the credit cards a battering."

"How was France?" I asked.

"Hectic," she replied, plonking a mug of coffee before me. "Here," she said, prising open the cake tin, "let's have some of this."

We buttered some slices and helped ourselves to the fruitcake. As soon as I popped the first piece into my mouth, I was transported back in time to rainy schooldays. We used to sit at the same kitchen table, eating big slabs of Mrs Whyte's fruitcake while we did our homework.

"I enjoyed it, but we had far too many visitors in a short space of time." She had only said this when her hand shot up to her mouth. "I don't mean that to sound as if I didn't want them. It's just that next summer, I'll space them out a little more."

"I don't know how you do it. You had your mother and Claire and then a whole string of other people for the entire month."

"I know, I know. Anyway, you live and learn. Next year I'll do things differently. We were so excited about getting the place that we wanted to show it off to everyone."

"Claire really enjoyed it."

Lainey looked at me questioningly. "Did she?"

"Of course she did," I said. "Why on earth wouldn't she?"

Lainey brushed some cake crumbs off the leg of her trousers. "She just seemed so preoccupied all the time. I thought she might have been sorry that she accepted the invitation."

A sombre tone had crept into her voice.

"Lainey, what do you mean?"

Lainey put her mug down and looked at me for a second, trying to decide whether to go on or not. She took a deep breath and continued. "I'm worried about her, Liz. I think she's going through a bad time and she doesn't seem to be able to talk to anyone."

I slapped my hands down on the table. "You're right," I said, shifting in my chair. "I've had a feeling for ages that something is wrong, but every time I try to approach her I seem to make things worse."

"Yes, I know," Lainey said, her face now crumpled into a frown. "Claire cuts herself off from people in a way that you just can't get close to her."

"Did anything happen in France?" I asked, hoping that Claire hadn't been rude to Lainey and insulted her hospitality.

"Not really," Lainey said unconvincingly.

"Come on, Lainey, tell me," I urged.

Again her forehead creased into deep lines and I could see she was picking her words carefully. "She's behaving oddly, Liz. It's like she's turning into a completely different person. I can't explain it very well but she seems like she's on the edge all the time. I don't think she relaxed for five minutes during the time in France. She was agitated and tetchy for no apparent reason, and when I tried to see what might be troubling her, she backed away completely. In fact, I was sorry I mentioned it at all. It kind of spoiled the weekend." Lainey's shoulders drooped under the strain. "I feel bad talking about her like this, but I think you should know, Liz. If anyone can get through to her, it's you."

I gave a sarcastic laugh at this. "God, Lainey, I'm the last person she seems to want to confide in. I can do nothing right in her eyes at the moment."

"Liz," Lainey said slowly, "I think she might have an eating disorder."

"What!" I said in a whisper.

"She got sick after almost every meal we had. She didn't tell me, but I could hear her."

"But she's put on weight lately – how could she be anorexic?" I asked, totally baffled.

"Well, it might be the other kind. Bulimia. Apparently bulimics stuff themselves and throw up after. Claire certainly seemed to eat everything, but I definitely know that she threw up after most of her meals."

"I had no idea," I said, reeling from the shock.

Lainey let out a long sigh. "I may be wrong about the eating disorder, but there is definitely something up with her."

I felt a lump form in my throat. "I can't seem to get through to her any more. I was only saying to Richard the other night that Claire seems to have pushed me out of her life over the past year or two, but it's been such a subtle process that I'm only beginning to notice now."

Lainey put her hand on my arm and gave it a squeeze. "You're not to start blaming yourself, Liz. Claire is responsible for her own life, and there's very little you can do if she is pushing you away."

I stared at the table and chewed my bottom lip, wondering whether to tell her or not.

"What?" Lainey asked, trying to read my thoughts.

"I shouldn't," I said.

"Go on," she said. Now it was her turn to prise it out of me.

"I had lunch with Claire and Rita and Daddy at the golf club last week, and something struck me for no reason really – it just occurred to me that Claire might be gay."

Lainey's eyes opened wide, she opened her mouth to say something, but closed it again.

"I know," I said with a weary smile. "It sounds preposterous, but when you put everything together it kind of makes sense."

"Put what together?" Lainey asked incredulously.

"Well, firstly, there's the man thing. You have to admit it's kind of weird that she doesn't seem to want to meet anyone. All those guys that I've tried to fix her up with, you'd think she'd have clicked with one of them. I don't mean marry them, but she just seems to have an aversion to any man."

"That's just because you try too hard to pair her off with them. She's just being stubborn."

"Secondly," I continued, "don't you think that she's beginning to look like a dyke?"

Lainey's eyes nearly fell out onto the table.

"Well, that hair cut and the shitty clothes she's been wearing. It's just not the Claire we used to know – perhaps she's trying to tell us without actually telling us."

"Oh Liz! What a notion! I hope you're wrong."

"The funny thing is, I don't care if she's gay or not. I just wish she'd talk to me and get it out in the open so we can get on with being sisters again."

Lainey looked at me sideways. "You really wouldn't mind?"

I shrugged my shoulders. "No. I really wouldn't." I thought of something and smiled. "As long as I'm not the one that has to tell Daddy and Rita."

Lainey laughed for a moment but her face fell back into a worried frown. "We'll just have to keep a close eye on her for the next while, make sure she's all right . . ." She broke off and hesitated before adding, "I never saw the resemblance before, Liz, until the weekend in France, but Claire is very like your mother."

Her words made me stiffen with fear. I was the one that was like Mum, Claire was like Daddy. They had the brown eyes and sallow skin, everyone remarked on it. I was the one with Mum's fair colouring and blue eyes – but only on the outside. I felt the back of my neck get clammy as I remembered the night of the barbecue in our house. Claire looking lost, drumming her fingers on the table, her thoughts miles away. She had reminded me of someone, but I'd pushed it to the back of my mind, not wanting to know who it was. The reality hit me like a body blow: it was my mother.

Then

Last week we went to our new house in Kerry. It was sunny and Mum made picnics and we ate our lunch on the beach most days. I taught Claire how to swim. Well, almost. She managed to splash about without her rubber ring for a moment before swallowing a mouthful of water. When we got out of the water and Mum wrapped us up in towels to keep warm, Claire told us that she'd swallowed a fish. Daddy laughed so loud that everyone on the beach turned to see what was so funny. I don't like the breakfasts in Kerry. In the mornings, the farmer from across the road leaves us a bucket of milk that comes straight out of the cows' dangly things. It's warm and frothy and smells of dirty socks. Daddy puts it on our cornflakes and they go all soggy and horrible and we have to eat up, because it's good for us. He doesn't even put it in his tea, so how would he know if it's good for us?

One evening, after dinner, Mum and Daddy went for a walk on the beach. My face burned with happiness when they asked me would we be all right on our own for a little while.

"Yes, of course," I answered quickly. "We'll stay here and colour. Take as long as you like."

Mum looked so pretty. Her golden hair was in a ponytail and her legs and arms were tanned from the sunny weather.

"Look after your sister," Daddy said. "We won't be long."

They walked out into the front garden and I heard the gate creak as they headed out onto the road to the beach.

143

Claire sat at the table, her head cocked to one side, lost in concentration. She was colouring a clown in the colouring book that Rita had given her to bring on holidays. Claire insisted on moving to the next page if she coloured outside the lines, so every picture needed the greatest care and attention.

I could feel a warm glow of satisfaction settle inside me. Mum and Daddy going for a walk together, and no Rita to spoil it.

I slid off my chair and went to tell Claire that I'd be back in a minute, but she was on a tricky bit of the clown's bow tie and I decided not to disturb her, for fear I'd cause her to go outside the lines. I tiptoed out the front door and down the garden path, climbing over the stone wall so I wouldn't make any noise with the gate. Mum and Daddy had disappeared around the bend of the road that led to the beach. I walked quickly, hoping that I wouldn't be spotted. We were not allowed anywhere near the beach on our own, and if Daddy saw me I would be punished. When I got to the bend in the road, I slowed down and looked around me. Any further, and I had broken the rules. I took one step, then another, then another. The sand dunes came into view and so did my parents. I crouched down behind the stone wall and slowly raised my head to have a look. My heart skipped a beat as I looked on from my hiding position. There they were, hand in hand, walking between the sand dunes out towards the beach. I bit down on my lip and tried to stop the tears that stung my eyes. I felt confused. Sad, happy but very confused. Why weren't they like that all the time? I tried to think of a time when I had seen Daddy holding Mum's hand, but I couldn't. They looked so lovely that I wanted to run up behind them and throw my arms around the two of them, but of course I couldn't. I waited until they were out of sight and rushed back along the road to the house. Just as I got to the garden wall, I heard the screaming. I could tell straightaway that it was Claire. I ran headlong up the garden path and burst into the kitchen to find Claire standing on her chair screaming hysterically.

"What is it?" I shouted.

She didn't answer. I followed the line of her shaking finger which was pointing to something in the corner of the room. There, looking at us with its head tilted sideways was a hen! It had crossed the road from the farmyard and walked straight into our house and through to the kitchen.

"Oh for goodness sake!" I said, helping Claire down from the chair. "Stop screaming. It's only a hen."

"It's going to bite me," sobbed Claire.

"No, it's not," I said firmly. "Hens don't have any teeth."

I opened the window and approached it gently. Then, hoping I was right about them not having any teeth, I picked it up, the way I saw the farmer's wife once do it, and threw the flapping bird out into the garden. Afterwards, I gave Claire a drink of Ribena and a biscuit to take her mind off the hen. The last thing I wanted was for Mum and Daddy to return to her hysterics.

I lay in bed that night with my window open, listening to the sound of the sea. Mum hadn't come into my room since she'd come home from hospital. I missed her, but I was glad she hadn't because it meant that she was with Daddy.

On our last day in Kerry, we went to the beach and Mum made a special picnic. There were no sandwiches, just biscuits and cake and red lemonade that had turned warm from the sun. Claire and I wore our matching blue swimsuits, and we made sandcastles with Daddy, while Mum stretched out on the deckchair and dozed in the sun. We swam in the sea, and Daddy waded out up to his chest with Claire sitting on his shoulders because she didn't like the waves. I dived into them, feeling the cold seawater gush up my nose and down the back of my throat. Back on the beach, Mum held her hand up to shade her eyes from the sun and waved at us from her deckchair. I felt sad because it was our last day. I didn't want to go home ever again; I wanted to stay the way we were, just the four of us for the rest of our lives. We dried off and flopped onto our damp sandy towels letting the sun warm us up. I think Daddy must have felt the same way as I did because I caught him looking at the three of us and smiling to himself. He lay back on his towel and put his hands behind his head.

"This is the life, eh?" he said. "All of us together on a lovely holiday."

Claire was sitting at Mum's feet, idly digging a hole with her spade.

"But we're not all together," she said.

Daddy lifted his head and looked over at her.

"Rita's not here," Claire said, dumping a spadeful of sand on to Mum's feet.

Daddy let his head flop back on to his towel. "Rita's not really one of the family, Claire – she's your aunt."

Claire stopped digging and glared over at Daddy. "Yes, she is. She is, Mum, isn't she? Rita is part of our family."

146

Mum was biting her thumbnail, trying to figure out how to answer Claire. I could see that the mention of Rita had upset her.

"She is, isn't she, Mum?" Claire persisted.

Daddy was still lying back on his towel, his eyes screwed up tight as if he was expecting someone to hit him.

"Yes, love," Mum said faintly. "I suppose she is."

Claire turned to Daddy and pointed her spade at him. "See, I told you. Rita is one of our family."

"Yes, very well," he snapped, keeping his eyes shut.

We all sat there in silence, waiting for the unpleasant moment to pass.

"Where's my bucket?" Claire asked. She didn't seem to even notice that she'd spoiled everything.

"Over there, beside the bag," Mum said, standing up from her chair. She muttered something about going for a walk and was halfway down to the water by the time Daddy lifted his head. He jumped up and looked after her.

"I'm going for a walk too," he said quickly. "Lizzy, look after your sister."

I watched him run down to Mum. When he reached her, he stopped and put his hand on her arm, but she shrugged it away and kept walking. My heart sank as I watched them begin to argue. Behind me, Claire filled her bucket with sand and hummed a song under her breath. She had ruined the last day of our holiday and I wanted to put my hands around her neck and choke her. I went over to her and bent down, as if to help fill the bucket.

"Look, Claire," I said.

She lifted her head to look at me and, as she did, I threw a fistful of sand in her eyes.

Now

The summer has gone and along with it our bright evenings and long sunny days. Soon the clock will go back, robbing us of another hour of precious daylight. How I hate this time of year when a chill stings the air and warns us that there is worse to come. One good thing the season has brought is a letter from the Health Board telling us that we are to begin our adoption course in four weeks' time. As I read the letter, an image of the most beautiful baby came into my head and my heart tightened at the prospect of bringing her home. To us, to where she belonged. My fleeting rush of euphoria subsided at the thought of Richard, and how to tell him about this course. Firstly, I had promised to wait until next year before we spoke about adopting again and, secondly, I hadn't mentioned anything about the preparation that was required for adopting. Richard just thought the baby would arrive, gift-wrapped and potty-trained. The course was starting at the end of October. Well, if you list the months in chronological order, the end of October is only eight weeks before next year. I would have to use this reasoning with Richard.

As for the course, the letter said that we would be one of four or five couples and it would comprise four sessions each lasting four hours. Ouch! I'd have to think of something very convincing to gloss over that one. No doubt Richard would think of millions of other things he had to do on those days. But first things first. I would have to find a way of telling him about our being accepted on to the course. When he got used to the idea, I would slip the other details in at a later time.

I chose Saturday night. Richard had played golf with Damian Jones and was in good form after an enjoyable day. I got some nice sea bass and a bottle of Sancerre and lit candles in the kitchen.

"This is very nice," he said, kissing me lightly on the cheek as he walked into the kitchen after his shower.

I felt like a modern-day witch, preparing my potion whilst plotting out my strategy.

I handed him the corkscrew. "Open the wine, I'm almost done here."

The meal was good and we talked about the possibility of getting something done with the garden for next year. Richard thought a pond or some sort of water feature would look nice. I let him talk, not saying much myself. My mind raced ahead to next year and the year after that. Water features in gardens are not practical when you have children. I would spend my time frantically trying to keep our little toddler away from the pond/fountain or whatever Richard had in mind.

"What's up?" he asked. "Not too gone on the water feature?"

I snapped out of it and smiled up at him. "I'm just thinking about children."

His face seemed to drop at the mere mention of the word.

"Children and water features aren't a good combination," I said.

Richard went back to eating his dinner and I could see a darkness enter his eyes.

"We've got a place on an adoption course, starting the end of next month," I blurted.

"What's an adoption course?" he asked, looking down at his plate.

"It's a kind of assessment and information process. It's just a few meetings over a few weeks and they talk us through the whole thing and some other couples take part as well . . ." My voice trailed off as I looked over at his expression of gloom.

"How many weeks exactly?" was all he could think of to say.

"Four weeks. One afternoon a week for a couple of hours."

Silence.

"I don't know if I could commit to –"

"Don't suggest that I do this alone!" I snapped. I had suddenly lost my desire to butter him up and wanted instead to throw my knife at him. "It's a few hours out of your busy schedule. Christ, Richard, when we do get this child, you'll be spending more than a couple of hours a month with her, so you had better get used to the idea of giving up some of your precious time for this!"

He looked over at me as if I'd bitten him and I felt annoyed with myself for losing it so early into the conversation.

"Liz, take it easy. I'm only thinking out loud. You spring this on me and expect me to deal with it instantly. I thought that we agreed not to talk about it again until next year." He spoke slowly, as if he was trying to talk me down off the ledge of a high building.

"This year, next year, what does it matter, Richard?" I said, letting fly again. "Do you really think that come the first of January you are going to wake up feeling any differently?"

"It's not like that," he said defensively. "Next year I plan on taking some time off and giving myself some space to think about all of this."

I stood up and took the plates off the table.

"Well, Richard, while you're thinking about it, some other couple will get our place on the adoption course and probably get the baby that was meant for us."

I threw the plates across the granite worktop, not caring whether I smashed them or not. Richard's head jerked back, shocked at my show of anger. I was behaving completely erratically and beginning to shock myself as well. I looked over at him and felt stupid for ruining what could have been a perfectly nice evening, if I'd kept my temper under control. I tuned around to face the sink and began to cry. Richard leapt up from his chair and approached me cautiously, in much the same way as he might approach a rabid dog.

He put his hand on my shoulder and left it there to see if I would swipe it away or turn into him. I considered both and decided on the latter. He took me into his arms and hugged me tightly.

"Liz, I'm sorry," he whispered. "I didn't mean to upset you. You just sprang it on me and I didn't have time to think."

"I know!" I cried. "I just wanted to say the right thing so that you'd agree. I've been building up to it all day, and now I've ruined it." I buried my face into his shoulder and sobbed my eyes out.

"Oh come on, Liz! Don't cry," he begged. "Sit back down and we'll talk about it." He led me to my chair and gently pushed me into it. He poured us both another glass of wine and sat back down. "Now, tell me the dates of this course and I'll check my diary."

I looked over at him, blinking the tears away. "Really?"

He reached across the table and took my hand. "I want you to be happy, Liz. It breaks my heart to see you like this. If adopting a child is what you really want, then I'll do it for your sake."

I gave a loud watery sniff and blew my nose into my napkin. "I feel so foolish," I said, in danger of bawling again. "I don't know what came over me. Now I feel as if I'm pushing you into a corner about this course."

Richard patted my hand. "No, you're not."

"It doesn't mean that we automatically get to adopt," I said. "It's just a course to give us some information and for them to find out about us."

"I know," Richard said soothingly.

"Maybe it'll help you to decide whether it's the right thing to do."

Richard tried to smile but his eyes clouded over with sadness. "Maybe," he said doubtfully.

All of a sudden it's becoming a real possibility instead of a distant pipe dream. We started our adoption course and that little baby lying in a cot in a Chinese orphanage moved just a tiny bit closer to us. Richard and I didn't talk very much about it after that night. He agreed to do the course and I gave him the dates and times and after that I was afraid to mention another thing in case he bottled out. I know that I'm forcing it upon him and it is so out of character for me, but I have such a strong feeling that I am doing the right thing. There were four couples, all of us shaking in our shoes as we were introduced to our social workers, who will be assessing us over the next few months to ascertain whether we are all responsible and competent enough to raise an adopted child. Richard hated every moment of it – so did I for that matter. But I don't envy the social workers and the task they've been given. How does anyone have the insight to judge whether a person will make a good or a bad parent? And why is it not necessary for every potential parent to go through the same rigours before they bring a child into the world? God knows, there are couples out there with armies of kids who wouldn't get through the first round of interviews with the adoption board. We were meant to be talking about why we wanted to adopt a child from a foreign country, yet the only thing I could think about was how unfair it all was. Why couldn't we go out for dinner on a Saturday night, go home, have sex and wake up pregnant like every other couple we knew did?

The two social workers who ran the course seemed very understanding and gave everyone the chance to speak and share their thoughts about what they had experienced in the adoption process so far.

I sat rigid in my chair, desperate to exude an air of intelligence and confidence. I felt overdressed compared to the other three potential adoptive mothers. Two of them wore jeans and shirts and the other one had gone for a plain shift dress. I looked as if I was going to meet with a head of state. At one stage of my preparations earlier that morning I had been wearing jeans with a white T-shirt, but I had decided against the casual look. I thought it might send out the wrong message. Instead, I had gone for a black trouser suit with skinny legs and high heels. To finish off the look,

I had worn a stiff white wrap-around shirt, starched to perfection. I looked like the type of career Mum that would drop her cute little adopted kid off at the crèche before sunrise every morning. To make matters worse, I had insisted that Richard wear a suit. I did this to try to hammer home the point that he was very respectable and was going to take these meetings very seriously.

"For God's sake, Liz," he said, as I made him change his tie for the third time, "it's just a bloody meeting. They're there to assess us, not our clothes."

"I know that," I said, picking a piece of fluff off his collar. "But it will do no harm to create a good first impression."

We were the last couple to arrive and my stomach heaved when I saw the other three couples sitting around in their weekend casuals.

We introduced ourselves and made our way over to the remaining two free seats.

"Bloody hell, Liz," Richard whispered through a forced grin, "we look like Posh and Becks."

The meeting was all about the importance of attachment. We were given printed handouts that had set out the topics we'd be discussing at each meeting. We were also told to keep a notebook at hand over the next few weeks in which we are to jot down our thoughts and questions on anything to do with adoption. Our two social workers were women, Val and Susan, and they conducted the session with professional detachment. Richard was asked to partner the woman in the shift dress while we were asked about loss and separation during our lives. We were to write down our thoughts first, then discuss it with our given partners and then to share our conclusions with the rest of the group. Some of them spoke at length about losing a parent, or in some cases both parents. At one stage, I was fighting against the lump in my throat as the husband of the woman in the shift dress (my partner) spoke about how he was still mourning the loss of his father who had died twenty-three years ago. He spoke with such genuine love for the man that it was impossible not to be touched in some way by his loss. I spoke briefly about the death of my mother, but kept it very brief and to the point, which is the only way I can talk about my mother. Anyway, it wasn't *Oprah*. Richard did the same when it came to sharing his experiences of loss. He shared the facts but not the emotions. When he had finished speaking, I looked over at him and gave him a nervous smile. He sat back in his chair and loosened his tie, looking like he had just done five rounds with Mike Tyson. I noticed with alarm that he had rolled his information leaflet into a long tube, and was squeezing down on it with what I guessed were very sweaty palms.

Then it was the turn of the woman in jeans, Cathy I think her name was. Even though Cathy had never experienced a bereavement first-hand, it didn't stop her speaking at length about it. Twenty minutes to be exact. She bleated on about how her best friend had lost a pal to cancer and how another mum she knew from her child's school had lost a parent recently. At this stage my thoughts had wandered miles away and I thought about whether I might cook or get a takeaway that evening.

I had begun to think about what I might do to try to woo the Browne account back to Task, when I was jolted back to the present. Did she just say she had a little girl?

I couldn't wait for her to finish, but I had to hang on for just a little longer while she rounded up with a story about how she had felt when her dog Roger had been mown down by a truck when she was five.

Susan and Val called the meeting to an end and everyone stood up very quickly and gathered their handbags and jackets. I edged across the room and sidled up to Cathy.

"Hi," she said with a smile. "I hope I didn't go on too long. He's always telling me off for talking too much," she said with a nod at her husband who was in conversation with Val on the other side of the room.

"No, not at all, it was very touching," I lied.

"Where are you hoping to adopt from?" she asked, lifting up a folder stuffed with pieces of paper.

"China," I answered. "What about you?"

"Same," she said with a beaming smile. "Who knows? Maybe our kids could be friends in years to come."

"Yes," I said doubtfully. "Did I hear you say you have a little girl?" I said, slipping it in coyly.

"Yes, three of them," she said proudly.

I tried unsuccessfully to keep the look of confusion off my face.

"Two are our natural children and the youngest is adopted. We've decided to go again," she said with a loud laugh.

"Lovely," I said with a simpering smile. I felt resentful towards her. She'd already adopted one child, so why didn't she give someone else a chance?

Richard stood behind her and jerked his head towards the door, desperate to leave.

"Well, we'll see you again at the next session," I said to

Cathy who had turned to wave at Richard, but he had already gone.

Out on the street, Richard pulled at his tie and opened the top buttons of his shirt.

"They're like the fucking Gestapo!"

I almost had to run to keep up with him. "They're just doing their job, Richard. They have to make sure that these children are going to caring responsible couples."

"Well, there must be a more dignified way of establishing that than stuffing us into a room full of people we have never met before and asking us to perform like monkeys."

I could see that it was going to be impossible to get him to attend the second meeting if this was the way he was behaving after only one.

"Come on, Richard. Calm down. It wasn't that bad."

He swung around to me wide-eyed. "Not that bad? If we'd stayed any longer in there they'd have been asking us about our sex lives."

I gave tight-lipped smile as I climbed into the passenger seat of the car. I'd neglected to mention to him that that's exactly what we'd be discussing with our social worker when they did their home visits.

Then

We are back in school again. I am in sixth class and next year I will start in secondary school and get to wear a different uniform. The secondary girls wear a navy jumper and a tartan skirt. I can't wait to be a secondary girl.

When we started back to school, Mum collected Claire

every day. I could see them from my classroom as they walked down the avenue holding hands and chatting. It made me want to be small again and have Mum collect me from school. Everything was great when we came home from Kerry. Mum seemed happy. Dad seemed happy. And Rita never called. But it didn't last for very long. Mum forgot to collect Claire one day and Sister Mary had to ring Mrs Whyte to come to the school. Now Mrs Whyte collects Claire every day. When I finish school, I walk home with Lainey and we stay in her house until Daddy gets home. The Whytes' house is like our new home. The only meal we don't eat there is breakfast. Mrs Whyte gives us our lunch and we all have dinner together. Sometimes Daddy even stays and has some dinner when he comes to collect us. Mrs Whyte drives us to school in the morning and gives us our lunches in Tupperware boxes.

When we go home in the evenings, we never know where we will find Mum. Sometimes the fire is lit and she's in the kitchen sitting at the table with a mug of coffee in front of her. I love these evenings, when I can tell her about what happened in school and show her the marks I got in my tests. But first I have to let Claire talk to her or she gets mad and screams over me. Mrs Whyte usually gives Daddy a plate of food to bring home to Mum because Mum sometimes forgets to eat. But she never touches the food. I always see Daddy scraping it into the bin the next morning. Mum is very thin and I wish she would eat something.

Recently, she hasn't been up when we get home. I know as soon as we get in the front door that she hasn't been up because the house is dark. On these evenings, I rush upstairs to my room to see how she is – she sleeps in my bed all the time now. She always seems so tired even though she sleeps all the time. I kick off my shoes and climb in beside her and if she's very tired we don't talk at all. We just lie there and stare at the shadows on the wall and say nothing.

Last night, when Daddy put Claire to bed, he called me downstairs.

I went into the kitchen with him and he asked me to sit down.

My stomach felt sick because I knew I didn't want to hear what he had to say.

He leaned against the sink and drummed his fingers together.

"Lizzy, you've probably noticed that your mother is quite sick again."

I nodded my head slowly and wanted to run from the room.

"I can't manage the two of you," he said in a strained voice. "And it's not fair on Mrs Whyte, expecting her to look after you all the time."

"She doesn't mind," I said quickly. "We're very good for her. Claire is always on her best behaviour and Mrs Whyte's always telling us how good we are."

Daddy raised his hand to stop me talking. "I know how good you are, Lizzy. You're the best girl in the world and you don't deserve all of this."

I didn't know what to say.

"Rita is going to come back to live with us and look after you and Claire and Mum, because your mother needs looking after too."

I gripped the seat of my chair and bit my lip.

"I know that you don't like Rita living with us, Lizzy.

But it's the only thing I can think of right now, until Mum is feeling better again."

A big tear plopped from my eye and I wiped it away before Daddy could see it.

"Couldn't we go to live with Lainey until Mum is better?" I asked in a whisper.

Daddy drew in a sharp breath. "No, dear, that isn't possible."

I knew there was no point in saying anything else. He had obviously made up his mind. He went to leave the kitchen and as he passed me he put his hand on the top of my head and let it rest there for a second before walking out.

So Rita is back. Her orange Ford Capri is parked in our driveway again and she has taken more time off work to look after us. I didn't go out to say hello on the morning she arrived. Claire ran into her arms and they kissed and hugged like mad. I felt sick listening to them. Rita calls Claire stupid names like "poppet" and "honeybunch".

I sat on the edge of my bed and made fists with my hands as their mad shrieks echoed through the hall downstairs. Mum turned to me in the bed and smiled.

"Go down and say hello to her."

I shook my head vigorously.

Mum reached over and took my hand in hers. "Don't be mad with her, Lizzy. Rita has a kind heart – she's come to look after us."

I looked at Mum sourly. Did she not realise what was happening? Perhaps she didn't care that Rita was going to steal Daddy away from her.

"I don't want to go down," I said. "I'll go down later."

Mum sat up and tousled my hair. "Hand me my dressing-gown then. I'd better get up before she finds me here."

I handed Mum her pink dressing-gown and noticed how dirty it was. The bed sheets were dirty too – they hadn't been changed since the summer. Mum's hair was greasy and she smelled like she hadn't washed in a long time. Rita came barging into the room and rushed over to the bed. Her eyes popped out and her fat little hand flew up to her bosom.

"Oh, my dear Maria!" she said, sitting down on the side of the bed, almost pushing me off it.

Mum gave her a weak smile.

Rita pushed Mum's hair off her forehead and looked at her in dismay. "Poor, poor Maria!" she crooned.

"Hello, Rita," Mum said, her eyes filling up with tears.

They hugged each other for ages and I looked on in total disgust. How could Mum be so nice to that cow?

Rita pulled back suddenly and looked from Mum to the bed sheets and back to Mum again.

"Now," she said in her bossy old voice. "We are going to get you into a nice bath and get your lovely hair washed. Okay?"

Mum shrugged her shoulders and didn't say yes or no.

Rita turned to me and without even saying hello she ordered me to run a bath. "With lots of nice bubbles!" she squealed after me.

Later that night we lay in bed together. Everything felt so clean. Rita had stripped my bed and put fresh sheets on. They were stiff and smelt of washing powder. Mum's hair was clean and glossy and I could smell the apple shampoo that Rita had used to wash it. When Mum had got into the bath I looked in through the crack in the door and saw Rita leaning over her with the bath-hose. Mum was lying back in the water while Rita washed her hair and told her how lovely she was going to look.

Part of me wanted to push Rita into the bath and drown her, but part of me felt choked up because she washed Mum's hair and spoke to her as if she really loved her.

Last night we stayed in Lainey's.

Daddy phoned Mrs Whyte and asked if she could keep the two of us overnight but Mrs Whyte didn't tell me why he had asked. I knew that something was wrong and I asked if I could go home for a few minutes to see if Mum was all right, but Mrs Whyte told me that I'd better not. We were allowed to stay up late because it was Friday and Mrs Whyte made pancakes with ice cream, but I couldn't eat them because I had that pain in my stomach again. Lainey's bedroom is at the front of the house, like mine, and when she fell asleep I crept out of bed and peered out through the curtains down to my house. Rita's car was there, but Daddy's was gone. I stood there for ages and wondered what to do. Mrs Whyte would be cross with me if I left the house without asking her, but I felt so worried about Mum. My breath made circles of fog on the windowpane and I began to shiver because I'd been standing there for so long.

Lainey sat up and looked over at me.

"What are you doing over there?"

"Nothing," I said.

"Should I get Mum?"

"No," I whispered, getting into bed beside her. The bed was warm and made me feel a little better. "I miss my mum," I said, not caring how babyish it sounded. It was the kind of thing I could tell Lainey because she'd never make me feel stupid for feeling that way.

"You'll see her in the morning. I'll go down with you as soon as we get up."

"Okay," I said, feeling a little happier. The pain in my stomach was still there and I tried to forget about it and go back to sleep.

Daddy was already downstairs when we got up. He was in the kitchen with Mrs Whyte and both of them looked as if they'd been crying. Daddy's nose was very red and the whites of his eyes were all bloodshot. I had woken early that morning with a buzzing inside my head that told me something bad had happened, and as soon as I saw their faces I knew.

"What's wrong?" I asked.

Mrs Whyte looked at Daddy and both of them looked down at me.

"Get Claire, Lizzy. We have to go home now."

Without asking any questions, I went out to the hall and called Claire.

She was standing at the top of the stairs in her pyjamas.

"We have to leave now," I told her.

Still in a half-sleep, she began to walk down the stairs towards me.

Daddy came out of the kitchen and waited for Claire to reach the end of the stairs before picking her up and turning to Mrs Whyte.

"Thanks again, Maura. I'll call you later."

Mrs Whyte just nodded her head and stared at him with watery eyes.

Back in our house, Rita was sitting at the kitchen table with a big ball of tissue bunched up in her fist. She jumped up when we entered the room and her eyes filled up with tears as she searched our faces.

"Girls," she whispered hoarsely.

Daddy took the two of us by the hand and led us to the table.

"Where's Mum?" I asked again. I had asked him about ten times on the walk back from Lainey's but he wouldn't answer me.

We sat down at the table and Rita fussed about at the cooker, warming milk to make us hot chocolate.

I knew. I knew. I knew.

"She's dead, isn't she?" I said, looking directly at Daddy.

He reached across the table and grabbed my hand. Rita dropped the tin of drinking chocolate and stared over at me in amazement.

"Yes, dear," he whispered, his voice quivering.

The pain in my tummy got worse and I felt like getting sick. "What happened?" I whispered.

Daddy tightened his grip on my hand. "Her heart stopped beating during the night. She's in heaven now, Lizzy."

Although I understood what had happened, his words didn't seem to make any sense.

The pain tightened in my stomach and I felt as if someone had lit a fire inside it. Rita put the mug of hot chocolate in front of me and the smell made me feel worse.

I stared into the mug and watched a crinkly layer form across the top of it.

"I want to go up to my room," I said, getting down from the chair.

Daddy and Rita exchanged worried glances.

"Won't you finish your drinking chocolate first?" asked Rita. I looked over at her and looked away again and she came over and took the mug away.

Upstairs in my room I stood at the side of the bed and looked into it, half hoping to see her there. The sheets were crumpled where she had lain but there was nobody there. I kicked off my shoes and got into bed and pulled her pillow over my face. I wanted to stay like that for the rest of my life, under her pillow, breathing in the smell of her apple shampoo mixed with my warm tears.

Now

The honeymoon is officially over. After holding out for a month longer than agreed, I am now part of the work force again. I have rejoined the real world, where people rise at dawn, and sit in two-hour traffic jams, and stand in line for twenty minutes at lunch-time just to buy a cup of coffee. I never seem to have less than two calls holding for me and my mobile phone rings incessantly. The funny thing is – I love it. I'd forgotten how much I enjoyed work. Everyone at Task gave me such a warm welcome back and I am also basking in the glory of being made partner.

Brian called a meeting yesterday with myself and Susie Wilkes. I am happy for Susie – she has at last got the promotion that she was passed over for last year. I have no doubt that her talents will now shine as head of the creative team. Susie is a no-holds-barred, tell-it-as-it-is kind of girl. Her mouth has landed her in trouble on numerous occasions over the years, mainly because she can never resist the urge to tell the truth, which is not always what people want to hear.

Brian conducted the meeting between calls, which is at the top of my list of things that annoy me about him. Why he can't tell his secretary to hold his calls until we're finished is beyond me.

He snapped his phone shut and continued with what he had started to say ten minutes earlier. "What was I saying? Oh yes! I've hired Matt L'Estrange from Warner's."

"I don't believe you!" I said, shocked to hear that Matt was leaving Warner's. He was one of the big guns there and I couldn't believe that he would even consider moving to Task.

Brian gave a smug grin. "Made him an offer he couldn't refuse."

"Christ, Brian," I exclaimed, "it must have been very attractive! I thought Matt had a job for life in Warner's."

"No one's sure of a job for life," Brian said abruptly. "Especially in this shitty business."

I gathered from this remark that he was still smarting from the David Fenlon affair.

"Matt L'Estrange," Susie said with a snort. "He sounds like something from a feckin' boy band."

"Not far off," I said with a smirk. Matt certainly had it all. Good looks, charming personality and a pretty nice guy, as far as I could tell. I had met him several times over the years and he had never failed to impress.

"I hope the two of you will make him feel welcome and

help out with any teething problems he might have in the first few weeks." Brian sat back and smiled at us.

Susie stood up and hauled her file of work off Brian's desk.

"Sure, boss," she said, heading for the door.

I went to follow but Brian jumped up and beckoned for me to stay.

He closed the door after Susie and turned to me.

"I want you to invite Jeff Williams out to lunch."

Jeff was the Managing Director of Browne's and was not my idea of a dream lunch date.

It was Brian who always dealt with Jeff when we had their account. Another thing that used to annoy the hell out of me! (I had only been back a few weeks and the list was growing rapidly.) Whenever there was a meeting with Jeff, Brian always muscled in and gave me the elbow at the last minute. He'd say things like, "I just cleared my diary for the rest of the day so I'll just go along and meet Jeff instead. You needn't bother." He was just short of patting me on the head and telling me to run along. Whenever I was included in a dinner or lunch meeting, Brian talked to Jeff as if I wasn't there. I often wondered if Jeff thought I was employed as a piece of eye candy that Brian brought along to meetings to decorate the table.

"Why me?" I asked. "Don't you want to look after it?"

Brian scowled at me. "No. I want you to invite him out for lunch. Tell him you're back at work again and that you want to make contact with your old clients. Make it sound casual."

"But he was *your* client, Brian," I reminded him. "Browne's was never my baby. And won't it look strange just me inviting him out to lunch? A little desperate perhaps?"

Brian looked over at me despairingly. "We are desperate! Browne's was our biggest account, you know that, Liz. We can't survive without them."

"Well," I stumbled, trying to think of any excuse not to have to go to lunch with Jeff Williams, "if I set up a lunch meeting, will you join us?"

"No!" snapped Brian. "I've done all I can to get them back. It's in your hands now."

I knew by his clipped tone that any attempt at further persuasion would be a waste of time.

"Right," I said with a sigh. "I'll give him a ring and see if he can fit me in for a spot of arse-licking."

Brian allowed himself a wicked grin. "That's my girl."

I went downstairs to the staff kitchen to fortify myself with some strong coffee before I made the call to Browne's. Susie was sitting at the table flicking through a magazine. A faint smile spread across my face as I thought of the perfect solution.

"Susie, you know Jeff Williams, don't you?"

"Mmh," she muttered, flicking over another page.

"I'm going to set up a lunch meeting with him next week. I was thinking of booking a table at Icon."

Susie looked up, eyebrows raised. "Very fancy."

I thought I'd throw in the bit about Icon because I'd heard her raving about the place a few days earlier. I walked over to the kettle and tried to keep my voice sounding casual.

"Why don't you join us?"

"Nah," she said, leafing through another few pages.

"Why not? I thought you loved Icon," I persisted.

"I do – when I'm out with the girls drinking *margaritas* and dancing on table-tops. But the invitation somehow loses its allure when you mention Jeff Williams."

"I'm sure he wouldn't mind if you ordered a few *margaritas,* but perhaps leave out the dancing on tables."

Susie threw her head back and gave a dirty guffaw. "Wouldn't it be a hoot? We could take the old stuffy shirt out and loosen him up a bit. God knows he could do with it! Send him back to the office pissed and covered in lipstick." Her blonde curls bounced around her shoulders as she burst out laughing.

I could see I was getting nowhere. "Oh, come on, Susie," I said, dispensing with my casual approach and getting down to some serious pleading. "You know him a lot better than I do. I need you to break the ice. Please say you'll come? I'll never forget it. I'll owe you big time."

Susie made a face. "He's such a boring old fart."

"Well, boring yes, but he's hardly old." I guessed that Jeff was somewhere in his early forties.

"You know what I mean," said Susie. "He's dull and settled and no fun at all. And those shirts he wears with the white collars. Ugh!"

Jeff's father had always worn those old-fashioned coloured shirts with white collars, and Jeff had carried on the tradition. Jeff's grandfather had founded the Browne's sportswear empire and Jeff was the third generation of the family to take over the helm. When it first opened, Browne's specialised in mainstream sportswear like rugby jerseys and tennis whites, but as sportswear became more popular they began to manufacture more modern garments. The company had expanded hugely in the past ten years, and there wasn't a teenager on the streets of Dublin who didn't own a Browne's hoodie or tracksuit pants. They had recently broken into the American market and had built a new state-of-the-art factory and outlet shop in the city centre.

The Browne account was something that had bothered me for a long time before I left Task. I had watched the company grow from a small factory in County Leitrim to what it was today. It seemed that everything about Browne's was moving onwards and upwards – except its image. Their advertising budget was never huge, and Brian was always content to work around it, therefore Browne's image had remained the same for years. I had always felt that the advertising needed to be more dynamic and aimed at their new customer base, young teenagers, who were prepared to part with a hundred euro for a washed-out hoodie that looked as if it had been through a boil wash. We should have been working on ad campaigns that featured hip sports, like skateboarding and surfing. Instead, Task had represented Browne's as an ancient institution and continued to feature middle-aged men in rugby shirts in all of their ad campaigns.

Susie closed her magazine and looked up at me.

"Say you'll come?" I said in my sweetest voice.

"Fine," she said, "but don't expect anything to come out of it. I hear that Browne's are putting their account out to tender next week, and Warner's are out to get it."

"I bet they are," I moaned. "I'm sure Brian poaching their golden boy has given them a real competitive edge."

"He just can't live with the notion that he's lost the account," Susie said, lowering her voice. "I wish he'd get over it and move on. It's not like we don't have any other clients."

"He's taken it badly all right," I agreed.

"You have no idea, Liz," she said, shaking her head slowly. "The guy is cracking up. Ever since you left there's been nothing but bad news. He actually cried the day he got the phone call to say we'd lost the Browne account. Imagine that, Liz! Brian Davies in tears. It was scary."

"God," I said with a slight gasp.

"It's been all doom and gloom around here, Liz. We're all so glad that you're back."

I gave her a smile. "Thanks, Susie. But I don't really know if my being back is going to make any difference."

"Are you joking?" She gave me a playful wallop with her magazine. "It's made a difference already. Old Misery Arse actually smiled at me this morning!" She raised her eyes upwards towards Brian's office. "That's because you're back."

"Thanks, Susie," I said with a smile.

"You're the glue that holds him and this place together. He literally fell apart during the time you were away."

"Poor old Brian," I muttered as Susie walked towards the door. Then I remembered what I was there for. "Eh, next Tuesday suit you for lunch with Williams?"

"Okay," she said, her face collapsing into a grimace. "I'll try not to get too excited about it, and don't expect me to assist you with any grovelling."

"Leave that to me," I said with a grin. "I'm very good at it."

I have no time for leisurely coffee mornings during the

week any more, so our girlie time has to be kept to weekends, when I am not working. We met in Daphne's early on Saturday morning, before the other weekenders grabbed all the good tables. Brenda came with me. Our plan was to load up on coffee and hit the shops for the afternoon. She was still battling with the last few pounds on her diet and emitted a quiet moan as the waitress handed us the menus.

"I love the scones here," she said, gazing longingly at the list of cakes and pastries on the menu. "But I'd better not." She closed the menu and put it down on the table gently as if it was a bomb about to explode in her hand.

"Have you eaten breakfast?" I asked.

"One shredded wheat," she said with pride.

"Well," I reasoned, "we are leaving here to go shopping for a few hours, and if you don't eat something you'll start to fade on me. So you'd better have a scone. It'll help to keep your energy up."

Brenda bit the side of her lip and stared down at the menu.

"You've done so well. You're dieting sensibly and keeping the weight off. So what if you've still a couple of pounds left to lose? You have to have to allow yourself some treats every now and again."

The waitress appeared at our table and waited for our order.

"I'll have a latte and a scone, please."

The waitress turned to Brenda and we both looked on in amusement as she twisted her hands together and smiled like a four-year-old on Christmas morning. "I'll have the same."

172

The waitress scribbled our order, grinning at Brenda's wild abandon.

"Good for you," I said. "Now enjoy it – and don't ruin it by feeling guilty."

"It's pathetic really," said Brenda. "This diet has taken over my life. Before, I never questioned how many Pringles or bars of chocolate I stuffed my face with. But now, a simple HobNob during a moment of weakness is enough to reduce me to tears."

"Christ, Brenda," I exclaimed. "You've let this weight thing become an obsession. Will you please believe me when I tell you that you look great! You've never looked better. The diet worked! Now get back to being Brenda again."

Brenda looked at me oddly and I realised that I was pointing my concern in the wrong direction. I was feeling nervous because Claire was coming and things were still very strained between us.

"Sorry. I don't mean to pontificate. I'm just using you to release some of my anxiety before Claire comes."

"What's up with her?"

"I don't really know. She hasn't fully forgiven me for trying to set her up with Damian Jones that night at my house."

"For Heaven's sake, Liz! You were only trying to set her up with a guy. I don't see why she got so upset."

"I know," I said. "But Claire didn't see it that way – she said I was interfering in her life."

The waitress arrived with our coffee and scones which gave me a chance to divert the conversation. I felt bad talking about Claire to Brenda. The two of them had never exactly hit it off and I knew that Brenda wouldn't have much sympathy for Claire.

Brenda piled a load of butter and jam onto her scone and smiled over at me. "You're right. It's time for me to get back to being Brenda the pig again!"

Lainey made her way over to us and sank into a chair.

"Good morning, early birds," she said, picking a raisin off my plate. "They look gorgeous. I'm starving! I think I'll order two."

Brenda looked over at me and groaned. "Silly cow," she muttered under her breath.

"What?" asked Lainey, wide-eyed.

"I had to go through a counselling session with Liz before I could bring myself to order one, just in case it might interfere with my new calorie-controlled lifestyle. And you breeze in like a bloody waif and order two! Honestly, it's just not fair."

"Well, if it makes you feel any better I'll put the other one in my bag and eat it on the way home in the car," said Lainey with a laugh.

"Yes, little Miss Greedy," I said. "That's a very good idea. Or better still, leave it for Claire."

Lainey's face darkened. "Claire just left a message on my mobile – she can't make it this morning."

I felt my heart sink and realised that although I was anxious about meeting her, I had been really looking forward to it. I thought that being together in a relaxed atmosphere might help us to move on from the place we had somehow found ourselves in.

Lainey gave me a sympathetic look. "I missed her call. I can't find a damn thing in this new bag and my mobile goes on to message minder after three rings. She said something about being needed at work this morning and that she'll try to catch up with us later."

"Okay," I said, trying not to show my disappointment. "I suppose we'll just have to let you eat two scones."

Lainey's coffee arrived and her face brightened as she pulled her chair closer to the table. "Can you keep a secret?" she asked with a grin.

"You know I can't," said Brenda, almost jumping off her chair with excitement. "But you'll have to tell me now. I hate suspense."

"If you breathe a word about this to anyone, I'll kill you!" Lainey said, trying to look serious.

We waited while she took a dainty sip of her cappuccino.

"Well, come on! Out with it!" Brenda demanded.

"Peter is forty next month and I'm having a surprise party for him."

"Great! It's been ages since I've been to a decent party," Brenda said. "Where are you having it?"

"At home," said Lainey excitedly. "It's going to be a nightmare to organise, but if I can manage to pull it off, it'll be worth it." She turned to Brenda. "I'll need you to do a bit of fibbing. Can you and Tom invite us to dinner in your house that night?"

"Sure."

"And, Liz, is there any way that Richard could ask Peter to play golf on the day of the party? I need to get him out of the house for a few hours."

"Yes," I said uncertainly. Trying to pin Richard down these days was impossible; he seemed so bogged down with work. "I'll make sure he keeps that day free."

Lainey beamed with delight. "I have it all organised. I'm getting a marquee and I've booked a great band. It should be a really good night."

"Right," said Brenda, slapping her hands down on the table. "No more scones for me. Liz, I want you to come and see a dress I tried on last week in Whistles. It's a bit tight around the tummy, but another month of starving should fix that. Sorry to muscle in on Peter's celebration, but I'm going to make this party my coming-out night. It will be the first time I've fitted into a size twelve dress since I got married."

Lainey waved her fist in the air like some mad American on a daytime talk show. "You go, girl!" she said with a laugh.

Then

My appendix burst. At first I kept vomiting and couldn't eat anything, but then the pain began to get worse. I wanted to get up and go to school but the pain was awful. The first time the doctor came, he said it was a bug and that I wasn't to eat anything, just take drinks. Rita boiled 7Up and kept mopping my forehead with a cold facecloth. I was so sick that I thought it was Mum sitting on the side of the bed, but when she got close and I smelled the cigarettes on her stinky breath, I knew it was only Rita – trying to pretend to be Mum.

The second time the doctor came the pain was so bad that I couldn't straighten my legs. He told Daddy and Rita to get me to the hospital immediately. I don't remember very much after that, because they operated on me as soon as I arrived.

I woke up sore as hell. The nurse told me that my appendix burst all over my insides and they had to do a big clean-up job. I had to stay in the hospital for ten days. Rita brought Claire in to see me after school every day. I hated the hospital and all the horrible smells that wafted through it. Like medicine and toilet and cooking smells all mixed together. My stitches hurt whenever I moved. They sewed me back together with brown criss-crossed thread like the bride of Frankenstein. Daddy came to visit me on his way home from work in the evenings. If I was sleeping, he would bend over and kiss my forehead and the tassles on his scarf would tickle my nose and wake me. He sat on the side of the bed and patted my hand. His face is always sad now – he looks the way I feel inside.

I didn't mind Rita and Claire leaving in the afternoons, but when Daddy stood up to leave at night, I felt like crying. I stopped myself though, because I know that he hates cry-babies. Except one evening I couldn't help it. He stood up to leave, and I grabbed his scarf and wrapped it around each hand, pulling him close to me.

"Don't go!" I pleaded.

His neck was locked tight in the scarf and our faces were almost touching. I would never have had the nerve to do this to him before, but that night I didn't care if he got cross. I wanted him to stay. I didn't want to be alone in that hospital with the sounds of babies' cries echoing down the corridor at night.

"Sweetheart," he said, his neck stuck tight in my noose, "I must go. The bell is ringing, hear? That means visiting time is over."

"Please, Daddy, take me home with you. I don't want to

stay here." I was crying now, big salty tears, unable to be brave anymore.

The fat night nurse came pounding into the room and stood there with her hands on her hips.

"Come along, Mr Kelly," she said in her loud nurse's voice. "It's time to leave now."

I pulled the scarf even tighter. I felt as if I'd die if I had to stay in that place another minute. "Please, please, Daddy! Take me home."

The scarf began to shudder in my hands and Daddy's head collapsed into the side of my neck. His shoulders rose and fell with the rhythm of his sobs and I put my arms around them and hugged him with all my might. I could see the nurse tilting her head to one side, looking at us in confusion.

"Two more minutes," she barked before marching out of the room in her squeaky white shoes.

Daddy sniffed loudly and I released him from my clutches, but kept a firm hold on the scarf.

"My poor Lizzy," he whispered, "what an awful time you've been through."

He began to stroke my head gently and I turned on my side and pulled him closer to me. His big hand was like a magic wand sweeping across my forehead, making all my pain vanish. The fat nurse came into the room again and before she had time to open her mouth, Daddy turned to her and said, "Leave us be," in his cross judge's voice.

The nurse opened her mouth but closed it quickly again and left the room.

My eyes grew heavy as his hand swept across my brow like a gentle tide and I fell deeper and deeper into a warm drowsy sleep. I woke the next morning to an empty room. Daddy was gone, but his scarf was still wound around my wrists.

I am home from hospital now but can't go back to school for another two weeks. I've got lots of presents for my appendix bursting. Daddy bought me a pink portable record player which is the best thing I've ever been given in my entire life. Rita brought me out to get my ears pierced but I changed my mind when we got to the jeweller's and I saw the size of the needle he was going to use.

"Go on," urged Rita impatiently. "It's only a little prick and then you can choose some lovely earrings."

I looked at the needle and felt my knees get weak.

"Oh, don't be a scaredy cat!" Rita said in a voice so loud that it made everyone in the shop gawk over at us. "Look," she said, jiggling her own hoopy earrings, "I got mine done when I was your age and it didn't hurt a bit."

I stood there like a big dummy and shook my head.

Rita got even more impatient.

I was sorry that I had let her talk me into it. I never wanted my ears pierced in the first place. It had been Rita's idea. Mum used to say that if God wanted little girls to wear earrings, he'd have made them with holes in their ears.

"I want to," Claire announced.

Rita turned to her and beamed. "But it's Lizzy's day out. You can get yours done when you're older. Isn't that right, Lizzy?"

The man stood there holding the needle looking like he didn't give a damn which of us got her ears pierced.

I shook my head again. "I don't want to."

"I want to. I want to!" Claire protested.

Rita threw her handbag on to the counter and glared at me. "Well, if madam has changed her mind, we may as well get yours done, Claire. Otherwise it'll have been a complete wasted journey."

Claire sat up on the high stool and held a mirror up while the man marked her ears with a biro. I turned away as he sank the needle into her ear lobes and waited for the screams, but when I turned back Claire was still sitting there smiling away as he put two little gold balls into her ears. They looked like the balls that Mum used to decorate the Christmas cake with.

Rita keeps talking about me behind my back. She thinks I'm not listening, but I am. I listen to her telephone conversations behind the kitchen door. She thinks my appendix burst because Mum died. What a load of rubbish! She uses words like "delayed reaction" and "trauma", whatever that means. I know she's talking about me because she lowers her voice when she says these things. When she moves on to how Claire is, she starts to talk normal again and says things like, "a little moppet," or "a ray of sunshine". She never uses words like that about me.

Mrs Whyte bought me a Ladybird dressing-gown. It's red and fluffy and has little ladybird buttons down the front of it. Claire howled the first night I wore it. She must have kept it up for almost an hour. Rita sat in her chair by the fire and made pleading faces at me.

"Couldn't you let her wear it just for a few moments?" she asked in her fake sweet voice. I pulled the dressing-gown tight around my body and fiddled with the red and black cord that tied around my waist.

"Nope," I answered.

180

I could tell that Rita thought I was being mean, but I didn't care. I wasn't taking it off for anyone. Claire's face was the same colour as the dressing-gown when she finally gave up and fell asleep on the couch beside me. For a moment I thought of giving her a go of it, and almost did, but I decided not to. I love it too much, and Claire is big enough now to learn that I'm not going to share everything with her.

Rita thinks she knows everything, but she doesn't. She thinks that my appendix was causing the pains in my stomach, but that's not true because I still get them.

"That's what was giving you all that trouble with eating," she said the other day when I wouldn't eat her lumpy custard. "Your appendix is gone now, Lizzie – you couldn't have any more pain."

I didn't bother arguing with her, but she's wrong. The appendix was a different pain – it was sharp and I could put my hand on the place where it hurt. I can't put my hand on this pain, or describe it either, because it's everywhere. And when I get it, I can't bear to look at Rita's horrible dinners.

"Daddy, can I go to boarding school?"

We were on our own for a change. Rita had gone to the shops with Claire and it was just me and Daddy in the house. Rita never seemed to be more than an inch away from him at any time and I never got a chance to talk to him alone.

His face tightened as he shook his newspaper and folded it over.

"Why on earth would you want to go to boarding school?" he asked.

"Karen Dowling from my class is going to board in a

school down the country. She says it's really nice and it has a swimming pool."

He frowned at me and turned his face towards the fire. He seemed to be more interested in staring at the flames than answering my question and after a few moments I wondered if he was going to say anything at all.

"She can come home –"

He turned his head quickly and spoke over me. "Aren't you happy in your own school?"

"Yes," I said, shrugging my shoulders. My own school hadn't really anything to do with why I was asking to go away.

"Well, why on earth would you want to move then?"

It was my turn to stare into the fire. Did he really want me to say it? Didn't he know already?

He began to shake out his newspaper again and I took it that the conversation had ended and went to get up.

"Lizzy," he said wearily, "believe me, I know how upset you are – but going away isn't going to help. You've suffered a terrible loss, we all have, and it will take time for life to get back to normal, but things will get better, I promise." He had rolled the newspaper into a long tube and was pressing it down against his knees.

I stood at the side of the couch and waited for him to finish so I could leave the room.

"Come here, love," he said, and waved his arm for me to go to him.

I walked over reluctantly and he put his arm around me.

"It breaks my heart to see you like this."

I looked down at the floor and thought of a thousand things I wanted to say but couldn't. I pulled my back up straight so his arm wouldn't touch me and when he saw this, he went back to rolling his newspaper.

"Can I go now?" I asked politely.

He looked at me with big sad eyes, but I didn't feel a bit sorry for him.

"Yes, Lizzy," he said with a long sigh. "Goodnight."

Upstairs in my bedroom I lay on my bed and ran my fingers up and down the ladybirds on my dressing-gown. I stared over at the wall and let my eyes close until they were tiny slits. The shadows of the tree blurred into each other and I could see Mum's face in amongst them, smiling out at me. The pain inside melted away and I stayed like that, perfectly still in case any movement would make her disappear. That is how I got to sleep every night.

Now

I arrived into work on Tuesday feeling nervous and jittery about our lunch date with Jeff Williams. I knew just how disappointed Brian would be if I didn't succeed in luring Browne's back to Task, yet it seemed like such an impossible challenge.

At eleven thirty, Susie stuck her head around my office door.

"I'm going to a meeting across town now. It shouldn't go on for too long, I'll see you in Icon about one-ish?"

"Forget about the 'ish'," I said smartly. "Just be there at one. I don't want to have to sit on my own with him."

"I'll do my best," sang Susie, as she disappeared around the other side of the door.

I sat at my desk, making a list of different suggestions I

could drop into our lunch conversation. Although Susie had told me that she was only going for the crab cakes, I knew that if I came up with some interesting ideas, she wouldn't be able to resist getting in on the conversation. But how to go about it without sounding desperate was the problem.

As lunch-time approached, I began to get flutters in my stomach. Jeff was so stand-offish, I knew I would end up blabbering like a fool, trying to fill in awkward silences while he sat there looking bored rigid, counting down the minutes before he could excuse himself and get back to work. At least Susie was going to be there to offer some entertainment, although I had warned her against exposing him to any of her filthy jokes. I decided to leave my car and call a cab – my stress levels were high enough without the added frenzy of trying to find parking in town. I was sitting in the back seat of the cab chewing my thumbnail when I heard the muffled ring of my mobile phone. After emptying the contents of the bag on to the seat beside me, I realised that the damn thing was in my jacket pocket.

I could see from the screen that it was Susie calling.

"Liz!" she wailed.

"Yes," I answered cautiously.

"Oh bloody hell, Liz, I've been clamped!"

"What?" I shouted down the phone.

"My car's been clamped. I'm on the quays now waiting for the bastards to come and unclamp it. By the looks of things, I could be waiting a while."

"Susie, for God's sake," I said impatiently. "Just leave it there and get a cab up to the restaurant."

Her signal began to break up.

"Say that again, I can't hear you."

"Get a cab and meet me in the restaurant," I said even louder.

"Liz, I can't. I need my car for this afternoon. I have a presentation to do this evening so I'll just have to wait here until they come.

I felt the perspiration break out at the back of my neck. "Did they give you any idea of how long it's going to be?"

"They said about thirty minutes."

"Ah Susie!" I exclaimed. "It's ten to one. We're meant to be meeting Williams in ten minutes."

I heard a loud breath of air being exhaled down her end of the phone.

"Liz, I didn't plan this," she snapped. "I would much rather be sitting down to lunch in Icon than standing on the side of the road waiting for these assholes to arrive and unclamp me."

"I know," I said with a sigh. "It would have to be today though."

"Yeh," she agreed. "Bad timing. Look, you go ahead and I'll try my best to catch up. If I don't appear, pass on my apologies to Jeff."

"Right," I said, trying to put aside my selfish disappoint-ment and sound sympathetic. "I hope they don't keep you waiting too long."

"Enjoy lunch and don't forget: you're not too proud to beg."

"Thanks, Susie. I'll try to keep that in mind," I said, snapping my phone shut.

Jeff William was already at the table when I arrived at Icon. He lifted his hand and gave me a brief wave. I went over to him and gushed an over-rehearsed apology for arriving late, without Susie.

"It's fine," he said with a smile. "Sit down and catch your breath. I was down this end of town for a meeting this morning so I was a bit early. Did you jog over?"

I realised that compared to his calm demeanour, I was practically hyperventilating.

Okay, Liz, I said to myself, chill out and stop behaving like he's the school headmaster.

I took a few deep breaths and gave him a strained smile, trying to stretch the creases out of my forehead.

"It's been kind of a hectic morning," I lied. "I'm still trying to catch up since I came back."

"How was your career break?" he asked.

"Oh, fine," I said, delighted with his choice of words. Career break sounded so much more dignified than she left to have a baby and came back because she couldn't have one.

"Did you get to do all those things people say they're going to do some day but never get around to?"

I tried to think of something interesting that I did during my eleven-month absence, but nothing came to mind. Shit! Why didn't I go backpacking to India or abseiling in the Rockies?

I had two failed IVF attempts didn't sound very interesting.

"I had a few projects that I finally got around to doing," I said, grabbing the menu so I could bury my head in it.

"Really," he persisted. "I envy you. What did you get up to?"

I silently panicked. "Weellll," I said, as if I was about to come out with something fascinating. "I did a lot of work on my garden. I designed it and landscaped it myself. That took quite a while to complete."

"And how it is looking now?" he asked enthusiastically.

"Oh, lovely," I said, thinking of the handful of semi-mature trees I had picked out and got the landscape company to plant.

"Anything else?"

Jesus, he wasn't giving up.

"I paint and –"

He sat upright on his chair and lowered his menu. "Wow, I'd love to be able to paint. Do you go to classes or do you just paint alone?"

"I started doing a class in watercolours, but I didn't keep it up. I enjoy painting alone – I find it's a really good way to switch off."

My God! Now I was lying to try to impress him. I had started a class in the local adult education centre but gave up after two weeks when I saw how brutal I was. I painted one picture of a pony that has been consigned to the utility room. It was hanging in the hall until the day one of Brenda's boys asked me why the horse had five legs.

"It's such a great thing to be able to do," Jeff said wistfully. "Just take some time out and enjoy life."

"Yes," I said, shaking my menu impatiently. "Do you know what you're having?"

As we gave our orders to the waitress I flicked through my mental filing cabinet for anything that could steer the conversation in another direction – for fear I began to tell him about my trek to the top of Kilimanjaro. That's the problem with me and fibbing, I can't tell little ones, they have to be big whoppers, and the more time I have to compose them – the bigger they become.

"Yes," he said, looking back to his menu. "I'll have the crab cakes and the duck to follow."

"Sounds good," I said, handing my menu to the waitress. "I'll have the same."

Jeff took his jacket off and hung it on the back of his chair. I managed to conceal a fleeting smirk as I thought of Susie, the deserter, and her comments about Jeff's shirts. Today's creation was a light pink with a white collar and cuffs.

There was a brief silence and I glanced over at the door, hoping that by some miracle I'd see Susie bursting through it and barging through the restaurant down to our table. But no such luck. The starters had yet to be served, so it was too early to start into begging him to give Task another chance – if he refused, I'd be stuck with him for another hour with nothing to say. Yet, I was anxious for him not to ask any more questions about my time out from work because I would either continue with the lies and get myself into a complete flap, or worse still, tell him the truth and have the poor chap squirming with embarrassment.

"How's Muriel?"

"Good, thank you," he answered stiffly.

Muriel was his wife and not someone I particularly cared for. She reached the peak of her modelling career ten years ago, by appearing on the cover of *Vogue* magazine. Her stunning good looks never failed to stop me in my tracks – she really was extraordinarily beautiful. We had crossed paths over the years at various functions, but I had never really taken to her. Whenever I spoke to her, I always got the feeling that she was looking over my shoulder to see if there was anyone more important in the room. When the modelling jobs began to dry up, Muriel turned her attention to fundraising, using her contacts in the fashion business to add a touch of glamour to the occasions. I'm sure her chosen charities benefited greatly from the lunches and balls she organised, but I always had my suspicions that Muriel's heart was never quite in the right place. Her charity events were really more about her, and once the photographers got the right shot of her designer gown specially flown in from Paris I doubt very much that Muriel gave a toss who was benefiting from the proceeds.

"I saw a photo of her in a magazine at the Ragtime Summer Ball." I tried to keep a straight face as I remembered how Lainey had outlined Muriel's collagen-enhanced lips with a red biro.

I could see that Jeff had nothing further to add regarding Muriel, and was relieved to see our food arriving.

He began to eat and I struggled to find something else to fill in a few more minutes of conversation.

"It's such a pity Susie didn't make it," I said, in a forced sing-song voice that made me sound like Rita.

Jeff's brow had wrinkled into a deep furrow as he cut into his crab cake. "Yes," he said flatly.

Well, I thought to myself, at least she would have filled in a few gaps. I was hoping to get more mileage out of Muriel, but obviously Jeff didn't like to get too personal.

He rested his fork on his plate and looked over at me for a few seconds.

I raised my eyebrows and gave a nervous smile.

"You're here to talk about the account," he said seriously.

I exhaled slowly, relieved to be done with the pretence. "Yes."

Again his brow furrowed and he lifted his fork and proceeded to eat.

"It's awkward, Liz," he said. "Browne's have been with you guys for so long, it was not a pleasant decision to have to make. But to be honest, Brian made it easy in the end."

I sat up in my chair. Oh no! I thought. Had Brian done something that he hadn't told me about?

"What do you mean?" I said slowly.

Jeff shrugged his shoulders and pushed his plate away. "The last presentation he made was nothing short of awful. I have to admit, I've been sorely disappointed with Task's representation of us for the past few years, but there was nothing I could do about it. My father controlled the company and he saw nothing wrong with the way our ad campaigns were run, but when he retired, it was the first thing that I wanted to change. I spoke to Brian in your absence about my thoughts on the matter, and he seemed to understand what I wanted, but when he came up with his final presentation – I realised that we just weren't speaking the same language."

I nodded my head as he spoke and tried to keep my anger under control. Brian never mentioned the fact that Jeff had voiced his disapproval. He had led me to believe that Browne's had simply pulled the rug from under Task without any warning.

I was still mulling this over in my mind when I realised that Jeff had stopped talking and was waiting for my reaction. I stopped nodding my head and tried to think of an appropriate reply that wouldn't make me sound as if I was hearing this for the first time.

"I was terribly disappointed to hear that you had left us, Jeff. Our companies have had such a long history. It was a blow for all of us in Task."

"I know," he said, looking at me with great intensity. "It wasn't a nice thing to have to do."

"I'll bet it wasn't," I said, trying to imagine the phone conversation between Brian and Jeff, with Brian trying to steady his voice as the axe landed.

"The thing is," he continued, "what was I supposed to do? Carry on with Task even though they didn't get what we are about? I don't think so. I have a vision for my company and I need to work with an agency that shares that vision. You must understand what I'm talking about, Liz."

It was like being let down gently by a man who had fallen in love with another woman. Jeff kept glancing over at me worriedly, to gauge my reaction, and all of a sudden I felt really sorry for him. Everyone at Task had an image of Jeff Williams as a hardnosed, ruthless bastard, who had severed links with us overnight. This man sitting opposite me couldn't have been more contrite over what he had done. Now was my chance to make a move, but it would have to be at Brian's expense. If I was to get anywhere with Jeff, I would have to use my position as partner to step outside the fray and take a risk.

"I understand your misgivings about the way we represented you."

Jeff looked over at me with a look of surprise on his face.

"It was something that had worried me for quite a while before I left Task."

There, I'd said it now. Well, Brian had told me to get this account back again, and if betraying his competency was the only way to do it – well, so be it.

"How so?" asked Jeff with interest.

"Your image is too old-fashioned. Your clothing is being bought by a younger person now, so why make commercials that are still targeting the old customer base?"

Jeff leaned across the table and his eyes lit up. "Exactly," he said, almost knocking over his glass of water.

"Browne's should be focusing on the young adults who fork out hundreds of euro on leisure wear every month, instead of trying to hold on to the ageing customer who might buy a new Airtex every summer."

His hands waved about in the air. "Yes. Yes, that's exactly what I said to Brian, but he just didn't seem to get it."

I'll kill him, I thought, as I took a sip of water.

The waitress arrived with our main courses which gave me a few moments to gather my thoughts. When she left, I continued with my pitch.

"Browne's billboards and commercials should feature surfers, snowboarders, the sort of sports that teenagers are into. It's time to drop the rugby players and golfers – you already have them as loyal customers. What you need is something to showcase your new ranges of leisure clothing. I was thinking of a campaign that might feature a polocrosse team."

"What's that?" said Jeff, looking baffled.

"It's like a mix between polo and lacrosse. It's played on horseback with lacrosse sticks."

"And what's a lacrosse stick?" Jeff asked, his brow knitted together with confusion.

I laughed, partly at his expression but mostly because I felt I was reeling him in with my idea.

He sat back and smiled. "I've heard of lacrosse before. I think my granny used to play on a team. But I've no idea how it's played."

"It's a bit like hockey, except the stick is longer with a net at the end. The player cradles the ball in the net and tries to drive it through the opponents' goal."

"And this polocrosse is lacrosse played on horseback?" He said this slowly, as if he was trying to get a mental image of it.

"Yes," I said excitedly. "There's a club down the road from where I live and on Saturday mornings I sometimes see them training when I go for a walk. It looks like such a fun sport."

Jeff shook his head and grinned. "Well, it's a new one on me. When did you come up with this?"

"One Saturday morning I was going for a walk and happened to see a team beginning a match. One of the girls looked stunning. Legs that went on forever and long blonde hair that was tied back in a ponytail. I stopped and looked on as she gracefully mounted a huge horse, with all the casual carelessness of a teenager. I noticed that she was wearing a Browne's hoodie, and it struck me that those few seconds I'd just witnessed would make a brilliant television commercial."

"Wow!" said Jeff, obviously pleased with my story. Of course, I hadn't seen a beautiful blonde teenager with fab legs. It had been a gawky brown-haired girl with braces and freckles, but I wasn't going to spoil the moment by telling him that.

I put my coffee cup down on the saucer. "What's the position on the account at the moment?"

Jeff breathed out through his nose noisily. "We've put it out to a few agencies and are awaiting some presentations over the next few weeks."

I felt a wave of relief wash over me. At least it hadn't gone to anyone else, yet.

"Give us another a shot at it," I asked quickly.

He looked at me but said nothing, his mouth held in a tight frown.

"Please, Jeff," I asked, keeping my voice as even as I could.

He emitted another loud sigh. "Liz, what's going to be different this time?" He said this with a weariness that indicated his complete lack of confidence in Task.

"I'll be looking after it," I said.

He pursed his lips and looked at me doubtfully. "I don't mean to underestimate you, but wouldn't it be Brian's input that would ultimately drive the campaign?"

"I'm a partner in the company now. And, believe me, Jeff, I will be the driving force behind the campaign this time."

Jeff examined the back of his hands which were resting on the table and I sat back and chewed the inside of my cheek.

"To be perfectly honest, Liz, I've had meetings with several agencies and although they haven't made their final presentations, the idea that has excited me most is yours. You can make a presentation, but I have to insist that it will be you and not Brian that's behind it."

"That's not a problem." My stomach tightened nervously at the thought of telling Brian.

"It's certainly most unusual. This polo lacrosse thing

sounds so odd. In fact if I didn't know you, I'd think you were making it up."

I looked at him and laughed. "It's called polocrosse." My nerves had calmed a little and I realised, much to my surprise, that I was enjoying his company. "I'm anxious to get a shot at the account again. It means such a lot to us – but I'm not so desperate that I'd actually invent a sport to get your attention."

Jeff smiled warmly, and I noticed that when he relaxed and stopped frowning, he was actually quite good-looking. "You never know," he said, with a hint of humour. "I hear that Brian was very upset about it. Are you sure he hasn't dreamt up this hockey polo thing to get his hands on the business again?"

"Don't worry. It's real," I assured him. "Why don't you call up to me some Saturday and I'll take you over to the stables?"

He didn't live too far away from me and I thought it would add a nice touch to our meeting. Show him how committed I was to the project.

His smile seemed strained all of a sudden and there was a slight hesitation before he answered.

Oh shit, I thought. Does he think I'm hitting on him?

"Yes, I could probably do that sometime," he said, but he looked as if he was trying to think of a reason not to.

I could feel my face getting red. He did know I was married, didn't he?

"Richard, my husband, he plays golf on a Saturday and I usually try to get out for a walk, shake off the cobwebs. You have met Richard, haven't you?" I blurted.

"No," he answered. "I don't believe I have."

"Well," I said, reaching for my handbag, "just have to visit the ladies'."

I walked away from the table, kicking myself for suggesting such a thing. How unprofessional was that? He couldn't have thought I was getting too familiar, could he?

In the ladies', I reapplied my lipstick, but grabbed a tissue and quickly wiped it off in case he thought I was tarting myself up for him. I took a deep breath and told myself to get a grip. This was a business meeting, and it had gone a lot better than I had anticipated. After only one meeting, Jeff had agreed to give me a shot at Browne's account. Brian would be ecstatic – that is, until I told him that he was to have nothing to do with it.

I went back out to the reception desk and produced my credit card. "Please put the bill on this," I told the girl behind the desk.

She smiled at me and pointed to the retreating figure of Jeff. "The gentleman's beaten you to it," she said with a smile.

I hurried after him.

"Jeff, there really was no need for you to do that, but thank you."

He put his jacket on and held mine for me while I slipped it around my shoulders.

"Don't mention it, Liz. Consider it a welcome-back gesture." Then he added hastily, "I mean a welcome back to work. I'll look at your proposals along with all the others but I can't promise anything, you understand?"

"Of course," I said.

"It's just that I don't want to get Brian's hopes up unnecessarily. I mean, I like your idea, I think it could really work. But I want you to be aware that the account is up for grabs to the best team."

We walked outside to the busy street and stood there for a few seconds.

"I enjoyed that, Liz. It's good to see you back again."

"Me too," I said in a businesslike tone, trying not to sound too familiar for fear he'd mistake it for flirting.

"Can I run you back to the office?"

"No, thanks. I've a few things to do before I go back," I lied, anxious to end our meeting before he had to start making excuses about not being able to meet me on a Saturday.

We had another adoption meeting. I don't relish the thought of them, but I accept that it's part of what we have to go through to get a baby, and just try to get on with it. Unfortunately I cannot say the same of Richard. To him, the whole process is intolerable. He hasn't actually said this, but I can tell by him that he is suffering through this just to keep me happy. I have begun to question whether this is right or not, and while it's most probably not right – I want a child so much that I am choosing to turn a blind eye to his exasperation. I know that Richard would stop the whole adoption thing quite gladly if I suggested it, but I am not going to, because at the end of the day I know he will grow to love this child. He just doesn't realise it right now.

I am terrified that Val and Susan, our social workers, will pick up on Richard's attitude and use it to strike us off the list. At the meetings my face hurts from smiling all the time, trying to compensate for Richard's sullenness. They've been trained in these areas and can easily identify telltale signs of not-so-eager-to-adopt-husbands that are attending the meetings only because their wives are going bonkers for a baby. Still, I think we've managed to hold it together quite well and I'm hoping that Richard's silence at these meetings will be put down to nerves.

The next hurdle I have to prepare for are the home visits. Val has told us that she will be our social worker and will interview us in our home to discuss more personal issues with us. But we'll just have to cross that bridge when we come to it.

Then

I am a teenager now.

I am thirteen and only have three more years to live in this house before I turn my back on it forever. My plan is to sneak out in the middle of the night on my sixteenth birthday. I want it to be like the Beatle's song. The one where the mum finds the note and breaks down at the top of the stairs, except it will be Rita in her flowery dressing-gown and rollers. She'll read the letter and shriek, "Daddy, our baby's gone!". And I *will* be gone, far away. I'll only tell Lainey where I'm going to, because if I told Claire she'd tell Daddy and Rita and they'd be after me before I got to the train station. I still haven't made up my mind where to go. I suppose I've plenty of time to think about it. It really all depends on how much money I have. I've started saving like mad. I have a Post Office account that Rita doesn't know about. Mum opened it for me when I made my First Communion. I steal money from Daddy's wallet every now and again. He never notices, and I lodge it to my account on the way home from school. So far I have saved forty pounds. Lainey knows about my plan, but she has promised not to tell anyone. I wish I could go tomorrow.

If I could do anything I wanted, I would go to live in London and get a job dancing on *Top of the Pops* with Pan's people, and go out with David Essex.

I got my first bra last week. Rita brought me shopping for clothes because the knee had come through my favourite pair of denims. They're called "Gentlefolk" jeans; Mum bought them for me just before she died. I still love them and wear them even though they are ripped at the knees and far too short for me. But Rita tut-tuts every time she sees me wearing them. "The neighbours will think we can't afford to dress you," she crows.

We went into lots of shops but I couldn't seem to find a pair that looked good on me. We finally ended up in Switzers department store. Rita picked up about ten different pairs of pukey trousers for me to try on but I hated everything she liked, because Rita's taste is stuck up her arse. Eventually, I settled for a pair of Levi's. They're not as nice as the Gentlefolk ones but they're all right. I got a pair of cowboy boots too which I really like. Then Rita brought me up to the underwear department and asked the shop assistant to measure me for a bra! I almost passed out with embarrassment. I had wanted one for ages, but didn't want to ask Rita. She'd only go mouthing it off to everyone. I could imagine her on the phone to her bridge cronies, "*Just imagine little Lizzy wanting a bra!*"

I didn't put up an argument. I just followed the lady into the fitting room and kept my vest on while she measured me. I stood like a statue with my arms in the air and looked up at the ceiling while she pulled a measuring tape from around her neck and sized me up.

"We have lovely little trainer bras just in," she said. "I'll go and get some different kinds and we'll see what you fit into."

She came back with three different bras. I tried on a pink one first, while the lady stood behind me and fastened it. "Let's see what your mum thinks of this one," she said, and was gone out the through the dressing-room curtain before I had a chance to put her straight. I don't know how anyone thinks that Rita could be my mum because we don't look anything like each other. I am skinny with fair hair and blue eyes – she is fat with dark hair and little mean black eyes. Rita oohed and aahed at the top of her voice in the changing room while I stood there and modelled the bra for her.

"It's such a special day," the lady said to Rita, "when a girl goes shopping with her mum for her first bra. She'll always remember it, you know."

I stood there, feeling goose-bumps erupt on my arms and waited for Rita to tell her that she wasn't my mother. But she just stood there and beamed over at me. I suppose she was waiting for me to smile back, to let her know it was all right for people to think that she's my mum, but I didn't.

"She's my aunt," I mumbled, and stormed back into the dressing-room.

"Ooh," the lady squeaked, "lovely!"

Back in the dressing-room I struggled back into my clothes and listened to Rita whispering outside. I could guess what she was saying. I wanted to run outside and strangle her with the bra, but I liked it too much. It's white and red gingham with a lace trim. Of course, when we got home, Claire wanted one too when she saw it, but it's one thing she definitely can't have because she's only nine and hasn't any boobies. I let her try it on last night and we fell about the place laughing. I stuffed a pair of school socks into each cup and Claire paraded around my bedroom singing, "I've got a bra-ah. I've got a bra-ah!"

Claire's asthma is really bad at the moment. Daddy has had to take her to hospital twice in the middle of the night because her face turned purple and he thought she'd stopped breathing. She has to take tablets that make her face look fat, but the doctor says that she will go back to looking normal again once the tablets are finished. Her face looks like a big moon. Rita thinks that Claire's asthma has got worse because of Mum. I heard her on the phone to her fat friend Carmel – they talk on the phone for hours almost every afternoon. Rita sits on the stairs in the hall, smoking her guts out and thinks that no one can hear her, but she talks so loud that I'm sure even Mrs Whyte can hear her. Claire's asthma has got worse all right, but it's not because of Mum. Is Rita so stupid that she can't see why Claire gets those attacks at night? It's because Rita is living with us. And because she sleeps in Daddy's room and pretends to be our mum and blows her filthy smoke all around the house.

Now

All systems are go for Peter's fortieth. The marquee, caterers and band have been booked and everything has gone without a hitch so far. Which is just as well, because Lainey sounded uncharacteristically frantic when she rang the

201

other day. I dread to think of what she'll be like if anything goes wrong.

"I keep waking at night and reaching for the notepad beside my bed to add to my list of things to do. Peter thinks I've lost it."

"What does he think you're writing?"

"Christmas lists," she said with a giggle.

"Oh God! He probably believes you, because you actually *are* one of those weirdos who start their Christmas shopping at the end of October every year."

I once caught her gift-wrapping Christmas presents in November.

"I've asked Richard to organise a round of golf on the afternoon of the party."

"There's no need," said Lainey. "I forgot to tell you, Peter's in the throes of moving office at the moment and the day of the party is the day that they're moving all the computer equipment. He'll be busy all afternoon. It couldn't have worked out better."

"Great," I said, feeling a little relieved as Richard hadn't actually confirmed the golfing arrangement. "Where's he moving to?"

"Haddington Place. In fact, the back of his new office looks right into Claire's apartments."

"Speaking of which, have you seen my sister lately?"

Lainey hesitated for a few moments.

"It's all right, Lainey. Just because she's taken a hump with me doesn't mean that you can't see her."

I knew from past experience that Lainey hated whenever myself and Claire fell out.

"I went to the pictures with her the other night. I rang

202

her and she sounded a bit down, so I just suggested it on the spur of the moment. I didn't think to call you."

I felt an old pang of jealousy stir inside me. It was the exact same way I used to feel when I was a teenager, and Claire would sneak out up to Lainey's house without telling me. I was reminded of my silly adolescent suspicions – when I used to think that Claire was trying to turn Lainey against me.

"It's all right," I said. "I doubt Claire would have wanted me to go anyway."

"So you haven't seen her recently?" Lainey asked, a note of concern creeping into her voice.

"No, I haven't," I said with a heavy sigh. "And it's not because I haven't tried. She's cancelled lunch twice. The first time she rang in the morning and said she was too busy. The second time I had just arrived in the restaurant when she called me on my mobile to tell me she had got stuck in court. To be honest, I think she was only making excuses. I think she's still mad at me."

"Oh, Liz. I hate to see the two of you not talking. Why don't you make one last effort to contact her? I think that whatever's going on between the two of you is really getting her down. She's not herself at all."

"Did she say anything?" I asked quickly. Part of me hoped that she had, yet at the same time I knew it would piss me off to hear that Claire had chosen to confide in Lainey and not me.

"Nothing," said Lainey. "I asked her had she seen you and she just said no, nothing else."

"I don't feel like arranging another lunch or coffee or dinner with her. I feel like a nuisance whenever I phone her. I don't know what's going on between the two of us – so I don't know how to go about fixing it."

"I know, Liz." Lainey sounded genuinely sympathetic. "I'm only saying it to you because I know how much you care about her."

"I suppose I do," I said wearily.

"Now," Lainey said, anxious to get back to more important matters, "I've picked some wines for the party and I want you to come over and taste them. I've tasted one and it's lovely, but I think it might be too strong. I don't want to end up serving rocket fuel."

"Well, you picked the right woman to come to," I said with a laugh. "When do you want me to come over?"

"Peter's out on Friday night – does that suit you?"

"Yes, I'll get a taxi so I can do the job properly."

I woke on Saturday morning with a blinding headache. I remembered Richard kissing me earlier in the morning before he headed out to play golf. I must have fallen back into a coma because when I came around for the second time, it was almost eleven o'clock. I jumped out of bed and nearly passed out as a wave of nausea rose upwards from my stomach. I clutched the edge of my bedside table and waited for it to pass. Brenda had accompanied me to Lainey's the night before, and we had sampled the birthday wines. In fact, I think we drank them all. Red, white, Italian, French – we left no bottle uncorked and I knew from the way my head pounded that I was about to pay dearly for my stupidity. I made my way into the shower and turned my face upwards, letting jets of cold water bounce off my throbbing forehead.

I had managed to get ahold of Claire earlier in the week, and while she wasn't able to make Lainey's on Friday night, she agreed to meet me for lunch on Saturday.

"Shit," I mumbled as I massaged a dollop of shampoo into my scalp. I really wasn't in the mood for Claire today.

I sat and waited in the restaurant where we'd agreed to meet. The smell of food was doing something strange to my stomach, I didn't know whether I wanted to devour a three-course lunch or throw up. I decided that some plain hot wholesome food would probably be a good idea, and ordered the lasagne. I spotted Claire coming in the door – she looked just as rough as I did and I guessed that she'd had a late one as well.

"Hi, stranger," I said, as she sat down opposite me. I wasn't in the humour for pussyfooting around her and thought I'd jump right in with a clever remark.

Claire gave me a nervy glance and managed a strained smile.

"Do you feel as bad as I do today?" I asked.

"What?" she asked, looking slightly confused.

I couldn't remember where she said she was going on Friday night, but her eyes were very puffed-looking, as if she'd been out on a bender.

"I'm diseased this morning. I stayed out far too late with Brenda, tasting wines in Lainey's for the party. What's your excuse?"

Claire looked at me as if she had no idea what I was talking about.

"Last night. Where were you? I take it you were out late. You don't exactly look as fresh as a daisy."

"Oh," she said, dismissing my attempt at being lighthearted. "I had to bring a client to the National Gallery dinner."

"Fun?" I asked, trying to force a smile out of her.

"No," she said grumpily. "You know how I hate those things. Having to spend an evening making small talk with some boring fart."

God, I thought. This was going to be hard work. "It's a pity you couldn't come last night. We had a good laugh, even if I am paying for it now."

"Mmh," she murmured, ignoring my last remark, as she glanced through the menu. "I think I'll just have a salad."

The waitress took her order and left us sitting in an uncomfortable silence. Claire looked around the restaurant, skilfully avoiding eye contact with me, therefore leaving it up to me to pursue any further conversation.

"It seems like ages since I've seen you," I said, trying not to make it sound like a swipe at her.

"Well, it has," she quipped. "Work has been manic — there don't seem to be enough days in the week."

"I know," I jumped in. "The time just seems to vanish since I started back at work — one week runs into another and I can't seem to find a minute to do anything."

"How's that going?" she asked.

"It's fine. It's as if I never left."

"But you're happy that you made the decision to return?" she asked, looking genuinely interested.

"Yes," I said. "I really am. I didn't think I'd settle in quite as easily, but, old habits die hard!"

A faint smile appeared at the corners of her mouth and I heaved a sigh of relief that her hostility appeared to be mellowing. Our lunch arrived and after a few mouthfuls, I knew I had made the right decision. The food began to settle that horrible nauseous feeling in the pit of my stomach and I realised that I was actually starving.

"Is Lainey still a nervous wreck about the party?" asked Claire.

I laughed. "Yes. Can you believe her? I've never seen her get so uptight over anything. I hope it all goes well and Peter gets a big surprise – or at least pretends to get a big surprise."

"Do you think he knows about it?"

"I don't know. It's kind of hard to organise a party in your own home for your husband without letting anything slip. I just hope that if he suspects anything, he keeps it to himself. She's gone to so much trouble to keep it a surprise."

"It's going to be so glamorous – I have to find something to wear," Claire groaned.

"No bother to you," I said, knowing how much my sister loved to shop.

I was almost finished wolfing the last of my lasagne when I noticed that Claire had spent the entire time pushing pieces of salad around her plate. She saw me looking at her food and put her cutlery down.

"Just have to visit the ladies'," she said. "Back in a sec."

I watched her walk away and thought of what Lainey had said, about Claire possibly having an eating disorder. I sat for a few moments before I decided to follow her. The restroom was very small. I looked around and saw that there were only three cubicles. A woman applied her lipstick at the mirror and walked out, leaving only me, and Claire, who was in the last loo. I looked under the door to check it was her and saw her shoes – facing the wrong direction. She wasn't sitting down, she was facing the toilet bowl and when the sound of the cistern from the adjoining toilet died down, I was sure that I could hear her retching. I tiptoed to her door and strained to hear what she was doing. A few seconds later the unmistakable sound of vomiting came from her cubicle. The toilet flushed and I jumped away from the door and waited for her to emerge. Claire stepped out, clutching a tissue to her mouth. She lifted her head slowly and a look of horror spread across her face when she saw me standing in front of her. The two of us looked at each other for a few seconds before saying anything.

"What's wrong?" I asked, my arms folded across my chest like a school matron.

"Nothing," she muttered under her breath and went over to the sink. She cupped her hands together and let them fill with water which she then splashed over her face.

"Claire, are you sick?" I asked hurriedly, afraid that we'd be interrupted any minute by another customer who wanted to use the loo.

Claire ignored me and pulled a paper towel from the dispenser.

I walked behind her, not giving her any time to make excuses.

"Claire, if you are sick you should tell me," I said, pulling off some more tissue for her.

She leaned against the sink and looked at herself in the mirror. All the colour had drained from her face and she look as white as a ghost.

"If you need help, you should tell me," I said softly.

"What kind of help?" she asked flatly, staring at her own reflection in the mirror.

"Why are you throwing up all the time? Do you have an eating disorder?"

She swung around to me as if I'd just hit her. "How do *you* know I throw up all the time?" she asked incredulously.

I grappled with what to say for a second, knowing that if I told the truth, I would be marching Lainey into it. But, there was no other way I could think of to get around it. This was my only opportunity to confront her and if it was at Lainey's expense, I was going to have to betray her confidence. "Lainey told me that you were sick all the time in France."

Claire put her hand on the washbasin as if to steady herself. I knew that I had said enough, and waited for her to reply. But there was no indignant denial; instead, she closed her eyes and began to cry. Her shoulders shuddered and she held up the crumpled ball of tissue to her mouth.

"Oh, Claire!" I rushed to her and put my arms around her.

I felt her body stiffen as she tried to control her tears. She pulled away from me and turned back to the mirror.

"Claire, I didn't mean to upset you," I pleaded. "I'm just worried about you – and I want to help you if I can. If there's something you're going through I want to be there for you."

"It's nothing," she said, straightening up. "I'm fine."

I could see the shutters coming down again and the brief flash of weakness I had witnessed was once again guarded behind a steely glare.

"You can relax, Liz," she said disdainfully. "It's my

asthma playing up again. The steroids are making me sick and bloated and depressed."

She fumbled about in her handbag for her compact and began to dab some colour back on to her cheeks.

"Why didn't you tell me?" I asked.

She let out a long sigh. "Because I kept telling myself that if I didn't dwell on it, it would just go away. But it didn't – it kept getting worse, and now I'm on these fucking steroids that make me throw up all the time *and* I look like an elephant."

"Claire," I said, reaching out tentatively and stroking her back, "I'm sorry."

Her shoulders hunched over as she tried to recoil from my touch.

"It's just one of life's shitty little trials, I suppose. I'll just have to put up with it." She closed the compact and put it back into her handbag.

"I wish you'd told me sooner."

"Why?" she snapped. "What on earth could you have done about it?"

I took my hand from her rigid back. "Nothing, I suppose," I said, trying to smile through my hurt.

"So, you and Lainey had it all worked out. I had an eating disorder. How interesting," she said with a bitter smile.

"We were concerned," I said, jumping to our defence.

"Well, you can tell her you were both wrong."

"I will," I said in a thin voice.

God, she could be so unforgiving.

"Claire, you have to understand that I care about you, and if I appear to pry into your life, it's only because you mean so much to me."

There, that did it. Her bottom lip began to quiver and the suit of armour fell away again for a fleeting second. "I know," she whispered.

"Okay," I said, giving her hand a squeeze. "I just want us to be friends."

Claire looked at me and nodded. "I know," she said again.

We stood there for a few seconds and said nothing. Claire withdrew her hand from mine and dabbed her eyes with a tissue.

"Do you feel up to having a coffee before we go?"

"Yes," she answered. "I'm fine now."

Back at the table, Claire resumed her composure.

"Why do you think the asthma is back?" I asked. It had been years since she had suffered from any serious attacks. I had almost forgotten that she'd ever had it.

Claire shrugged her shoulders. "Who knows?" she said despondently. "These things can flare up at any time in your life."

"Remember when Daddy used to have to run to the hospital with you in the middle of the night?"

She smiled as she remembered the frantic car rides.

"And the counting game with the inhaler. I still have that inhaler in a box somewhere, along with your Peter Rabbit."

Claire face softened. "Peter Rabbit," she whispered.

"You know, they say that recurring illnesses can be brought on by stress or trauma. I know your asthma got really bad after Mum died. It used to drive me mad when Rita said so, but she was probably right. It was the shock of losing Mum. Are you stressed out at work at the moment? Maybe you should take some time off."

Claire shifted uneasily in her chair. It was always the same when I made any mention of Mum – she would change the subject immediately.

"How's the adoption going?" she asked, as if I hadn't said anything.

"Slowly!" I answered, allowing her to veer off the subject of Mum. "It's amazing just how many obstacles they can find to put in our way. We haven't even got halfway through the process and already Richard has had enough. It's really got me thinking how unfair life is. Here we are crying out for a baby and we've to go through this ridiculous ordeal to get one, and there are criminals and crackheads out there just churning out one kid after another and nobody bats an eyelid."

"And how's Richard coping with the whole thing?"

I threw my eyes up to heaven. "Richard just wants a mail-order baby to be sent by FedEx and signed for. The entire process is just a big inconvenience for him."

"But he wants a child?" Claire asked with a certain curiosity.

"Oh yes," I said, far too quickly. "Of course he does."
Of course he does. Of course he does.

I suddenly felt like a big hypocrite. Why should I expect Claire to confide in me when I wasn't prepared to open up to her?

I felt the need to lie, to cover up the fact that Richard really didn't care whether we had a baby or not. I looked over at Claire and stopped myself from saying anything else when I saw the look of sympathy in her eyes.

We walked outside and I turned to her and hugged her.

"I'm glad we met," I said. "I've missed you."

Claire smiled uneasily and looked as if she was going to cry again. "I've missed you too," she said.

"Do you need a lift? The car is around the corner."

"No," she said. "I think I'll walk. I could do with the exercise."

I stood and watched her light blue raincoat flap about in the wind as she turned the corner out of sight, and I was struck with a sinking feeling of disappointment.

My sister was always going to be unhappy. It was part of who she was and there was never going to be anything I could do to change that.

Matt L'Estrange, our new colleague and partner, joined the firm last week. Brian led him through the office and introduced him to the team. Matt smiled and shook hands and generally created a glowing first impression with his movie star smile. I'd had dealings with Matt in the past and so was not quite as disarmed with his charm as Susie was. For a moment I thought she was going to curtsey to him when he passed by. As soon as the introductions were out of the way, Brian steered Matt away from the main working area and down the hall to his office.

Susie stretched both arms out across her desk and let her head flop down on them.

"Jesus! He's a ride!" she squealed.

Her head popped up again and she looked out the door as the two men walked away. "Hallelujah! Finally, a good-looking man in the office. Monday mornings won't be such a drag any more."

"Shut up, Susie," I hissed, afraid that they would hear her, but they were well out of earshot.

"I suppose he's happily married with ten kids," she groaned. "Mind you, if he is, he's not wearing a wedding ring."

"Actually, as far as I know, he's single. He was living with a girl, but I think that's broken up."

Susie wound a curl around her forefinger. "Well, in that case, you can pass the word around to the other female members of staff: I saw him first."

"Right," I said. "I'll go and pin a memo on the notice-board."

We haven't even presented our pitch to Browne's and Brian is already trying to muscle in on it. I hadn't planned on actually telling him what Jeff said, about me handling the account – of course that's if we even get it. But yesterday my back was against the wall and I had no choice. I called a meeting about the Browne's presentation and discussed my idea of doing a polocrosse shoot. Brian's been walking around like a Cheshire cat, grinning from ear to ear at the prospect of getting Browne's back on board.

I had my photos of a polocrosse match and my flip-chart of ideas and I threw them out to the group at breakneck speed. I just knew this idea was going to work and that Jeff was going to like it. But with each sentence I spoke, Brian's face grew more and more despondent, until I couldn't bear his disapproving glare any longer.

"Brian!" I snapped. "Do you want to add something to this?"

He looked over at me with a cold stare. "I don't see it working," he said, looking around the group for a reaction.

"Well, let her finish," said Susie.

Brian ignored Susie's comment and looked to Matt for some support. Matt sat back and shrugged. "It could be interesting," he said.

Brian flopped back in his chair and exhaled loudly. "Liz, you know the Browne account. You know that they expect a certain kind of representation. It's a label that caters for middle-aged rugby players and golfers. Why would you want to try to win them back with an off-the-wall sport for kids?"

"Brian, I think you're missing the point here. We lost the Browne account because Task was doing exactly what you've said – making boring commercials for a middle-aged market that they already had sewn up. They want to widen their market, reach out to a younger buyer and that's what this presentation is trying to achieve."

Brian sat forward and laced his fingers together. "We can't take any chances on this one, Liz. We are trying to get these people to come back to us and veering off on a whacky path like that is too risky. If it was any other account, I'd give you free rein with it, you know that. But this is too important. We need to change – I agree with you on that score, but not so radically."

I stood there, squeezing my pen between my thumb and forefinger, trying to contain my frustration. Brian slapped his hands together which signalled the end of our meeting.

"It's back to the drawing board," he said, gathering his papers together. "We'll have another meeting next Monday and see if there are any new ideas to discuss. And put your thinking caps on, lads – we've got to work fast on this one."

Susie and Matt left the office, while I hung back, taking more time than necessary to gather my things. Brian closed the door and walked over to me with a sympathetic smile.

"Sorry, Liz, but that just isn't going to work. There was no other way to say it."

"You could have let me finish," I said.

He threw his hands up in the air. "Liz, you know there's no time to waste on this. We have two weeks to come up with something. We can't afford the time to spend on ideas that won't work."

I took a deep breath and tried to stay cool. "Actually, Brian, if you had let me continue, I would have rounded off the presentation by saying that Jeff Williams thinks it's a great idea."

His mouth fell open slightly. "You never told —"

"I never told you because you never gave me a chance to finish. I discussed my ideas with Jeff and he seemed very excited about it." I tried to keep any trace of gloating out of my voice.

"Why didn't you tell me this before now?" he asked, his mouth held tightly with disapproval.

"Because I wanted it to be part of my presentation. I wanted to end with the fact that Jeff had given it the thumbs up, but you wouldn't even let me finish."

Brian pulled the flip-chart from under my arm and put it down on his desk. He leaned over it and began to thumb through the pages, looking totally baffled.

"You're completely serious about this, Liz? He really did like it?"

"Yes!" I snapped, feeling my frustration rise again. "He did."

Brian straightened up and ran his hand through his hair. "I suppose we'd better continue with it so. Arrange a shoot wherever the game takes place, and I just hope to God that we're doing the right thing."

"Okay," I said, picking up the chart, trying to ignore his tone of complete and utter doubt in me.

"Maybe I'll arrange another meeting with Jeff Williams. I might bring Matt along."

Here we go, I thought. Squeeze me out and make way for the boys.

I turned to Brian as if I'd forgotten a minor detail. "Jeff has asked that I head up this campaign, so if there are any further meetings with him, I think I should be included."

Brian took a step backwards and stared at me.

"I didn't think I would have to deliver that to you so bluntly," I said, holding his stare, "but I can see my idea getting hijacked if I don't speak up now."

I could see the hairs on the back of his neck bristling. "I wasn't trying to hijack anything. I was simply suggesting that now that Matt is a partner he should meet with Jeff – it would be a good excuse to touch base with him again."

Usually I would crack a smile here, to show him that there was no offence taken, but I kept my stony glare intact. "Brian, I didn't come back as partner just to get a bigger salary. I want to be treated as one – and that means being included in everything. I know it's going to be hard for you – you've never had a woman partner in the firm before – but it's hard for me as well. I want you to have faith in me and allow me the freedom that will enable me to work without constraints. I don't want to have to do battle with you for every idea I want to act on. I want this to work, Brian."

He looked around the room, not knowing how to react

to my rant. Eventually, when he realised that he would have to say something, he came across to me and patted me awkwardly on the arm.

"I didn't mean to undermine you, Liz. I have complete faith in you. If you feel that this idea is going to work, then run with it. I'll let the others know."

I tried to wipe the smug grin off my face as I walked back to my office, but it just wouldn't go away.

Then

I feel sick because I smoked a cigarette on the way home from school today. Johnny Devlin started chatting to us as we walked down the road. He was showing off like mad because he'd just bought ten Sweet Afton. He fancies Lainey, but she's not interested in him. I like his friend Gary Kilroy. We stood in behind a bush and they lit up. The guys were trying to act real casual, like they did it every day but I could tell that they were really nervous. I think I'll take it up, even though it makes me feel shit, because it definitely makes you look really cool. The only thing that stops me is when I see Rita belching out mouthfuls of smoke, because it doesn't make her look very cool. But, it's different for teenagers.

Lainey took a puff of Johnny's fag, but she started to cough and handed it back.

"It's all wet at the end," she said, with her face screwed up.

The lads laughed at her and handed it to me. I took it and pulled in a small mouthful of smoke and felt it burn the back of my throat. I inhaled as deeply as I could, and to my relief, I blew it back out without coughing my guts up. I passed it back to Lainey but she shook her head. I took another drag and then another and I could see that the lads were impressed. It made me feel so sophisticated – until now. My face has turned a funny shade of green and all I want to do is throw up. But I am determined to keep trying until I can smoke a whole cigarette without feeling sick. I've pulled the curtains on my bedroom window so I can't see the shadows of the tree on the wall. I don't think Mum would have liked me smoking.

I am grounded for a week and it's all Rita's fault. There was a disco in the tennis club and everyone was allowed to go, that is everyone except me. Lainey's mum said that she could go, but when she spoke to Rita, she suddenly changed her mind. Dad didn't seem to care whether I went or not, until he spoke to Rita. Then he decided that I was too young for discos. I'm in second year for heaven's sake! Some of the first years were even allowed to go. I pleaded and pleaded, but it was no use, Rita wouldn't budge. So, instead of fighting, I decided to lie. I pretended that Mrs Byrne down the road had asked me to baby-sit on Friday night. Lainey told her mum that she was baby-sitting with me. We left the house in our sweatshirts and jeans and changed into different clothes behind the bushes at the end of Lainey's front garden. We shivered and giggled like mad as we crouched down in the dark and pulled on our disco clothes. We both wore our Sasperilla satin jeans. Mine are turquoise and Lainey's are bright pink. Lainey's are so tight on her that she had to lie on the ground while I sat on top of her and forced the zip up. On our way down the road,

Lainey realised that she had put her top on back to front, which made us go hysterical. The disco was great fun. I brought a packet of Sweet Afton and smoked three of them in the loo without coughing at all. I'm getting lots of practice smoking Rita's fags behind the bike shed in the back garden

When the slow set came on, Gary Kilroy asked me to dance to "Je t'aime". I could feel my knees turn to jelly as he wrapped his arms around my waist. We didn't talk at all, and as the song went on he tightened his grip on me and we kissed. It was my first French kiss and it made me feel so dizzy that I thought I'd faint. We rolled our tongues around each other's mouths and I was almost afraid to breathe. I kept my eyes shut for most of it, but I opened them for a second to see if Lainey was looking at us, and she was! Later in the toilet she came rushing up to me, dying to hear what it was like.

"Oh my God, Lizzy! You French-kissed him!"

I stood there grinning like an idiot.

"Well? What was it like?" she asked, waving her hands about impatiently.

"Brilliant," I gasped.

She leaned against the washbasin and took out her lip-gloss that she'd got free with *Jackie*. "Lizzy! I can't believe you French-kissed him – you're so lucky!"

"Did you not do it with Johnny?" I asked. I knew he was going to try to because Gary had told me.

"No," she said, wrinkling up her nose. "I mean, he's nice but I don't like him enough to give him a Frenchy."

She rolled the glass ball of the lip-gloss across her mouth and handed it to me. "Here, you might need some of this in case he tries to kiss you again. It's cherry flavour."

I rolled it across my mouth and smacked my gluey lips together.

When the next slow set started, Gary appeared again. We danced together for two more songs. "I'm Not in Love" by 10cc and "Freebird" by Lynard Skynnard, and we kissed our way through both of them. We even stayed kissing for the fast part of Freebird.

Gary walked us part of the way home. The tennis club is only a few minutes away, but when we got close to our house I told him to go, in case we were spotted. Just as well he went, because when we turned the corner on to our road, Rita and Mrs Whyte were standing outside the Byrnes' house. Rita stood with her hands on her hips like the town sheriff about to pull a gun on us.

"Oh shit," I said, as I felt the thrill of the evening fade away.

"Get down here this minute!" Rita roared at the top of her voice.

Lainey burst into tears. "Oh no! We'll be killed."

We walked up to them and stood there waiting for all hell to break loose.

"You liar," Rita said, without waiting to hear any explanations. Not that I had any to offer.

"Lainey," said Mrs Whyte, looking as if she was about to pass out with worry, "where have you been?"

"Oh Mum, sorry. I'm so sorry," Lainey blurted between sobs. "We went to the tennis club disco. I'm so sorry, Mum."

Mrs Whyte put her arms around Lainey's shoulders and patted her back. "You shouldn't have lied to me. I've been so worried about you."

"I know," gulped Lainey.

Mrs Whyte looked at Rita and nodded her head. "I think we've all had enough excitement for one evening. I'll see you tomorrow."

She walked up the road towards her house with her arm still around a hysterical Lainey.

I looked at them and thought, why can't I just burst into tears and say sorry? I really wanted to, but I knew that no matter how hard I tried, there was no way I could turn on any tears — or say sorry.

Rita turned to me and stared at me with her mean little stony eyes. "Happy now?" she asked, her hands still on her hips.

"What?" I said.

She nodded her head towards the retreating figures of Lainey and her mother. "Happy that you've led her astray as well?"

"I didn't make her go," I retorted.

"Don't give me that," said Rita, throwing her head back. "You devious little cow! Lainey would never have done something like that without you to egg her on."

I stared at her but kept my mouth shut.

"Your father isn't home yet, but you can be sure that I'm going to tell him what you did tonight. He's going to be so annoyed with you, madam."

She turned towards our house and began to walk up the road. I followed, but kept a few paces behind her. She opened the front door and we both walked into the hall. I remembered our clothes that were still hidden in a bag behind Mrs Whyte's rose bushes, but I didn't think it was the right time to mention it. I put my hand on the banister and went to go to my room. Rita turned around and stared at me.

"Your poor mother would be so disappointed with you."

I felt my heart lurch forward in my chest and my eyes stung with angry tears. How dare she mention Mum like that! I had reached the third step of the stairs and stopped to look down at her. Her mean little eyes were full of spite as she glared at me.

"Fuck off!" I hissed, before bounding up the rest of the stairs and into my room.

Now

Our first home visit was last Saturday. Inside, I was a nervous wreck but decided not to share my feelings with Richard. I busied myself by scouring the house from top to bottom. If there was any reason why we weren't fit to adopt a baby, it wasn't going to be because my house wasn't clean enough. I scrubbed, polished and vacuumed without as much as a whisper about how nervous I was feeling. I remained perfectly calm but, to my utter surprise, Richard was a basket-case. For the week before the visit, he didn't sleep at all. He tossed and turned every night, keeping me awake. On the night before the visit, I ordered him into the spare room so at least one of us could get some sleep.

As it turned out, there was nothing to worry about. Val arrived and we showed her around our extremely clean house. She loved the curtains in our bedroom and I gave her the name of the lady who made them for me, anything to stall the inevitable. We sat in the living-room and she asked more of the same kind of questions that we'd covered in the adoption course and Richard seemed to relax a little as the interview proceeded. We had been told that there would be some pretty intimate questions about our private lives, but Val was obviously saving them for a later date. When we were finished, I showed her out to her car. I tried to stay quiet and not babble too much, but I couldn't resist the opportunity to siphon some information from her.

"How do you think it's going so far?" I asked tentatively.

Val turned to me and shrugged her shoulders with a smile. "I can't comment on anything, Liz."

It was like asking the driving inspector if you'd passed your test before you got back to the centre.

"I understand. You're just doing your job," I said. "But I'm so anxious to know how the whole thing is going. Are we doing okay?"

Again Val gave a strained smile. "So far, so good. And that's as much as I can say without getting into trouble."

I smiled back. "Thanks," I said gratefully. "Did you get the referees' letters?" I had reminded Brenda and Lainey not to delay about getting them in. Val flicked through her notes.

"Brenda and Tom Power have furnished us with one, but the other couple haven't. Maybe you'd remind them about it?"

"Sure," I said, making a mental note to throttle Lainey. She'd been so wrapped up in the party preparations that she'd probably thrown the forms into a drawer and forgotten about them."

Richard was lying back in the armchair when I returned to the living room. He looked pale and had big dark circles under his eyes from lack of sleep. I sat down and put my arms around his neck and kissed him.

"That wasn't so bad, was it?"

He smiled weakly. "No, I suppose it wasn't."

Poor Richard, I could tell that it had drained him completely.

"Thank you," I whispered. "I know how much you hate it, but it'll all be worth it in the end."

He put his arm around me and pulled me close. "Oh Liz," he said wearily, "I hope so."

After the visit, Richard decided to go into the office for a while. Normally I'd moan about him working on Saturdays, but after going through such a stressful morning, I didn't mind what he did for the rest of the day. When he left, I wandered around the house for a while, feeling at a bit of a loose end. It was too late to go into town and the house certainly didn't need any more cleaning, so I decided to call over to Daddy and Rita. I hadn't seen them in weeks and I'd bought some spring bulbs for planting that I wanted to give them. It was a perfect late autumn day and I knew that Rita would be in the garden. I turned the radio on in the car and mellowed out as I drove further out of suburbia and down the leafy roads that led to their house. The trees were bathed in the crisp afternoon sunlight that turned the leaves a rich shade of russet.

To my surprise, the door was answered by Claire. She looked slightly put out to see me, as if I was muscling in on her time. I shoved a tray of bulbs into her hand and went out to get more from the car.

"I thought you had your interview today," she said.

"I did. It only lasted an hour."

"Is that Daddy's?" I asked, pointing to the baggy jumper she was wearing.

She pulled at it self-consciously. "No. I'm helping Rita with the vegetable patch – she's let it go wild." Then she added sarcastically, "If I'd known you were coming I would have got dressed up for the occasion."

We walked down to the kitchen. Through the window, I could see Rita straightening up from her crouching position at the vegetable patch, her two hands massaging the small of her back. Her eyes widened when she saw me and she came flying up the garden and in to meet me.

"Lizzy! I didn't know you were calling today."

"Neither did I," I said, placing the tray of bulbs down on the drainer.

"How did the interview go?" she asked.

"Fine," I said. "It was just more of the same old thing."

Rita gave a giggle and wiped her mucky hands on the front of her jumper. "I can't believe the two of you will be getting a baby soon. You know, I've never seen your Dad get so excited about anything before! He's really looking forward to being a granddad."

I felt slightly awkward at her show of enthusiasm. Did that mean Rita was going to be the grandmother? I'd spent all my life making sure that nobody thought she was my mother and now she'd probably end up being grandmother to my child. It felt a bit odd, but there was too much water under the bridge to start being petty about it.

"How do you feel about being a granny?" I asked, letting her know that it was all right to assume the title.

Her face broke into a beaming smile and she clapped her hands together. "I can't wait!" she exclaimed.

Claire leaned against the kitchen table looking miserable and I felt my excitement dissolve into guilt. It had never been any different. Like the bicycle and the dressing-gown, and everything else I had ever been given that she'd wanted. Her envy had always managed to sour the moment. But this time – just for once, could she not have put aside her covetousness and been happy for me?

The party was a resounding success. A very unsuspecting Peter arrived home from moving office all day to the sight of a marquee in his back garden, filled with family, friends and a twelve-piece swing band. The poor guy almost had to be picked up off the floor. Thankfully he was moving office that day and not relying on my husband to take him off golfing, because as it turned out, Richard had to go to London for the day and wasn't back in time to be there for the surprise. He arrived later in the evening. I took a taxi with Brenda and Tom at seven o'clock – we had been warned by Lainey not to arrive a minute later than seven thirty. The place was buzzing as we walked in the door. The band was tuning up in the marquee and caterers were bustling about the place putting last minute touches to the tables. Luckily the day had been mild and the rain that had been threatening all evening had decided to hold off. Lainey tripped down the stairs looking positively regal in a black halter-neck evening gown. However, as soon as she opened her mouth, her air of grace and poise immediately vanished. The poor girl was rattling with nerves.

"You didn't leave the car outside?" she shouted frantically. "He'll recognise your cars. I've told everyone to park around the corner or better still, out on the main road."

Tom went over to her and placed his hand on her shoulder. "Calm down, woman. We came in a taxi and I didn't see any cars outside. Now pour yourself a drink and relax. The place looks great," he said, looking around at the balloons and party banners that decked the hall. He steered Lainey towards the kitchen and we followed. After a few sips of wine, the doorbell went and Lainey almost spilt the drink over herself in the rush to get to the door. Half an hour later, almost everyone had arrived and the party was in full swing out in the marquee. I stayed in the front room with Lainey and kept a lookout for Peter. She stood at the window nervously chewing her thumbnail.

Richard called me on my mobile to say he was at the airport and would be along soon.

Through the window I spotted Claire walking up the driveway.

Lainey waved and gestured to her to hurry up.

Claire looked really well. Her hair had grown a little since her last disastrous chop, and her coppery highlights had been touched up. Her skin had a flawless glow, as if she'd just had a facial. She wore a smocked top over black trousers which didn't exactly do anything for her figure, but it was the first time in ages that I'd seen her look so well.

"Hi," she said as she walked into the room. "Where will I leave this?" She held out a gift-wrapped box.

Lainey looked around from the window. "Hi, just leave it in the hall," she said dismissively, and turned back to her post at the window.

"Where is everyone?" Claire asked.

"Out in the marquee," I said.

"Okay. I'll just leave this in the hall and go on out,"

Claire said, looking a bit put out at Lainey's ungracious welcome.

Very nervous, I mouthed at her behind Lainey's back.

"Are Brenda and Tom here?" Claire asked.

"Yes. They're out in the marquee."

"Richard?"

I rolled my eyes up to heaven. "Not yet. Soon, I hope."

Claire left the room and Lainey went back to staring out the window.

It probably wasn't a great time to ask, but I was anxious about the reference and felt I mightn't have a chance to ask Lainey later. "Did you write my reference yet?"

Lainey swung around looking distracted.

"The reference for the adoption board," I said.

"Yes, I know," she said. "I did, but the printer is broken. I meant to ask Peter to do it in work, but I forgot."

"You can write it by hand, it doesn't have to be type-written."

"It looks better typed," she said. "My handwriting is atrocious – they'd never be able to make it out."

"Well, I know you've got a lot on your mind right now, but would you put it at the top of your list after tonight?" I asked.

"Yeah," she said absently. Then she stood on tiptoe as a car drove down the road. "Shit, I hope Richard doesn't walk in at the same time as Peter."

Shit, I thought to myself. Knowing Richard's sense of timing, that's exactly what would happen but our fears were allayed when Lainey jumped back from the curtain like a scalded cat.

"It's him!" she squealed. "Quick!" She pulled me up

from the couch. "Get out to the marquee and tell everyone to be quiet."

He didn't have a clue. He stood there at the door of the marquee in his dusty sweatshirt and trousers with his mouth wide open. It took him a few seconds to realise that the party was for him. Lainey was suddenly her old self again, mission accomplished. Peter ran upstairs and changed into the clothes that had been carefully chosen and left out for him. He appeared ten minutes later to a loud cheer and the band broke into their first song.

It was after ten by the time Richard arrived. He tapped me on the shoulder and kissed the back of my neck. "You look lovely," he said, looking over the new dress I had bought for the party.

"What kept you?" I asked.

"I went home to dump the car and call a taxi, but it never arrived."

"So how did you get here?"

"I had to drive."

"Well, you can leave it here and we'll get a taxi home." Richard shrugged his shoulders. "I don't mind driving."

"But that means you can't have a drink," I said.

A waiter came around with a tray of wine and Richard grabbed himself one. "I'll have one glass while I decide."

The dancing was in full swing and I looked around and spotted Brenda and Tom strutting their stuff on the dance floor. Brenda looked radiant in her size twelve red silk dress. I was so happy that she had achieved her goal. Fitting into a dress seemed so trite compared to most people's problems, but I knew how much it meant to her. Tom was doing his best impression of Tom Jones and looked as if he was going to have a heart attack at any moment. After two songs, I saw Brenda pointing to her shoes, gesturing that she'd had enough dancing. Tom looked around and spotted Claire, who was talking to Mrs Whyte. He weaved through the couples on the dance floor and pulled a very reluctant Claire back out to partner him. After another few swing numbers, the band slowed down and I recognised the first notes of "Moon River". Richard was talking to Peter and looked across at me with a smile. It was our song. It had been Mum's favourite song and it was what I had asked the band to play for the first dance at our wedding reception. I smiled across at him and he put down his glass and came over.

"Come on," he said, taking my hand and leading me on to the dance floor.

The dancers had thinned out and there were about twenty couples swaying to the music. Tom had managed to keep ahold on Claire but when she saw us coming she took the opportunity to slide out of his grip.

"Hey," he protested, "I didn't say you could go."

Brenda appeared and took Claire's place and Claire disappeared into the crowd.

I closed my eyes and let my head rest on Richard's shoulder.

How long had it been since we had danced together? It seemed like forever.

I put my mouth against his ear and whispered, "I love you".

He tightened his grip around my waist and held me close until the music ended.

The band took a well-deserved break while the food was

served and when the main course was finished, there was a loud drum roll as the birthday cake was wheeled out on a trolley. There were hoots and roars as Peter tried his best to make a speech, thanking Lainey for such a wonderful evening. As the band got going again, Brenda came up to me.

"Isn't this a great party?" I shouted over the music.

Brenda looked worried and pulled me towards the door of the marquee. I followed her out to the garden.

"Will you go upstairs and talk to Claire. I think she's upset about something," she said.

"What's wrong?" I asked, putting my glass of wine down on the patio table.

Brenda looked up at a bedroom window. "I don't know. I went into the girl's room to get my mobile phone out of my jacket and found her there, crying."

"Oh no!" I gasped.

"She brushed me off and said that she's fine, but I think you'd better go up to her."

"Thanks, Brenda," I said.

Jenny and Alannah were spending the night with school-friends and the guests were using the downstairs toilets, so upstairs was empty and eerily quiet after the din of the party. My ears were ringing from the loud music. I pushed open the bedroom door and found Claire wiping her eyes with a tissue. Her glowing complexion had turned red and blotchy from crying.

"Claire," I said softly, "what on earth's wrong with you?"

She jumped up and took a few steps back as though she was annoyed to see me.

"Nothing!" she snapped.

"Oh, come on," I said as gently as I could. "You're sitting here sobbing in the middle of a party – of course there's something wrong."

She hung her head and wiped away another tear. "I just feel awful," she said in a choked voice. "I felt another attack coming on and I panicked. I ran up here to find my inhaler and I just . . ." She stopped and blinked back her tears.

I walked across the room and went to put my arms around her but she turned away.

"I don't want to ruin the evening for you," she said, grabbing her coat. "I'm going to call a taxi and go home. You go back down and please don't make a fuss."

"Don't leave," I said. "Come back down and we'll have a drink."

"Liz," she pleaded, "I just want to go home."

I could see there was no point in trying to persuade her to stay. "Okay, but don't get a taxi on your own. I'll leave with you."

"No," she said crossly. "You go back downstairs and let me slip out quietly without anyone noticing."

I couldn't let her leave alone, not when she was so upset.

Then I remembered Richard wasn't drinking.

"You go down and wait outside the front door and I'll get Richard to drive you home. That way, you won't have to wait around for a taxi."

She waved her hands in the air frantically. "Liz, I just want to go home. Now will you stop interfering and let me out of here."

I decided to ignore her protestations and turned to leave.

"Richard will be out at the front door in a minute. If you're not there, I'm going to follow you home myself."

I closed the door and didn't listen to anything further that she had to say. Tom was holding court out on the patio, surrounded by a group of men who were laughing raucously as he told one of his dirty jokes. Richard stood at the edge of the group and I pulled at his elbow to get his attention.

"Richard did you have any more to drink?" I asked.

"No," he said, still laughing at whatever Tom had said. "I'm going to drive."

"Claire's upset about something. I found her crying in the bedroom upstairs. She wants to get a taxi on her own and I don't think it's a good idea. Would you mind running her home?"

His smile faded and he frowned at me and bit down on his lower lip.

"I know it's a pain, but I really don't want her to leave on her own."

"What's wrong with her?" he asked gruffly.

"She's had an asthma attack and she's just upset. You know Claire!" I said with mild exasperation. "Will you?" I urged, afraid that if I wasted any more time explaining that she'd leave on her own.

"Okay," he said reluctantly.

"Thanks, sweetheart." I gave him a quick peck on the cheek. "She's at the front door."

He muttered something under his breath and marched into the kitchen and out to the hall where Claire was waiting.

A few seconds later I was pulled on to the dance floor by Tom who was now in full party mode. His tie was hanging loose around his neck and his shirt was open down to his chest. He nearly broke my wrist swinging me around the place like a rag-doll, and I was very relieved a few minutes later when Brenda and Lainey got up to join us.

"Here," I shouted, pushing Tom over to Brenda. "Throw your wife around the floor for a while."

Lainey squeezed my arm and leaned into me. "Where's Claire?" she asked.

I went to shout an explanation into her ear, but decided against it. "Don't ask," I mouthed over the din.

Our eyes met and Lainey shook her head disapprovingly. I shrugged my shoulders and started to dance again – it was a party, and I was glad that Claire had left. I felt that I needed a night off from my sister and all of her problems.

The band played their final number at two and I wasn't sorry to see them packing up. My ears sounded like they'd had cymbals crashing against them all evening. A lot of the guests had left and the last few of us sat around a table for a late night chat. Lainey and Peter were like two lovebirds – Peter hadn't stopped thanking her and praising her all evening. The combination of alcohol and delayed shock had left him feeling very emotional and his speech had become slightly slurred.

"Isn't she the best in the world?" he said to me with a big dopey grin.

Lainey swatted him away from her playfully. "Peter! Stop it. You're embarrassing me."

Peter took her hand and kissed it. "She's the best. Isn't she, Liz?"

I laughed at his complete adoration. "Yes, she is," I agreed. "I wish I'd married her myself."

Lainey looked around the table. "Speaking of which, where *is* your husband?"

"He gave Claire a lift home earlier. She wasn't feeling well."

Tom belted out the first few lines of "Strangers in the Night" and Brenda gave a loud groan. "Oh Tom, don't start singing now!" she said.

Lainey raised her eyebrows and gave me a quizzical look, and for once I was quite happy to suffer Tom's drunken singing. It was late and I was too tired to start defending Claire.

We eventually climbed into a taxi just after three o'clock.

Tom was clutching a bunch of balloons that he had taken for the boys. There were too many of them to fit into the back of the taxi so Tom pulled down the window and let them float outside while he held on to the string. Brenda gave out to him for the entire journey and complained of the cold, but Tom was determined to get those balloons home one way or another.

Richard was in bed when I got back. He would have had to pass our house on the way back from Claire's and I guessed that he'd decided to call it a night. Damn Claire, I thought, as I let my dress slide to the floor. I had bought some very sexy underwear and stood in front of the wardrobe mirror admiring it. Richard stirred in the bed and opened one eye.

"Hi," I whispered, climbing on to the bed beside him.

"Hi," he said hoarsely.

I kissed his lips slowly and realised that I was more than a little drunk. "Oh baby, I love you so much. Thank you so much for taking Claire home."

"Did you have a good time?" he asked.

"Yes," I said, getting in beside him. "It's a pity you didn't come back."

I put my arms around his neck and pulled him close to me. He rested his head against the silk bustier top I was still wearing and I stroked the back of his neck.

"I didn't think there was any point. It was getting late."

I kissed the top of his head. "How was she?"

"She didn't open her mouth for the whole journey home. I just left her off at her apartment and came back here."

I felt the strap of my bustier fall away from my shoulder and I moved closer to Richard and ran my hand down the front of his chest. The wine had boosted my libido and made me feel a little more daring than usual. My fingers brushed lightly down past his stomach, but he stopped me. He took ahold of my hand and laced his fingers through mine. "Do you mind if we leave it tonight?" he said sleepily. "I'm shattered."

"No. It's fine," I whispered.

He kissed my forehead and rolled back over onto his side. Moments later he was sound asleep again. The stiff-boned bodice was sticking into my ribs, and I decided that there wasn't much point in wearing it any longer. I climbed out of bed and went into the bathroom to change into my pyjamas. A wave of nausea swept over me and I leaned on the sink heavily and stared at my reflection. My mascara had run and I looked utterly pathetic, standing there in my tarty underwear. I felt annoyed and sad and lonely and drunk and as I reached for a packet of make-up wipes I began to cry for no reason at all.

Then

Today we put flowers on Mum's grave. Daddy brings us every year on her birthday, just the three of us, Rita doesn't come. It is almost four years since she died. I brought yellow roses from Mrs Whyte's garden, because I know Mum liked them. Claire bought her red tulips. Daddy always puts a single white rose on her grave. After, we went to Captain America's for tea and Daddy gave me a lecture on how I should be studying harder for my Inter Cert. Claire is so lucky – she has no exams and gets hardly any homework. I get tons of homework and now Daddy has organised Mr Cooke to come to the house on Wednesday evenings to give me and Lainey grinds in maths and science. Mr Cooke is small and bald and his nose whistles when he breathes out, and I spend my time trying not to laugh because Lainey makes faces behind his back. As if that wasn't enough, I'm expected to study at the weekends *and* I'm not allowed out on Sundays.

I've been going out with Gary Kilroy for exactly one year. We bought each other Claddagh rings to mark our anniversary. Rita didn't know about Gary until two months ago. I didn't want to tell her I had a boyfriend because I knew she'd stick her big nose in and ruin things for us – and that's exactly what she did. Bloody Lainey told her mother that I was going out with Gary, and Mrs Whyte let it slip to Rita. She didn't do it on purpose; she's not like that. It's just that sometimes she can be a bit flaky and say things she's not meant to say. She'd forgotten that Lainey had told her to keep it a secret. Rita thinks I've only been going out with Gary for a month – she'd do her nut if she knew how long we've really been together. She says that I'm too young to have a boyfriend, but I know that the main reason she doesn't like it is because he comes from the cottages behind the tennis club. If I was going out with one of her snooty friends' sons, she wouldn't mind at all. She's always telling me to give her fat friend Carmel's son a ring to arrange a game of tennis. Not that I would in a million years – he looks exactly like Carmel, except he's got acne. It's such a pain in the arse, Rita knowing about us now. It means that we have to sneak around all the time. Gary is two years older than me and is leaving school this year to train as a carpenter with his dad. We are going to put our savings together when I am sixteen (a year and two months away) and move to London. I don't talk about it any more to Lainey in case she tells her mum. The reason why Daddy is watching me like a hawk is because Rita told him about Gary and he agrees that I am far too young to have a boyfriend.

I'm so in love with Gary. I have his photo under my mattress and every night before I go to sleep I take it out and look at it. I know that Mum would like him. Sometimes I feel that she's looking in at me from her place in the shadows and I get a feeling that she likes him. He is the best friend I've ever had. I told him everything about Mum and Daddy and Rita and I didn't feel a bit embarrassed about it because he understands me. Sometimes I don't have to say anything at all and he knows exactly what I'm thinking. It doesn't bother me that he's from the cottages and his family don't have as much money as mine. Only snobs like Rita would be bothered by things like that.

Claire is nosing around my bedroom all the time.

Yesterday I caught her reading my diary. I sneaked up behind her and pulled it out of her hands, and whacked her over the head with it. I have it hidden behind my wardrobe now, because Claire would go blabbing her head off to Rita if she read anything about my plans. Claire is about the most annoying little sister anyone could ever have. She spends her life going through my stuff, trying on my clothes and jewellery, messing with my make-up. I know she's taken things, like my gold belt and the silver necklace that Mrs Whyte gave me for my birthday. I've searched her room and can't find them, but I know it's her that's taken them because she's a little thief. Lainey is so lucky that she doesn't have a sister. Rita will make my life a misery now that she knows about Gary. Already, she's sticking her head out of the kitchen every time I leave the house.

"Where are you off to?" she asks, with her pencilled-in eyebrows arched as high as they can go.

Gary sometimes borrows his brother's motorbike and we go for a ride on it. The other day, we were stopped at traffic lights on the main road and who pulled up beside us? Only Daddy! I buried my face in Gary's back and prayed that the lights would go green. Gary kept shouting at me to stop pinching his waist – he didn't realise who was parked just inches away. Thankfully Daddy didn't see us. Just as well, because he would have hauled me off the bike and made a complete show of me. Since Rita found out about us, we have to arrange to meet in secret and I have to lie my head off all the time. But I don't care. I love him and nothing is going to stop us being together.

Now

The morning after the party, I woke with a pounding headache. The bed was empty and I couldn't remember if Richard had told me what his plans were for the day. I crawled out of bed and threw myself under the shower, adjusting the water knob to cold to punish myself for drinking so much. I dressed, dried my hair and applied a thin layer of make-up which made me look marginally better. Down in the kitchen, I was surprised to see Richard sitting at the table, reading the morning papers. He had been out to our local deli and brought back all sorts of goodies to help tackle the hangover he quite rightly presumed I would have. He jumped up and kissed me and proceeded to brew a pot of strong coffee.

"God," I croaked, "was I really drunk last night?"

He turned to me and suppressed a smile. "Eh, yes."

"Oh, I feel awful," I said, tearing off the end of an apricot croissant and stuffing it into my mouth.

"Well, this should soak up some of the alcohol. Sit down," he ordered, as he brought the coffee pot to the table.

I gladly obeyed, and collapsed into a chair. "It wasn't much of a night for *you*," I said sympathetically. "You'd really only arrived when you had to bring Claire home."

He poured himself a cup of coffee and shrugged his shoulders. "I didn't mind. I was tired; the meeting in London went on for hours and I'd had an early start to the day."

"It's a pity. It really was a great night – at least I think it was."

I suddenly had a flashback of Tom hurling me around the dance floor after he'd asked the band to play the music from *Riverdance*.

I took a sip of my coffee and felt immediately better. "You make great coffee," I said, smiling over at him. "Tell me, how was Claire on the way home?"

He flicked over to the sports section of the newspaper. "I told you last night, she didn't say a word. We drove home in silence, she got out of the car when we got to her apartment and then she thanked me for the lift."

"Did you go in with her?"

Richard rolled his eyes up to heaven. "No, I didn't go in with her. I drove into the carpark and stayed there until she was safely inside her front door. Honestly, Liz, sometimes you treat her as if she's slightly retarded. How do you think she gets home every other night?"

"She didn't say what was bothering her?"

Richard licked his thumb and flicked over a page. "No," he said slowly, "she didn't say anything."

I poured another cup of coffee.

"I can't help worrying about her, Richard. She's just so . . ." I tried to think of what I was trying to say.

"So what?" he asked, looking up from the paper.

"I don't know. I'm too hungover to think straight."

"Well, if you ask me, she's a spoilt brat that gets far too much attention from everyone. Why did she go to the party if she was planning to have one of her little turns?"

"Oh Richard, don't be so hard on her. Claire is just different – she's a lot more fragile than most people."

Richard gave a little snort. "Fragile! She takes advantage of your good nature and you fall for it every time."

I wasn't going to get into an argument about it. Richard was obviously annoyed about having to leave the party early to drive Claire home, and, in hindsight, it had been unfair of me to ask. I reached over and put my hand on his.

"I really appreciate your taking her home last night."

His gaze had drifted back down to the newspaper and he gave a quick nod of his head in reply to my gesture.

Later that day I tried to phone Claire, but her landline rang out and as usual she had her mobile powered off. After ringing several times during the afternoon and evening, I finally got through to her just before I went to bed. She answered the phone and her voice sounded groggy, as if she'd been asleep.

"Hi," I said. "Did I wake you?"

"No, I was just lying on the couch watching TV."

"How are you?"

"Okay."

I was obviously going to have to push her for any further information.

"I just wanted to see how you were. You seemed so distraught last night."

I could sense her bristling down the phone line.

"I'm fine now. It was just another asthma attack – they make me feel so bad. I'm just tired of feeling sick all the time, that's all."

"I see," I said, doubtfully.

"Did you enjoy the rest of the night?" she asked, trying to deflect my probing.

"Yes, it was a great party. Lainey did a really fantastic job. Everyone had a ball."

"What time did you get home at?"

"After three," I groaned.

"Did Richard go back?"

"No," I said. "He was wrecked. He just went home."

A few seconds of awkward silence followed.

"I'm sorry if I ruined his evening," she said eventually.

"It's all right," I jumped in, not wanting her to feel bad. "I think Richard would have left early anyway. You just gave him a good excuse."

Claire went quiet again.

"So, everything's okay?" I ventured.

"Yes," she said quietly.

"Claire, if there was anything up, you'd tell me, wouldn't you?"

"Anything, like what?" she asked defensively.

"I don't know," I said, trying to decide whether to risk upsetting her again. "It's just that you've been so miserable and I feel that you're isolating yourself from me. Lately I feel like I'm just a nuisance. Whenever I try to be there for you or help in any way, you seem to want to keep me at a safe distance."

I heard her exhale loudly.

"Exactly what kind of help do you think I might need, Liz?"

Oh no, this was just what I didn't want to happen.

"I'm just saying that if you had anything on your mind, I hope you feel that you could come to me and talk about it. I'm your sister and nothing you say is going to make me judge you."

"What are you talking about?" she said, raising her voice.

Well, I'd got that far, I thought, I may as well continue.

"The thought has occurred to me lately that, well maybe, you might be gay, and if you are it's all right. You can tell me, Claire."

At first there was just silence, but after a few seconds she let out a series of sharp nasal bursts. I couldn't figure out whether she was laughing or crying, or having another asthma attack.

"Claire?"

"Oh Liz," she gulped.

"What? Please tell me, am I right?"

"You think you know me so well, Liz, but you don't know anything." She spat the words out like poison arrows.

"Claire, don't get like that. I'm only trying to —"

"Trying to what?" she said angrily. "What gives you the right to constantly interfere in my life? Do you think you own me?"

I bit down on my clenched fist and tried to think of the right thing to say. One wrong word and I knew the line would go dead and I would lose any chance of getting through to her. I tried to erase any trace of hysteria from my voice. "Claire, there's no need to get so upset. I just wanted you to know that you can talk to me about anything, that's all."

This only made her worse.

"What makes you think that I'd want to talk to *you*?"

Her stinging comment was like a slap across the face.

"I don't know," I said shakily. "Look, this isn't why I rang you. I just wanted to see if you were all right. I'm sorry if I've upset you."

A sharp click on the line told me that she had hung up.

I was left leaning against the bed, clutching the phone to my chest.

Richard walked into the bedroom and stared over at me."

"What is it?" he asked.

I turned off the phone and threw it onto the bed and straightened up, trying to disguise the awful hurt I felt inside. "Oh, nothing," I said with a sigh. "That was Claire. I was trying to get her to talk about what's bothering her but she bit the face off me."

"What did you say to her?"

"I think she's using the asthma as an excuse – she lived with it for all of her childhood years and it's not something that ever caused her that much distress. I think there's something more serious upsetting her and she won't admit it."

Richard stared at the carpet and frowned.

"Richard, I think she might be suffering from her nerves. I didn't see it until Lainey pointed it out to me, but Claire's behaviour is beginning to remind me of the way Mum used to be, and it terrifies me."

"Did you say that to her?" he asked.

"No, I asked her if she was gay, and she flew off the handle."

Richard's eyes opened wide. "You asked her if she was gay?" he exclaimed, trying to suppress a grin.

"Yes. Why? Do you think it was wrong of me?" I needed him to tell me that it had been the right thing to do, but I knew by the look on his face that I was not going to get that reassurance.

"Liz," he said, shaking his head, "will you leave it out?

If she is gay, — is your knowing going to make any difference? Surely Claire will tell you in her own time.".

He moved over to where I was standing and put his arms around me. "You have to stop worrying about her. If Claire needs your help she'll ask for it in her own time — why don't you just back off and let her sort things out for herself."

"But she seems so . . ."

I didn't get a chance to say anything else. Richard put his mouth against my ear and said, "Stop worrying, love." He began to kiss the side of my neck and his hands slid up and down my back slowly. He pulled me down onto the bed and loosened my shirt.

"Can I take you up on last night's offer?" he whispered into my ear.

I smiled at him and moved closer. He was right. I would just have to back off and give Claire some space.

Brian organised another lunch with Jeff Williams and invited Matt and me to join them. Personally, I didn't think it was a good idea as we hadn't had time to work on a presentation, and didn't have much to talk about. But Brian has a different take on the situation. He thinks that by love-bombing Jeff with lunch and dinner invitations to the best restaurants in town, it might help us to secure the account. We met in a very swanky restaurant around the corner from Browne's head office, and Brian made a big fuss of introducing Matt, our new superhero. I could tell by Jeff's reaction that he wasn't too impressed. He looked as though he might have preferred to spend the afternoon cleaning out the drawers of his desk, rather than listening to Brian spouting his usual crap.

After the sailing talk, (Brian and Jeff belonged to the same club), and the same boring golf stories we'd all heard a hundred times, Brian finally got down to business.

"So, Liz talked you through the proposed presentation?"

"She did," said Jeff, shaking himself out of a trance and smiling over at me. "It sounds very interesting. I'm looking forward to the presentation."

"We're going to do a shoot up at the stables next week," Brian said.

"Great," said Jeff.

"Now," Brian said, leaning his body into the table, "I think an all-round sports commercial would look really good. You know, a bit of the horsey stuff," he said dismissively, "and then," he continued, as if he expected a drum roll to begin "a quick succession of different sports shots."

Jeff leaned his elbows on the table and cupped his chin in the palm of his hand. He looked totally bored at this suggestion. I sat up in my chair and tried not to show my anger at being sidelined by Brian once again.

"I thought what I discussed with Liz seemed like a good idea. Why don't you just go with the polocrosse idea?"

Brian's mouth tightened. "Oh, we will," he assured Jeff. "It's just that Matt was thinking that we could broaden it a little, bring in a few more sports, make it a bit more interesting."

Matt was thinking? Why hadn't they talked to me about this? I looked over at Matt and he returned my stony glare with a simpering smile. I wanted to reach across the table and poke my fork down his throat.

Jeff looked over at me questioningly. I could tell that he

was just as puzzled as I was at this turn of events. We had discussed my idea, he'd agreed to let Task make a presentation and now Brian was bombarding him with a pile of shite. Unlike me, Jeff wasn't aware that Brian suffered from a syndrome that didn't allow him to accept other people's ideas. (Especially if the aforementioned people happened to be female.) If Brian didn't invent it – then it simply wasn't worth considering.

"Liz, what do you think?" Jeff asked.

Brian straightened up in his seat and eyeballed me. I gave him a look that said *don't think for one moment that I'm going to go along with this crap.*

"I think my original idea for a commercial that just features the polocrosse storyline would work best." I tried to seem measured and decisive, even managing to force a little smile.

Jeff now turned his body to face me and totally ignored the other two, who were exchanging shifty glances.

"Yes," said Jeff. "I have to say, it sounds far more interesting."

"Right, right," said Brian, pouring himself a glass of water.

"When do you think you'll be ready to make the presentation? I think it's only fair to let you know that we have three other agencies that will be making theirs over the next week or two."

All of his conversation was directed at me and I sat there trying to disguise the look of malicious pleasure that rose up inside. "We should be ready in about two weeks' time."

"Great!" Jeff said, throwing his napkin onto the table. "I still haven't made it up to watch the polocrosse matches on a

Saturday, but I'll give you a shout and maybe you can come up with me. Now, if you guys will excuse me, I've got to run."

"Of course," I said, flashing a wicked smile across at the other two.

I was just about to leave the office when my mobile phone rang. I was more than surprised to see it was Daddy's number calling, as he never ever rang my mobile – or my land-line come to think of it. He was never a telephone person, unless he had an important message.

"Hi, Daddy," I said.

"Lizzy!" he roared down the line. As a result of never making personal calls, he spoke as if he was standing on the summit of Mount Everest.

"Yes, it's me."

"Ah yes. Now, what do you think of this?" he asked in a clipped tone. "It's Rita's birthday soon, as you know, and I want to take you and Claire and Richard, if he's free of course, to a hotel for a weekend to celebrate."

I think this was the first time that my father had ever taken such an initiative. Rita had always organised his life, right down to what socks he puts on in the mornings. Making decisions that pertained to family life is something that only happened when Mum was still alive. I don't think Daddy has taken on even the most basic domestic task for the past thirty years.

"Wow! What's brought this on?" I asked with a laugh.

Daddy gave a loud guffaw. I could tell he was chuffed with himself.

"My friend, Dermot, from the golf club did the same for

the wife's birthday. He brought the family down to the Lakeview Falls for a weekend. It was a great success. I thought I'd do the same."

"Oh Daddy, that's so kind of you. I hear it's a beautiful place. Does Rita know about it?"

"Not yet. I want to settle on a date that we can all make it, and then I'll tell her."

"When were you thinking of?" I asked, pulling out my diary.

"Well, I was thinking of the second weekend in December. That's Saturday the 12th, how does that sound?"

I looked at that week and saw that we had nothing on. "That sounds fine, Daddy. I'll have to check with Richard and get back to you."

"Very good," he shouted.

"What about Claire? Have you checked with her?"

"Yes," he said. "She's free too."

The tightness that had formed in my chest eased away at his reply. At least if she'd agreed to come it meant that she wasn't still mad with me.

"Why don't you keep it a surprise for Rita?" I suggested.

"Eh?" he asked, sounding slightly baffled.

"Don't say anything about it. Just pack a bag for her and don't tell her where we're going."

"Don't tell her?" he asked, dumbfounded.

I tried to picture Daddy packing his own bag and then having to pack one for Rita and I knew it was a terrible idea. He most likely didn't know which drawer his own underwear was kept in, let alone Rita's.

"Actually, it probably wouldn't work. You'd be better off telling her beforehand," I replied quickly.

I could hear him breathe a sigh of relief on the other end of the phone. Me and my big mouth! Why did I always have to complicate matters?

"Well, get back to me and confirm those dates. Bye, bye."

Then

When I lie on my bed and gaze into the shadows of the chestnut tree I can see my mother's face. It's the only time I can remember what she looks like. If I try to imagine her face when I'm anywhere else, I can't do it. It's as if she only exists in the shadows of the tree. I carry her photo in my wallet so I can always keep her with me, but it makes me scared that I can't picture her when I'm away from my bedroom. I can see Gary in the shadows as well. I kiss him before I go to sleep at night.

We have been together for a year and a half. The longest that anyone in my class has ever gone out with a boy. Rita and Daddy are not a bit happy, but there's nothing they can do about it. Gary has a job now and earns his own money. I will be sixteen on my next birthday and Gary is almost eighteen. We don't have enough money saved to run away yet, but we plan on doing it just as soon as we can.

Daddy has threatened to send me away to boarding school if I don't improve on my grades at school. I failed maths and geography in my Inter Cert and he went completely bonkers. I hate school. Why should I waste my time studying things that I'm never going to use again? I want to be a dress designer or a hairdresser and I certainly won't need science or biology to do either. Lainey got A's in practically every subject, which made it even worse for me.

"Look at how well Lainey did," Rita shrieked, over and over again, the day we got our results.

"Well, I'm not as clever as she is," I tried to explain.

"Nonsense!" Daddy roared. "She put in the effort and you didn't. It's as simple as that."

"Running around with that tearaway, that's what distracted you," Rita said, delighted to get a swipe in at Gary.

"You can tell that damn Romeo that you won't be seeing him any more," Daddy said, wagging his finger at me. "It's boarding school for you, young lady, if you don't pull up your socks."

Typical. When I wanted to go to boarding school, he wouldn't send me. Now, I'd kill myself if they sent me away.

Lainey has turned into the greatest square ever – she does nothing but swot all the time. I told her about Gary wanting to go all the way and I'm so sorry I did. I thought that she'd be a good person to talk to about it, but she was horrified that I'd even consider doing such a thing. It was thick of me to think she'd ever understand how I feel, because she's never been in love. But I'm still sorry I told her. She made me feel like such a slut. Lainey's never actually said anything, but I can tell that she doesn't like Gary very much.

Our school isn't a convent any more. It changed over to a community school and the younger classes have boys in them. Claire has boys in her class but she doesn't speak to any of them. She says they're all retards. The head nun has been replaced by a headmaster and he hasn't a clue what's going on half the time. There are millions more kids in the school and they've built on a whole new block of classrooms. Daddy isn't happy at all. He thinks it's far too big.

It's really easy to bunk off. If I go in for the first class and sign the resister it means that I can take the rest of the day off and no one seems to notice. Gary gets a half-day on Wednesdays and we go to his house because his Mum and Dad are out at work.

We smoke cigarettes and lie on his bed and talk about what we'll do when we get our own flat. We kiss for hours on end. Gary wants to go all the way, but I'm too scared that I'll get pregnant. I've promised that when we go to London, I'll go on the pill and we'll be able to do it as much as we like. Sometimes Gary gets into a sulk about it, but mostly he's sweet and understanding. I live for Wednesday afternoons.

The Kilroys' house is a lot different than mine. It's really small and he has to share a bedroom with his two younger brothers. They only have three rooms downstairs and all three would fit into our kitchen. Their furniture is really old and the sofa in their telly room is full of holes. I suppose they're quite poor, but it doesn't bother me. Rita says that if I married Gary I'd be really unhappy because we wouldn't be able to afford a nice house or a car, but I think if you love someone, none of that matters. Mrs Kilroy is a cleaning lady, and when we were young, she used to clean our house. Rita is mortified about that. I heard her on the phone to her fat friend, Carmel.

"Maureen Kilroy's boy. Yes, her. I know. I can't believe it either. Sometimes I think she does these things on purpose."

Oh, yes, Rita, I felt like saying, but I couldn't, because I wasn't meant to be eavesdropping. I'm only going out with

Gary to get at you. Honestly, sometimes I think she's totally thick.

Claire knows that I bunk off, but I've told her that if she opens her mouth I'll never let her borrow my clogs or use my sparkly nail varnish again.

Apart from Wednesdays, I have to sneak out at weekends to see Gary because Daddy thinks that I broke it off with him. After my Inter Cert results, he was really serious about sending me to boarding school. He'd been on to schools down in the bog asking whether they had a place for me. I begged him to give me another chance and told him that it was all off with Gary. It's easier to let them think that, otherwise they'll just blame him for every little thing I do wrong. It's such a pain, because he can't ring the house. We have a code that we sometimes use in an emergency. Gary rings the phone twice and then hangs up. I wait until the coast is clear and then ring him and pretend I'm on to Lainey. I have to be careful though, because I've caught Rita hovering around the hall, listening to my conversation. She knows that I'm still seeing him, but I think she's turning a blind eye. There are some days I think I'll just die if I don't see Gary. All I do is think about him when I'm not with him.

Last night I almost died. I woke up in the middle of the night to find Gary tapping on my bedroom window. He had climbed the chestnut tree and swung himself over on to the porch roof that's just below my bedroom window. My curtains were open and I thought I was dreaming, until he started tapping at the window again. I jumped up and pushed the window open, almost knocking him backwards. He climbed into the room and kissed me.

"Gary," I whispered, "what are you doing?"

"I wanted to see you." He stood there in the darkness and I could feel my heart pounding.

"If Daddy finds you here, he'll kill us."

Gary kissed me and I forgot about the danger I was in and wrapped my arms tightly around him.

"Lizzy, I can't get used to seeing you once a week. We'll have to get out of this place."

"I know." My heart felt like it was about to explode from wanting him.

We stayed by the window in case someone heard us and he had to make a run for it. "Are they the shadows you told me about?" he asked, looking over at the wall.

"Yes," I whispered, feeling a bit stupid. The shadows on the wall looked just like any other ordinary shadows a tree would cast.

"Show me where I am in them," he said, pulling me closer to him.

"No," I whispered urgently. "It takes ages. You have to lie back and concentrate."

He pulled me towards my bed. "C'mon then. Let's lie down and look at them."

The hair at the back of my neck felt clammy. The thrill of seeing him was quickly wearing off and I was filled with dread of what would happen if we were caught. Daddy would probably call the police.

"Gary, you have to go," I pleaded. "My life won't be worth living if we're caught."

He pulled me closer and we kissed again.

"I love you, Lizzy. I can't live without you."

Outside in the hall, a floorboard creaked and we jumped away from each other.

"You better go," I said in a strangled voice. "I love you too, but you have to get out." Gary began to climb out the window but stopped when he was halfway out. "Lizzy?"

"What?" I said, looking over at the door, waiting for it to burst open.

"Promise that you'll definitely come to London with me as soon as we can afford it?"

"I promise, Gary. Now go, please."

He disappeared out the window and I hopped back into bed and closed my eyes, but no one came in. After a few minutes my heart stopped pounding and I lay there basking in the aftermath of the few precious moments we'd had together. I turned over and closed my eyes and imagined that he was still beside me, holding me in his arms.

Now

A letter arrived from the Health Board this morning and I almost broke a knuckle in my haste to open it. It contained a brief note to say that Val would be making her second home visit to us on Sat 12th Dec. I immediately began to make plans on how to cosy up the house and make it look warm and Christmassy and a potential haven for our future child. My mind raced ahead as I thought of how I would put the Christmas tree up early and get Richard to fetch the outdoor lights from the attic and put them on the bay trees at the front door. I'd get some cinnamon-scented candles, and, oh yes, buy a Christmas CD so I could have Bing crooning in the background while I talked about what brilliant parents we are going to be. There was something about the date that bothered me but I couldn't think of anything that might be happening. It was only later in the day, when I was sitting at my desk flicking through my diary, that I remembered Saturday 12th December was Rita's birthday. We were going away for the weekend. I flew into a mad panic trying to decide who could be put off most easily. Daddy would be devastated if we told him we couldn't go. I can't remember the last time I saw him get so worked up about anything. He'd already called me about five times over the silliest things about his plans for the weekend. Only yesterday he'd phoned me to ask what time he'd book the restaurant for dinner on the Saturday night, and whether we should bring a birthday cake or order one from the hotel kitchen. I could just imagine his disappointment if I called him to tell him that we couldn't make it. On the other hand, would it look bad if I was to put off the social worker's house visit? Would it make us look like we were too busy to put aside a Saturday in our hectic lives to discuss getting a baby? I had phoned Richard several times, and with each conversation he became more useless.

"I really don't know what we should do," was his first reply.

His second was even worse. "I'll have a think about it and call you back." Which, of course, he never did.

My third attempt to discuss it with him ended with me losing my temper.

"It's up to you, Liz. Whatever you want to do," he said in his best non-committal tone.

"No, Richard!" I shrieked. "This is not up to me. It's up to *us* to decide what's best to do!"

So after chewing my fingernails for the entire morning I decided, without consulting Richard, to ring Val and explain the situation. Besides, I had come to the conclusion that it would look good. Wasn't this all about family and how important it is to us?

My decision paid off.

"Oh, that's no problem," Val said casually when I phoned her.

"It's just that Daddy has put so much time and effort into the weekend and it would break his heart if we were to let him down," I gushed.

"I believe the Lakefalls is beautiful. Lucky you! Enjoy it."

"You know, we're free any other weekend besides the 12th," I said, hoping that she wasn't going to put us to the end of some list and make us wait until next year to do her visit.

"Well," she said slowly, "let me just look at my diary and see what I can do."

I heard the sound of pages turning.

"I can do it the following weekend. That's Saturday the 19th, if it's not too close to Christmas for you?"

"No! Not at all, that's perfect."

"Okay, I'll send out a letter confirming a time and I'll see you then."

"Thank you so much, Val."

"No problem, enjoy your weekend."

I put the phone down, chuffed with myself. That meant she'd be visiting us on Christmas week. I made a note in my diary to call Lainey and ask her for some advice on how to decorate the house tastefully. If left to my own devices, I would probably end up going overboard and have the place looking like Santa's Grotto.

I decided to pop into Lainey's on the way home from the

office. I knew Peter was away and Richard had called me earlier in the day to say that he wouldn't be home in time for dinner. Alannah spotted me from the kitchen window and ran down the hall to answer the door. I had only put one foot inside the door when she took my hand and pulled me towards the kitchen, ranting and raving about the new dog they were getting.

"It looks just like Trixie, and we're getting a pink collar for her," she gushed excitedly.

In the kitchen, Lainey stood at the table coaxing Jenny to finish up the remaining vegetables on her plate. She turned and smiled at me, then wagged a finger at Alannah.

"Didn't I say that there's to be no more talk about the dog! We haven't made a decision about it yet."

Alannah immediately put her hand up to her mouth. "Sorry, Mummy," she said. "But it's only Liz, and she won't tell anyone. Sure you won't?" she pleaded.

"Of course not," I reassured her. I looked across at Lainey and she rolled her eyes up to heaven.

"Run along, girls, and let me have a few minutes with Liz," she said, removing the dinner plates from the kitchen table.

They both took off down the hall, their whispers punctuated with giggles as they ran into the den.

Lainey gave me a look of exasperation. "I'm going to kill Peter."

"Why?"

"Some guy he works with has a wife that breeds West Highland Terriers, and he's only gone and promised the girls that they can have one."

I tried to keep a straight face. "Well, I believe they *are* the latest fashion accessory at the moment."

Lainey looked at me scornfully. "Zip it, smarty pants! I don't think cleaning up pee and poo for the next six months is going to be very fashionable."

Poor Lainey, she looked as if her whole world had been turned upside down.

"The girls seem very excited," I said, trying to find an upside. "And they say that it's very good for a child's development when there's a pet in the house. Especially a dog." I couldn't actually remember where I'd heard this, but it sounded good.

"Yes, yes, I know," Lainey said, as if she'd heard it all a thousand times. "It's just that I've never liked dogs very much."

"But what about Trixie?" Mrs Whyte's Westie was loved by everyone, especially Lainey's girls.

"Trixie is fine because he lives at my mum's house. I've never said it to the girls, but I don't really like Trixie very much. He smells, and I hate when Mum asks me to mind him. I really am pissed off with Peter for walking me into this."

It was so unusual to hear Lainey giving out about Peter and using bad language into the bargain! It was wrong of course to promise the kiddies a dog without talking about it first, but it was just about the first time I'd heard of Peter putting a foot out of place.

"Well, he probably decided that there was no point talking to you, given the way you feel about the creatures."

"He could have tried," she replied.

"Oh, you know what a softie Peter is. He probably saw the little pups and got carried away when he thought of how the girls would love one."

Lainey became more animated on hearing this. "Yes,

that's exactly what happened. He had to collect something at the dog breeder's house." She said this as if the dog breeder was some kind of criminal. "The girls happened to be with him and they saw the pups and –"

"Well, there you go!" I said, throwing my hands in the air. "He didn't exactly go and order a puppy without telling you. It was a spur of the moment thing. They saw the little puppies, and what with Trixie being a Westie too. Come on, Lainey! You above anyone else should know how Peter is. He probably just couldn't say no to the girls."

Lainey mulled over my words for a few seconds and her face softened slightly. "I suppose you're right."

"It's only a dog. You'll probably end up loving it," I said hopefully.

"Yeah, right!" she replied.

"Think of all the exercise you'll get walking it every day. And you can dress it in one of those Burberry doggie jackets."

Lainey smiled over at me. "Well done for fighting Peter Chambers' corner. I must tell him that he owes you one."

"Well, think about it. When was the last time he did anything out of order?"

Lainey pursed her lips and looked like she was having difficulty calling anything to mind.

"See!" I said. "You can't even think of one thing. Give the guy a break."

"You've no idea the fights we've had over this mutt," she said, walking over to the cooker. "But you're right. It's only a bloody dog. It's not the end of the world."

She opened the oven door and the smell of something delicious filled the kitchen.

"Will you stay and have some stuffed mushrooms? I can't seem to get the hang of cooking for just one person. I've made far too many."

"Perfect," I said, accepting her invitation. "Richard is out for the evening and it sounds more appetising than a toasted cheese sandwich."

It had been almost a month since Peter's party but we had only seen each other once or twice, so there was still plenty of post-mortem gossip to cover. Lainey told me about her neighbour, a separated woman who had made a play for the husband of another woman who lived around the corner. Peter had ended up pulling the two of them apart after we'd left.

I laughed at the thought of Peter trying to referee a punch-up with two mad women.

"I'm sorry I missed that," I said. "But I'd had enough, and Tom and Brenda were leaving so I had to go with them."

Lainey's laughter evaporated, and her mouth tightened. "It's a pity that Richard had to miss the party. Claire should have called a taxi if she wanted to leave."

"I know," I said, trying to explain what happened. "But Richard had been up since the crack of dawn and he was exhausted anyway. And Claire seemed to be in such a state that I couldn't let her go home on her own."

Lainey didn't say anything.

"Richard didn't mind," I added.

Her silence made me feel I had to justify the matter further.

"I'd already had too much to drink. I couldn't have driven her myself, and Richard really didn't mind."

Lainey's forehead wrinkled into a tense frown.

"What?"

"It was selfish of Claire," she said quietly.

"She wasn't well."

"Then she shouldn't have come and ruined your night."

"She didn't ruin my night," I protested.

"Stop making excuses for her!" Lainey snapped. "Richard is your husband and he should have been at the party having a good time with you, not ferrying your sister around the place."

I was taken aback at her annoyance. We had only talked briefly about what had happened to Claire at the party, and Lainey hadn't seemed too bothered about it. At least that's what I had thought, but I was obviously mistaken

"Are you annoyed about Richard leaving early?" I asked, suddenly realising that it may have appeared really rude of him.

"It's not that," Lainey said, twisting her hands around each other as if searching for the right words to say. "You get little enough time to spend together and he should have been here. It was wrong of Claire to ask him to take her home."

I quickly jumped to her defence. "Claire didn't ask Richard to take her home. I did."

Lainey looked at me with large disbelieving eyes. "Liz! For heaven's sake!"

"What?"

Our empty plates lay before us. Lainey stood up and began to clear them away. I felt my face redden, even though she was standing at the sink with her back to me, I could sense her anger, yet had no idea what I had done to upset her.

"What?" I asked again.

Lainey put the plates down and leaned forwards with her

hands on the edge of the sink, and for a minute I thought she was going to cry.

"Look, I apologise for Richard leaving the party. It was my fault, I didn't think of how rude it would look. I should have taken Claire home myself."

Lainey spun around and glared at me. "Liz, shut up! It's not you I'm annoyed with. It's Claire. I mean, why the hell should *anyone* have taken her home?"

"She wasn't —"

Lainey put her hand up. "Stop it!" she snapped. "I don't want to hear you make any more excuses for her."

"I'm not making excuses for her," I answered indignantly.

"Yes, you are." Lainey said, staring down at the floor. "And it's time you stopped."

I could feel my heart pounding at this unexpected dressing-down I was being subjected to. "Lainey, you know what Claire is like."

Lainey kept her eyes on the floor and chewed her lower lip.

"She needs minding," I concluded.

Lainey looked over and gave me a weak smile. "Everyone does, even you."

I smiled back, relieved to see her softer side emerge.

"I mean it, Liz," she continued. "I think it's time you stood back and looked at Claire in a different light. She's far tougher than you think she is — you've just never stopped mothering her for long enough to see it."

Mother. The very word still touches something deep inside me, like a forgotten bruise, and presses down hard until it starts to hurt again.

"Old habits," I said quietly.

Lainey came over from the sink and sat back down beside me. "You have to start putting yourself first, Liz — because that's what Claire does. That's what everyone does. You have to start looking out for yourself."

"What do you mean?" I had no idea what she was trying to say.

Lainey drew a breath, as if deciding whether to continue or not. "You get so caught up in Claire's life, and you seem to think that she's to be pitied all of the time. It's poor Claire this, and poor Claire that. It's bullshit, Liz."

I couldn't believe I was hearing this.

Lainey grabbed my hand and held it firmly. "Claire is a grown woman who can make her own choices in life — and if some of them haven't worked out, well, that's her own fault." She kept a grip of my hand, as if waiting for my reply.

"I know I tend to be a bit protective of her, but it's always been that way. And I do pity her because she seems to be so alone right now."

I didn't get a chance to finish, because she squeezed my hand tightly and jumped in again.

"You see! There you go again, feeling sorry for her! Liz, you've got to stop it, because she's taking advantage of you."

I swallowed loudly. Wasn't that what Richard had said recently?

"Richard said the same thing," I said.

Lainey released her grip on my hand and nodded her head. "You're too good to her, Liz. It's in your nature, and it's something I've always loved about you. But, it makes me mad to see someone constantly take it for granted."

I suddenly saw myself the way others might. Was it me, and not Claire, that everyone pitied? But I was the capable one. Always on hand to pick up the pieces of my oddball family. Perhaps I was the only one who thought of me in that way. It was strange to hear Lainey talk about Claire putting herself first and taking advantage of me, when she knew, more than anyone else in the world, what Claire was really like. It was as if she was trying to tell me that she knew Claire better than I did.

"In her defence," I said quickly, before Lainey could interrupt me, "she wanted to get a taxi home the night of the party, but I wouldn't hear of it. I asked Richard to bring her home because he'd just arrived and hadn't had anything to drink."

Lainey stayed quiet and listened.

"I'm sorry if you and Peter were insulted about him leaving. I never thought about how it would look."

Lainey gave a loud sigh. "Liz, I told you, this is not about the party. And we weren't insulted about Richard leaving."

"It was rude," I continued, "especially after all the effort you'd put into the night. You and Peter are our closest friends and Richard should have been here."

That wasn't really true. We both knew that Richard and Peter were only friends because they had to be. Friends by association, not by choice.

Lainey got up to make some coffee and we both said nothing as the noise of the boiling kettle filled the room.

When she set the cups on the table, Lainey looked down at me. Her face looked strained, as if she hadn't had enough sleep. "I don't want you to be mad with me for saying those things about Claire."

267

"I'm not," I said, trying to hide the fact that I was.

"I feel that I'm close enough to you to point it out."

"Yes, I know."

We drank our coffee and Alannah and Jenny came in to show us the picture of the dog they had drawn. I tried to suppress a grin as Lainey said things like, "We're not definitely getting it," and "The lady might change her mind and want to keep it". But the girls jumped up and down screaming, "We *are* getting it! Daddy said we are!"

Just before I left, I remembered to ask Lainey about the reference. I had meant to ask Val about it on the phone, but it had slipped my mind.

"Did you get the reference done yet?"

Lainey took my coat from the cloakroom and seemed to get flustered. "Shit," she muttered. "Sorry, Liz. It's just that we've been so busy lately. Neither of us have had a chance to sit down and do it."

"Lainey," I said, "it's been over two months since they sent the form to you. What can be so difficult about filling in a few details?"

"It's not just a few details," she said. "It's quite an in-depth questionnaire. It requires the two of us sitting down for an evening and wording it correctly."

"No, it doesn't," I argued. "Brenda and Tom completed it and returned it within a week." Christ! Lainey had to do everything with bells on. "It's only a bloody reference. Now will both of you get a move on and do it!"

"I'll sit on Peter this weekend and make sure he finds the time."

It was so out of character for Lainey. If she was five minutes late for a coffee morning she sent a note of apology! She was almost two months behind in getting this reference done, yet she brushed it off as if it were nothing.

After three aborted attempts, due to foul weather, we finally shot our presentation at the polocrosse grounds. The skies cleared and turned a crisp winter blue as we worked flat out to get the right shots. We saw the finished tape yesterday and everyone agrees that it will be a sure winner when we make our presentation to Browne's next week. Matt has been very detached and quiet about the project lately. Perhaps he (quite rightly) sees it as my baby and has decided to take a back seat. I thought I'd like Matt more than I do, but I feel slightly disappointed with him. His Mr Nice Guy image is exactly that, just an image. The more I get to know him the more I distrust him. I can't help feeling that lurking behind that suave façade is a sneaky little git. It's always a dangerous thing, when good looks belie a bad character. Susie has chosen to see nothing but his good traits and has all but thrown herself at him. She now arrives into work every day wearing another creation from the new wardrobe of clothes she has purchased since Matt's arrival. No more saggy-bottomed jeans and gone-grey-in-the-wash shirts. Our Susie now struts into the office wearing sharp tailored Armani trousers and the tightest Lycra tops that reveal her many acres of cleavage. The usually frizzy hair is now coiffed into sleek glossy curls that tumble down around her shoulders in a sex-kittenish way. She's also developed a most annoying habit of twirling these curls around her fingers during meetings, especially when Matt happens to be sitting opposite her. The other day I caught her sucking the end of a pencil in a most provocative way and couldn't help but notice that Matt was staring right over at her, grinning, like a wolf about to pounce on its prey. I have to keep my negative thoughts about Matt to myself as Susie seems to be so completely smitten with him. Although how she could be is beyond me! He's only short of slapping some of the female staff on the bottom as he swaggers past them. And what's more annoying is that his unashamed vanity seems to be totally acceptable to all the ladies, encouraged with longing glances and misty-eyed smiles. Personally, it makes me want to puke. The other day I heard him call Susie "babe". Funny, he hasn't dared try any of his old-fashioned charm on me. I waited to see what her reaction would be but Susie stood there batting her eyelids at the endearment. Call me a prude, but isn't there something kind of smarmy about a man who refers to his female work colleague as "babe"?

What amazes me about Susie is that if any other guy in the office attempted to call her "babe", even as a joke, I think she'd flatten him. But Matt is different – she's fallen completely under his spell.

"How can you let him call you that?" I asked rather tetchily the other day. Matt had left the office after a meeting saying "See ya, babe" – to Susie, of course.

Susie smiled and twisted a curl around her index finger. "Jealous?" she asked, raising an eyebrow.

I forced myself to share the humour and managed a weak smile. "No. I'm all sorted in that department. But I have to say I shudder when I hear him calling you *babe*."

Susie gave a throaty laugh. "It's been eighteen months since I've had sex! Believe me, I'll answer to anything."

"Susie," I hissed, gesturing to her to keep her voice down as my door was still open.

She laughed again, her eyes sparkling with happiness.

"Do you really like him?" I asked.

She got up and went to the door and closed it gently. Then leaning against it she gave a dreamy sigh and grinned at me. "Not a word, all right?" she said firmly.

I nodded, waiting for her to fill me in.

She took another deep breath and the buttons on her very tight blouse looked like they were about to pop. "He's asked me out," she gasped.

"Oh," was all I could think of to say.

"Well, don't get too excited for me," she exclaimed. "He's only the most gorgeous hunk on the planet and he's asked *me* out."

"I am excited for you, Susie," I said, trying to sound convincing.

"No, you're not," she quite rightly observed. "You don't like him, do you?"

"I do. I do like him," I blurted. "I still have to get to know him – he hasn't been here long enough for me to form any kind of an opinion." I was talking too fast, always a dead giveaway that I'm trying to dig my way out of a hole.

Susie eyes narrowed. "Trust me, he's delightful, and he's all mine!" she shrieked, punching the air with her fists. "I feel like the luckiest woman alive."

"He's the lucky one, Susie," I said, trying to make up for my earlier despondency. "Look at you. You look fabulous lately. You could have any man you wanted."

Susie's head fell to one side. "Really?" she said, putting a finger to her chin. "Then I wonder why they aren't lining

271

up on the street outside. Or jamming up my phone line with messages."

I smiled at her playful sarcasm.

"Come off it, Liz!" she roared. "I'm thirty-five years old. I was one step away from joining a nunnery till Matt came along."

"Well, I'm very glad he did because you would have made a terrible nun."

She left the door and came over to my desk and perched on the edge of it. "Now," she said in a very business-like tone, "what would you think of some Botox?"

"Me?" I squeaked.

"Not for you," she said, rolling her eyes up to heaven. "For me!"

She ran a finger along her forehead. "See here? All the lines that have appeared lately due to me getting stressed about never getting laid again. Do you think I should get them zapped?"

"Susie!" I exclaimed. "Surely you wouldn't consider it."

She threw me a scornful look. "Of course I would. I'm trying to bag a man here, Liz. A man who usually dates twenty-year-old models. I need as much help as I can get."

I gave a prissy little sniff. "Well, don't you think that injecting yourself with botulism is going a bit too far?"

"No," she replied.

"Susie, you look great just the way you are. I don't see any lines on your face. You have beautiful skin. Anyway, can't you end up disfigured from getting that stuff?"

She gave a snort and looked at me in dismay. "Liz, would you ever get real! Half the women in this business are

Botoxed up to their eyeballs. It's no big deal. You make it sound like open heart surgery."

"No, they're not," I said dismissively.

"Yes, they are," she insisted. "I know for a fact that Barbara in accounts and Joan in reception have had it done."

"No!" I gasped.

Susie threw her head back and laughed at the look of horror that spread across my face. "Anyway, back to me," she continued. "I was thinking of a few shots across my forehead and maybe some collagen injections in my lips."

"Ugh!" I said, recoiling in my chair.

Susie stood up and threw her hands in the air. "Oh, forget it!" she said in exasperation. "I'm wasting my time here."

"I'm afraid so. I think you're lovely the way you are, and if it isn't good enough for Mr L'Estrange, then he's certainly not worth wasting your time over."

Susie walked towards the door and looked back over her shoulder. "Yeah, yeah," she said sarcastically. "I'll keep slapping on the Pond's cold cream in the hope that I'll wake up some morning looking ten years younger."

I couldn't help feeling a sense of disappointment as she left the room. I liked Susie and I didn't want to see her ending up with a creep – she deserved so much better. Not that Matt was a creep. Like I'd said to her, I'd hardly had time to get to know him, but there was something about him I hadn't warmed to. I felt mean, hoping that their date would go badly, but Susie needed to meet a nice guy and I doubt that she was going to find that in Matt. Besides, if Brian found out that there was a romance about to take off, he'd hit the roof. The only person allowed to have affairs in our office was him.

Then

I am halfway through fifth year and have failed four subjects in my Christmas exams. My year head, Mrs Talbot, called Daddy in for a chat and I am in deep shit. Not only did she tell him how badly I had done in all of my exams, she also showed him my attendance records for the year, along with all of the sick notes which have his signature forged on them. I have never seen him so angry before. I sat beside him while Mrs Talbot went through each and every sick note, asking Daddy whether he had signed them or not. Daddy leaned across the desk and fumbled through the bundle of notes, his face getting paler with each one. I have become so good at forging his signature that there were one or two notes where he wasn't quite sure whether he had signed them or not. After a while, Mrs Talbot turned to me and told me to sit outside in the corridor while both of them had a word in private. I sat outside and prayed like I've never prayed before. Please God, don't let him send me to boarding school. I'd seen a leaflet lying around his study for a boarding school in Kerry. It looks like a cross between a mental institute and a prison camp. There are bars on the windows – I suppose they're needed to stop the boarders from jumping to their deaths.

They came out of the office and Daddy glowered over at me. I jumped up off my chair and stood to attention.

"Get your things," he barked. "You're coming home."

Mrs Talbot was cowering behind him and glanced over at me pityingly.

I grabbed my things from the locker room and joined him out in the car. We drove away from the school without saying anything but after a few minutes he broke the awful silence.

"What are you doing?" he asked. He didn't sound cross any more, just hurt.

"Nothing," I mumbled.

He pulled over to the side of the road and turned around to look at me.

"Lizzy," he said, "why are you doing this?"

What a stupid question. How was I meant to answer that? I don't know why I do half the things I do. I sat there and blinked nervously.

"Are you unhappy?" he asked.

Oh God. What was I supposed to say? Of course I'm unhappy. I want to run away to London with Gary but I'm scared to do it before I do my Leaving Cert because you'd have the police out looking for me. I could hardly tell him that, not after what he'd just heard from Mrs Talbot. I was in enough trouble already, so I shrugged my shoulders and said nothing.

Daddy ran his hand across his forehead and looked out the window. I felt a dull sickening feeling in the pit of my stomach.

"This is not normal behaviour for a young lady," he said quietly. "Something is making you pull against me and I need to know what it is."

I pursed my lips and stared down at my shoes.

"We try our best Lizzy, Rita and I." He gulped loudly and my heart began to beat loudly as I saw tears glisten in his eyes.

"I know," I said quickly, and tried to think of anything else I could say that would stop him getting upset. "I'll never do it again."

He looked at me, the way I imagine he looks at the criminals in his courtroom before handing down a long sentence. "You're throwing your life away. I know that you're still running around with that boy from the cottages."

Gary! His name is Gary.

"Have you ever stopped to think of what would happen if you ended up with him?"

"Yes," I said bravely.

Daddy breathed sharply through his nose. "I don't think you have, Lizzy, because if you really thought about it, you wouldn't be with him."

I stared straight ahead and waited for him to continue.

"He works as a labourer, is that right?"

Yes, m'lord, I wanted to say. But I just nodded.

"How much does he earn a week?"

"I don't know," I said, my voice rising just a little with annoyance. I didn't go around counting out his wage packet.

"Very little, would be my guess," said Daddy.

I stared over at him, confused at where this conversation was leading. Part of me was delighted, relieved almost, that Daddy was finally accepting the fact that I was still with Gary.

"Lizzy, you're getting to an age where you have to make your own choices in life and believe me it's very easy to make the wrong ones."

Splats of rain began to hit the windscreen and Daddy turned on the wipers.

"You'll be what? Seventeen? Next birthday."

"Yes." Daddy was never sure of our ages.

"You've got to think ahead, Lizzy, and decide what kind of a life you want. Do you want to live in a nice house and have the money to do the things you want?"

"Yes," I answered.

"Would you like to have children some day and be able to give them all the things that you had?"

I nodded sullenly as I realised where this conversation was taking us.

Daddy shifted in his seat so he was looking directly at me. "If you stay with this lad, you'll never have anything."

I felt a lump form in my throat. How could he speak so callously about Gary? As if how much he earned could have anything to do with the way I felt about him.

"You may think I'm being cruel, but I am only being realistic."

My heart felt heavy with all the things I wanted to say. This was my chance to try to get Daddy to understand how serious we were about each other.

"I want to go to London with him when I finish school."

As soon as the words had left my mouth I was sorry. Within seconds, his whole expression had changed. He sank back into his seat and his face crumpled in despair.

"Lizzy, that's impossible," he said quietly.

Tears began to sting my eyes. "But, Daddy," I whined, "we've been planning this for a year. Gary's got a job on his uncle's building site – he could have gone already, but he's waiting until I finish school."

Daddy turned his head slowly and looked at me wide-eyed. "It's out of the question. Lizzy. Have you lost your mind?" he said with sharp impatience. "Run off to London with some builder's labourer! Have you gone completely mad?"

I shouldn't have told him. Big tears ran down my cheeks as I thought of the consequences. Gary would be so mad with me for ruining everything.

Daddy shook his head crossly, oblivious to my tears. "Where did you propose to live when you got to London?"

"We'd get a flat," I sniffed.

"A cold-water flat in Kilburn is about all you could afford and I doubt very much that you'd be happy there, Lizzy. Did this fellow ever have any plans to marry you or were you just going to shack up together?" His voice has getting sharper as he thought about it.

"I could get a job," I said weakly in my defence.

"Haa!" he said loudly. "And what kind of job do you think you might get? If you continue the way you are going, you won't even have a Leaving Certificate when you finish school. I don't think there are many jobs out there for girls with no qualifications, unless you want to clean houses for a living."

I gave him a hateful stare. This of course was a dig at Gary's mum. I wanted to tell him what a horrible snob I thought he was but it wasn't the right time.

He took a deep breath and put his hands on the wheel. "It's only fair to let you know that we are looking into other schools at the moment. It will break my heart to send you away, Lizzy, but if that's what it takes to get you to knuckle down, then so be it."

He waited for my reaction but I bit down on my lip and said nothing. I'd just run away some night – and there was nothing he could do to stop me.

He turned the key and the engine started up. "Meanwhile, if I hear that that lad has been next or near you – I'll knock his block off."

I want to kill myself.

Everything about my life is crap at the moment.

I have only seen Gary once in the past two weeks. I told him about Dad being called up to the school and all the horrible things he'd said. Well, I didn't tell him everything. I was too ashamed to repeat what he'd said about me ending up cleaning houses. Gary thinks that Dad is a prick and he wants me to come to London now. He's sick of waiting around. His own Dad is not paying him enough – he could earn twice as much in London. Last Saturday night, I pretended that I was baby-sitting and met Gary in the pub to talk about what we were going to do. Gary was grumpy and smoked one cigarette after another, squashing the butts on top of each other in the ashtray. Things aren't the same any more. All we seem to have to talk about these days are our problems and Gary is always in bad humour. I sat at the back of the pub and jumped every time the door opened in case it was a friend of Rita's that might tell her they'd seen me.

"For fuck's sake, will you relax," Gary said, setting our drinks down on the table.

"I can't! I'm afraid someone will see us."

He stared down into his pint and frowned. "This is shit, Liz. Let's just go to London now. There's nothing here for me."

I wanted nothing else, but I knew I wouldn't have the nerve when it came to it. "Gary, it's only another year. Then I'll be finished school and we can go."

He chewed his thumbnail and said nothing.

I put my arm through his and moved my stool a little closer to him. We finished our drinks without saying very much. I felt so angry and frustrated with Daddy for being so unreasonable. What was wrong with being with somebody you loved? Why didn't anyone understand? After our third drink Gary snapped out of his humour and cheered up a bit. At closing time he went up to the bar and bought a half bottle of vodka.

"Mam and Dad are away for the night. Will you come back for a while?"

I looked at my watch. It was eleven o'clock. I usually came back from baby-sitting at about half past twelve. That is, when I was really baby-sitting. I figured it would be safe to go back to Gary's for an hour.

We walked along the road to his house wrapped around each other. I felt better that his spirits had lifted as I was feeling so guilty at being the cause of all his misery.

We stopped and kissed and I felt that there was nowhere else in the world I wanted to be, but with him.

"Gary," I whispered into his ear, "I'm so sorry for ruining everything."

He took my face in his hands and kissed me. "It's all right, Liz. I don't want to go without you. I'll wait. It'll be fine."

His house was in darkness which felt weird. The Kilroys' house was usually full of people. Gary turned on the hall light and I took my coat off.

"Where is everyone?" I asked.

He grinned at me. "Free house for the weekend."

"You never told me."

"What was the point?" he said scornfully. "You can only manage to sneak out for a couple of hours a week."

I felt my heart sink again at the reminder of my house arrest. "I know. I'm sorry."

Gary stepped over to me and we kissed again. "Let's go upstairs," he said.

We lay on his bed and drank the vodka with some flat coke he had found downstairs.

"I want to stay here forever," I said, resting my head on his chest.

He moved his hand under my shirt and his touch sent a shiver through my body.

We kissed slowly, and I could feel every nerve in my body tingling as he touched my naked skin. He undressed me, and I lay back and didn't try to stop him. He took off his shirt and the feel of his warm bare skin on top of mine was overwhelming.

"I love you, Gary," I moaned over and over again as I gave myself up to him.

Later on, as I walked towards home, I looked up and saw that Lainey's bedroom light was still on. I stopped outside her house and gathered a handful of pebbles to throw up at her window. I didn't want to go home to bed. What had happened was too big and important and I desperately wanted someone to talk to. Then, I thought of how Lainey would react to my news. The look of horror that would spread across her face as I told her what we'd just done. I let the pebbles fall from my hand and continued towards home. It was the first time in my life that I felt I couldn't talk to her about something and it made me feel sad that we were growing apart.

Now

We decided to meet in our usual spot in Daphne's coffee shop an hour earlier. Saturday Christmas shoppers were out in their droves even though it was only the end of

November. It had been Lainey's idea and I smiled at her forward thinking as I pulled into a parking space right outside the door. Another hour and I'd have to park half a mile away. Inside the cosy shop the tables were decorated with festive candles and the aroma of freshly baked bread was heavenly. Brenda and Lainey were already seated and I made my way over to the table.

"Great idea, Lainey," I said as I sank into a chair. "It's nice and quiet in here."

"I'm full of them," she said with a wave of her hand.

"The calm before the storm," Brenda said with a grimace. "I have to battle my way through every toyshop in town this afternoon to find what the boys want."

"What do they want?" Lainey asked.

"Oh, some warrior game that you can only get by standing in line for hours in a computer shop on the other side of town," Brenda said, rolling her eyes. "What about the girls?"

"They're not too difficult this year. Apart from about a million pink doggie accessories, Alannah wants a doll's house and Jenny wants a bike."

"You're getting a dog?" Brenda squealed excitedly.

Lainey shook her head and began to tell Brenda about the Westie saga. I took up the menu and drifted off with my thoughts. Hearing the two of them talk about Christmas presents for their children had sent a pang of envy through me. How many more Christmases would I have to endure before I could leave a gift under the tree for my own child? I tried to concentrate on the menu and stop myself being dragged under by the sudden wave of depression.

"So we're getting it on Christmas week. Which is

exactly the time of year that parents are not meant to give their children pets, but I'm hoping that we'll be giving it back in January."

Brenda laughed. "Oh Lainey! How will you cope with a little mutt chewing everything in sight? Your beautiful house will be ruined!"

Lainey put her hands up to stop Brenda going any further. "Thank you. I'm well aware of what I'm in for. I just hope that Peter is well prepared for all the shitty mess that will come with the little bugger."

A waitress came to the table to take our order.

"Will we go ahead or wait for Claire?" Brenda asked as she glanced at the menu.

"I didn't get a chance to phone Claire." Lainey turned to the waitress. "A latte and cranberry muffin, please."

"Oh," said Brenda, "should I give her a quick bell now?"

"There's hardly any point now," I said. "By the time she gets over here we'll be finished."

"I did try to call her but there was no answer and it just went out of my head after that," said Lainey.

"Poor Claire," said Brenda. "She never seems to have any free time these days – her work just takes over. I haven't seen her in ages."

"Mmh," said Lainey, sounding unconvinced.

"Well, I'll give her a ring later on," said Brenda. "I'm going to have you all over to dinner some night before Christmas."

"Lovely," said Lainey.

"About time," said Brenda. "I've been talking about it for the last six months. In fact we should decide on a night now. Next weekend is out; Tom's mother is coming to stay," she said grimacing. "How about the following weekend?"

"Great," said Lainey.

"Can't," I said. "We're going away for Rita's birthday."

"Really?" said Lainey. "Where are you going?"

"Daddy is taking us down to the Lakeview Falls for the weekend."

"Wow!" Lainey knew how humdrum Daddy and Rita's life was and was understandably surprised to hear of his burst of spontaneity. "Who thought of that?"

"Daddy," I said. "All on his own. He called me up and said that he was booking it for the five of us."

"I'd love to go down there," said Brenda. "I've heard it's out of this world."

"The five of you?" Lainey asked, sounding surprised.

"Yes, Richard's coming too."

"And Claire?"

"Well, I haven't spoken to her about it, but Daddy tells me she is coming."

"Why wouldn't Claire go down?" asked Brenda.

"Oh, I don't know!" Lainey exclaimed. "I thought she might be too busy with Christmas coming and everything."

Brenda looked puzzled. "Claire doesn't even have to buy a bag of Brussels sprouts at Christmas time. Why would she be too busy?"

"I meant with work," said Lainey tetchily.

"Well," I said, "as far as I'm aware, she's joining us."

Brenda looked from me to Lainey and shook her head. "All right," she said. "That rules out the weekend of the 11th."

She flicked through her diary looking for another suitable date. I glanced over at Lainey and detected a shift in her humour. Her brow was knit into a tight frown and she seemed to want to avoid my gaze. The waitress set a tray on the table and Lainey reached across and began to arrange our cups and plates.

"Okay," said Brenda, waving her teaspoon in the air. "I can do the following weekend, but only on the Friday night. We've got Tom's office party on the Saturday."

"That's sounds good. I'll check with Peter and ring you later."

"Oh, Brenda," I groaned, "sorry to be so awkward, but the day after that we're having another home visit from our social worker, and I don't want to be bleary-eyed for it. Do you mind if we change to another night?"

Brenda exhaled deeply in mock annoyance. "What a little pain in the arse you are, Liz!"

I grinned. "I know, but I believe these visits get more up close and personal as they go along and I just know that I'm going to be uptight the night before."

"It's fine," said Brenda, snapping her diary closed. "Nobody can say I didn't try! We'll just have to leave it till after Christmas. Or, you could invite your social worker to join us for dinner and we'll tell her what you're really like!"

"Thanks," I said. "By the way, Lainey, would you give me a hand to decorate the house before she comes?"

"You're decorating the house for her!" shouted Brenda at the top of her voice.

"I mean Christmas decorations. I always seem to make a mess of it and your house looks so nice every year."

"Of course I will," said Lainey. "I'll come over a few days before and do it – I think I might do Mum's as well while I'm at it. I'm terrified she'll break a leg getting up to the attic for the Christmas decorations."

"Thanks," I said.

"How personal do they get?" asked Lainey.

"Oh God, I think they ask just about anything they want. A woman in our group sessions told me that she was asked how often they had intercourse. And to make matters worse, herself and her husband gave different answers!"

A crumb flew out of Brenda's mouth as she burst out laughing.

Lainey clasped a hand to her chest. "They do not ask you things like that!" she gasped.

"Yes, they do. And worse by all accounts."

"That's scandalous. Poor Liz, no wonder you don't want to go out the night before. It sounds worse than the Spanish Inquisition."

"Oh, to be honest, I'm not going to get myself into knots over it. It has to be done, and I'm just going to get on with it."

"That's the right attitude," said Brenda, leaning across towards me. "Just keep thinking about that baby and consider it part of your labour."

"How does Richard feel about it?" asked Lainey.

"Sure he can boast about what a great sex life the pair of you have," said Brenda with a wink.

Lainey looked over at her and frowned. "How would you know?"

"We can hear them at it every other night. They're like a pair of rabbits."

Lainey tried not to smile but she couldn't help it. I pasted a smile across my face and didn't tell her that it had been almost six weeks since my husband had laid a hand on me. After more coffee and some idle gossip from Brenda about a Charity Queen that had run off with Paddy Stone, the richest man in the country, Lainey looked at her watch and gathered her things together.

"Right, it's time to hit the shops before they fill up."

"I suppose you're right," groaned Brenda. "Isn't it a pity we can't stay here all day? We always seem to be in such a rush."

We said our goodbyes outside Daphne's and just as I was pulling out of my car space I remembered what had been at the back of my mind all morning. I had meant to ask Lainey about the reference.

We had arranged to meet for drinks in the lounge of the Lakeview Falls at seven. The stand-off with Claire had continued and as usual it was left to me to break the ice. There was no point in taking three cars down to Kerry and I knew that Daddy and Rita were leaving first thing Friday morning. Richard had promised to be home at lunch-time and I had taken the day off. I rang Claire the night before to make our peace and offer her a lift. The first few seconds were stilted and clumsy. We spoke at the same time and then waited in silence for the other to continue.

"How have you been?" I asked.

"Not great," she answered quietly.

My heart sank with guilt. I hadn't called her for weeks to let her cool off.

"I'm sorry to hear that. Is the asthma bad?"

"Yes, I've had a few more attacks."

"Why didn't you call me?"

"I didn't want to bother you. I feel bad about the night of the party – I shouldn't have dragged Richard away."

I didn't want to even talk about the night of the party. I'd had enough harsh words from Richard and Lainey.

"Please forget about it," I said. "Will you be all right to come away for the weekend?"

"I've just been on to Rita," said Claire. "I can't go. I'm not feeling up to it. I feel bad for disappointing them but I'm so tired, and the weekends are the only time I get to rest properly."

"What about work?" I asked. "Have you missed much?"

"They've been really good about it. I'm doing a lot from home at the moment."

"Claire, I'm really disappointed too." There I was feeling sorry for her again, but I couldn't help it. My heart went out to her. "I was really looking forward to spending some time together."

"I know," she replied. "So was I."

"I'm sorry for what I said, about you being gay."

An awkward moment passed while Claire cleared her throat.

"It was out of order and I apologise."

"It's okay," Claire said softly.

"Can we meet up when I come back?"

"Sure."

"Rita has invited us for Christmas Day. Will you be going?"

There was a slight pause and I heard her draw a breath. "Yes," she answered. "I will."

Inside our walk-in wardrobe, I reached up and pulled Richard's large suitcase until it tilted down towards me. Usually we brought our own luggage on trips away but we were only going to be away for two nights and this one was big enough to share. I wiped away the film of dust that had settled on top of it and pulled off the airline tag from our trip to Italy which was still tied to the handle. I pulled our clothes from the wardrobe and began to pack, all the time thinking of Claire.

Richard's car came roaring into the driveway at two o'clock.

I stood in the hall tapping my foot on the tiles. "Come on, Richard. It's a five-hour drive, get a move on."

"Ten minutes," he said, bounding up the stairs. "Just give me ten minutes."

Half an hour later, we were on the road. I stared at the fields as we left the city behind and headed south. Richard was never a great talker while he drove, and I took advantage of the few hours of peace. I closed my eyes and tried to clear all thoughts of Claire from my mind for the weekend, but it was impossible.

"Claire's not coming," I said.

Richard hit a knob on the radio and changed the station. "Isn't she?" he asked.

"No," I sighed. "She's not feeling well."

"Really," he remarked while he leaned across the steering wheel to rub a smudge on the windscreen. He clicked open the glove compartment and fumbled around inside it. "Honey, there's a cloth in there somewhere. Will you get it for me?"

I found a cloth and handed it to him and went back to staring out the window.

We arrived at the hotel with just enough time to unpack

and get down to the lounge to meet Daddy and Rita. Daddy sat in a wing-backed chair like lord of the manor, while Rita sat beside him, her cheeks glowing after a glass of sherry. We hugged and kissed each other.

"Thanks for the invitation, Denis," said Richard, shaking Daddy's hand stiffly. "It's a lovely place."

Daddy looked around and smiled. "It's nice all right."

"It's beautiful," I agreed. "Our room is like a palace – we have a balcony overlooking the lake."

Rita's smile was a mile wide. "We have a suite!"

"Wow! How'd you manage that?"

She was positively bursting with excitement. "Your father told them that it was my birthday and they upgraded us."

"Well done, Daddy," I said, smiling over at him.

After a drink in the bar, we went in for dinner but had to wait for a while as Richard made a call to a client in Dubai. I could see that Daddy wasn't impressed but he managed to contain his disapproval.

The following day Daddy and Richard spent the morning waiting for the rain to ease off before they got off for a round of golf. Rita and I had booked ourselves into the health spa for a full day of pampering. I doubt very much that Rita had ever been to a health spa before – she spent most of the time tightening the belt of her robe looking terrified that she might be showing any flesh. At the end of the afternoon we both looked like scarecrows. Our hair was plastered to our heads with essential oils and our faces were bright red after all the potions that had been slapped on them. We reclined on heated loungers in the chill-out room that overlooked the lake.

"This is so relaxing," said Rita with a satisfied sigh.

I kept my head tilted back in order to balance the cooling gel mask that covered my eyes. "Certainly is," I agreed.

"It's such a pity that Claire didn't make it," she said.

"I know," I answered.

"Have you seen much of her lately?"

I could tell by Rita's wary tone that she had noticed there was something wrong between us.

"No," I answered.

She was quiet for a few moments.

"Neither have we."

I wanted to keep it to myself and not spoil Rita's weekend by worrying her, but it seemed that there was no one else to talk to about it. Richard was totally uninterested and Lainey seemed to get pissed off at the mere mention of Claire's name.

"I think she's going through a tough patch at the moment."

I heard Rita shuffle about on her lounger. "What do you mean?"

"Did she tell you her asthma is bad?"

"Yes," said Rita. "She told me she's had a few bouts of it lately."

"It's got quite bad recently – she seems to be suffering from pretty awful attacks. We were at a party recently and she had to leave because of it."

Rita was quiet again. I heard more rustling and guessed that she was tightening her robe again.

"Between you and me . . ." this had always been a favourite opening line with Rita "your father is very hurt that she didn't come down this weekend. Don't mention it, but I thought I'd let you know. He's quite upset about it."

The last thing I felt like doing was making excuses for her, but I didn't like to think of Daddy being upset on his special weekend.

"I really don't think she was up to it. She told me last night that she was working from home at the moment because it's so bad." I took the eye mask off and looked over at Rita.

"I worry about her," she said. "I think she's avoiding us and I can't understand why."

"Yes," I agreed. "I feel the same way. But every time I try to get her to talk she pushes me away again."

Rita's face was screwed up with worry. "Don't tell your father this. But I called over to her twice last week and she didn't answer the door. I know she was in – I could see the lights on and her car was parked outside. She even posted my birthday present this year instead of calling with it."

I felt my stomach lurch with fear. Why had we left her all alone for the weekend when we knew that something was wrong? I tried to hide my concern from Rita.

"I'm going to make it my business to see her first thing next week and sort it out once and for all," I said. "I'll get to the bottom of it, so don't spoil your weekend worrying about it."

We left the chill-out area and I raced back to the room to phone Claire. The hotel was in a valley and none of us had any mobile coverage. What if she'd been trying to reach me? I had a horrible feeling that she might have tried to do something stupid while we were all away. I bit down on my bottom lip and prayed that she'd answer.

"Hello?"

"Claire? Are you all right?"

"Liz? What's wrong?"

I realised that I was shouting. "Nothing," I said, trying to steady my voice. "I'm just calling to see how you are."

"Fine," she said. "What time is it?"

I looked over at the clock. "Almost five."

"Jesus," she muttered, "I must have fallen asleep."

"How are you feeling?"

"I'm fine. Just wrecked, catching up on some sleep. What's the place like?"

She sounded fine. My heart slowed down and I began to feel a bit foolish.

"It's beautiful. We just spent the afternoon in the health spa."

"Lucky you," she said.

"We miss you."

There was a brief silence.

"We'll do it again another time," she said. "Give Rita my love and wish her a happy birthday tonight."

Richard came into the room as I put the phone down.

"Who's that?" he asked as he unzipped his wet rain jacket.

"Reception," I lied. I didn't want anything to ruin what had turned out to be a lovely weekend. We had needed the time together and for the first time in months I felt that Richard had really relaxed and switched off. We'd made love the night before and stayed in bed till eleven that morning. I wasn't in the mood for discussing Claire and I suspected he wasn't either.

When it came to checking out on Sunday morning, Daddy

and Richard almost came to fisticuffs at the hotel reception desk. Earlier that morning Richard had said that he couldn't possibly stick Daddy with such a huge bill. I had noticed that the prices in the restaurant and health spa were sky high and agreed that we should pay our own bill, even though we risked incurring the wrath of my father. While I packed our things, Richard left to settle the bill in reception. Thirty minutes later, he still hadn't come back to the room, so I decided to take the luggage down to the car myself. Passing through reception I was surprised to see that the place had been transformed from an oasis of tranquillity to one of complete mayhem. I could hear Daddy's voice booming over everyone else's.

"Completely out of order!" he barked. "This was meant to be my treat!"

Rita stood behind him wringing her hands together.

The reception desk was thronged with irate residents waiting impatiently to check out.

I saw Richard leaning over the desk talking to a very nervous-looking member of staff. I made my way up to him, tapping him gently on the arm.

"What's going on?" I asked.

The receptionist looked down and began to tap furiously on a calculator.

Richard turned to me and threw his hands in the air. "The bloody computer system has gone down and there are two girls trying to sort out a million bills."

The girl looked up from her calculations and smiled apologetically.

"Your father is livid. I should have let him pay the damn bill – poor Rita is trying to calm him down. I thought I'd have this sorted out before they appeared, but it's taking forever."

On hearing this, the poor girl seemed to hit a wrong button on the calculator. She closed her eyes tightly for a second and appeared to start over again. Richard bunched his hands into fists and looked as if he was going to hit her. Murmurs of "bloody ridiculous" and "typical" could be heard floating across the hotel lobby. My heart went out to the two young girls who were frantically trying to manage an impossible situation. I left Richard to sort out the bill and made my way over to Daddy and Rita.

"Ridiculous," he shouted. "I invite you away on a weekend and you pay your own bill."

"Daddy, we had a marvellous time. It was such a great idea, but we couldn't possibly let you get the bill."

He had a thunderous look on his face. Richard had upstaged him and I could see he was furious.

"I wanted to treat you this weekend, damn it!"

Richard appeared, stuffing his credit card back into his wallet. "Honestly, Denis, I couldn't let you get that. I really appreciate the gesture, but it was too much."

I thrust a suitcase into Richard's hands and pushed him towards the door. He gladly took it and scurried out to the car park.

I kissed Daddy on the cheek and slipped my arm through his. "It was the best weekend I've had in a very long time." I saw the beginnings of a smile. "I think we should do it every year for Rita's birthday."

"Hmm," he said. "Well, next year you're not coming if you don't let me pay."

"Deal," I said and breathed a sigh of relief along with

Rita. After all, she had to sit in a car with him for the next five hours.

Then

My room has never been so clean. I have vaccumed and dusted and scrubbed everything in sight and it is gleaming. From now on I will never drop any clothes on the floor – I'll hang them up as soon as I take them off. Everything on my dressing-table is lined up in the proper order. My perfumes are in one line, I only have three bottles, *Charlie, 4711* and some really stinky stuff called *Kiku* that Rita bought me for my birthday last year. I did have some other bottles but I can't find them. My make-up is in another line, and my jewellery has been untangled and placed in my musical jewellery box. I have counted each piece, so I'll know if Claire takes anything. She takes things from my room all the time but I can never prove it because she's such a clever little liar.

I may as well be living in a prison camp. I can't leave the house without giving Rita a detailed account of where I'm going and what I am doing. From now on, whenever I miss any time from school, Mrs Talbot told Daddy that she would contact him personally and let him know. I really wish I could run away and never come back to this house again. I hate my family. Claire is being a little bitch. She's really enjoying the fact that I'm in so much trouble. But, I have to be nice to her, which is killing me, because I depend on her to get my notes to Gary. I still pretend that I'm baby-sitting on Saturday nights, not every Saturday, but every second one. They still haven't copped on that I'm lying – it's about the only thing left that they haven't found out about. Claire has to pass Gary's house every Tuesday on her way to a violin class. I give her the notes, which I write on my lavender notelets, and she posts them into his letterbox. Sometimes Gary answers the door and she hands them to him, but she never tells me anything about what he says to her. She's standing beside the love of my life, who I'm not allowed to see and she won't even give me the slightest idea of how he is.

"What did he say?" I ask, almost jumping on her for the tiniest bit of information.

Claire always shrugs her shoulders and says, "Nothing."

I follow her around the house and pester her to tell me something.

"He didn't say anything. He just took the note and closed the door."

"Did he say 'thank you'? Did he smile at you? Did he seem like he was in good form? Did he look miserable?"

"Shut up!" Claire eventually ends up shouting at me. "He just took the note and closed the door."

"If you dare read those notes, I'll think of something really horrible to do to you!" I try to sound as fierce as I can. I know I'm taking a big chance using Claire to get messages to Gary, but there's no one else. She's such a little nosey parker, I'm sure she's itching to know what's in them, but Gary says that so far they've all been sealed when he gets them. Still, there's no harm letting her know that I'll kill her if she tries anything, just in case her curiosity gets the better of her.

So that's what we are reduced to. Me sending notes through my little sister, in order to meet up with Gary. The past three times we've met up have been in a pub near his house – it's a grotty little place but at least I know that I won't be spotted. If I get caught sneaking out to meet Gary, Daddy will lock me up for the rest of my life.

God, it's so depressing, I don't think I can take it any more.

Gary is always in foul humour and I don't blame him. Who in their right mind would want to sit in McGinn's Bar on a Saturday night? But it won't be for much longer because I'm going to London with him, and whatever happens I know for sure that life couldn't be much shittier than it is now. So what if I have to clean houses? At least I'll be with him. The only thing is, now that I've made up my mind to do it, Gary seems to be getting edgy about the whole thing. He keeps saying things like, "What'll happen when your old man finds out?" and "Maybe you should forget about it for a while".

I haven't asked him why he says 'you', and not 'we'. Surely he wouldn't go without me?

I'm not really speaking to Lainey at the moment. We didn't exactly have an argument, but we got annoyed with each other and neither of us have phoned or called to each other since. It happened a while ago, just after all the trouble at school. She called around one evening just as I had finished cleaning out my bedroom.

"My God!" she exclaimed. "What happened?"

I stood in the middle of the room and looked around proudly. "It's the new me! I'm going to be tidy from now on."

She walked around and surveyed the result of my hard work.

"Was that chair always there?" she asked.

"Yes, but it was always covered with clothes. I almost forgot it was there myself."

She plonked down into it. "I heard about Mrs Talbot calling in your dad. Did you get murdered?"

I sat down on the edge of my bed, careful not to disturb the freshly ironed duvet cover that I had struggled to put on. "Why do you think my room is so clean?" I asked. "I've nothing else to do! They follow me around like little spies. Every time the phone rings for me, I can see Rita's big ears wiggling at the other side of the door, hoping she'll catch me out so she can report back to Daddy."

Lainey wore a grave expression on her face as she listened to me. "Perhaps it mightn't be a bad idea to take a break for a while, at least until things cool down a bit."

"I can't take a break, Lainey. It's far too serious for that," I said, feeling exasperated with her for suggesting something so stupid.

Her eyes opened wide. Resting her elbows on her knees, she leaned forward and cupped her face between her hands. Lainey hasn't really gone out with anyone for more than a month or two, so she doesn't understand what it's like for me.

I could feel my face going red.

Lainey's eyes opened wider. "Liz, how serious?"

I struggled about whether to tell her or not. Then I foolishly decided to trust her with my secret.

I jumped up and crossed the room, opening my bedroom door to see if Claire might be earwigging outside. She does that all the time, but there was no one there. Then I went back to the bed and poised myself to tell all.

"Remember the way I always said I was going to move

to London with Gary? Well, we're going very soon, but I'm not telling anyone except you."

Her mouth fell open. "Liz," she whispered, "have you gone completely mad?"

I giggled at her shocked expression. "We've thought this through for a long time – it's not a spur-of-the-moment decision." I said this in a very grave and superior way. Our plans to run away had made me feel like a woman of the world, and Lainey suddenly looked very young and inexperienced to me.

"Liz, you don't know him well enough to run off just like that," she whispered loudly.

"Oh for God's sake, Lainey, we've been together for almost two years. We know each other inside out."

"You've been dating for two years – living together is an entirely different thing."

I bristled at her pointed disapproval. Why did she always have to look down her nose at anything that had to do with Gary?

"What do you mean?" I asked.

"Well . . . for a start, you'll be sleeping with him. You'll practically be married to him and you're far too young."

I gave a quick smirk at her innocence. "We've already slept together, and I know that I love him. I couldn't ever be with anyone else."

She sat like a statue, staring over at me, and blinked a few times.

"Well," I said, feeling really awkward, "say something."

Lainey swallowed loudly and gave me a tense smile and I knew right then that I shouldn't have opened my mouth.

"You've slept with him," she said flatly.

"Yep."

"How many times?" she asked.

"Just once."

"Are you on the pill?"

"No."

"Aren't you afraid of getting pregnant?"

Oh God! I really was sorry I'd said anything. I'd forgotten how judgemental she could be.

"We just got carried away one night. It was so special I couldn't stop myself and I'm not pregnant. Lainey, can't you just be happy for me?"

Lainey took a deep breath and picked at some fluff that was coming through a hole on the arm of the chair. "I'm not happy for you because I think you're making a mistake."

"Why?" I asked in a high-pitched voice.

"Because I don't think you should run off with him. I think it's going to be a disaster and you'll come out of it the worst."

"What do you mean?" I wanted to run across and slap her for being such a prissy cow.

"If it doesn't work out, which it probably won't, he'll take off and be able to find work and somewhere to stay – doesn't he have an uncle over there?"

I nodded crossly.

"You'll end up hurt and coming home with your tail between your legs. Don't go, Liz, please. I really don't want to see you get hurt."

"You never liked Gary, did you?"

Lainey looked away and said nothing. She didn't have to. Her silence answered my question.

She glanced at her watch and stood up. "I'd better go," she said.

I stayed sitting and didn't look up at her. "Don't tell anyone," I mumbled.

"I won't," she said quietly, "but I really wish you hadn't told me."

I stayed in my room wanting to hurl myself at the wall for being so stupid. Why did I even think she'd understand? At least I didn't have to worry about her telling anyone. I could always trust Lainey to keep her mouth shut.

I lay back on my bed, not caring whether I crumpled the duvet cover or not. I turned off the bedside lamp and stared ahead at the shadows on the wall.

"Mum," I whispered, "am I doing the right thing?"

The shadows of the branches swayed about carelessly in the stiff breeze, as if they didn't give a damn what I did.

"Mum," I whispered again, "I love him so much."

Now

The week has been a blur. The office has been crazy – not only are we pitching for the Browne account but there are three other presentations to be made before the Christmas holidays. Brian has been so wrapped up in getting Browne's back that our other accounts have been neglected and every one is playing catch-up. I haven't been able to keep my mind focused on work because of this blasted home visit that's looming over me. I arrived home on Friday evening feeling shattered and stepped into the hallway only to find it had been completely transformed. I'd forgotten about my arrangement with Lainey. Earlier in the week I had left out a key for her, and that afternoon she had let herself in and performed miracles with the piles of decorations, both new and old, that I had left out. Not only had she used my things, she had also added a few of her own as well. The banister was festooned with pine branches intertwined with a wide red satin ribbon and fairy lights. In the front room, the tree, which I had left with only fairy lights adorning it, had been made-over with a truly magic touch. I usually stood back and fired the decorations at it – but Lainey must have measured the distance from branch to branch and every fairy and silver bauble seemed to be in perfect symmetry. I plugged in the lights and looked on in wonder as it came to life before my eyes. I silently gave thanks for being blessed with such a great friend.

The phone rang and I was more than surprised to see Claire's number come up on the screen.

"Hi," I said, feeling guilty that I hadn't called her after the weekend. "How are you?"

"A lot better, thanks," she said. "How was the weekend?"

"Really lovely, it's a pity you missed it. We should all try to do it again soon. Daddy and Rita really enjoyed it too."

"Are you going over to them for Christmas Day?" she asked.

"Yes. Aren't you?"

I was so used to her cancelling out on arrangements lately that I fully expected her to say no.

"Yes, of course."

"Great. I probably won't see you till then. I'm up to my eyes at the moment."

"Work busy?"

"Yes. I have this home visit tomorrow and a big presentation on Wednesday, so I'm like a headless chicken at the moment."

"What's a home visit?"

Shit! I hadn't really wanted to go into the whole adoption thing with her. We were skating on thin ice as it was. I didn't want to say anything that might seem insensitive.

"It's a visit from a social worker. To do with the adoption."

Claire fell silent for a moment. "I didn't think you'd reached that stage yet."

"Yes," I said, desperately trying to think of something that would veer us off the subject. "When are you breaking up for Christmas?"

"I'm not sure," she answered. "I've been doing a lot from home so I probably won't bother going in next week but I was hoping to meet up with you before Christmas Day."

I was going to be too busy early in the week preparing for the presentation on Wednesday. That only left Thursday which was Christmas Eve. I had last minute shopping to do and Brenda's drinks party was that evening.

"Sorry, Claire," I said, "I'm just too busy. I'll see you at Brenda's on Christmas Eve."

"Okay," she said, sounding disappointed.

There was nothing I could do and I refused to feel bad about it. After all, she'd broken so many arrangements with me over the past few weeks that she'd just have to wait until I had the time to see her.

I drove Richard mad that night with one question after another, trying to prepare him for the interview with Val.

"Please try to smile more, Richard," I said, as I turned off the bedside light.

"Jesus, is there anything else you'd like me to do? Maybe

I should sing a song or do a tap dance for her. I'll smile as much as I usually do," he grumbled.

Which is never, I thought to myself.

I lay back and didn't say anything else. There was no point arguing at this stage, and risk having him sulking the following day. Richard can be quite short with people without meaning to, and I know there have been times that he's been taken up the wrong way. Our cleaning lady left us because she said that Richard was rude to her. He didn't mean to be rude – he only asked her not to clean his desk in the study, but it was the way he asked her. He can come across as being a bit abrupt sometimes – it's one of his faults. I knew that if Val asked him something of a delicate nature that Richard could easily appear brusque and uncooperative. I just hoped he'd remember to smile, I thought as I drifted off to sleep. He had such a lovely smile it would win anyone over.

I opened my eyes and looked at the clock. It was a quarter to nine. Val would be calling in two and a half hours. I tiptoed into the bathroom and had my shower. Then I pulled on my dressing-gown and went downstairs to make some coffee. The smell of pine cones and cinnamon wafted around the house. I turned on the Christmas-tree lights and the lights on the banisters to create an instant atmosphere of a perfect Yuletide home. The morning paper came through the letterbox and I brought it into the kitchen and flicked through the pages, but couldn't concentrate on reading anything. At ten o'clock I heard Richard closing the door of our en-suite. It was so typical. He always got up before nine on Saturdays, but on this particular one, he'd decided to sleep late. I waited patiently downstairs until I heard him on the landing. Then, I grabbed a cloth and some detergent and ran upstairs to clean out the bathroom. I wanted the house to look neat and tidy and I knew that Richard would leave his wet towels lying on the bathroom floor.

We passed on the stairs and he glanced down at my rubber gloves and muttered, "Good morning." I could see he wasn't in a very good mood and decided to ignore it.

"Hi," I said brightly. "There's coffee in the pot. I'll be down in a second."

After giving the bathroom a thorough going-over, I went back down to the kitchen to find Richard clicking off his phone.

"Who was that?" I asked.

"The office," he said crossly. "Damian wants a file that I brought home with me."

"Well, I hope you didn't tell him he could come over!" I shrieked like a madwoman, waving the floppy rubber gloves about. "I don't want anyone calling here this morning. We've enough to contend with without unexpected callers."

Richard looked at me as if I'd lost it. "Calm down, Liz," he said slowly. "I said I'd meet up with him later. Christ's sake, you'd think the fucking Queen of England was calling."

I fired the rubber gloves into the press under the sink and snapped it closed before the avalanche of cleaning bottles I had stuffed in earlier came tumbling out onto the floor.

Shit, I said to myself. *Stay calm or you'll blow it.*

The last thing I wanted was Val to arrive and catch us in the middle of a shouting match. It was half past ten. Only another forty-five minutes to kill.

"I'm going upstairs to get dressed," I said quietly.

I gave the upstairs bedrooms one last check, just in case Val did another inspection. They looked perfect. In our own bedroom I spotted the suitcase in the corner and went to call Richard, but thought the better of it. The shelf, which I had managed to pull it down from, was too high for me to put it up again. I had asked Richard as soon as I'd unpacked it after our weekend to put it away, but there it was, still standing exactly where I'd left it. I held it over my head and tried in vain to shove it up on the shelf in the wardrobe but I wasn't tall enough for the task. What I really wanted to do was kick it around the room and curse my husband for being such a shithead. But instead, I slid it under the bed out of sight. I stayed upstairs for longer than I needed to. I figured it would be better to give Richard some time alone before Val arrived. At exactly eleven fifteen, I heard her car pull up outside and my heart began to race. I jumped up, gave myself a final examination in the mirror and decided that I looked too casual. I went to pull my jumper off, but the doorbell rang and I realised I wouldn't have time to change. I smoothed it down again, ran a comb through my tossed hair and charged down the stairs like a lunatic.

"Val," I said, trying not to appear fussed and breathless.

"Hi there," she said, stepping into the hall. "Wow! That's lovely," she said, pointing to the banisters. "It's so unusual."

"Thanks," I said with a guilty grin. Thankfully she didn't ask if I'd made it, because I had already decided to lie and say yes.

I brought her into the kitchen where Richard was sitting

exactly where I'd left him. He stood up stiffly and shook Val's hand. I'd forgotten to tell him not to shake her hand; it looked too businesslike. I made some more coffee and we chatted a bit about where we were in the process and what else was to come. Well, Val and I chatted, Richard looked as if he'd been struck dumb.

"I know this seems very odd," Val said, "but I'm afraid it has to be done. I want to interview you both separately. Is that all right with the two of you?"

"Yes," I said, before she'd finished her sentence.

"Richard?"

Richard looked over at her and shrugged his shoulders. "Sure," he answered casually.

"Would you like to look over the house again," I offered.

Val gave me a smile. "No, that's not necessary, Liz. Who wants to go first?"

I looked at Richard and decided to nominate him, just in case he got one of his important phone calls and decided to leave while I was in with Val.

"Richard, you go first," I said.

He looked at me as if I was about to push him off a cliff.

"Do you want to go into the front room?" I asked. "I've lit a fire."

"Great," said Val, standing. "Thank you."

Richard stood up and followed her out into the hall.

"Would you like more coffee?" I asked.

Val raised a hand as she walked into the front room. "No, thanks. I'm fine."

The door closed and I sat down at the kitchen table and began to bite my nails. Fifteen minutes later, I couldn't stand it any longer and decided to hang out a wash to pass some time. Another fifteen minutes passed and there was still no sign of them finishing up. I opened the kitchen door quietly and tiptoed out to the hall. I stood to the side of the front-room door and held my breath in order to listen. My chest tightened when I heard Richard's voice: it was raised and sounded angry. Val seemed to be trying to talk over him in a flatter more even tone, but there was no mistaking the sound of Richard's sharpness. I felt myself stiffen with fear. What were they talking about? I heard the sound of a case snapping closed and scurried back to the kitchen, but just as I'd reached the door, Richard came thundering out of the front room. He stopped when he saw me, and threw his hands in the air. His face was red and he looked as if he was struggling to hold back his tears.

"What's wrong?" I whispered.

He stood there looking at me and opened his mouth to speak, but nothing came out.

"Richard, what happened?" I asked, feeling my heart begin to sink.

"I can't do this, Liz," he said with tears in his eyes. "Sorry."

Before I could reply to this, he turned around and walked out the door.

I heard the sound of his car starting up and the roar of the engine as he drove away from the house. I was left at the kitchen door with my mouth open.

Val came out from the front room and looked over at me. "Come in, Liz," she said.

I walked mechanically into the room and sat down on a chair, still trying to take in what had just happened. Val sat down opposite me and waited a few moments before she spoke.

"Richard seems very upset about something. Can you tell me what it is?"

I looked at her blankly. "No."

We sat in silence and I stared out the window in the hope that he'd change his mind and come back again.

"Nice Christmas tree," Val said gently, shaking me out of my trance.

"Thank you," I said with a forced smile.

"Liz, this happens quite a lot. Couples rush into adoption and halfway through the process they find that they're not quite as prepared as they thought they were."

I looked over at her and shook my head. "We are more than prepared, Val. I know whatever happened this morning with Richard was probably just down to nerves. He's a very reserved person and he doesn't take kindly to being questioned about delicate matters. Please, Val, let's do it again and see how he gets on."

Val stayed quiet for a few seconds before clearing her throat. "Liz, I must report what happened in this interview. It's not a good sign when one party storms out like that. You really have to talk things out with Richard and see what it is that he really wants."

"Of course it's what he wants. It's what both of us have always wanted," I said. I felt eerily calm inside as I lied. My voice was measured and even, giving the impression that I was in total control of my emotions. It was as if I had discovered an inner pool of strength which was stopping me from going to pieces in front of her.

"I found him unresponsive. He wouldn't cooperate.

Why do you think that was?" The sympathetic tone had drifted out of her voice and she sounded firmer, less personal.

"Richard can be a difficult man," I said. "He can be gruff and standoffish and people can take him up the wrong way."

Val sat forward and nodded.

"He has a problem opening up to people. Being asked such personal questions by a stranger is something he's had a problem with from the beginning of this process."

"It's something that he should have come to terms with by now," she said.

I looked over at her pleadingly. "We both really want this baby," I said. But my words sounded hollow and untrue.

She gave me a sympathetic smile but said nothing.

We both heard a car pull up outside and Val stood up quickly. I breathed out with relief. At least if Richard came back and apologised for walking out, we'd have some chance of redeeming ourselves with her.

"Richard," I muttered under my breath as I walked over to the window.

"There's really no point in any more discussion today," she said, walking towards the door.

I looked out and my heart sank when I saw that it wasn't his car. I walked out to the hall behind Val and waited while she pulled on her coat. Over her shoulder, through the frosted glass, I could see a figure approaching the front door.

"The two of you need to sit down and talk about this before we go any further," she said as she adjusted her scarf.

I nodded my head and glanced over at the door again as the doorbell rang.

"I'll be in touch after the holidays. Happy Christmas, Liz."

I opened the door to let her out and found myself standing face to face with Jeff Williams. I stared at him in horror as Val stepped between the two of us and nodded at him before hurrying out to her car.

"Is this a bad time?" Jeff asked.

"No," I said faintly. I had no idea why he might be calling.

"I couldn't get through to your mobile and I don't know your land-line number," he explained.

I stood there nodding, frozen to the spot.

He put his hands up and grimaced. "Honestly, if this is a bad time just tell me. I was passing and I'm not sure where the polocrosse grounds are, so I thought I'd call in. It was probably very unprofessional of me."

I jolted back into the present. Of course, the stables. I'd told him I'd bring him up some Saturday. *Shit!*

"Oh yes," I said, stepping back. "Come in for a second. I'll just grab a jacket."

He stepped into hall while I ran upstairs. I fumbled through my wardrobe for a warm jacket and stopped for a second, burying my head into the rack of clothes.

Don't cry. Don't cry.

All I wanted to do was crawl into bed and bury myself under the duvet for the rest of the day – what the hell was Jeff doing, calling to me in the middle of a nervous breakdown? Tears stung the back of my eyes, but I blinked them away and went back downstairs. Jeff stood in the hall with his hands in his pockets, oblivious to the calamity that had just taken place.

"That's nice," he said, nodding to Lainey's banister creation.

"Thank you," I muttered, heading towards the door.

I sat into the front seat of his Jaguar. The sharp musky scent of his cologne hung in the air and I inhaled deeply trying to keep myself together. Thankfully, the stables were only a mile up the road, and Jeff did most of the talking as we drove. We made our way over the mucky ground to where a match was taking place. We leaned over the fence and looked on for a while without saying anything. The brisk wind whipped around us and I pulled my jacket tight against the cold. This was my chance to make a pitch and reel him in, but I couldn't bring myself to speak.

"Okay, I believe you now," he said, turning to me with a smile.

I stared at him blankly.

"I've asked about twenty people in the past few weeks and none of them have ever heard of the game. I thought you were having me on!"

What was it that made me crack? I had been doing so well up to that point.

Maybe it was the fact that he said something funny and nice to me. Or the way the skin around his eyes crinkled when he smiled. Whatever it was, I felt my chin begin to quiver and without any warning, big fat tears began to roll down my cheeks.

Jeff looked horrified. "Liz, what's wrong?" he said, putting his hand on my shoulder.

I tried to get a grip of myself and find that pool of inner

strength that I'd had in abundance half an hour earlier, but it had abandoned me. I tried to talk but only blubbery nonsense came out.

Jeff put his arm around my shoulders and walked me back to his car.

He opened the door for me and I collapsed into the front seat in a complete state. While he walked around to his own door I gulped in big lungfuls of air to try and stop the awful hysteria that had gripped me, but it only resulted in my nose beginning to run. He sat in and closed the door and looked over at me.

"I'll just take you home," he said.

My eyes filled up with tears again until he was just a blur and I nodded my head.

He pulled up outside the house and I clutched the bundle of Kleenex he'd handed to me. I felt so stupid, I couldn't look at him.

"Liz. I'm so sorry for calling like that. You should have told me to go away."

I tried to look up at him and smile but my face just distorted into an ugly grimace.

"Bye," was all I managed to gasp as I scrambled out of the car and ran towards the safety of my front door.

Then

Gary is gone. I want to kill myself. Rita and Daddy have ruined my life, especially that cow Rita. Why wasn't it her that died and not Mum? Surely God made a big mistake that night and took the wrong sister? How did we ever let her push her way into our family?

Claire started reading my notes and Gary didn't notice that the envelopes weren't sealed when she delivered them to him. I got careless with what I wrote and little Miss Nosey Parker began to piece things together. About three weeks ago I got home from school and Rita was standing in the hall glaring at me.

"What?" I said, staring her down. Recently she's always got something to nag me about when I come in from school, so I didn't take much notice of her.

"Come inside," she said, turning to walk back into the kitchen.

I followed her and nearly got sick when I saw my lavender envelope lying on the kitchen table. I recognised it immediately – it was the last one I'd sent to Gary because I'd drawn a heart on the back of it.

Rita's pudgy little fingers tore the note from the envelope, and she held it up to read:

"Dear Gary, I can get out on Saturday night. I'll pretend to baby-sit again and I'll see you in McGinn's around nine. This is one of the last times we'll have to meet like this and I can't wait. I can't wait just to be with you night and day. I have withdrawn all my money from the Post Office today and we can go in another few weeks. I'll talk to you about it on Saturday night. I love you forever. Liz."

She dropped the letter onto the kitchen table and stared down at it.

"What the hell are you doing, young lady?" she shouted.

I stood there like a dummy with the words of the letter still ringing in my ears. How could I have been so stupid? Writing all of that down and giving it to Claire.

Rita grabbed the letter and crumpled it in her fist. "You

little bitch!" she hissed. "You're nothing but trouble from one end of the day to the other. I'd swear you're doing this out of spite."

I looked at her scornfully. "Oh yeah, I'm doing it just to get at you, Rita."

She flung the ball of paper at me and it hit the side of my head. "Get out of here before I slap your brazen face!" she roared.

I'd never seen her so mad before. Her face was bright red and for a moment I thought she was really going to take a swing at me.

"Your father's on the way home. He'll have a thing or two to say to you."

"You told Daddy!" I exclaimed.

"Of course I told him!" she shouted. "I think he deserves to know that his daughter is making a show of herself running about with some ruffian. I'm sure he'll be interested to know where you were going."

"I hate you!" I shouted, before I ran from the kitchen. I bolted upstairs to my room and saw Claire standing just inside her bedroom door, looking terrified.

I stepped up to her and grabbed her by the scruff of the neck but Rita came bounding up the stairs behind me.

"You leave her alone, you big bully!" she shouted.

I pushed Claire backwards and glowered at her. "You're dead," I whispered, before stamping into my room and slamming the door with full force.

Once inside, I threw myself on the bed and felt the whole world come crashing down around me. I cried out loud like a baby, whacking my pillow with big angry thumps. Why did everyone in my family want to ruin my life? My anger turned to despair as I thought of the plans we'd made that had gone up in smoke.

Daddy did come home early, but he never came up to me. I thought of packing a suitcase that night and sneaking up to Gary's. Now I wish I had.

Nobody said anything about it the following day, which I thought was very strange. Daddy was gone when I got up and Rita didn't speak to me over breakfast.

The next day was just the same.

The following day, Gary's letter arrived, telling me that he had gone to London without me. Daddy had gone straight to the Kilroys' house when Rita read him the letter over the phone and he'd told Gary's parents what we were doing. I don't know what else was said. Gary was very vague about it in his letter. But he did tell me that his parents gave him the money to go to London on condition that he promised never to see me again. He wrote the letter the night before he left and his mother posted it to me. I don't even have an address for him. I can't believe he went without me. I keep praying every night that he'll write, but it's been three weeks now and I've heard nothing. I can't stand to even look at anyone in this house; they all make me sick. Rita is walking around like the cat that got the cream – she has this nasty little smile that appears whenever I'm in trouble, and it's permanently pasted across her face these days. Daddy hasn't said a word about it. He's probably riddled with guilt after doing such a horrible thing. As soon as I'm eighteen, which will be in eleven months, I'll walk out that door and never come back, and they'll all be sorry they were such shits to me. I'll find out where Gary is if it kills me. I'll get his address from his mother and I'll follow him to London and never come back to this house again.

Now

After his walkout, Richard stayed away from the house all day and didn't return until later that evening. I had cried my eyes out for most of the afternoon and by the time he came in I felt completely worn out. He threw his keys on the hall table and came into the front room quietly. I was lying on the couch with a blanket thrown over my legs, staring blankly at a Christmas variety show.

He collapsed into an armchair and ran his hands through his hair.

"I'm sorry," he said softly.

I didn't look up. It wasn't enough. Nothing he said would make up for what he'd done.

"Liz," he said pleadingly, "we've got to talk about this."

I hit the button on the remote and turned off the television.

"No, Richard," I corrected him. "*You* have to talk about this. It's something you should have done long before now."

"I know," he said. "I just didn't know how."

I looked over at him and bit my lip to stop myself from crying again. "Richard, why can't you talk to me?" He looked as if he didn't understand what I'd said. "Am I unapproachable? Am I so wrapped up in myself that you can't get through to me?"

"No, Liz, it's not that," he said.

"Well, tell me what it is, because you don't seem to be

318

able to communicate with me any more. Please, Richard, tell me what it is that I'm doing wrong."

"It's not you, Liz. You mustn't think that," he said, looking down at the floor.

"Well, what is it? I'm confused," I said, my voice beginning to shake.

He looked up at the ceiling and pursed his lips, staying silent for a few seconds, as if he was trying to search for the right words.

"Just say it, Richard. Tell me what the problem is."

He looked over at me and my heart sank when I saw the hopeless expression on his face.

"I don't want to adopt a child." His shoulders collapsed as he said this. "It's no good trying any more; I can't keep up the pretence. I feel like a fraud, lying through my teeth to those social workers about wanting this child, when nothing could be further from the truth. I'm sorry, Liz. I thought I could go along with it for your sake, but I just can't do it."

I sat rigid, not able to move a muscle. Deep down, I'd been waiting for this moment for a long time, but hearing him say it shattered the tiny bit of hope I'd been holding out for.

He gripped the arms of his chair and waited for my reaction.

I couldn't speak. I couldn't think of a single word to say. All I could think of was how could he be so cruel as to back out now, when he had promised to go along with it for my sake. I had buried my head in the sand about all his reservations about this adoption with only that shred of a promise to cling to – that he'd do it for my sake.

Without saying anything, I stood up and left the room.

Upstairs, I rummaged through my bedside drawer and found some sleeping tablets. I took one and lay down, and waited for sleep to dull my senses, anything that would help escape the nightmare that was unfolding. When I woke early the next morning, I saw that Richard had not come to bed.

On Wednesday, we made our presentation to Browne's. It was decided after much discussion that we would present it in their offices. Brian stalked me twenty-four hours a day, and by Wednesday I came very close to telling him to shove it. I had my own problems to deal with and I didn't think I could bear another moment of his mind-bending persistence.

"If we don't get this, we're screwed," is all he'd said for the past two weeks, giving the team no credit whatsoever for all the hard work they've put into winning back the account.

Susie is on another planet. Contrary to my wishes, her date with Matt went really well and she's grinning from ear to ear, and driving me round the bend into the bargain. She's made so many screw-ups this week that I'm about to throttle her.

"Susie!" I snapped, my patience giving out on me. "Keep your mind on the job. You do realise that we're making our pitch tomorrow?"

Susie had been going over her part of the presentation when she'd stopped in mid-flow to tell me about something really stupid that Matt had said. My sharp words had no effect whatsoever – she just smiled dreamily and pulled up a chair.

"Oh, sod the presentation! I'm in love!"

I shook my head. "Couldn't you have timed it a little

better? We need you to be on the ball tomorrow. Not all goofy and grinny like a lovestruck teenager."

She flicked her hair and giggled.

"Susie! I mean it. You've got to pull yourself together."

Her smile remained fixed. There was nothing anyone could say to burst her bubble. She was in that very annoying lovesick zone where perfectly sensible adults are transformed into babbling idiots.

"He's asked me to move in with him," she whispered excitedly.

"Isn't that a bit soon?" I asked.

"Well, I won't do it for a while. He's just split up with someone and she's left all her stuff in his apartment. But as soon as that's all sorted out, I'll think about it. I wouldn't like to move in with some other girl's things all around the place," she said, with her nose wrinkled up.

"When did he break up with her?"

Susie twirled her hair around her finger and shrugged her shoulders. "I'm not sure – not too long ago," she said coyly.

"Susie, don't do anything hasty. Don't forget you have to work with him every day – it could be awkward if things don't work out."

She dismissed my matronly advice with a wave of her hand. "I know, I know," she said. "We've talked it through and we both know the risk we're taking. But," she said this with a breathy sigh, "he's worth it."

"I hope so," I said, as my eyebrow shot up involuntarily.

Susie sat forward and her face lit up. "Oh Liz, he's fantastic! I've never had so much sex in my whole life."

I lifted a hand to shut her up. The last thing I wanted to

hear was how great her sex life was, especially since my own husband had given up sleeping with me.

"Too much information. Now get on with it," I quipped, pointing to the flip chart.

Wednesday morning was manic. I got up half an hour earlier to prepare for the day ahead, which was probably not a good idea, as Richard was still in the house. Usually he was gone by the time I got up. We hadn't seen each other since Saturday night and I had decided, for a change, to let him make the first move. We'd had arguments and disagreements in the past and over the years they had taken on a familiar pattern. He would move into the spare room for a night or two until the bad feeling had blown over. But, it was always me who made the first move to patch things up, usually by suggesting that he come back to our bedroom. This time, I was leaving it up to him. This time, I wasn't in any hurry to invite him back to bed because I felt we needed some space between us. I was still in denial about his not wanting to adopt a child, still clinging to the shred of hope that he might just change his mind to save our marriage.

Richard was dumping his plate in the sink when I walked into the kitchen.

I stopped at the door and he raised his head, looking almost frightened to see me.

"Hi."

"Hi," I said, standing at the door awkwardly.

He brushed some crumbs from his hands and stood there looking at me.

"Big day today?"

I smiled weakly, amazed that he'd remembered. "Yes."

"Well, good luck with it."

"Thanks," I said. It was the day before Christmas Eve and it suddenly dawned on me that I still hadn't bought him a present. I felt a lump form in my throat and wished that he'd just go. As soon as this goddamn presentation was over I'd get back to my own life and sort things out, but until then I couldn't deal with any more confrontation.

He took his briefcase from the kitchen table and walked towards me, kissing my cheek as he passed. Our eyes met for a second and I let my hand rest on the lapel of his jacket.

"Brenda and Tom are having drinks tomorrow evening. Will you come?" I tried to keep any hint of desperation out of my voice even though that is exactly how I felt. If he said no, it would mean that there would be no chance of reconciliation between us before Christmas.

"Sure. What time?"

"Early. About six thirty," I blurted eagerly.

"Shields are having a lunch for their legal team tomorrow which will probably go on for a few hours, but I'll try to get home early."

"Right," I said, thinking that a night out would surely be the start to a truce.

He hesitated for a moment. "There's a law library dinner this evening. I probably won't be home till late."

"Okay," I said.

"Best of luck today," he said, kissing my cheek again.

Our eyes met again for a split second – and a strange feeling rose up inside me, but I pushed it back down again.

Brian was acting like a complete pig to everyone. I got into the office at ten past eight to be greeted with much rolling of eyes from the staff who were already there. One of the girls from the post room was in tears at the coffee machine over something Brian had shouted at her. I poured myself a cup of our dishwater-flavoured coffee and went up to my office to hide. After a few sips, I pushed the polystyrene cup of grey liquid away from me. I had a knot in my stomach that was making me feel ill. I dreaded the prospect of meeting Jeff Williams again after making such a fool of myself with him. He had called the office twice on Monday morning looking for me but I'd diverted his calls to Brian's phone. I rested my elbows on the desk and buried my face in my hands. What the hell was happening to me? Was I imagining things, or was my marriage really in trouble? I jumped as the phone beside me rang out.

"Yes."

"You in?"

"Yes, Brian. I'm in."

"Well why didn't you tell me? I'm trying to do about ten friggin' things at once. You'd think those other two bastards would have come in early this morning."

I smiled to myself. Those 'bastards', were probably still loving it up one last time before they got up.

"Brian, we've plenty of time. Stop panicking. The presentation's not until twelve and everything is sorted. What did you say to Jill in the post room? She was crying when I came in."

He fell silent for a moment. Always a sure sign that he was guilty.

"What the fuck is she crying for? All I did was tell her to wake up and stop putting Matt's post in my basket."

"Yes," I said doubtfully. "And I bet you said it really politely."

"I want to see the film one more time. See if we can add anything else to the dialogue. Do you have the disc?"

"Yes."

"Well, bring it up and we'll have another look."

"I'll bring it up after you go down to Jill and apologise for snapping at her."

"What!"

"You heard me," I said firmly.

"Ah Jaysus!" he exclaimed, before slamming down the phone.

After much discussion and general messing about, it was decided that Susie and Matt would go in one car with all the equipment for the presentation. Brian and I drove separately as he was going directly to a Christmas lunch after we made the pitch. Browne's offices were only a few miles away but I was glad to have some time on my own. I couldn't have listened to Brian jabbering on for another second. We all pulled into the Browne's carpark at the same time and helped unload the paraphernalia from the back of Matt's car. On the way up in the lift we wished each other luck.

"Of course, don't mention the war," Susie said.

"Oh Christ, yeah," agreed Brian.

Matt gave a wicked grin.

"What war?" I asked.

The three of them looked at me wide-eyed.

"You didn't hear?"

"What?" I asked.

"Jeff Williams' wife has run off with Paddy Stone. It was all over the Sunday papers last week."

"Oh my God!" I said, remembering how Brenda had mentioned something about it. I hadn't made the connection with Muriel Williams — Brenda had just referred to her as a Charity Queen.

"Muriel has run off!"

"Yes," said Susie. "Apparently it's been going on for ages. Paddy Stone sponsored all her charity balls during the year."

"Yeah," said Matt, guffawing stupidly. "One good ball deserves another!"

Susie took a breath and began to fill me in on the details but, just as she did, the lift stopped and the doors opened.

"Zip it," Brian hissed out of the corner of his mouth.

Poor Jeff, I thought, as we sat waiting for him in his office. Not only did he have to suffer the indignity of his wife running off with another guy — he had to suffer it in public, with idiots like Matt L'Estrange making wisecracks about it.

Brian rubbed his sweaty hands on the legs of his trousers and looked anxiously towards the door. "Tactics," he said, nodding over at me. "Bastard's probably in the jacks reading the paper."

"Calm down," I said. "We're five minutes early. He's probably in another meeting."

The door opened and a very haggard-looking Jeff walked into the office with his team. Brian almost knocked his chair over as he jumped up to make his over-enthusiastic introductions. After plenty of backslapping, we settled down and all eyes turned to Susie as she stood by the flip chart and began her surprisingly professional pitch, given the state of her brain. As she turned over to the second page of the chart, she tossed her hair playfully over her shoulders, revealing a purple mark that peeped out from the side of her collar. I gripped the edges of my chair as she unwittingly displayed her freshly sucked love bite to the room full of men. I looked around furtively, to see if anyone had noticed, but to my immense relief, everyone seemed to be concentrating on the chart. Except Matt. He met my eye and gave me a sneery smile which I returned with a glare of disgust that said: *You dirty little pervert.* The two-minute show reel felt like an eternity and I braced myself to pounce as the room lights were turned up.

I grabbed Susie's elbow as she stepped back to the table and pulled her down on the chair beside me. "We can all see your love bite. Pull up your collar!" I hissed.

Her hand flew up to her neck and she pulled up her collar as if she was about to do an Elvis impersonation. "Shit," she mumbled under her breath.

I was so preoccupied with hiding the love bite, that it took me a few seconds to notice the reaction to the presentation. With the love bite crisis averted, I glanced at the faces across from me and could tell immediately that they liked it.

"Well done," Jeff said. "That looked great."

His team of henchmen nodded in agreement.

Jeff looked over at me. I quickly looked away as I felt my face begin to burn.

Brian spouted off for a couple of minutes and I kept my gaze fixed downwards, for fear our eyes would meet again. I felt like such a fool every time I thought of what had happened.

After the meeting Matt and Susie gathered everything together and left just before Brian and me. I thought I'd better wait and try to coax him out – otherwise he'd be there till Christmas Day, telling them how brilliant our agency was and how they'd be crazy not to go with our campaign. When we got down to the carpark, Brian checked his watch and saw that he was already late for his lunch date. I looked over at my car and realised that some one had parked me in.

"I can't help you, Liz," said Brian, rattling his keys. "I'm late as it is. Go back inside and ask reception who owns the car."

My stomach lurched when I saw it was a blue Jaguar. The same blue Jaguar I'd made a twit of myself in last Saturday.

I went back into the building and almost bumped into Jeff as he was walking out.

"Is that your car I'm blocking?" he asked.

"Yes," I said timidly.

"Sorry," he said. "I thought it might be one of your cars. I was just coming down to move it."

Although I couldn't see it, I knew my face had turned bright red again.

We walked over to the cars and when he reached his, Jeff stopped and looked at me.

"I'm so sorry about the other day . . ." I stammered.

But he didn't give me a chance to finish.

"No, Liz, I'm the one who should be sorry. I should have called you beforehand. I don't know what I was thinking."

I looked down at the ground and nodded through my embarrassment, not knowing what to say.

"Look, would you have time to come for a coffee?" he asked.

There was a nervous tension between us and I should have wanted to run a mile, but there was something about him that I really liked. I wanted to go, but I was worried that it might seem inappropriate.

"It's fine if you don't –" he began.

"I would," I cut in.

We both gave a short laugh of relief, and once again I sat into his car, albeit with a little more composure than last time, and we drove towards the city centre.

He picked a quiet low-key place that was only half-full even though it was Christmas week. Probably a deliberate move seeing that my company had just made a pitch for his business, not to mention that his wife had just run off. If anyone saw us it would certainly set tongues wagging.

We sat at the back of the cafe and ordered some coffee and paninis.

He looked across at me and smiled that smile again. I don't know what it was about it but it made me feel special and I blushed for allowing myself to even think like that. The dark patches of skin under his eyes were presumably from worry or sleepless nights. Something I knew plenty about.

"We'd better not talk business. But I'll just say that I was really pleased with that presentation."

"Great," I said. "Brian will be pleased."

He shook his head and smiled again at the mention of Brian. He stared down at the tablecloth and seemed to drift off for a few seconds.

"I suppose you heard that Muriel left me," he said flatly.

"I . . . I . . ." Shit, I didn't know what to say. Was I supposed to know? Then I remembered Susie saying something about the Sunday papers. "I've just heard about it. I'm so sorry."

Jeff shrugged his shoulders. The smile had faded from his face and he looked totally miserable.

"It happened two months ago. The papers just got wind of it recently and it's become a source of great entertainment. The funny thing is – I think it was Muriel who informed them."

What a cow, I thought.

"Do you have children?" I asked.

"Thankfully no. It's bad enough having to cope with it as an adult. I can't imagine what it would do to a child."

"Has it been awful?"

He looked up at me. "Which part? My wife running off in the full glare of the media, or not having children?"

"I'm sorry," I said quickly. "I didn't meant to pry."

The waitress set our food before us and we stopped talking until she left.

Jeff sighed deeply. "Not having any children was something that didn't bother me until recently. Muriel announced two years after we got married that she didn't want children, and I just accepted it and went along with her. It's only lately when I see my friends with their families that I know I missed out on something really special. To be honest, our marriage should have ended years ago. I've been fooling myself for a long time."

"Sounds like she should have married my husband," I said with a bitter laugh.

"How come?"

I began to discuss the problems in my marriage with a

person that I hardly knew, and once I started I found that I couldn't stop. We were still sitting there two hours later while the waitress set the tables up for dinner. I told Jeff more than I had ever told anyone about Richard and the problems we were experiencing. We talked openly about our marriages as if we'd known each other forever. I told him why I'd been so upset when he'd called to the house. He didn't make any judgements or try to hand out any advice. Instead, he listened, which was just what I needed, to talk my heart out and finally get it all off my chest. As we stood to leave I felt the knot in stomach return and I realised that I didn't want to go home.

Outside on the street it was beginning to get dark. Carol singers filled the air with festive songs and Christmas lights lit up the busy shop fronts, reminding me that I had still more shopping to do.

"Can I leave my car in your car park till later? I need to go shopping."

"Of course," said Jeff, pulling his collar up against the chill that had set in.

I looked at him and tried to smile. It seemed so pointless wishing him a Happy Christmas when I knew it was probably going to be dismal.

"Happy Christmas," I said anyway.

He gave me that smile again. "I feel a lot better after talking to you," he said.

I could feel butterflies in my stomach, like I used to when I first dated Richard.

"Good luck with everything, Liz. I hope things work out for you." He said this with genuine concern, as if he really meant it.

I found myself gazing into his eyes and couldn't pull myself away.

He bent down to kiss me and as I turned my face to offer my cheek, our lips brushed together briefly.

"Happy Christmas," he whispered.

He walked away and disappeared into the crowd, leaving me standing in a daze in the middle of the pavement. I stared after him and felt a surge of happiness rise up inside me, as I was pushed left and then right by the busy shoppers that jostled by.

Then

My new school is called Our Lady of the Wayside. It is on a lake in Killarney and all of the inmates only get to go home twice a year. I am repeating fifth year, so I will be imprisoned for two years before I am released back into society. I don't really mind too much. I thought I'd hate it a lot more, but the nuns are all right and the girls in my dorm aren't too bad. Most of them are swotty spotty squares who walk about the place clutching bundles of books to their flat little chests, but Julie is good fun. Her parents sent her here because she was expelled from her convent in Waterford for getting into a fight with another girl. I heard about it from some of the other girls in the dorm, and by all accounts it was pretty vicious. But, the other girl did steal Julie's boyfriend which was a pretty crap thing to do, and Julie let her have it. Julie's sister sends her cigarettes, hidden in boxes of biscuits, and we sit on the windowsill in the dorm when everyone's gone to sleep and blow our smoke out the window. We'll be expelled if we're caught, but I'll take my chances. A girl's got to have some kicks in her life and they are few and far between in this boghole.

Daddy and Rita have complained to the head nun that I haven't written any letters to them since I arrived. Sister Brigid has given me a demerit for it, which means I miss my Saturday trip to the shop in the village, but I don't care. Julie will get me my bits and pieces and smuggle them back in. As far as I'm concerned, Daddy and Rita can drop dead if they think I'm going to write to them.

We have this really nice nun called Sister Bosco. I wonder if you get to pick your own name when you become a nun. If so, she picked a really weird one. It isn't even a woman's name – it's short for John Bosco – apparently he was a saint or something. I think she should think of changing it because it makes her sound like that puppet on TV. Daddy obviously filled Sister Bosco in on my trouble at home and she's tried to talk to me about love and forgiveness. Normally I switch off when I hear anyone talking like that, especially when they're referring to my family. But Sister Bosco has a special way about her – it's like she's too nice to ignore. Julie says that Bosco's on the lookout for recruits! She says that the convent is running short of nuns and they'll take any mad thing that applies.

Gary left at the beginning of the summer and I never heard a thing from him. I sat in my bedroom and cried for weeks. Every day I watched the postman as he delivered his letters to our road, but nothing ever came from London. I got so desperate that I called to his house and asked Mrs Kilroy for his address, but she gave me a dirty look and closed the door in my face.

When I got my summer holidays I stayed in my room

every day, moping about, trying to think of ways to poison my family. No one understood how I felt. Daddy hardly ever came near me. Rita lost her patience with me constantly and did nothing but shout all the time, but I just ignored her. I didn't speak a word to her for six weeks. Claire avoided me and when she had the misfortune to bump into me on the stairs or in the kitchen I'd give her a good thump, to remind her that it was all her fault.

I lay on my bed at night, staring at the shadows of the tree on the wall. For the first time, I wondered if Mum was really looking down on me, because if she was, then surely she would have done something to stop Gary from leaving. Still, it didn't stop me being hypnotised by the sway of the branches. In the evenings, just before it got dark, I would lie on my bed and fall into a trance as I stared at the shadows dancing on the wall. It was the only time I felt any peace inside.

In the middle of July, Rita decided to redecorate the house. She turned the place upside down and had an army of painters and decorators crawling all over the place every day. They arrived first thing every morning and the noise of hammers and drills drove me crazy. It took over every room in the house, nowhere was safe.

"Don't touch the banisters," Rita would bark one day. The next would be, "Don't rub against the front door," or "Mind the skirting boards." The sound of her shrill voice was almost as bad as the drilling and banging.

I couldn't take it any more so I moved up to Lainey's.

I lay on my bed in Lainey's room and poured my heart out about Gary and how my family had ruined my life. I could tell that Lainey was sick of hearing about it, but it didn't stop me moaning. It wasn't her that had lost the love of her life, so she could damn well put up with it and listen to me.

"Come on, Liz," she said one day. "Let's go for a swim."

The bedroom was hot and airless and the sun was splitting the stones outside.

"It's so boring here." she said. "Get up and do something. It'll make you feel better. There's a crowd going down to the beach this afternoon. Mum said she'll drive us."

"I don't want to," I said, turning over on my side.

"Well, I'm not staying in all day. It's too hot. You'll be on your own all afternoon."

I felt listless. I'd grown so lazy that just getting up off the bed seemed like such an ordeal.

"Really, Liz, you'd better think about pulling yourself together," said Lainey. "It's time you moved on with your life."

I threw her a withering look and wondered how anyone could be so cruel.

"Please," she said. "Please come to the beach today. It'll do you good to get out for a while. Mum is really worried about you."

At least Mrs Whyte cared about me – she was about the only one who did. She had cooked my favourite meals and even brought them up to me on a tray when I didn't feel like getting up.

The sun was shining directly in through the bedroom window and I felt a trickle of sweat on the back of my neck. I thought about going to the beach. It would mean getting up and moving about, but, I hated to admit, Lainey was probably right.

It would do me good to out for a change.

"Come on," pleaded Lainey. "Get up."

I sat up and let my legs dangle over the side of the bed.

"I'll have to go home and get my togs and a towel."

Lainey smiled down at me and clapped her hands. "Go on. Mum is making lunch and then she'll give us a lift."

She pushed me towards the door and steered me down the stairs. I blinked in the bright sunshine as I stepped out into the garden. The pungent smell of Mrs Whyte's roses filled the drowsy air and I could hear the drone of machinery in the distance.

I started down the road towards my house and tried to think of when I'd last been there. Four, possibly five days. I couldn't remember.

As I turned into our driveway I saw the last of the tree being felled. I put my hand on the gate and felt my knees go weak as I looked on in disbelief. Two men in helmets and visors were standing looking down at the stump which was all that remained of the chestnut tree. Rita stood at the front door shading her eyes from the sun.

I ran blindly towards them, the sound of my screams filling the air. After that, I don't really remember what happened. According to Claire, I attacked Rita like a wild animal. For weeks afterwards she bore the scratches and bruises to prove it. I believe I also bit her.

I hope I did.

I was whisked down here within weeks of it happening.

I was almost glad in a way and didn't put up much of a fight. I couldn't bear to sleep in my room any more. At night when I woke and saw the blank wall it frightened me, as if a part of me had been taken away. I hated being in that room on my own. I even went into Claire's room some nights and slept with her.

The night before I left, Claire did something really strange. She came into my room carrying all the things she had stolen from me over the years – perfumes, necklaces, pens, lip-gloss, combs and lots of other things. She didn't say anything. She just walked in, her arms heaped high with all of the stuff and set them down on my bed along with her precious Peter Rabbit.

Mrs Whyte came down with Lainey and they both bawled and started me crying as well. Mrs Whyte had made a big fruitcake for me. We stood in the hall, hugging each other while Daddy and Rita looked on in stony silence.

The following day, as I was packing the last few things I looked at the heap of bits and pieces that Claire had brought into me. At the time, I had searched high and low for some of the items when they'd gone missing, but none of them seemed important any more. Even though Claire had caused most of my problems, I couldn't bring myself to take her Peter Rabbit because I knew how much she loved it. Before I left, I put it back on her bed, but when I got to the convent and started to unpack, I found it, stuffed under the clothes in my suitcase.

Sister Bosco has a way of getting things out of you without asking any questions. They're probably told how to do it in nun camp, or wherever they go to train. I can just imagine them lining up, being taught to fold their arms and make their hands disappear up the sleeves of their habits. Then when they've got the hang of that, they're trained to incline their heads a little to one side and wait for the student to start blabbering. I can't believe I did it, but I told her about the tree and why it was so special to me – it just came out one day while I was helping her to carry some books to the convent. I'd never told anyone before, only Gary, because it sounded so stupid, but Sister Bosco seemed to understand.

We dropped the books on the desk in her office and her hands disappeared up her sleeves as she folded her arms. I was standing quite close to her and her big blues eyes looked huge behind her thick glasses. Her dainty little nose twitched slightly as she mulled over what I'd said.

"Do you really believe that she existed in the shadows?" she asked gently.

I shrugged my shoulders and felt like I was going to cry.

"Your father told me about what happened with your aunt. Is that why you attacked her? Because she had the tree cut down?"

I nodded my head and gulped back the lump that had formed in my throat.

"Did you ever tell any of your family about what you saw in the shadows?"

Again I could only answer by shaking my head from side to side.

"Poor Lizzy," she said, taking me by the hand, "what a terrible shock it must have been."

With her free hand she pulled a tissue from her deep pocket and handed it to me.

I wiped the tears from my face and tried to sniffle back the ones that hadn't escaped yet. I was standing so close to her that I could see the fine silvery grey hairs at the top of her forehead that were too short to fit under her veil.

Sister Bosco's head tilted to one side and she smiled at

me. "You're growing into such a fine girl," she said, squeezing my hand tightly. "And I know that it's not easy. Growing up is difficult. It's hard to leave certain things behind, yet we have to learn to let go in order to move on."

A strand of hair fell across my face and she lifted her hand and brushed it behind my ear.

"Do you understand what I'm saying?"

"Yes," I whispered.

"You must trust me, Lizzy, when I tell you that the only place your mother ever existed is here." She guided my hand upwards and placed it across my heart. "You can imagine her in shadows or trees or anywhere you wish. But the only place she truly exists is in your heart, and that is where she'll always be."

When I went back to the dorm, I didn't tell Julie or anyone why I'd been crying, but I felt a lot better after that talk. Like she'd taken a big brick off my shoulder and tossed it in the lake. Two weeks later a long letter arrived from Rita saying how sorry she was about the tree. I don't know if Sister Bosco told them about our talk – if she did I should probably be annoyed with her, but I'm not. I'm tired of being annoyed all the time. Rita wrote a lot of other stuff in her letter about how she blamed herself for my anger and how sorry she was for making me so unhappy. She sounded like she genuinely wanted to make up and be friends and it made me feel kind of sad about everything that had happened. Even though I'd hated her more than was humanly possible, she really wasn't the worst in the world. I knew I'd never be close to Rita or like her very much for that matter, but I've decided that when I go home I'm going to make an effort to get on with her. I suppose that's what Sister Bosco meant about letting go.

Now

I sat beside the fire surrounded with the gifts I'd bought, still feeling slightly dazed from the conversation I'd had with Jeff. Normally whenever I opened up to people, I was filled with remorse afterwards, for revealing so much of myself, but with Jeff it had seemed so natural. I gazed into the fire and wondered where he had gone after he'd left me. Like me, he had probably returned to an empty house. Muriel had already packed up and moved into Paddy Stone's Arcadian mansion complete with helipad.

I tied a ribbon around the gift-wrapped perfume and moisturiser that I had hastily chosen for Rita. I had opted for the safe choice of a cashmere cardigan for Claire because I couldn't think of anything else she'd like. Poor Daddy! Once again I had ended up in the sports department and bought him a new pair of golf shoes.

I finished wrapping the various toys I had bought for Lainey's and Brenda's kids and put them under the tree. I had bought Richard a palm computer which I'd heard him talk about, but I didn't want to put it under the tree. When it came to birthday and Christmas presents, Richard reverted to being three years old again. There had been times when I'd caught him picking holes in wrapping paper just to have a sneak preview of what he was getting before the big day arrived. Mind you, considering the turn our relationship had taken, I doubt that he expected to get anything this year, but old habits die hard. I brought his present upstairs and pushed it under my side of the bed. I figured it was safe as houses there, given that he wasn't even sleeping in it.

On my way back downstairs I heard the thud of the post

as it was dropped through the letterbox. There were a few Christmas cards, which I opened and read. One was from Brenda and Tom; they had let the boys sign it and I smiled at the smudged and shaky handwriting. Another was from Richard's sister in Canada, which I left in a prominent position on the hall table so he'd see it and know she'd written. I noticed the letter at the back of the pile had the Lakeview Falls logo. I guessed it was probably their new brochure and tariff which I had requested a copy of, after Lainey's suggestion of a girls' weekend in the spring. I opened the envelope and was surprised to see that it was a letter of apology, stating that due to the mix-up at reception on the morning of our departure, there had been an error in our final account. The accounts department had neglected to include one evening meal and a telephone bill from our invoice. Attached was the restaurant docket along with the itemised telephone bill. I glanced at both and recognised the lobster bisque starter and pheasant that I had stuffed myself with on the Saturday night. A quick look at the telephone bill confused me slightly. I knew Richard had called a client in Dubai at least twice. I remember how Daddy had moaned about him having to nip back to the room before we sat down to dinner. In fact, due to the time difference, he'd had to leave our company on both nights to make his calls. But there were no overseas calls recorded on the bill. Instead, there were only five calls – all to Claire's number. I knew immediately that this was wrong as I had only called her once and could see where it was printed. Saturday 6.10 p.m. Duration of call: 5:02.

I reached for the phone to ring the Lakeview Falls. I figured I might as well sort it out as Richard's calls would have cost a lot more. As I waited for a reply, I began to study the bill closer.

"Good afternoon. Lakeview Falls Hotel. How may I help you?" came a voice on the other end of the line.

"Yes, hello, this is Liz Joyce," I said, trying to control my voice. "I stayed in your hotel on the 11th of this month and I've just received a telephone bill from you."

"Oh, yes," she said breezily. "That was the weekend our system crashed. I'm afraid there were a few errors made with the accounts that weekend. I hope it hasn't inconvenienced you."

My eyes were locked on the telephone bill.

"My husband made some overseas calls that haven't been included on the bill. There are five calls to the same local number, and I know I only phoned this number once. Perhaps you could check this with your accounts department."

"If you'll just hold the line, I'll check it for you right away."

My hand began to shake as the numbers danced before my eyes. I saw that my call to Claire on the Saturday evening was the shortest on the bill. The one made at 8:10 p.m. later that night was 15:07 minutes long. I began to breathe in short gasps as if someone was trying to strangle me.

There was a click on the line as the receptionist resumed our call.

"I've just checked that bill out, Mrs Joyce. There were no overseas calls made from your room that weekend. Just those five calls to the same Dublin number."

I tried to answer but nothing came out.

"You stayed in room 208, is that correct?"

"Yes," I replied faintly.

I looked back down at the page in my hands and felt my mouth go dry. 8:10 p.m. on the Saturday night was about the same time that Richard had excused himself to make his call. Except it hadn't been to Dubai.

"Are you happy enough with that, Mrs Joyce?" came the receptionist's puzzled voice.

"Thank you," I managed to say, before hanging up.

I felt my legs give way from under me and I sank to the floor, clutching the pages to my chest.

I bit down hard on my closed fist as my mind flooded with all of the things I'd chosen to ignore over the past few months. It was as if someone had gripped the back of my head and was forcing me to look at something I didn't want to see. All the times that Claire had tried to avoid me. Richard's coldness towards me. His move out of the bedroom. I let out a low moan as I thought of the morning he had stormed out of Val's home visit. Was that the reason he didn't want to go ahead with the adoption? I thought of the way he had looked at me earlier that morning, and knew that what I had seen was a glimpse of his thinly veiled deceit.

My thoughts turned to Lainey. Hadn't I known, somewhere deep down, that she was hiding something from me? I pulled myself up off the floor and stumbled into the kitchen. I grabbed my bag from the table and ran outside to the car. I started the engine but my leg was shaking so badly that I could hardly keep it on the accelerator. I leaned my head on the steering wheel and started to cry, all the time thinking, this couldn't possibly be happening to me.

"Do you know something?" I cried when she opened the door.

The two curious faces of Jenny and Alannah peered out at me from behind their mother.

"Girls, go upstairs for a while and let me talk to Auntie Liz," Lainey said calmly, batting the girls away from her without taking her eyes off me.

I had forgotten to put my coat on and I stood in the porch shivering from the cold and the shock.

Lainey looked as if she was going to be sick. "Come in," she said.

"No!" I stood where I was and began to cry again. "Tell me the truth, Lainey. Why wouldn't you write the reference for me?"

She stood in the hall and I watched the colour drain from her face.

"Why?" I shouted.

Her head drooped slightly and she put her hand to her mouth as if she was afraid of what she'd say.

"Why?" I shouted at her again.

Her mouth moved but no words came out. She didn't have to say anything – the expression on her face said it all.

I turned to leave but her hand shot out and grabbed me.

"Please, Liz, come in. We have to talk about this."

I tried to pull away from her grasp but she held on to my arm with a firm grip. She pulled me forcefully into the hall and shut the door behind me. My sobs grew louder as she steered me into the kitchen and pushed me down into a chair.

"Lainey," I warned her, raising my voice again, "tell me what you know."

She looked towards the door, terrified the girls would come in and see me in such a state, but I didn't care. She walked over and shut the door gently.

"Why wouldn't you write the reference?" I shouted.

She wrung her hands together and looked down at the floor.

"I didn't write it," she said faintly, "because I think that Richard may be cheating on you."

"How long have you known?" I said, wiping the back of my hand across my runny nose.

"Since Peter moved into his new offices. Around the time we had the party."

I looked around wildly. "The party," I whispered to myself. "The party when Claire got upset and Richard had to take her home."

Lainey's face had collapsed inwards and she shook her head grimly. "I don't know anything for sure, Liz," she said gently. "All I know is that Peter has seen Richard going in and out of Claire's place quite regularly. He can see her apartment from his office window."

Hearing her speak the words made it all the more real and I felt like I'd been kicked in the head.

"Why didn't you tell me?" I asked hoarsely

Lainey shook her head again. "I didn't know what to do, Liz. I had planned to wait until after Christmas and tell you then. I've been trying to get through to Claire, to hear it from her, but she won't answer my calls."

"She wanted to see me this week," I muttered, remembering our last phone call.

Lainey came over to me and hunkered down. "Look, Liz. There might be a simple explanation for this. Peter said

345

the other night that they might be only working on the same case. We could be jumping to conclusions."

My mind rolled back over the last few months and I wondered how I could have been so blind.

"That's why she didn't come on the weekend," I whispered to myself. "It's why she didn't want me to set her up with anyone else – she already had Richard."

"Now, you can't say that for certain," said Lainey gently, handing me a tissue.

I slapped her hand away and jumped up from the chair.

"You knew about them!" I screamed at her. "You could have told me about it months ago, but you let it go on under my nose."

Lainey straightened up and took a step back.

"Liz," she said, tears filling her eyes, "I didn't know what to do. I wanted to say something, but I'm still not certain that there's anything going on between them."

I pushed past her and stormed out to the hall.

"Liz, where are you going?" she said, running after me.

I opened the front door and walked towards my car. A freezing fog was beginning to descend and the cold air stung my face.

"Please, Liz, come back inside. You're too upset to drive anywhere," she pleaded.

I reached out to open the car door and swung around to face her.

"I thought you were my friend."

It was the worst thing I could think of to say to her, knowing how much it would hurt.

I pulled out of the driveway and left her standing there. As I pulled away from the house I could see her in the rear-view mirror, standing alone in the driveway with her face buried in her hands.

I drove towards Claire's apartment oblivious to the other cars on the road. My trembling hands gripped the steering wheel until my knuckles were white. As I approached her road I slowed down and pulled into a parking spot. I sat in the darkness and tried to prepare myself for what I was going to find. Part of me wanted to turn around and go home, and keep pretending. It was easier that way – hadn't I been doing it for months? The shrill ring of my phone startled me and I fumbled about in my bag for it. I was about to reject the call, when I saw that it wasn't Lainey calling.

The number was withheld. Richard was the only person I knew with a withheld number and I pressed the answer button and waited.

"Liz?"

"Richard?" I said, feeling my eyes fill up again.

"It's Jeff."

"Oh," I gasped. "Hi."

"Are you all right? You sound funny."

"No," I answered, sniffing loudly. "I'm fine."

"I just thought I'd let you know that we're giving the account to Task. I'll make a call to Brian in the morning, but I wanted to let you know first."

I had just won back the Browne account. It should have been a cause for celebration, but it didn't mean a thing to me. My life was falling apart as we spoke.

"Great," I whispered.

"Sorry?" he said.

"That's great," I repeated a little louder.

"Liz, are you alone?"

"Yes," I said, sniffing again.

"Is something wrong?"

"I'm not too sure. I'm about to find out."

"Do you want to talk about it?"

"No," I said quickly. "Look, Jeff, I have to go. Thanks for letting me know. I really appreciate it."

I snapped the phone shut and waited for a break in the traffic before pulling back out onto the road again. As I pulled into the carpark at the back of Claire's apartment block, I struggled against the urge to throw up as I spotted Richard's Mercedes parked outside. I parked behind it and turned off the engine. All of a sudden I felt scared. Wasn't this all I needed to know? Perhaps they were working together on something and both had forgotten to mention it. I forced myself to get out of the car, knowing that there was only one way to find out what was going on. I punched the code into the front door and went inside to the foyer. The elevator was already on the ground floor and I stepped into it and pressed the button for the third floor. Outside her front door, I leaned against the wall and shut my eyes tightly, praying that there would be a simple explanation that would allow me to go back to my real life again. I pressed on the doorbell and waited.

I could hear panicked voices as the intercom clicked on and I looked directly into the camera. No one answered. I banged on the door with my fist.

"Open the door!" I shouted.

I kept banging until it opened.

Richard stood at the door and stared back at me in shock.

I pushed past him and walked through the hall into the living-room.

He closed the front door and followed me into the room. Claire was nowhere to be seen. He stopped as he entered the room and looked behind him anxiously.

We stood there, both of us lost for words as the reality of the nightmare unfolded.

"Richard, what are you doing here?" I pushed the words out, knowing that the answer would probably end our marriage.

He rocked backwards and forwards and stared at me without saying anything.

"Richard," I said, my voice rising with fear.

He looked around at the door again nervously waiting for Claire to appear.

"Where's Claire," I demanded.

He put his hand out to stop me but I pushed him aside and went back into the hall.

"Claire!" I shouted, "Claire, get out here!"

I heard a sound in the bedroom and threw the door open.

At first it was only her back I saw as she fumbled around frantically for something in the wardrobe. She was wearing tracksuit bottoms with only a bra on top.

"Claire!" I roared, as I entered the room.

She kept her back to me and froze. Her head drooped downwards as she gripped the side of the wardrobe door. After a few seconds, she turned slowly and I stumbled backwards in shock feeling the door handle dig into the small of my back. I didn't lift my head to look at her face. My eyes were fixed on the taut shiny skin that was stretched over the dome of her pregnant stomach. Her hand looked so tiny as she tried to hide the swollen mound of her baby from me. Their baby.

The door was eased open gently behind me and I stepped forward to let Richard into the room.

"Liz!" he cried. "Jesus, Liz! I didn't want you to find out like this."

I turned around slowly and looked at him. His shoulders shook violently with the force of his sobs. I turned back to face Claire. This time I looked at her face, but she wouldn't meet my gaze. Her eyes were cast downwards as she cradled her stomach.

"Liz," Richard pleaded, as he followed me out into the hall. "Liz, I never meant to hurt you."

My trembling fingers pressed the button of the elevator and it opened immediately. As the doors closed, I saw Richard walking towards me his arms outstretched.

"Liz, please!" he cried.

I ignored his pleading and turned my back on him as the doors slid shut between us.

Then

Summer is here. The girls in the dorm are wild with excitement as they pack their cases to go home. There are whoops and screams coming from the bathrooms as each girl tries to claim her towels and shampoos. Outside the sun is shining. It glistens and bounces off the surface of the lake like big diamonds. I'm looking forward to going home, but I'll miss this place, even though I'll be moaning my head off when I come back in September. I'll miss Julie and the other girls and I'll really miss Sister Bosco. Not that I'd admit that to anyone. Christ! They'd think I was a right geek if they heard me saying that. Sister Bosco always cries whenever we break up for holidays. She stands on the convent steps hugging and kissing us while the other stony-faced crows look on in disgust. Bosco says that we're like her children and I know what she means, because she feels a bit like a mother to us. I think I'll write to her over the summer – nobody would ever find out and I know it would mean a lot to her. After all, what the hell does she do when we're not around to annoy her? The floors won't need to be polished because we won't be tramping around on them, and there are only so many prayers you can say in a day, even if you are a nun.

Julie should write to her as well. I tried to drop a hint the other night when lights went out, but I could hear her snorting in the dark.

"What kind of a feckin eejit would write a letter to a nun!"

But she should, because if any other nun had caught us that night, we would certainly have been expelled. Well, Julie would definitely have been kicked out – I may have been given another chance as I don't have that many demerits on my record but Julie has millions. Mother Superior called Julie up to her office one day and told her that if she got into any more trouble, she'd be on the first train home. She's already been suspended for a week for sneaking out at night to meet a boy in the village. Her father killed her and threatened to send her to live with her aunt who's a missionary in the Congo. That really put the wind up her. Usually Julie gives everyone the two fingers and doesn't give a curse about what they say, but she was really terrified that he would send her away. Anyway, on the night in question, when everyone was asleep, we tiptoed over to the window and lit up a cigarette. The convent windows are huge and we sat on the sill and threw our legs out into the darkness. Our dorm was on the ground floor. There was only one cigarette left in the pack, so we took turns blowing the smoke out into the night air. Julie was telling me about the boy she'd been seeing from the village. Shay Hennessy is his name, and he's barred from going within a mile of the convent gates since they found out that Julie was sneaking out to meet him. We were stifling our laughs, trying not to wake anyone, when we heard a snap, like the sound of a twig being walked on. We looked out to see if anyone was coming, but the path that ran alongside the window was clear.

"C'mon," said Julie. She took a last drag of the damp butt and swung her legs back into the dorm. But just as she went to take the cigarette away from her lips and fire it into the darkness, a figure appeared a few feet from the window and we were face to face with the ghostly figure of a nun.

"Jesus!" I heard Julie mutter under her breath.

We both stood like statues, frozen with fear as we watched the figure come closer.

Julie hid the burning cigarette behind her back and for a split second I thought we'd get away with it. We could say that we were just getting some air. But when I looked over at Julie and saw the plumes of smoke leaking from her nostrils, I knew the game was up.

"Throw that cigarette out here before you set the dormitory on fire," came the voice of Sister Bosco.

Julie threw the butt out the window and Sister Bosco squashed it under her foot.

"What do you think you're doing?" she said in a hoarse whisper. "Julie, do you realise what this means?"

Julie's hand shot up to her forehead and she burst out crying. "Oh God, they'll really send me to the missions now!" she wailed.

"Sssh!" someone hissed from the other end of the dorm.

Sister Bosco beckoned to us to climb out the window and join her. "Come on," she said. "Out here, or you'll wake everyone and cause a stir."

We balanced on the window ledge and jumped out onto the path beside her in our pyjamas. Sister Bosco looked around nervously and pushed us around the corner where the bicycle sheds were.

"I'm ashamed of the two of you," she scolded. "And you, Julie! As if you weren't in enough trouble already."

Julie erupted into another burst of tears.

"Please, Sister," she pleaded, "I'll do anything you ask. Just don't tell. You spoke to my Dad. He told you where he's sending me if I get in any more trouble. Please, Sister, don't do it!"

"Perhaps, Julie, you'd be happier out in the Congo. After all, you'd be gone from here which seems to be all you've ever wanted since you came to us."

"I don't, Sister. I don't want to leave," Julie blurted.

Sister Bosco looked at her and sighed. "Julie child, I don't think you really know what it is you want."

Julie didn't have an answer to this and I put an arm around her shaking shoulders to stop her blubbering.

"As for you, Liz," she said, turning to me. "I thought by now you'd have learned some sense."

I kept my arm around Julie's shoulders. "Sorry, Sister," I whispered.

She looked at the two of us and shook her head slowly. "You are two very silly girls," she said. "Risking expulsion for the sake of a cigarette."

"Sorry, Sister," we said in unison.

"You'd better get back to your dorm before the three of

us are caught," she said, looking around to see if anyone had spotted us.

We turned to go, but stopped as she began to speak again.

"You are two bright girls who are throwing a good education away. You both had disgraceful results in your Christmas exams." She came up behind us and put a hand on each of our shoulders. "Your summer exams start in three weeks. There's still enough time to bury your heads in the books and improve. I'll be watching closely, and if your grades are still as bad as they were last term – I will report what happened tonight." Sister Bosco tightened her grip. "However, if I see a great improvement in your grades, I'm prepared to forget what happened – we'll put it down to pre-exam nerves."

We both turned and went to put our arms around her.

"No hugs tonight," she said, pushing us back towards the dorm. "You don't deserve any, and I can smell that dirty nicotine from your breath. Wash your teeth and say your prayers before you go to bed.

The exams are over now and we must have done pretty well, because it's the last day of term and our reports have already been posted home. If Sister Bosco was going to spill the beans, she'd have done it by now. It was funny to see us during those three weeks before the exams. All the other girls thought we'd gone mad. Julie was doing extra hours in the library, asking all the swotty girls to help her with her maths.

I stayed up late every night trying to catch up on all the work I hadn't done, cursing myself for not paying attention when it was being taught in class.

I hope Julie does well in her report. I'd miss her so much if she was sent away. Her parents collected her earlier this morning and I miss her already. Before she left, we promised each other that we'll stop messing next year and be really good. Julie says she's going to buy flat shoes and navy knickers and try to fit in with all the other geeks when she goes into sixth year.

Down in the front hall the excitement has reached fever pitch. Girls shriek as they see their parents' cars appear up the winding driveway. They hug and kiss and cry as they lug their heavy suitcases out the door. I feel a knot in my stomach as I look out for Daddy's car, but I don't see it. I haven't seen them since Christmas and I'm feeling nervous about meeting them again. It's like I don't really belong to their family any more – I'm an outsider that no one knows what to do with. At least we've made our peace with each other, so there's no fighting any more.

Rita brought up the business about the tree again when I went home for the Christmas holidays. She stood beside the fire in the front room one evening, wringing her hands together anxiously as she explained how she never would have cut the tree down had she known what it meant to me. It was blocking light from the front of the house and she'd simply decided to get rid of it. She said she hadn't intended to be malicious or upset me in any way. Big tears glittered in her eyes as she spoke and I cringed inside as I thought of how I'd attacked her that day in the garden.

I apologised as well. Told her I was sorry about all the trouble I'd caused.

Christmas was quite nice. I'd been dreading it, but my chat with Rita cleared the air and everyone seemed to have put the ordeal behind them. Claire didn't leave my side for a moment. At nights she came into my bed and I hadn't the heart to boot her out, even though she is thirteen and getting a bit old for that carry-on. But, I suppose it's lonely for her now, being all alone in the house without a sister.

It was great to see Lainey again. I stayed some nights in her house and we talked for hours, until Mrs Whyte had to bang on the door and tell us to shut up. Lainey told me that she'd seen Gary in town – he must have been home for Christmas as well. I hardly ever think about him any more. Much as I hate to admit it, Lainey was probably right when she said it wouldn't have worked. Looking back now, I don't think I would have been very happy moving to London with him.

I've tried to let the memory go, but I still can't get used to not having the shadows of the tree on my bedroom wall. I miss them, but I know now that Mum still remains in my heart and will always be there, long after the ghosts of the shadows have faded.

As of now

As of now my life is perfect. That is, I am under no illusion that at any given time it may revert to being a disaster again, but right now things couldn't be better. I have left my old life behind and sometimes, when I think about it, I find it hard to believe that I ever lived it.

Today is a beautiful day. Clara and Mia are playing on the swing and their hysterical laughter fills every corner of the garden. I come out of the kitchen and approach them slowly, but they remain unaware of me. I pull the camera from my pocket and stoop to take a photo and I am suddenly overwhelmed with happiness. I stop, holding the camera in mid-air and try to immerse myself in the feeling, because now I know that moments like these are gifts. Happiness is not a God-given right, but fragments in time that fall into our lives, often unbidden. These moments are delicate and transient, and I want desperately to savour each one that falls my way from now on.

My daughter Mia is wearing her swimsuit while her cousin Clara, who is two years older and significantly taller, is soaking her with the garden hose.

Click. I take the photo and check the image on the screen. It seems like only yesterday since myself and Claire ran around the same garden, shrieking with childish abandon as we played our innocent summer games. Now it is the turn of our children, and although they are only games, they must be taught to play fairly. It is our responsibility to teach them the rules and, unlike our own parents, we will try not make them up as we go along.

Where to begin?

I don't want to talk about the misery that I indulged in after Richard left, except to say that it consumed me, ate me up, like a worm inside an apple. I spent every living moment apportioning the blame.

I blamed Lainey for not telling me what she knew, and didn't speak to her for months. I blamed Daddy and Rita for rearing the monster that was my sister.

But mostly I blamed myself. Believing, had I been a better wife, that Richard wouldn't have done such a terrible thing.

I know now that that is rubbish. But, at the time, I latched on to this reasoning and wouldn't let go.

It wasn't until Daddy called over about a month after it happened and pounded on my door till I let him in, that I realised that everyone and no one was to blame. I didn't speak to anyone that Christmas. I unplugged the phone and locked the doors so that Richard couldn't gain access. He did try a couple of times but I ignored his persistent bell-ringing and listened as his car tore away from the house.

I left it up to the happy couple to tell Daddy and Rita what had happened. Needless to say, they were horrified.

The day that Daddy called, I was still in bed, hoping that he'd give up and leave, but his banging only grew louder. I pulled myself from the bed and went downstairs. I opened the door and we both got a fright when we saw each other. I'd barely eaten or washed for two weeks and he had turned into a feeble old man.

"Lizzy," he whispered, "are you all right?"

I turned and walked back upstairs, unable to cope with anyone else's reaction. Daddy stepped inside, closing the door behind him and followed me up the stairs. I went back into the stuffy overheated bedroom, pulled back the covers and climbed into the comfort of my bed. Daddy sat down on the edge of the mattress and put his hand on my shoulder.

"It's been such a blow to us, Lizzy," he said. "I can't imagine what it's been like for you."

He pulled a linen handkerchief from his pocket. He wiped his eyes and blew his nose loudly before stuffing it back into his pocket.

"Oh Lizzy," he whispered, "I've failed you terribly."

I looked up at him blankly and saw the pools of sadness reflected in his watery eyes.

"I have not come here to make excuses for Claire. What she did is unforgivable. But I do think there's a reason why she behaves the way she does. I've never talked to you about things that happened in the past. I wanted to shelter you from any more pain. But I think we should talk about it now."

I waited listlessly for him to continue.

"When Claire was born, your mother was at her worst."

It made me stiffen in the bed. Daddy had only mentioned her name a handful of times since her death. It was as if her very existence was wiped from our lives without trace. The mention of Mum's name in our house was always enough to drive someone from the room and so her memory was snuffed out in a vain attempt to gloss over the cracks in our family.

"Maria's depression deepened during the pregnancy and she blamed Claire for it. She wouldn't even hold her after the birth." He fished around for his handkerchief again and wiped the end of his nose with it. "She neglected Claire when they came home from hospital. She left her lying in her cot all day, not feeding her or changing her nappy. Sometimes, she'd take you out and leave Claire in the house all alone."

I sat up and stared at him in disbelief.

"You're too young to remember these things, Lizzy."

"She'd never have done that!" But as I said this, I felt something tug at the back of my mind as I remembered the constant crying from the cot upstairs. There was always crying.

He looked down at me and stroked my cheek. "You were more like a mother to Claire," he said with a sad smile. "I don't know what she would have done without you."

My thoughts clouded over and images collided in my head, of a time I had chosen to forget, a time that seemed so distant I wondered if it had happened at all.

I remembered the big steel nappy pins in my small hands. I had to be careful not to stick it into Baby Claire's tummy because that made her cry even more. But that meant the nappy would be loose and she'd wet her cot again.

"She was so very sick and I didn't see it," he said, shaking his head. "I was too busy with my own life to stop and see what was happening. You were doing such a good job, looking after Claire and your mother that it took me longer to notice."

I remembered the smell of the milky vomit that left stains on my uniform jumper. Baby Claire always burped up her bottle in the mornings when I was rushing out to school.

"It's difficult for you to understand, Lizzy. You had such a different relationship with your mother. You were the only one who could reach her – she lived for you."

I felt a lump rise in my throat. I was so desperately afraid that he was going to take her from me, tell me that she'd done the same to me.

"She lived her life through you, and I shouldn't have allowed it. You were only a child trying to cope with a very difficult situation. You saw how your mother rejected Claire and you tried to compensate for her."

My body felt weak as he told me what I'd always known – Mum had loved me and not Claire. I can't say I forgave Claire at that moment, I sometimes wonder if I ever have, but it made me realise the contempt that had been bred into her towards me.

"Claire only ever wanted to emulate you. She thought that by being like you that we'd love her more and although Rita tried to make her feel special, it was never enough." He said this looking utterly defeated. "She only ever wanted what you had, and nothing else would do."

"Does she remember how Mum treated her?"

Daddy sighed. "She's never spoken about it and I've never had the heart to bring it up with her. She was only seven when Maria died so I doubt she remembers too much." He stared at a spot just over my shoulder as he said this, lost in the pain of the memory. "By that stage they were rarely in the same room together. Maria had removed herself from everyone in the family except you."

I shot him a look of resentment. "Wasn't there a good reason why she removed herself from you?"

Daddy wrung his hands together. "Our marriage was over long before Rita arrived. It wasn't planned – I asked her to stay because the two of you needed looking after and things just happened."

"Under her nose!" I shouted. "How dare you come here trying to explain your mistakes on the back of what Claire has done! Can't you see what *you've* done? Part of what's happened is your fault as well. Claire's just a case of history repeating itself!"

"It's entirely my fault. That's what I came here to say to you," he said, hanging his head.

"No," I said, sitting up and clenching my fists angrily. "It's Rita's fault as well. The two of you set an example that Claire has followed. It's disgusting. I'm ashamed to be part of your family."

"I'll go now," he said, standing up slowly.

He looked at me for a second, then looked away again, his face crumpled up with anguish.

I collapsed back down on the pillow and closed my eyes as I listened to his footsteps leaving the hallway.

I had a similar scene with Lainey, but she was harder to shake off. Every time I answered the phone or the door, she was there. Her fierce relentlessness finally wore me down – I was too exhausted to remain angry with her and I badly needed a friend. The day I heard that Claire had given birth to a baby girl, I honestly wondered if it was worth going on. I doubt I would have had it not been for Lainey.

I heard about the birth from Rita – she had drawn the short straw and been given the onerous task of telling me. Rita and Daddy had to split their time between the two of us – never mentioning Claire's or Richard's name when I was in their presence, or the name of their new granddaughter. I realised very quickly after Richard left, that the most devastating thing about what he'd done was that I wouldn't get to have my child. I say my child, because it had never been his. I just hadn't faced up to it at the time. It was while I was saying this to Lainey one day that she suggested the possibility of a single parent adoption. I tried to push the idea out of my mind, but it wouldn't go away. I spent months trying to get on with my life but the thought of this baby kept making its way back into the core of my thoughts, and somehow I knew it was something I had to do.

After a gruelling reassessment, the adoption board finally deemed me to be a suitable candidate, and I began the process of adopting my beautiful daughter Maria. I called her Maria after Mum, but she has renamed herself Mia since she started talking, as she can't seem to get her tongue around Maria, and everyone agrees that Mia suits her better. The moment I saw her, my life changed forever. Everything bad that had happened in the past didn't matter any more because finding my daughter gave me the strength to move on and let go of the hurt and anger that had lodged itself so deeply inside me.

Lainey made the trip to China with me and was there for me to lean on, every step of the way. I could only have done it with her at my side and it was an experience that brought the two of us even closer together. She is Mia's godmother and they both adore each other. Daddy and Rita wanted to come to China as well, but I managed to persuade them not to. It was such a huge gesture on their part, considering how a car journey to Kerry sends them into a complete spin. I was really touched by their kindness, but I would have ended up taking care of them and was far too nervous about the trip to think of anyone else. They were waiting at the airport when we arrived home and the two of them almost smothered Mia with tears and kisses as they wrestled her from my arms. Their joy at her arrival came as a complete surprise and it made me realise just how much they had wanted this for me.

When we got home from China, Rita told me that Claire and Richard had split up. Their daughter Clara was only two and Richard had left them to move in with a junior counsel who was devilling for him. I heard that Claire was devastated. Lainey didn't speak to her any more. Neither did Brenda. The only people who saw her were Daddy and Rita, and it was clear that they felt very uncomfortable talking about her to me. Not that I ever wanted to know much, but hearing that Richard had walked out and left her with their child, made me feel very sorry for her. I also became aware of how much I missed her. Even though she'd hurt me so badly, she was still my sister and that bond was hard to break. It seemed that when Richard removed himself from the equation the possibility that we could go back to being sisters again became a faint hope.

It was the reason I decided to contact her again. Regardless of what had happened between us, Mia and Clara have only each other as cousins, and it would have been unfair to deprive them of that. It didn't all happen overnight. It took months of miserable meetings, full of silence and resentment as we introduced our daughters to each other and looked on as they played happily together, oblivious to the past events that had shaped their innocent lives.

I look out the window to check up on the girls and see that they are lying on the rug at the bottom of the garden, idly chatting to each other. It's at times like these that I know we made the right decision. My relationship with Claire will never be the same again, there will always be a barrier of hurt and distrust, but I don't want it to affect our children.

Claire moved in with Daddy and Rita after Richard left. I thought she was mad at the time, but it has worked out quite well. Rita minds Clara during the day while Claire works and it's given Daddy a new lease of life. He's gone from being a growling curmudgeon to a doting old softie. The other day he looked after the two girls for the afternoon. When I went to pick up Mia I found him running around the back garden like a lunatic, with a bed sheet thrown over his head. The girls ran away from him and screamed with delight as he got tangled up in the clothes-line. I watched from the kitchen window and laughed at how ridiculous he looked and tried to think of a time when he played with us like that, but I couldn't. I suppose that's the nature of life itself. You watch the little things slip away and by the time you realise they're special, they've vanished, gone forever. Daddy says that having grandchildren has made him realise how much he missed out on when we were young and that he's making up for lost time, enjoying a second chance.

Brian Davies dragged me back to Task even though I resigned after that awful Christmas. He wouldn't hear of it! At the time, I didn't know my own mind and so allowed myself to be shunted back and propped up at my desk like a dummy. Looking back now, it was the best thing I could have done and I think Brian knew that at the time. He was always looking out for me and only ever had my best interest at heart, but he drove me mad telling me that he knew exactly what I was going through. I wanted to scream at him every time he said, "I've been there, Liz. I know how rough it is – just hang on in there. Things will get better."

You've no idea how I feel, I wanted to scream. He had walked out on his family. How did he think that his situation bore any resemblance to mine? Eventually I couldn't listen to him any more and snapped at him one day after he'd told me he knew just how I felt.

"Actually, Brian, you don't."

He looked over at me and went to say something, but I put my hand up to stop him saying anything further.

"You walked out on your wife. You made a decision and acted upon it. I on the other hand did nothing of the sort – so please stop saying that we have this *thing* in common, because we don't."

I saw the beginning of a smile cross his face and left his office before he had a chance to compare my sudden flashes of anger with something he had also experienced during his divorce.

Someone who did know what I was going through, to a certain extent, was Jeff Williams. He heard about what happened through Brian and, apart from one or two phone calls to see how I was, he mostly stayed away for the first few months. Not that I wanted him anywhere near me. I felt hollow inside, and was incapable of even considering the possibility of another relationship. However, we had to work together and during the time that followed we became very close to each other. Jeff's divorce was followed closely by the media and was aired in public as Muriel ruthlessly sank her stilettos into his jugular. The court case was lengthy as her demands for spousal support grew more unreasonable – but the judge was fair and she got no more than what she deserved.

Although it was a single parent adoption, Jeff lived every step of it with me and had a special bond with Mia from the first time he saw her. It was only when I travelled to China for six weeks to get Mia that I knew I really wanted to be with him.

Richard walked away from our marriage overnight, and there was no legal mess to contend with. At least he was generous in that respect, and I was informed by our solicitor shortly after our separation that he had signed the house over to me. I decided to sell up and start anew – it was far too big anyway. It sold within the first week on the market and I bought a smaller house close to Lainey.

Much to my surprise, Susie and Matt stayed together. It got off to a shaky start and was an on-again off-again relationship for the first year or so. But, they both managed to hang in there and sort things out and all of Susie's wishes came true when they were married a few weeks ago. The wedding was more like an advertising convention and the antics became more raucous as the night went on. I had been sitting beside a speaker all night and had gone partially deaf from the noise of the band. There was a chorus of cheers and roars as Matt proceeded to remove Susie's garter with his teeth.

I touched Jeff's elbow and without saying anything, nodded towards the door. He could read my thoughts and willingly led the way.

I climbed into the car, my feet throbbing from the ridiculously high heels I'd worn.

"Your place or mine?" he asked as we pulled out of the hotel car park.

"We can stay in mine. Lainey has Mia for the night, so we can have a lie-in tomorrow morning."

He slowed down and looked over at me. "It's a bit silly, isn't it?"

"What?"

"This shifting between houses all the time. Half my stuff at your place, half your stuff at mine. Why can't we just have one house that the three of us live in?"

I looked at him and his face broke into a smile.

"What are you saying, Jeff?" I asked.

He pulled over and turned off the engine.

"I'm saying I want to marry you and I'm hoping you'll say yes, because we've wasted enough time already. I love you, Liz, and I want to spend the rest of my life with you."

I was hoarse from trying to talk to people over the noise of the music all night, and a strangled yelp came from the back of my throat as I threw my arms around his neck.

"I'll take that as a yes then," he said, laughing at my reaction.

"Yes, yes, yes!" I shrieked.

He pulled back and we stopped talking and looked at each other. For just a moment, we stayed perfectly still and felt its presence. It fluttered in the air, sparkling in the darkness that hung between us and we both reached out, grasping the delicate thread of happiness that would lead us to a better place.

THE END

Direct to your home!

If you enjoyed this book why not
visit our website:

www.poolbeg.com

and get another book delivered straight to
your home or to a friend's home!

www.poolbeg.com

All orders are despatched within 24 hours.

Also published by Poolbeg.com

A Life Left Untold

GER GALLAGHER

"My eyes filled with tears and all the conflicting emotions I had for her somersaulted through my head. I loved her. I hated her. I resented her. And now, looking at her lying on the dirty crumpled sheets, I mostly pitied her."

Iris Fortune never questions why her alcoholic mother Grace seems to have no love for her, while her grandmother Lily has enough obsessive love for two parents. Just who is Iris's father, how can she overcome the die that fate cast for her mother, and would she recognise happiness if it fell in her lap?

When Lily dies and her lifelong friend Sarah reveals some hidden details about the past, Iris has to decide whether to protect her mother or reveal the truth.
Keeping secrets can be dangerous, and when they work their way to the surface all hell can break loose.

A novel about three generations of women whose lives have been dramatically shaped by a secret from the past.

ISBN 978-1-84223-252-1

Also published by Poolbeg.com

Broken Passions

GER GALLAGHER

Anna Barry is running Jacob's shoe shop on Sackville
Street and keeping house for her father and brother
Seán in 1920's Dublin.

Anna is stepping out with Joe Maguire, a man her
brother and father regard as a hero in the fight for a
United Ireland, but does she really love him? When he
proposes, Anna succumbs to family pressure and
accepts despite her reservations.

When Anna's boss has a stroke, his son Daniel must
abandon his studies in England to run the shop. Anna
and Daniel are irresistibly drawn to each other and so
begins a secret love affair. For what would her father
do to Anna if he were to discover the relationship?
And Daniel's family would never accept a humble
shop girl.

As Joe, Seán and the Anti-Treaty Forces prepare for
war in the Four Courts, Anna and Daniel, consumed
with their passion for one another, must fight for
their future.

ISBN 978-1-84223-262-0